CHILDREN OF SATURN

A Novel

John Neeleman

OPEN
BOOKS

To Gwendolyn, to all my children—Olivia, Emily, Ethan, Jack, and Victoria—and to my parents, who taught me to love books.

"Presently journalists exercise formidable powers, as though they were kings' ministers. Every day they ascend the orator's tribune, and among them are stentorian voices which make themselves heard in the kingdom's eighty-three departments. Places to hear these orators cost only two sous; journals denounce, they decree, they rule in unforeseen matters, they absolve or condemn. Fifty broadsheets enlighten the world each day, punctually as the sun."

—From no. 17 of Camille Desmoulins's Paris gazette

"We know nothing of Thomas Paine's private life."

—Mary Wollstonecraft

PROLOGUE

IT IS THE AFTERNOON of Sunday, July 12, 1789, and Camille Desmoulins is in the Palais-Royal. He is alone. Camille is vain and mindful of his appearance. He is wearing a blue coat with gilt buttons, buckskin breeches and well-polished boots, a perfectly white waistcoat, a shiny hat, and he holds a cane with mother-of-pearl and a gold knob. He has a dark complexion and an ambiguously feminine essence. His big dark eyes are extraordinarily bright and expressive, below a smooth and prominent forehead. His mouth is large and sensuous, his curled black hair so long that it falls over his shoulders, loose and unpowdered—as is the custom now among the republicans—and he is slightly built and not tall, though athletic in his movements and bearing.

Irresistibly, the public is drawn to the Palais-Royal, a public space built to appear like a magnificent rectangular château. Within there are vast and majestic courtyards and gardens surrounded by arcades, beneath which there are innumerable shops resplendent with treasures of the world displayed in a most alluring fashion, lit up by lamps that enhance their bright and dazzling colors. Crowds of people are flowing through these galleries; they are walking up and down for the sole purpose of looking at each other. So, too, there are coffee houses, taverns, pubs, and cafés, the foremost in Paris, which are all full of people.

There is a terrible din; people are quarreling and making speeches, reading aloud at the tops of their voices the latest news and argumentation from the newspapers concerning the movement that is now called the French Revolution. Along the promenade that fronts the boutiques and galleries, professional escorts, legs and arms bare and with feathery headdresses, are strolling and making contacts and assignations.

Here, then, is also a gathering place for thieves, crooks, cheaters, fornicators, and the men and women who plot the royalty's very destruction—just across the Rue Saint-Honoré from the king's Tuileries Palace (it is vacant, for the royal family is ensconced in Versailles).

More irony: the man who imagined and financed the development of this place is the king's estranged cousin, Louis Philippe Joseph, the Duke of Orléans, who has now renamed himself Egalité, and here he holds court among the enemies of the king. Within the House of Bourbon, the Orléanses are the pedigree's inferior branch; they would succeed to the throne only if their more exalted cousins die out. Philippe and Louis XVI have never gotten along. But if Philippe has designs on the throne, the motive is hidden, for overtly he is in thrall of the ideas of philosopher Jean-Jacques Rousseau and a member of the Jacobins, the revolutionary political club. He has made the Palais-Royal into the club's nerve center and, as such, the bastion for the people's rebellion. Is his aim, as rival royalty, to replace King Louis XVI, or, as a true revolutionary, to destroy the monarchy altogether? Time will tell.

Now Camille is outside the galleries, making his way within the columns of chestnut trees of a Palais-Royal garden, where calm and shadows are to be found. He hears from within the arcades the sensuous sound of fine music; a gentle breeze makes the bright green leaves on the trees rustle and brings relief on this warm afternoon.

"What now, Camille?" These words are spoken from the shadows. The words have a singsong, unpleasant, pedantic edge. Camille's reverie is broken. Marat. He stands a few paces away—slovenly in appearance, posture bent, a dirty red kerchief binding his scalp, two pistols on his belt, and diseased, blistered skin. Camille braces himself. He knows that Jean-Paul Marat is a good judge of Camille's character and plays upon his vanity and insecurity.

Marat is called the "Friend of the People," the same name as his newspaper, which competes with Camille's. But Camille does not regard him a friend. It is Marat's sardonic jabs more than the hideous appearance that put Camille ill at ease.

Camille gazes at him, his look asking, *What do you mean?*

"Necker," says Marat. "Haven't you heard? The king has dismissed Necker. Foullon will replace him."

Suddenly, Camille's mind is ablaze. Swiss Minister of Finance Jacques Necker, the lone liberal among the king's ministers, is now gone. Necker, who wished to reform the French monarchy to resemble the British constitutional monarchy. But he is now replaced by Joseph Foullon, who said, *Let the people eat grass.*

Camille's thoughts race, yet he is silent. Stricken by intense emotion, his stutter is insurmountable. He is trembling, his eyes misty.

"Struck dumb, eh, Camille. Don't concern yourself. Notwithstanding the boldness and originality of your pen, you are ever under the ascendancy of others. Now is the time for a coup d'état. Leave that to men of action. Men who express, arouse, and also act upon the will of the people. Revolutions cannot be made with rosewater, after all. *Adieu.*" Marat is gone as suddenly as he appeared.

Camille arrives at his destination; he is in front of the Café de Foy. It is about half past three. The news is released and on everyone's lips: Necker, the people's minister, the savior of France, has been dismissed by the king! His replacement is Joseph Foullon, who said, *Let the people eat grass.*

All of his friends who are prominent Jacobin Club members are here. His boyhood friend, Maximilien Robespierre, is with Philippe, Duke of Orléans (Egalité), and the lawyer Georges Danton. They are not seated at their usual table. They are standing. Camille sees that they are too anxious to sit. Monstrous Danton, with rampant black mane, billowing linen shirt, arms spread, and fingers splayed, is howling emphatically at Robespierre—Robespierre erect in his usual blue waistcoat; arms folded; his hair neatly drawn, ponytailed and powered; a pale grimace. These three men are among those to whom Camille subordinates himself—as

Marat would put it. Robespierre is a delegate to the revolutionary legislature now known as the National Assembly.

Yet today Camille is heedless of the great men. For now is not time to deliberate, but to fulminate. He is enraged, and rage is the surest counteractant to obsequiousness. Camille is suddenly rushing about outside the Café de Foy, face ablaze, hair streaming, shouting, pumping his arms. He has discarded the cane, lost his hat, seized two pistols; he does not think where from. They are now brandished in each hand. In his eye corner Camille sees a dark and red colored smear, musketed Gendarmerie, bayonets aloft; he is unafraid. The king's police are numerous here today, but they cannot take him, not if they want to remain alive.

Friends (not the great men themselves) help Camille climb up on a table and then onto a chair placed on the table. Someone holds the chair while Camille stands upon it, holding the pistols aloft and crying out to the milling crowd. This time, he speaks without stammering.

"Friends! Shall we die like hunted hares? Like sheep bleating for mercy, hounded into their pinfold where there is no mercy to be had, but only a whetted knife? The hour is come; the supreme hour of Frenchman and Man; when oppressors have dared to drive their oppression to conclusion. And for the oppressed, the choice is this: swift death, or deliverance forever! Let such hour be welcome! For us, it seems to me, one cry only befits: To Arms! Let universal Paris, universal France, sound only: To arms!"

And "To arms!" yells one great responsive voice, the combined innumerable voices.

Camille looks upon the multitude now gathered before him, and he sees the rage, and he feels its energy. He has, he sees, evoked elemental powers in this great moment.

"Friends," cries Camille, "we need some rallying sign! Cockades; green ones; the color of hope!" Always, there must be some sign. Thus do the people snatch green tree leaves, green ribbons from the neighboring shops, all green things, to turn into cockades—a flight of locusts!

Camille descends from his table and he is stifled with embraces, wetted with comingled tears. He is handed a bit of green ribbon, which he sticks in his hat. Now the multitude spills from the Palais-Royal, and they smash through the streets, armed with muskets, axes, staves, farm implements, anything that man may devise as weapon.

Camille sees that somewhere the multitude has seized a wax-bust of Necker, and a wax-bust of Egalité, erstwhile Duke of Orléans, advocates of the people, now covered with crape, as in funeral procession, or like supplicants appealing to heaven. For always there must be idols. And now, to the Bastille, all intrepid Parisians!

―――――――

Later, after nightfall, the crowd has laid siege to the Bastille. Near the frayed edge of the crowd, among the cautious and the fearful, Camille sees a familiar face; a woman. She is dressed in a light and simple chemise à la reine (still more irony: the style introduced by Queen Marie Antoinette in rebellion against the highly structured garments worn by the French court)—thin muslin layers loosely draped around her shapely body and belted around the waist with a sash—and a plumed hat.

It is his good friend, Olympe de Gouges, and she is arm in arm with a similarly outfitted woman. Olympe sees him and she smiles brightly, lets go of her friend's arm and moves toward him. Her smile, painted bright red, turns impish. She is perhaps ten years older than Camille, nearly forty, which is an element of his attraction to her. Her exquisite, feminine features both disguise and enhance her celebrity in the Paris salons. Olympe has had many powerful and wealthy lovers, whose support have enabled her in leisure to write a multitude of well-known socially conscious works, including essays, manifestos, literary treatises, political pamphlets, and plays, establishing a formidable literary reputation of her own. She has been received in Paris's most prestigious artistic and philosophical salons and become friends with many important writers and politicians.

Indeed, Camille now recognizes her companion. It is Baroness de Staël, the grown and married daughter of Jacques Necker. Her mother, Madame Necker, is hostess of one of the most popular salons of Paris, in the mansion that she has restored, furnished, and decorated to magnificence—they call it a palace—and it is there that Camille met the daughter, when visiting with Robespierre, and also developed his intimate friendship with Madame de Gouges.

When she is nearby, she says in a low voice, "Are you alone? Would you like to meet later?" The rich timbre of her voice, even as whisper, betokens her prestige in artistic and intellectual circles.

"Yes!" he cries above the din.

It seems hardly more than a minute has passed since their eyes first met and she says, "I'll see you at my place. I need to go back to my friend."

"When shall we meet?"

"After I arrive, whenever that may be."

When she arrives, alone, darkness has fallen; he is seated on the floor beside the entry, waiting.

Next day, from the window of her apartment that enables a view of the Bastille, the two of them watch the momentous event that Camille set in motion. Yes, a condition of egotism has him believe that the destruction of the Bastille will have been his doing.

The forbidding, hoary Bastille fortress-cum-prison is a just symbol of the revolution's mark—four hundred year-old, eighty foot towers individually named—La Chapelle, Trésor, Comté, Bazinière, Bertaudière, and Liberté—adjoined by stone walls of like height. A mob, growing ever denser, is pushing forward to the edge of a moat, swirling mass of cockaded hats and heaving shoulders now stretched as far as the Rue des Tournelles. The drawbridges for pedestrians and for carriages are pulled up.

Behind Camille and Olympe lays an unmade bed where, like bindweeds, they grappled naked, before jumping out to watch the spectacle before them.

Back in his apartment, after leaving Olympe, Camille writes to his father:

You made an error when you would not recommend me to the people who would have elected me. But it doesn't matter now. I have written my name on our Revolution in letters larger than those of all our deputies from Picardy.

Camille has always felt too inferior to Robespierre to be envious. They were schoolmates at the Lycée Louis-le-Grand in Paris, an elite school whose alumni include Voltaire and the Marquis de Sade. Camille was his usual sidekick. The friendship was possible only because Robespierre is older, was two years ahead of Camille. What oddity, their friendship. Pretty Camille, all too human, emotionally intense, a good hater equally prone to sudden loves and infatuations, philanderer, and his pal, the proud and serious Robespierre, ascetic, a paltry wardrobe, perfectly at home amid the high and dismal walls of black and gloomy Louis-le-Grand, its moss-grown playgrounds, smoky classrooms, Robespierre inevitably alone unless beside frothy Camille. At Louis-le-Grand, both Camille and Robespierre trained as lawyers. But while Robespierre emerged the top student in his class, collecting all of the prizes, Camille had little aptitude for law. Camille discovered a gift for writing. Still, Camille believes that with his father's support, he too could be elected as a representative to the National Assembly, from his ancestral village of Guise. His father declined to support him—they are at odds over Camille's radical journalism—which was fatal to his nomination.

———

Amid the multitude, the body and head of Monsieur Foullon are introduced in triumph, the head on a pike, his mouth stuffed with hay, the body dragged naked through the streets of Paris. Gracious God, the people!

PART I

CHAPTER 1

A RECURRING DREAM: IN silhouette against the sun atop the chalk ridge visible from the Paine cottage, three men hanging, their bodies left to swing. A gibbet was installed on that chalk ridge, so the sight renewed itself again and again. Still a young child, it brought this to mind: *Then were there two thieves crucified with Him, one on the right hand, and another on the left.* Or: *they crucified two rebels with Him, one on His right and one on His left.* Rebels or thieves, which one was it? Thomas wondered. And what was Jesus if not a rebel?

In deep sleep, a hard nudge—and Thomas Paine is awake. Lafayette is leaning over the bed, wrapped in a black banyan, a frown on the patrician face. It is June 21, 1791, and Paine is in Paris seeing to the translation of his book *Rights of Man*. He is Lafayette's guest—that same Lafayette who, though a French aristocrat, became convinced at nineteen years old that the American cause in the War of Independence was right and could change the world forever, came to the New World seeking glory in it, and became a general in the Continental Army and a friend of Washington and Jefferson and the other founders of the American republic and a hero in the United States.

Lafayette exclaims, "The birds are flown!" He is frantic. Louis XVI and Antoinette are gone, with their entire household; they have fled. Next month, July 14, Parisians will celebrate two years since the storming of the Bastille. It was not three months later, October 5, 1789, that women led the March to Versailles and the crowd forced the king and his family to return with them to Paris. Ever since, they have been virtual prisoners in their Tulieres Palace. Now they have escaped. As Lafayette is the officer in charge of the king's guard, the Jacobins are surely saying that he is incompetent or a traitor or both. Lafayette has been acclaimed by the National Assembly as the commander-in-chief of the National Guard of France; it is an armed force established to maintain order, and under the control of the Assembly. It is Lafayette himself who named this armed force and made its symbol: a blue, white, and red cockade.

Paine proudly regards himself a commoner, a Thetford, England-born, naturalized American. He is equally proud that he has left his common roots behind. He became famous when he was nearly forty because when he arrived in America, the majority of its citizens were divided—or indifferent—about war with Britain, and the simple eloquence of Paine's pamphlet *Common Sense*, published in 1776, at once impelled Americans of every class to rally to the cause of American independence: *The cause of America is, in a great measure, the cause of all mankind*, he wrote. Yet like Lafayette, he has returned to his homeland. Paine's primary residence is now again in London. Now it seems fateful— indeed miraculous (though he reminds himself that he does not believe in such fantasies)—that he now finds himself in the same role he played in the American Revolution.

Paine wants to console his friend. He replies, "It is for the best. I hope there will be no attempt to recall them. You see the absurdity of your system of government; here will be a whole nation disturbed by the folly of one man."

Leaving the house together, they make a fine pair. The general walks emphatically erect. He is wearing a coat with a high double collar and broad lapels that is lavishly embroidered in gold that matches medals on the lapels and the big brass buttons.

4

A lace jabot decorates his breast. He is bare headed except for a wig with a queue.

At fifty-four, Paine is still in his prime—about five feet ten inches and physically fit. He is broad-shouldered, though latterly stooped a little, and his face is not lined. A weakness for spirits has not spoiled his complexion or physique. His eye emanates the muse's inner fire. He is dressed like a gentleman of the old French school, though simply, and his hair is elegantly ponytailed—there is no wig—with side curls and powdered. He is wearing a cocked hat.

Outside they are met by Jean-Sylvain Bailly, the mayor of Paris; Viscount Alexandre de Beauharnais, the President of the Assembly; and Lafayette's and the other men's aides-de-camp and a small army of bodyguards. Their mood is grim. Lafayette is anxious.

But to Paine, everything is working out. Paris looks so beautiful this morning. The cityscape and the day are full of promise. He can hardly hide his happiness.

They walk to the Tuileries Palace, where a placard, *For Rent*, hangs on the wrought iron gate before the spectacular gardens and the domed edifice. Beauharnais reads a proclamation. Paine's French is limited but he understands the message to be, essentially, that the government will continue to function, yet without a king. No truer words were ever spoken, he thinks.

From there he follows Lafayette to the magnificent city hall, which the Parisians call the Hôtel de Ville. Crowds are gathered out front. And there the people taunt Lafayette as a collaborator of the king. Deputy to the Paris Commune Georges Danton—broad, a fleshy, pock-marked face, and spectral, his long hair hanging undressed, as always physically imposing and now more daunting than ever, elevated by a makeshift platform of some kind—points a thick finger at Lafayette and shouts that he is "a traitor or a fool." That much Paine can clearly understand. Jacobins have established the revolutionary Paris Commune to govern Paris as the Assembly is supposed to govern France, with the mayor the executive, and deliberating in the Hôtel de Ville. But it is much more radical and pragmatic than the Assembly, firmly in control of the Jacobins.

Paine finds a friend, the young Scottish pamphleteer and radical Thomas Christie, and they warmly greet one another, and Paine allows Lafayette to disappear. All around them men are dressed in a ridiculous uniform—a calico hip-length waistcoat of coarse wool with broad tricolor stripes called a carmagnole and a red bonnet, "the cap of liberty," emblazoned with the ubiquitous tricolor cockade. Christie is wearing just the cockade on his cocked hat. Paine wants no part of it; entirely new in his experience, this organized uniformity among civilians feels like a new means of oppression, a new subordination to authoritarian power.

A fist boxes his cheek and he falls; a foot kicks him hard. He lays on the pavement buckled in pain, his healthy cheek against the cobbles, tasting blood. He raises his arms to cover his face. He hears shouts of "Aristocrat!" He feels more hard kicks to his ribs and his stomach and arms.

He hears Christie vainly pleading, hysterically shouting—in his Scot's English—that the man they are killing is the famous philosopher Thomas Paine, an American and an advocate of liberty, a scourge of kings and the very opposite of an aristocrat. His writings ignited the revolution in America! He is like Camille Desmoulins!

Over a forearm he sees a boot's toe box, blunt deadly weapon, rise up and swing at his head. An arm partially deflects it and and the edge strikes him above the eye. His eyes are filled with warm liquid. A well-placed blow to the head will now kill him. He hugs his wounded head, sees sparkles and prisms. In his mouth there is a taste like iron.

All at once Paine hears nearby a volley of French words spoken reproachfully and the battering stops. Strong arms lift him to his feet and he stands bent and nauseated and wobbly. He spits red mucus onto the pavement. He is face to face with a gentleman, perhaps thirty years of age, who is himself fully dressed in that same ridiculous uniform, though appearing perfectly dapper. Physically diminutive, elegant, and refined in his manner, he is radiating surprising power and authority. His handsome face is flushed, though otherwise he is fully in control of his person. Paine recognizes

Nicolas de Bonneville, whose press is publishing *Rights of Man!*

"Thomas Paine!" the other man says, now appearing concerned and then relieved. Bonneville is a founder of Cirque, the influential revolutionary club, and from his press in the Palais-Royal, he publishes books and newspapers that promote his public and clandestine revolutionary activities, including *Rights of Man*. Bonneville's face again shows heartfelt concern.

"How did you get here?" Bonneville asks.

"Lafayette brought me."

"Damn him, he left you. Come with me to my apartment. We must get you off the streets."

Paine realizes that his shirt is badly torn, his chest and a shoulder are exposed, and blood is clotted in his chest hairs. His own cocked hat is gone. Somebody hands him a red bonnet bearing the cockade and he puts it on.

Bonneville lives over six miles away, in the Palais-Royal, but a coach could not maneuver the narrow streets amid the crowds. They must walk.

The sun is bright, hot, and joyless. The streets are filled with armed citizens. The people run wildly through the streets. They carry every conceivable variety of arm—rifles with or without bayonets, pistols, sabers, swords, pikes, knives, scythes, saws, iron crows, and wooden billets. Paine and Bonneville are at sea amid the crazed and fanatical, boiling and bloodthirsty populace of Paris, the offensive body odors of the dirty and sweating multitude and the stench of human excrement streaming down the steaming gutters.

Eventually Paine draws closer to Bonneville and speaks to him quietly, choking on his words. "I fear what would have befallen me were it not for your intervention, my friend."

Bonneville replies, "A Frenchman knows nothing else, only tyranny and oppression, for this has been our history. Here, liberty means the freedom to oppress others. The revolution will remain a lie until there is established a republican form of government. That will not be possible until the people have enough to eat."

Bonneville nods in the direction of a queue they are passing, of maybe a hundred citizens holding fast to a rope that extends to a baker's door. Armed National Guardsmen stand nearby to maintain order. They are pushing and cursing one another.

At last they reach the gardens of Palais-Royal. They climb the steps to Bonneville's apartment, which overlooks the gardens and the cafés. He opens the unlocked door and shouts, "Marguerite! Come quickly! I am with a special guest and he is hurt."

A woman appears—a young woman. Paine has never before seen her. A pretty face with a prominent nose and golden eyes, a cascade of curled bright red hair; she is petite, with bare arms; a simple unadorned blue dress cut low at the neckline; the dress highlights her narrow waist and the supple lines of her body; her jaw line is exquisite. She is surprised—her lovely lips are parted.

"Meet Thomas Paine. I rescued him from the *sans-culottes*. They mistook him for an aristocrat." He turns to Paine and says, "Marguerite is your greatest admirer. She has read everything you have published and practically committed *Rights of Man* to memory. She has been very excited about our publishing the French version. She has made it her own special project."

Carefully she removes his ruined shirt, murmuring sympathy. His chest and midriff are bare, but between Paine and Marguerite there is no shame, not a hint of awkwardness. She brings warm water, linens, fresh clothes, and, finally, cognac. She washes him and tends to his wounds.

Now he is clean and wearing a fresh shirt and seated drinking a glass of cognac in Bonneville's parlor, chatting with Nicolas and the woman. She is Marguerite Brazier, and he has learned that the two of them live here together. Evidently they are not married.

Paine is pleased to recognize an educated and worldly woman. Notwithstanding her youth, she is unfailingly self-possessed and at ease. He feels at home with her, as though they have been friends for a very long time. He has all but forgotten about his wounds.

Now she is looking at him, a prolonged and steady gaze. He feels his own eyes drawn to her, a charming woman, with red curling hair, with bare arms and shoulders, and with a pleasant curve of the lips. He feels she is perhaps the most beautiful woman he has ever seen.

All at once feeling uneasy, he looks up and examines an engraving on the wall. In classical style, it features a black man and a black woman and the legends:

He: I am thy equal. Color is nothing, the heart is all, is it not, my brother? And she: In freedom as thou art: The French republic in accord with nature has willed it: am I not thy sister?

She follows his gaze and says, "Nicolas's brother François made it."

"It is extraordinarily fine," he says, "and the idea is exemplary."

He notices another engraving on the wall: A woman is sleeping on a bed, lying on her back. Her gown intimately enfolds her voluptuous figure. Her head and shoulders are draped over the end of the bed; her long neck is exposed and her hair is hanging down. Seated on her midriff is a demon, an incubus that is staring at whoever is examining the engraving. Curtains drape behind the bed; they are parted and emerging from the parting is the head of a horse with bulging eyes appearing sightless.

Paine points at it and says, "Henry Fuseli is my friend." He is the artist. "If you have not seen the original painting, you must."

"I have not been to London," she says.

"I have seen it," Nicolas remarks.

Paine hardly hears his comment for he is looking at Marguerite. He says, "When you make it there, I will show it to you. When it is not exhibited, he keeps it in his drawing room. I will get him to do your portrait too."

She blushes. They discuss the possible meanings of Fuseli's painting. She says, "Maybe Mr. Fuseli himself does not know what his painting means. We now understand the power of reason and it is thrilling to us. What most excites is not the clarity, as much as the mysteries revealed by reason. Nothing is so mysterious as the human mind and character."

He regards her insight as extraordinarily clever and he tells her so. This leads to a discussion about the new movement in art—lush with nature, and there are multitudes of imaginary beings and mythological images.

Next they discuss the business that has brought him to France: the intangible war he is waging with Edmund Burke. He is pleased that she is extremely aware of the story behind *Rights of Man* and of the treatise itself, which Paine originally issued in response to Burke.

Burke fired the first shot with his *Reflections on the Revolution in France*, in which he stated that "we fear God, we look up with awe to kings; with affection to parliaments; with duty to magistrates; with reverence to priests; and with respect to nobility. Why? Because when such ideas are brought before our minds, it is natural to be so affected."

When he read Burke's pamphlet, Paine recoiled, literally reeling physically as though wounded, for he had regarded Burke a friend and political ally, someone who is beloved in the United States for his support of the cause of the American Revolution both as a member of the House of Commons and as a philosopher.

Paine recounts to Nicolas and Marguerite how he confronted Burke outside St. Stephen's Chapel in London following an adjournment of the House of Commons. Burke remained calm, replying, "Paine, you and I, we want essentially the same end; it is the pace of change, and degree of moderation, or revolution, that separates us."

How could they seek the same end if Burke favors retaining a monarchy—albeit greatly reduced—for England and for France, and a Church of England? When Paine tells Marguerite this, she enthusiastically agrees.

She says, "*Rights of Man* exposes monarchies and churches and aristocrats as the source of human misery and thus evil."

"Yes," Paine replies, "and only by the consent of its citizens may governments have a right to arise, and this is the only principle on which they have a right to exist. The Prime Minister, the parliament, the monarchy, and the Church of England themselves are not immune from scrutiny. And as these institutions are the source, rather than in opposition to poverty and oppression, the people are fully justified in revoking their consent that these institutions exist."

"These ideas preceded your writings," says Marguerite, "from John Locke and others. Yet only you have gotten to grips with the real problem of man-made poverty and injustice everywhere. Your *Rights of Man, Part the Second* is truly the first work to put forth programs for a representative government in combination with enumerated social programs financed by progressive tax measures to remedy the awful poverty of commoners. It is a work of genius that surpasses even the original part. Here in France it is being read and praised, condemned and argued about everywhere, it seems, among rich and poor, among the powerful, nobility, merchants, peasants, and criminals alike."

Paine sees that truly she has absorbed every particle of his books, and this is a delight to him.

While they talk, Nicolas remains mostly silent, and Paine is all the time admiring her—mostly her intelligence, her culture, and the directness and sincerity with which she expresses her interest in him. He wonders about her inner life and her life here with Nicolas, and he thinks that she is indeed a marvelous mystery, and he wonders if it is ever possible for anyone to really know another person.

They stop talking. She turns away, slightly, yet enough to avoid his gaze, as though momentarily diffident. There is a hint of blush. She says, "But why did you leave the United States?"

She has sensed that the question may vex him, and it does a little. Originally, his idea for a single-arch iron bridge brought him back to Europe, and he tried, unsuccessfully, to find backers for his plans. Then he could not bring himself to part with London. Truth be told, he has returned to London again and again, ever since he first went there at age twenty-one. He loves that most worldly of all cities, and the longer he spent in the United States—where packs of hogs forage in the streets of Philadelphia, Boston, and New York, and open garbage heaps are everywhere—his longing for it only grew stronger. But these are ignoble reasons.

"My hope," he says, "is to see the restoration of republicanism at its source, in Europe, and to be instrumental in that rebirth."

"But your work is not finished in America. The slaves are not free. Women remain unemancipated. Businessmen and landowners are the new aristocracy."

"We must continuously strive for progress," he says. "We will not live to see the world reach the limit of goodness. Yet America has progressed further than Europe, for Europe is still feudal and still has kings and state religions."

"But I fear," she says, "that here you may find obstacles that did not impede you in America. There, you inhabited a new world. Here, since Augustus we Europeans have been yoked by authority. We know nothing but authority. We have not governed ourselves. Look at the Jacobins. I fear that Danton, Robespierre, and Marat wish to forge a new triumvirate. Today you bore the brunt of a fanaticism in the streets that I find terrifying, to be honest. Your writings are vital, but I fear that they may await later generations to bring about real-life progress."

Now he is more than a little vexed. But he resolves not to argue with her. He is too taken by her charms. "Well," he replies, "maybe so. But if so, my ill-conceived return to Europe has resulted in the happy coincidence of this meeting with you, and the same is true about my near-death experience today and the injuries I have sustained."

Nicolas gets up and leaves the room to fetch more cognac. She is still looking at Paine, and she says, "At last I lay eyes on a great man; I am acquainted with a great man."

Paine does not blush nor does he humbly protest. He says, though he knows full well what she means, "Nicolas is a great man."

"Until you arrived, there were no great men in France. Not since Voltaire."

Now blushing, he says, "Nicolas . . . he saved my life."

"He is a good and capable man. But he is not great. Socrates was a great man, and so are you."

CHAPTER 2

AT NIGHTFALL, PAINE IS seated in the Palais-Royal drinking straw-colored cognac at a table otherwise occupied entirely by women. (Nicolas has preferred to stay in the apartment immersed in his books and papers. There is much to say about today's events, and he wants to be among the first to publish it.) They are seated in the patio before the Joinville colonnade, linked with the Rue de Beaujolais. Before them, the sign *Café du Chartres* is on the façade where the café opens through three arches onto the gardens of the Palais-Royal.

Paine is enjoying himself, notwithstanding the horrors that he experienced a few hours ago, and that his right eye is turning black and swelling shut and a cheek is badly bruised. He has been sipping cognac almost continuously since Marguerite served him that first glass at Bonneville's apartment, and he feels luxuriously relieved and at ease, resolved to enjoy this moment of life. Marguerite is seated beside him and she is a chief source of his enjoyment. The clinking sound of glass and cutlery is accompanied by the usual rumble of conversation. Conversation has been humming around their table at the Café du Chartres.

Except for Marguerite, the women are drinking wine; she, like Paine, is sipping a cognac. Marguerite and a couple of others are also smoking pipes. Paine does not smoke. The women wear simple gowns that hang straight and plain from a bodice cut short at a high waistline — there are subtle differences in design and color, but it is possible to make certain generalizations about their style of dress. There is no trimming except for the fichu that finishes the necklines. They wear cockades at the left side above the heart, as though they were tricolored flowers. There are no corsets or stays, and so is the powder gone: their hair shows its natural color—even gray, as the case may be—worn low in front and hung in clusters of curls behind.

The atmosphere in the Palais-Royal is celebratory, though Paine perceives a dangerous edge to the festivity. The energy is especially high following the day's momentous event, and the gardens and the surrounding stone arcade enclosing the cafés and shops are overflowing with people. Here, deep within the center of Paris, it seems that a metaphysical magma chamber has burst forth this raging torrent of human lava.

Marguerite says, smiling brightly, "The Palais-Royal has become a place where all desires can be gratified as soon as conceived!"

Now Paine is holding forth. He explains that France is in need of a constitution modeled on the American one.

One of the women, her name is Olympe de Gouges, replies, "Yes, France needs a government modeled on the American system—yet still superior." Her English is heavily accented. She is beautiful—tall, with an oval face, brown eyes, an aquiline nose, and abundant dark hair. She has a lorgnette that she keeps lifting to signify her attention when someone else speaks. He cannot tell her age but clearly Marguerite is younger.

"Yes," Paine says, "the American system is deeply flawed. It is unfinished, for slavery remains a thriving institution there."

"I have always been outraged by this—the whole history of it," says Gouges. "As I was growing up, I heard them spoken of like beasts, beings whom heaven had cursed; but as I grew older, I saw that it was force and prejudice that had condemned them to this horrid slavery, for which the unjust and powerful interests of whites are alone responsible, and nature plays no role. Oh, Mr. Paine! We will congratulate you for your constitution that gives black men their rights, should such a happy day come for them. But it will be a sad day for all women—white and black—if men

14

are still unjust toward us. We are ourselves but your slaves. Let us be your voluntary companions who help you create a worthy constitution, Mr. Paine."

"It is my dearest wish. All of you here would, for me, be ideal compatriots."

"Do I sense a note of condescension in what you say? Do you believe that we are not made to be as ambitious as you are?"

"I believe that women do not differ from men in this respect. I expect no less."

"Yet you have named your book *Rights of Man.*"

"It is a figure of speech. As you well know, when in the abstract we say 'men,' we include women."

"Your figure of speech itself betrays the world's eternal injustice toward women. Mr. Paine, can it be that women desire success, a fortune, and a good name less than men do? Actually, it is as natural to women as to men."

"Please, call me Thomas. Olympe, your very life attests the truth of what you say."

Earlier, as they were anticipating this gathering, Marguerite reprised for him Olympe de Gouges's interesting biography. She was born Marie Gouze, legally the daughter of a butcher surnamed Gouze, and Anne Olympe, a maidservant, but in actuality the illegitimate love child of her mother and Jean-Jacques Lefranc, the Marquis de Pompignan, a famous French man of letters who was a bachelor when Olympe was born. Her legal father did not attend her baptism and died two years later. She was close to her biological father throughout her childhood and he provided for her education. But eventually the marquis married a woman of his own class, had a son, and renounced Marie as his daughter, to her amazement. Marie and her mother were nearly destitute, and so at age sixteen she married a minor government official from Paris at her mother's behest and against her will. But the husband soon died and immediately thereafter she came to Paris to work as a courtesan.

The tradition upon undertaking this trade is that the initiate change her name, and so she became Olympe de Gouges, taking her mother's maiden name as her own given name, with slight modification, adjusting her own surname, and adding "de" to give it a faux aristocratic element.

She is nearing completion of her protest piece, against, ironically, the Assembly's *Declaration of the Rights of Man and of the Citizen*, which she has titled, *Declaration of the Rights of Men and Women, and the Male and Female Citizens.* Throughout the piece she has changed the references to "men" in the original document changed to "men and women." It will cause a sensation, Marguerite tells him. She knows the first few lines by heart and recites them to him: "*Man, are you capable of being just? It is a woman who asks you this question. Tell me, what gives you sovereign empire over my sex?*"

Now Olympe says, "Thomas, why then do women not receive the same education and the same means to acquire it as men? As a young woman, I married, and my good fortune was that my husband soon died. I resolved never again to marry. My advice to all unmarried women is that they should not marry! Never! When I married I understood that my life, my liberty, my property was no longer mine; leaving childhood, I was turned over to a despot whom my heart regarded as repulsive. The most beautiful days of my life would slip away in moans and tears. It is not nature whom we have to blame for our lot. Everywhere, the laws favor men at the expense of women, because everywhere power is in the hands of men!"

Paine replies, "Here in France, we can create the perfect society. I am committed to pursuing the ideal that you describe—a utopia for women."

"Do you know what that word means? It comes from Greek, Mr. Paine."

"Utopia? I didn't know it was Greek."

"It means 'nowhere.'"

She has vexed him and he feels like fleeing. But Jacques Pierre Brissot arrives to the rescue. Visitors are repeatedly attending their table. Especially among the writers, Paine is much admired, and word about the *sans-culottes'* mayhem with him has gotten out.

There are many who want to wish him well.

Brissot stands by Paine, and before him he holds his Quaker's hat, nervously rotating the brim in his hands.

Brissot says his chief preoccupation is human rights. He is a French republican, and has founded an anti-slavery club. Like Paine, he takes the habitable globe as his country. Paine knows him from his visits to the United States—at one time he planned to settle there with his wife and children—and London.

Brissot is timid and awkward, and he and the women barely acknowledge one another, though Paine sees that they are acquaintances. Nobody offers him a seat. He wears a dark suit, plain and modest, frayed at the collar. He is slight in frame, short, and his shoulders cave inward. But improbably he has become a household name in France for his fiery speeches at the Jacobin Club, his pamphlets, and his journalism, and he is a member of the Assembly. He has founded a newspaper, the *French Patriot*.

Brissot expresses horror at the attack on Paine, and wishes him a quick recovery. "I heard that it happened at the Hôtel de Ville," he says.

"Yes."

"Danton was there."

"Yes. He was shouting, and taunted Lafayette. This was why the general left."

Brissot shakes his head disapprovingly.

"And what will France become now that the king is gone?" Paine says. "I say let him go. Good riddance."

"Good riddance, yes. Good riddance. I wish it were that simple. Certainly, their destination is Austria, the court of Antoinette's brother, the Holy Roman Emperor! They will invade France to overthrow the revolutionary government and reclaim their throne, restore the power of the monarchy and the nobility. That is their plan, I assure you; not to retire from the throne. France must declare war on Austria at once. It is better to make our enemy's country the theater of war than our own."

"Do not lightly plunge France into war. Our cause is worth the price of war, but is it really necessary? Is France ready to wage war on the Holy Roman Empire?"

Brissot's eyes flash and he brandishes a finger at Paine. Suddenly his faced is flushed, as though from too much drink. "War!" he says. "That is the wish of all friends of liberty spread out across the face of Europe; a war of expiation—now we have good reason to attack and overthrow the tyrants all across Europe! A holy war to renew the naturally human face of the world and plant the standard of liberty over the palaces of kings, the harems of sultans, the châteaux of petty feudal tyrants, the temples of popes and muftis. Your own good United States required such a war."

Paine is enjoying the rhetoric, but Brissot abruptly stops. He bows curtly at a handsome young man who has just arrived and stands beside him. "Hello, Camille," says Brissot, now again nervous.

All at once Paine confronts his alter ego. Camille Desmoulins, like Paine in America, is the revoltion's mouthpiece. Paine has been well aware of this handsome youth and his reputation. He sees Marguerite gazing at Camille, her smile effulgent. It occurs to him that in truth there may be another in France whom she regards a great man: he who gave the seismic oration that impelled the mob to the Bastille.

Camille removes his hat, places it on the table, takes Paine's right hand and clasps it, bowing deeply. It appears he is about to kiss the hand, but his head drops beneath the conjoined hands. "You are my hero," he says in English, rising. "In all my doings I have tried to emulate your achievement with *Common Sense*. It is the greatest narrative ever written, intellectually impeccable, and in the language of common men and women. We owe our own revolution to it."

Seemingly all of the world is wondering how Thomas Paine, the son of a corset stay-maker from Thetford, a tiny village, a former stay-maker himself, reinvented himself as Thomas Paine, who by his words, in *Common Sense,* and now *Rights of Man,* incited the masses of under-educated to assault the *anciens régimes* across two continents. Paine believes that the power of his words comes only from human reason. Yet Paine is surprised; he had thought that Camille spoke little English.

"We haven't spoken before," says Paine. "I did not know you could speak English so well."

"But he is so outlandishly intelligent, how could he not?" says Marguerite.

Camille raises a splayed hand. "Y-y-yes, I do, but not so well. I try hard." He is speaking deliberately, quelling his stammer. "I talk to my friends, I pick it up little by little, b-b-but I don't speak as well as my friends do, Marguerite, Brissot, Danton. Marguerite here has taught me, we speak it," says Camille. "She is better educated than any of us."

"She has helped us all," interjects Olympe, "and with good reason. A respectable public intellectual must know English."

Camille dips his head. "Of course, it is the language of liberty, of Hume, Franklin, Jefferson, and Paine."

Brissot waves goodbye and leaves. Camille leans forward and inspects Paine's injuries. "I'm, I am so sorry this happened to you," he says, straightening. "The *sans-culottes* have suffered so much, they are very angry. I'm glad you have Marguerite here to look after you." He is looking at Marguerite. Her eyes are smiling. "He is staying with you?" Camille says to her.

"Yes. We have persuaded him not to return to Lafayette's place. It is not the best place for him right now. Nicolas gave up his study with the bed chamber. Next we will persuade him to stay in Paris."

"Excellent." He looks at Paine. "I used to live with them."

"I fear Paris is not a good fit for me," says Paine, surprised that he is suddenly blushing. "It is not like England or the United States."

"Yes," Camille says to him. "It is quite different. But it is hard to resist Marguerite's charms."

Marguerite speaks French to Camille and he likewise responds. She is animated, and Paine can see that she is very much enjoying this exchange. She pretends to plead with him, and he declines whatever it is she wishes. She levels good-natured insults. He makes her laugh, and her eyes are shining.

She turns to Paine. "I am asking him to dine with us. He refuses. He prefers the set at Café de Foy. Danton is there. And Philippe may show his face there, but not here. We are dismissed as cloistered intellectuals. We're irrelevant."

Camille seizes a nearby empty chair, swings it so the back is in front and sits down between them, straddling the chair just outside their circle. He says, "So my friend Brissot is advocating for war."

"Yes," says Paine. "What do you think about that?"

"W-we . . . ah, we must make every effort to avoid war. As usual, Brissot is dogmatic, and impractical. Brissot brings rigid puritanism and the zeal of a monk to this cause we share of overthrowing monarchy and state religion. Shall we forge a republican continent out of Europe? We must first get our own house in order. The people are hungry. W-we need to relieve the people's suffering; we need a constitution and a functioning republic before we can consider the luxury of war to make a continental republic. And if we militarize the country, we cede power to the generals, who may be disguised royalists, or, worse, we will get Caesar, a dictator. What do you think about this war that Brissot advocates, Paine?"

"I think that wars happen because of wicked leaders. Bad government. Foolish leaders who blunder are the reasons war occurs. Heedless of war's awful consequences. The fly-blown corpses of young men, trampled crops, burned cities, rape. Muskets, swords, armor, cannon, these are not natural features of human beings. They are perversions. Yet the evil that men do means that there can be such thing as a just war. No?"

Olympe says, "Brissot says that Louis Capet will return with his brother-in-law and an awful Holy Roman army to restore the royalty here." After the events of today, everyone is resolved from now on to call the fleeing king Louis Capet, his common name.

"Perhaps," says Camille, "in that event, we may have no choice but to go to war. But meantime, we should try to avoid it, and we should let the king go. At the Cordeliers Club, we put up a placard today: 'If among us there be found a traitor and who could regret kings, and who could wish a master, let the wretch die in the midst of torments.'" He laughs.

"Ha!" exclaims Marguerite. "Voltaire's Brutus! His very words. How clever."

Camille winks at her and continues. "Unfortunately, Lafayette has sent the National Guard after him. The general wants to redeem himself, even if it is a disservice to his countrymen. If the king is captured, what shall we do with him? Danton vows that he will stand trial for treason."

Marguerite is smiling blissfully at Camille. Paine is stung by that wink and her reaction. He says emphatically, "Capet's life must be spared. France cannot stoop so low as to kill the king." Killing the king seems a farfetched possibility. Yet more than a century ago, the British tried and executed for treason Charles I—the traitorous act being his efforts to retain his office. Paine has heard murmurings that France cannot progress to true republicanism while the king still lives and his death may be "cruel necessity," as Oliver Cromwell remarked over King Charles's grave. Now, after the king's escape to Antionette's homeland in the heart of the Holy Roman Empire, it would not take an inventive prosecutor to charge the king with treason.

"Of course," says Camille amiably, "I very much oppose penalty of death for anyone, even for the perfidious king. His life should be spared. So, what shall we do with him? It will be a misfortune if this faithless man is brought back to us. He would come like Thersites, an ugly buffoon to shed the great tear of which Homer speaks. If he is brought back, I shall make a motion in the Assembly that he be three days exposed to public ridicule, with a red handkerchief on his head, and then conducted to the frontier for exile."

Everyone at the table laughs, Marguerite loudest of all. She looks adoringly at him. Paine is galled by that look.

"France needs a constitution like the American one," says Paine, again emphatically, now sounding nearly vengeful.

"Of course," Camille replies.

They talk for a while longer, the others joining the discussion.

Eventually, Camille stands and says, "I must go."

Marguerite gives him a wounded look. "Where is Lucile?" she says.

"I don't know. I don't want to know." He smiles and winks at her. "I think she is at her parents' house."

"When are you going to have a baby?"

"I don't know if we should bring a child into a world such as we have now. Where is Nicolas?"

She gestures with her head in the direction of their apartment. "Working."

"He needs to spend more time in the streets, with the people. That is what I tell Robespierre too."

Paine is chagrined, and disappointed with himself, that he is envious of Camille, of his youthful charms, his elegance and easy amorality, and Marguerite's attraction to him. When Paine was his age, his life was beset by poverty and grief and hapless struggle. Since unexpected fame rewarded his labors in America, Paine has carefully cultivated the image of an ascetic. He cannot be seen as a man corrupted by greed or lust or deluded by romance: He is a man of reason, like Lucretius. Paine regards himself a virtuous man in the way that Aristotle defined virtue as the highest aim of a man's professional life—someone so devoted to civic service that he became revered in his lifetime, and after death was remembered by history for his great and generous work. Yet he cannot help himself. Sometimes he is beset by longing and regret.

"Ah, my friends!" Nicolas de Condorcet's stout body now stands before them. Condorcet is Paine's dear old friend. Paine loves Condorcet. He is an influential advocate for freedom of speech, free and equal public instruction, a constitutional democratic government modeled on the United States, a liberal economy, and equal rights for women and people of all races. He is a delegate to the Assembly and a famous scientist and philosopher; he has published mathematical and philosophical treatises that will withstand the ages.

Paine turns to Condorcet and says, "I want to form a club that we will call 'The Republican Club,' and it will issue a newspaper called *The Republican*. Our first action will be to declare the need for a constitution like in the United States."

"France already has enough clubs like that. I'll speak to Danton about getting you a forum at the Cordeliers Club, and to Robespierre about the Jacobin Club. Brissot can arrange it at the Jacobin Club, for that matter."

"Our club will be different. The narrow focus will be to promulgate a new constitution modeled on the American one. Who has said publicly that France must become a republic? Nobody. The purpose of our Republican Club will be to proclaim that republican government is essential and to make a case for a republican France. Nicolas and I will schedule a meeting soon. I'm sure Brissot will join us. Will you come?"

Actually, Paine despairs that his Republican Club is possible. He sees that there are no natural leaders among his circle—Paine is a philosopher and a writer, after all. Brissot comes closest. They will have to rely upon him. Condorcet, like Bonneville, is a scholar who prefers a cloistered life of study. Though a famous scholar, he is painfully shy, wholly lacking in social polish. He is stout and has a gauche way of standing—as though he is a priest bowed before an altar—he bites his lips and chews his fingernails, and has chalk powder in his ears. His voice lacks intonation. Olympe or Marguerite, or Condorcet's beautiful and brilliant wife Sophie, who maintains a widely admired and attended salon, would be fitter leaders. But France is not yet so enlightened as to tolerate any woman in politics.

"Of course," says Condorcet, "if you want me to."

Suddenly, Paine's mood again rises. He has found his community, he tells himself. Here is the meaning of life. Society among educated, like minded people who share his belief in liberty, and the importance of each individual human being, no matter how low his status or means or level of piety. There could be no better refuge for Paine at this moment than the Palais-Royal: he perceives a public sphere of enlightenment; a site of openness, tolerance, and civility, and a space for rational debate.

———————

It is a time of high energy, and frequently Nicolas and Marguerite host their revolutionary friends. Marguerite is inquisitive, tireless, and confident in the power of her beauty and her charms and her smiles. She gives suppers, entertaining their political allies, and plays the clavichord.

When she is not entertaining friends, she takes Paine to visit the salons, coffee houses, fashionable cafés, theaters, gaming rooms, and clubs within and outside the Palais-Royal. Nicolas prefers to live in a solitary manner, absorbed with his reading and writing, while Marguerite is more outgoing and gregarious, like Paine.

At night Paine lies awake in bed and wonders if they are lovers. He imagines creaks and moans, but hears no sound providing irrefutable confirmation.

———————

From Nicolas de Bonneville's newspaper, *The Mouth of Iron*:

No more kings, no more man-eaters for us! The name has been frequently changed, but the thing itself has been retained. Now let us have no regent, no dictator, no protector, no Orléans, no Lafayette! Must a nation be under tutelage forever? Let our departments unite and declare that they will have neither tyrant nor king, neither protector nor regent, nor any of those semblances of royalty whose shadow is as fatal to the public welfare as the accursed upas-tree is fatal to those that come beneath its shade.

———————

From Jean-Paul Marat's newspaper, *The Friend of the People*:

There is only one means left to pull you back from the precipice to which your unworthy leaders have led you, and that's to imme-diately name a military tribune, a supreme dictator, to put down the principal known traitors. Let the Tribune be named today. Let your choice fall upon the citizen who has, until this day, shown the most enlightenment, zeal and fidelity. Swear to him an inviolable devotion and obey him religiously in all he commands you in order to shed yourselves of your mortal enemies.

June 25, 1791. Paine will never forget the awful silence. Assembly deputies and six thousand armed citizens escort the royal family back to Paris.

The royal couple and their children were disguised as common travelers but their coach was laden and slow and they required extra horses and changes of horses, as they could not live without the usual comforts. Jean-Baptiste Drouet, the postmaster of Sainte-Menehould, recognized the king from his portrait printed on an assignat in his possession. He rode ahead to Varennes, and the royal family was arrested there after they took lodgings and a night's sleep. They had traveled one hundred and sixty-five miles, and were within thirty-one miles of their ultimate destination, the royalist citadel of Montmédy in Austria, Antoinette's homeland. Their intention was clear: to return as invaders to reclaim the throne.

All of Paris appears of one mind in their hatred of the king. The streets are thronged with men and women, and the garden walls, the windows, the balconies, and the roofs are packed with citizens watching the king's procession, escorted by municipal officers, National Guardsmen gunners, gendarmes, hussars. The carriage advances slowly. Hats remain in place, not one removed to show respect. Guns and swords are crossed in defiance of the king.

News moves rapidly through the crowd that Antoinette's face is lined and her hair is gray. In the space of a week she has become an old woman.

———————

They are just the two of them, Paine and Marguerite, seated at a small table in the Café du Chartres, drinking cognac.

"Is Nicolas your fiancé?" he asks.

"No. I have no plans to marry. Not him, not anyone."

"Are you lovers?"

"Of course, you silly man; a woman needs her lovers, just as any man does. Who is yours?"

"I have no lovers. Not for a long time. My calling does not allow for it."

"I don't believe you. If what you say is true, it is not healthy. You must have a lover."

———————

Socrates was a great man, and so are you. Her flattery has made him believe that he can accomplish anything here that he did in America. Paine sits in Nicolas's study, at the desk beside the window, wishing for a cooling breeze, distracted by the people in the streets. He stares at the blank page, blocked. Paine is resolved to write a *Common Sense* for France. And if he possesses enough faith in himself to believe this is possible, is it not without reason? Is it not his very genius for explaining modern, patrician ideas in essays that any plebeian can read and understand that have made him famous? Only he was able to arouse common men to the cause of independence from England. It was his words, in *Common Sense*, that incited common Americans to rebel against their mother country.

A single phrase from *Common Sense* stands out in his mind: *For all men being originally equals, no one by birth could have the right to set up his own family in perpetual preference to all others forever.* Inspiration takes root and begins to grow. He dips the pen into the well of ink. He begins to write, the sentences spilling forth, like a living thing. "Let France then, arrived at the age of reason, no longer be deluded by the sound of words, and let her deliberately examine, if a king, however insignificant and contemptible in himself, may not at the same time be extremely dangerous. . . ." He calls this work *The Republican Proclamation.*

It is after midnight when Paine and his companions leave the Palais-Royal and emerge onto the streets, surrounded by high buildings, streetlamps, and the lights of shops and houses and gleaming fine carriages at rest. They are all three of them nearly drunk—Marguerite, Paine, and Achille Duchâtelet, a young French noble. Marguerite is at Paine's side, wrapped in a cloak that covers her head, and bearing a can of paste and a brush. Paine carries hundreds of copies of his *Proclamation,* as does Duchâtelet. The three of them have taken it upon themselves to placard the city's buildings with this document. They have decided that a Frenchman must put his name as the author of the *Proclamation,* and Duchâtelet gamely agreed. At seventeen he served under Lafayette in the United States. He is Paine's enthusiastic admirer, imbued with republican principles. He devoured Paine's books and the *Proclamation.* He is brave, open, honest, and generous; he has education, taste, and polish, and is unfailingly amiable. But he is heedlessly impetuous, ambitious for miliatary glory, as his noble birth has superseded the necessity of discretion.

When they are in open spaces, the squares and the gardens, the cobbles and the water are spread out before them gleaming.

Paine could not feel more vigorous and alert. He inhales a vaporous elixir of eternal life and joy.

He asks her, "Are you afraid?"

"I am not afraid," she answers.

She seems bright and animated in a way that is extraordinary, even for her. Paine does not leave her side, and during their night's work he is nearly oblivious of the earnest Duchâtelet. He feels he is discovering a new facet of her personality, and his own; he will know her better after tonight.

At last, their subversive work is nearly done. Paris is placarded with the *Proclamation* signed by Duchâtelet. Upon returning to the neighborhood of the Palais-Royal and the Tuileries Palace, they cover the doors of the Salle du Manège where the Assembly meets. Here he and Marguerite are laughing out loud, nearly stumbling over one another and themselves.

They bid goodbye to Duchâtelet. Inside the Palais-Royal he slips his hands inside the hood that covers her head, and she moves against him. He kisses her on the lips and she kisses him back full on the lips, the lips parted. Neither of them has anything to say and they go quietly to their own beds.

———

Paine and Marguerite are in Nicolas's book shop talking, she is behind the counter, when Marat enterers. It is extraordinary, considering that he and Bonneville loathe one another. His face is blotched and mottled and scabbed; he walks in his irregular nervous way.

"The republican placards have been taken down," he says. "Today the Assembly denounced whoever it was that was behind them." Marat's tone of voice is pedantic, a faintly disgusted sing-song. "We debated whether to prosecute this Duchâtelet. Condorcet persuaded us not to make a martyr of him, and that he most certainly is not responsible. The content and style of writing could not be that of this callow Duchâtelet. He is somebody's dupe." Marat looks at Paine. "Is it possible that you believe in a republic? You are too enlightened to be the dupe of such a fantastic dream."

Marguerite replies for him, "He is no dupe, for he was enlightened enough to have imagined and single handedly created the proclamation that inspired the Americans to revolt from England and establish their own republic."

When he is gone, Marguerite says, "He makes my blood run cold." She picks up a newspaper from the stacks and looks closely at it, and then she reads out loud, "He says, 'Select, a true Frenchman and a true patriot, the citizen who has displayed the most intelligence, the most zeal, fidelity, and disinterestedness, take him at once, or the Revolutionary cause is lost.' He nominates himself dictator."

In the coming days they talk continuously, as though they were new lovers, but she will not engage him about two subjects—her age or her origins. Nobody, she says, not even Nicolas, knows about her past, and she wants to keep it that way. He suspects lowly or scandalous origins; but he does not care. His own roots are common. Yet her education is impeccable, even by the nobility's standards.

The Assembly's reaction to Paine's *Proclamation* has soured him on France. And while sharing a home with his friend Bonneville, he cannot bring himself to act further on his fanciful infatuation with Marguerite. His infatuation with this young woman is an ignoble reason to remain in France. Suddenly a letter from Mary Wollstonecraft arrives, misaddressed to and finally delivered from Lafayette's apartment. It says, "You must return to London at once. *Rights of Man* is now erupting in popularity among the people. Your hour has arrived!" His hour in Britain has arrived, but soberly, Paine realizes he must be there with his publisher and supporters to confront the inevitable backlash.

When he is about to mount the carriage steps and leave for London, he turns and says goodbye to Marguerite, she kisses his lips, in full view of Nicolas, who appears impassive. Paine appreciates that Nicolas and Marguerite belong to one another, and they will be together, and he will be left alone, as always.

"You'd better return," says Nicolas. "Your friends are going to need you to share your enlightenment."

"I will return," says Paine, "to see the monarchy abolished." He is still gazing into her eyes. So too he feels an attraction to her that will not dissipate even when stretched as far as London.

After Paine returns to London, in the coming days, weeks, and months extending to more than a year, he imagines Marguerite as Artemis depicted in a picture he once saw displayed in a London gallery. She is fair as alabaster, her skin glows as though bathed in moonlight; she has a tall body, slim hips, an upper body that evinces manly strength, arresting gold eyes, and a high forehead. Her red hair is long with braided strands. She carries a silver bow with gold arrows, and she wears a white and green toga and a silver moon diadem.

CHAPTER 3

JULY 10, 1791: CAMILLE is at the Jacobin Club. The club is so named because it holds its meetings in a former hall of the Convent of Jacobins (the sobriquet for the Dominican order in Paris), in the Rue Saint-Honoré. Like the royalty's indoor riding academy requisitioned by the National Assembly, the Salle du Manège, this hall was chosen as the only space available to house so large a crowd as needed for its immense gatherings. Before the revolution, no space was needed for large indoor gatherings because the government prohibited them. Tonight, the galleries are filled to capacity—eight hundred onlookers—and below them the ground floor of the hall is filled with hundreds of the club's members. Everyone in the hall is wearing the red cap of liberty with the tricolor cockade. Outside, there is a crowd bunched around the entrance, disappointed that there is insufficient room for them in the hall. The hall is noisy and humid.

Marat, the club president, steps to the tribune and suddenly there is silence. Marat is not just Camille's chief rival as a radical journalist and pamphleteer. Camille appreciates that Marat is an effective politician beloved in the streets of Paris—the name of his journal, *The Friend of the People*, truly describes him. Born a noble, the common people adoringly regard Marat as a traitor to his class. He was once a well-known doctor in London who published admired books on science and philosophy. Now Marat's radical polemics surpass any peer's, advocating the most direct means to rectifying historical injustices—violent redistribution of property. He once wrote to his working class readers, *Five or six hundred heads cut off would have assured your repose, freedom, and happiness. A false humanity has held your arms and suspended your blows; because of this millions of your brothers will lose their lives.* Camille also regards Marat as a self-promoter extraordinaire. Marat's extreme politics and writing made him a special target of the king's police, and many times Camille has heard him boast to rapt listeners, "Exposed to a thousand dangers, encompassed by spies, police-agents, and assassins, I hurried from retreat to retreat, often unable to sleep for two consecutive nights in the same bed." According to Marat, to evade arrest, he sometimes descended into sewers, and lived in cellars, writing day and night in subterranean retreats, by miserable light. Yet now he moves about freely, above ground, protected by a burgeoning armed squad Camille has observed as comprised of foreign vagabonds, dregs of all nations, convicted murderers, and other perpetrators of violent crimes.

But Marat's persona remains impoverished and unrefined notwithstanding his current security and a new domestic arrangement with a twenty-six-year-old bride (of noble upbringing). Tonight, he wears his regular tattered waistcoat over his naked breast.

He begins to speak. Here his voice lacks the usual singsong, pedantic tone. There is the usual rasp, but the tenor is avuncular; he is addressing not the other club members, but the gallery—these are his children.

Then Robespierre advances to the tribune. Everyone stands, and there is thunderous cheering and stamping of the feet, and whistling. His costume is the same as always, and, as always, precise, modest, and scrupulously clean. He wears a bright blue coat buttoned over the hips and open at the chest, displaying a white waistcoat and yellow breeches, with white stockings, and shoes with silver buckles. His powdered hair is turned up in clusters over his temples.

At the tribune he stands with his chest thrown out and shoulders squared; his words are emitted like lightning bolts. The intonation is thunderous, crackling, hard-edged, and self-assured, arousing moans and howls of wonder and enthusiastic roars and applause—not any ordinary applause, but ritual response.

Robespierre was once derided for his weak voice. He is a learner.

The cheering from the galleries is notably high-pitched, because of the extraordinary proportion of women. Camille senses holy fury ready to rip apart any dissenter. Tonight Robespierre is railing repeatedly against *la philosophe* and *les philosophes*, against all of those known for their *intelligence artificielle* gained from books. He finishes, and the stamping, cheering, and applause are climactic.

Once the noise has died down, Brissot moves quickly to the tribune, absent introduction, and begins to speak. It is difficult to hear all his words because of crowd noise. He refers to Robespierre repeatedly by name, and he speaks of those such as Rousseau, whose virtues are distinguished by their *intelligence special*, their *genie*, and their *idées fondamentales* gained from much study and reflection.

He exclaims enthusiastically about the Assembly's *Declaration of the Rights of Man and of the Citizen* and the future constitution. His pronouncements are first met with gentle murmuring, working up to loud interjections, and culminating in thunderous stamping, hissing, and denunciation that is uninterrupted. Finally, his voice is drowned out and he is forced to quit his oration prematurely. Camille is aware that the heckling started with compensated Robespierre and Marat plants.

July 14: It is nearly dawn and the Palais-Royal is now quiet. Camille and Danton are alone, seated at a table in the Café de Foy. Danton seizes the bottle and pours wine into Camille's glass and then his, finishing it off.

In the Cordeliers district of Paris, on the Left Bank of the Seine, where Camille has set up home on the Place de l'Odéon, and lives very well thanks to Lucile's dowry of one hundred thousand francs, he finds relief from Robespierre's austerity in Danton, who lives nearby, and also a lawyer turned revolutionary. The two of them founded the Cordeliers Club—its meetings are held in the Cordeliers Convent. Camille and Danton founded the Cordeliers as a satellite if not a rival of the Jacobin Club.

Danton is sensual, mysteriously possessed of money enough to live lavishly, and physically imposing. His very attraction derives not only from his humor and oratory and irreverence, but as well from his weird ugliness. There is a deep scar across his lips, and his nose is bent and misshapen from a youthful encounter with a bull—a badge of his rural upbringing. Smallpox ruined his complexion. His bulbous cheeks give him the look of an enormous cherub. He is a giant, and his thick, long hair hangs shaggy and undressed.

They are discussing the day's unhappy event. The unthinkable has happened. The Assembly has, by majority vote, reinstated Louis Capet as king, because he has capitulated to the idea of establishing a constitutional monarchy, and because, it is now clear, bourgeois and aristocratic elements still hold sway in the Assembly. A new constitution will be adopted, and in return the Assembly will also grant the king immunity from prosecution for his desertion and apparent treason. The Assembly will announce that the royal family was "kidnapped" by Austrian agents. More than anything, it seems, what everyone now wants is stability.

But following the royals' attempted escape, Camille and Danton now want no less than their abdication. Robespierre wants the king and queen tried for treason. The Assembly, however, rejected motions made by Marat and Robespierre.

Danton changes the subject. He says, "I want to discuss a sensitive matter with you. About your wife and General Arthur Dillon."

"How disappointing," says Camille, "I was hoping we could talk about something interesting."

"He is a royalist."

"Still, he is my friend."

"Do you know Dillon well?"

"Of course I know him. He is a royalist, yet have I not said that I regard him my friend?" Dillon is about ten years older than Camille. It is a complicated friendship. Dillon represents Martinique in the Assembly—while retaining his noble status.

Camille met Dillon in the heady days of 1789 following the storming of the Bastille, at one of the popular Paris salons. Initially, he regarded the general a valuable contact, and Camille was much taken with his wife, a beautiful and wealthy French Creole from Martinique, Laure de Girardin de Montgérald, the Comtesse de la Touche.

Irish by descent, Dillon's good looks and aristocratic manner are bred in the bone. Camille was captivated by the tales of heroism and French colonization in the tropical New World—the white sands and densely forested volcanoes and mountains descending steeply to the clear blue seas.

The general was likewise drawn to Camille, though less by Camille's skill and reputation as a subversive writer than the bold and quick action, and the enormous risk a man such as Camille, a man of letters, took on July 12, 1789, in the Palais-Royal, which changed the course of French and world history. The general never tires of questioning him about it, which is very gratifying to Camille.

"Does your wife often see Dillon?" says Danton.

After they became friends, Camille began to see that the general was evidently fond of Lucile, whom he dazzled with his wit and preternatural good looks. She likes him too. They flirt. Camille has facilitated their growing intimacy, and privately encourages the general to pursue her, partially as a gesture of friendship and political alliance, but also for the sheer sake of Camille's own perversity, and because insofar as his marital vows are concerned, he is not a hypocrite. His own liberation would grow in equal measure with hers. Thus he is untroubled, a little titillated, actually, at the rumors that he knows Danton is about to address.

"I don't think she has seen him four times in her life," Camille says.

"Since you take it so philosophically, you must know that Dillon betrays you as surely as he will betray the Republic."

"How do you know this?"

"Everyone gossips about it."

"If everyone says so, then it must be that my wife and General Dillon have been unfaithful to me. I see plainly that you do not know my wife as you think you do. You are correct. I am untroubled by the rumors."

Camille happens to know that the rumors are false. Lucile is like her well-married mother, whom Camille relentlessly pursued, and who rebuffed Camille before he fell in love with the daughter. Lucile will endlessly flirt with the general, meet privately with him, sip wine and cognac with him, dress in her finest for him, listen rapt to the vivid tales of his adventures, touch his hand and grasp his forearm, hug him, and give him her best smiles—because she likes him and enjoys his company, and she is ambitious for her husband. But alas for the general, ultimately all she gives is tantalizing but excruciatingly unfulfilled anticipation.

"You are not a handsome fellow," says Danton. Camille can see that behind a flat aspect, Georges is barely concealing a smile. His eyes are twinkling.

"Far from it."

"Your wife is lovely, Dillon is still handsome, and women are so fickle."

"Some, at least."

"I am sorry for you. I hope you will remain so philosophical if I tell you that I am envious of Dillon. I, too, am your friend, and you know I am besotted with your wife."

"You know me, you are my closest friend. Believe me," continues Camille, "if Dillon betrays the Republic as he betrays me, I will answer for his innocence. As for your interest in my wife, as I said, apparently you do not know her as well as you think you do . . . B-but I'm flattered. G-go ahead; see if you can interest her. And Georges"—here, Camille takes Danton's forearm—"we are not friends in the same way that Dillon and I are. We share a destiny."

Later that day, Camille, Danton, and Robespierre meet in Camille's drawing room. They are unable to meet at their usual place, the Café de Foy, as they must maintain strict secrecy. Robespierre lives with his sister Charlotte, and they could not avoid her officious intrusions. Danton lives in a comfortable house like Camille's, but there is a noisy baby. So Robespierre collected Danton and brought him to Camille's drawing room. Camille knows that Lucile is pretending to be fast asleep, but is actually not far off, eavesdropping. She wants him to do whatever is necessary to advance the revolution.

Lucile's dowry financed this room's fine furnishings and elegance. There is a white marble fireplace with a bright, lively fire, a crystal chandelier, padded linen walls, and silver trimmed drapes. There is a lacquered harpsichord. The fire has made the room comfortably warm. Camille is seated in an armchair of wood and silk upholstery that is among several pieces of furniture that are in the style popular before 1789. Robespierre and Danton each sits in a matching chair that lacks the arms. This is the first time that the two great men have together been in Camille's house. Camille is anxious; he feels vaguely that though they are political allies, these two most important friends of his harbor a secret dislike for one another.

Usually, Robespierre has the anxious but rather gentle look of a domestic cat, but today he has the fierce and wiley look of a wild cat. Indeed, something feline resides in the shape of the head and character of the face—a small mouth, almond-shaped eyes, arching brows, and the profile of a back-sloping forehead declining into a long but not too prominent nose; green eyes and pale complexion. Camille has seen that feline face change character in interesting ways. He has also seen—though rarely—the savage look of a tiger.

"Neither Danton nor I can start a revolution against the Assembly," says Robespierre. "It would be an act of insurrection, not against the king, but the revolutionary legislature. We cannot be seen to undermine the institution that stands for the revolution, yet legislated this!" His scowl deepens. "We would deserve to be arrested. But you, Camille, you are unrestrained, because you are a journalist, and the government cannot be seen to abridge your freedom of speech. So, too, the people will remember, it was you who initiated the uprising against the Bastille. You are perfect for this place and time. Now, this falls to you."

"So what is our plan?" says Camille.

"The plan is that the Cordeliers Club will placard the city with a petition demanding the king's abdication. It will also announce a demonstration, on July 17, at the altar of the homeland."

The altar of the homeland is where the Fête de la Fédération was celebrated last year to honor the anniversary of the storming of the Bastille. The altar and the stadium were built in anticipation of last year's event.

"The substance of the petition," continues Robespierre, "will be to charge that Louis Capet's crime is proven, that Capet has abdicated; to demand that the Assembly accept his abdication, that he be tried for treason, and to call for a new, reconstituted legislative body that will proceed in the nation's best interest, issuing a judgment against Capet and replacing the king with a newly designated executive power."

"This is the same as Brissot originally proposed," says Camille. "The Jacobin Club was to placard the city and man the demonstration."

A flicker of annoyance on Robespierre's countenance. He replies, "I interceded and persuaded Brissot that Assembly members could not undermine the Assembly or its decrees."

Camille feels that, most of all, Robespierre did not want Brissot to lead a popular uprising. He loathes Brissot and considers him not an ally but a rival. For that matter, Camille realizes, Robespierre may not want Danton to lead a popular uprising for a similar reason.

Robespierre drones on, describing details of the plan. Camille's anxiety is rising. Before an audience, usually his stammer impedes him, so many thoughts and emotions assail him. More important, he himself fears arrest. That he is a writer will not immunize him from arrest. Perhaps the contrary is true.

At this moment, he is keenly aware of the exquisite little home that surrounds him, Lucile in the next room, sleeping or an ear cocked, this precious home life with Lucile and their plans for a family of their own. Camille is looking at Robespierre's slender, pale, almost feminine hands, as though they were playing at cards and his friend were dealing. It is uncanny that Robespierre is forever scheming, yet always he absents himself from the action.

Camille has lost track of the conversation. Robespierre has stopped talking, he and Danton are looking at Camille and expecting him to say something. He must say something, and he summons the words, "What do you supppose we can expect from Lafayette and his National Guards? I believe the general regards himself de facto Prime Minister and wants to maintain the new order."

"Where is Paine?" says Danton. "Perhaps he can have a word with Lafayette, size him up, urge restraint whatever may be a foot. We do want the demonstration to be peaceful."

"Paine has returned to London," replies Camille.

"We need to get him back here," says Danton.

Robespierre is looking annoyed at this digression, his small mouth pursed. He says sharply, "Camille, you don't look so well. Maybe you aren't the right man for this."

Camille is racking his brain for a clever repartee in response to Robespierre's admonition. Before he can answer Danton says, "Max, Camille and I both lead the Cordeliers Club. I want to do this with Camille. We will be calling for abolition of the Assembly. I am not a member, and I do not feel beholden to it. As for the possibility of my arrest, I can't ask others to risk what I myself would not suffer."

Robespierre stares at Danton. Robespierre smiles faintly, and his look is returned to that of the domestic cat. There is a pause, Camille hoping he will agree. "Very well," Robespierre says. "Suit yourselves."

Camille is relieved.

"And one more thing." Robespierre looks back at Camille and says, "Camille, keep writing your articles."

Camille has already written several belittling the king. Most are not factual reportage so much as satirical commentary.

"Of course. I didn't realize you followed them."

"I follow everything you do, Camille. You know that."

No. 83:

When Louis XVI re-entered his apartment at the Tuileries, he threw himself into an armchair, saying, "It's devilish hot," then, "That was a journey. However, I have had it in my head to do it for a long time." Afterwards, looking towards the National Guardsmen who were present, he said, "I have done a foolish thing, I admit. But must I not have my follies, like other people? Come along, bring me a chicken." One of his valets came in. "Ah, there you are," he said, "and here I am." They brought the chicken, and Louis XVI ate and drank with an appetite that would have done honor to the King of Cockayne.

No. 84:

The Assembly has treated the king, an accused person, too well. They ought not to have awaited his convenience, to have permitted a criminal to take a bath when the commissioners were coming, and waited in the ante-room until his bell rang for the Assembly to be admitted, like bath attendants. Did any one ever see judges writing their names in the lodge-keeper's book at a prison, by way of humbly asking the accused to favor them with an audience, and to name the hour? Such subservience never was heard of before.

Sunday, July 17: It is said that the vast stadium surrounding the Champ-de-Mars has a seating capacity of one hundred thousand, and Camille estimates some fifty thousand are present. Since it is Sunday, all work places and theaters are closed. Paris has burst forth this raging torrent through its thousand avenues. Upon the platform is a maelstrom of patriots and patriotesses signing the petition for the king's abdication set forth at the head of a long scroll, now unfurled and bearing the ever increasing number of signatures, now about six thousand. All the present revolutionaries have signed, some in bold and flowery strokes; from the populace there are many signatures in the form of an "X" as they are disproportionately from the illiterate poor.

Camille stands on the crowded wooden platform bearing the altar and the tribune for the speakers, watching the crowd. On the field, people are standing, milling about, parading, mostly in Sunday best. Men in cocked hats, women in bonnets and bearing flowers and garlands—and men and women alike are wearing the tricolor cockade. Children—girls, their hair done in ringlets and wearing immaculate dresses—and boys in suspendered breeches—all as well bearing the cockade one place or another on their diminutive bodies. Most are residents of Paris, but many come from surrounding areas also to protest the Assembly's unholy compromise allowing Louis Capet to remain king. Camille can see that many young people are also here for lack of anything better to do.

Flags gently fluttering show the tricolor; he sees here and there a few of England and the United States. It is past seven in the evening. Camille and Danton have given their speeches. Others are now speaking. All have delivered harangues. Everyone has been emotional and with the crowd roaring its approval.

Camille ought to be relieved and pleased. Yet he is filled with foreboding. Two wretches were discovered hiding within the platform and, in a fury, the crowd accused them as spies or setting about to inflict terror. But the pair had no weapons and no gunpowder. To Camille they appeared mere lowlifes, inhabitants of the street, two evidently mean individuals, one with a wooden leg. Yet the boiling crowd hanged them from lampposts. Danton ordered the bodies dispatched to a guardhouse before the great mass of people arrived. It was a bad omen and has added to Camille's worries. Surely a price must be paid for this bloodshed.

At one end of the field, there is a triumphal arch. What is this? At the other, open end, Camille now sees armed National Guardsmen. Lafayette is at the front, wearing his great plumed bicorne. Rank upon rank follows Lafayette, and for standards they carry red flags, symbol of martial law. People are dispersing. Yet tens of thousands of throats howl in angry derision at this intrusion of National Guardsmen and the imposition of martial law. Camille is transfixed. Rocks are hurling, pelting Lafayette. There's the crackle of a pistol-shot and Lafayette ducks. "Fire!" he shouts. National Guardsmen level muskets, firing volley upon volley. Crack! Crack! Crack!

Camille is still standing, dazed. The whole body of the gathering seems to shudder and then convulse. He perceives shrieking and shouting and more crack! crack! crack! He sees people falling, joining a different world. What reason could underlie this horror? He abides in an age of reason in which the savagery of men is unabated. His brain bursts into flame. He is choked. It is love that strangles him. Thought of Lucille and the family they plan. The prospect that this hitherto unappreciated happiness might be lost assails with such power that he begins to cry.

A ball hums close by his left ear, and he dives to the earth and lays flat. He gets up on his forearms and looks at a man who sits near him hunched. Camille smells gun smoke. He sees a bloody hole in the sittting man's neck and Camille now notices that he wears a crimson bib and then a bullet hole in his forehead. He hears screaming and shouting and sees a child in suspenders stands alone crying. The dead lay strewn on the field still in their finery, where they had been frolicking moments before they were cut down. Camille stands and sees that bodies lie heaped on the steps and the dais; a blood mist rises, and commingled blood is splattered and pooled on the alter, the dais, and the steps. Shock and grief give way to fear and panic, and Camille begins to run, heedless that he might be a target.

Camille is running fast as he can, fleeing. His destination is the Jacobin Club.

Later, Robespierre stands at the tribune in the Jacobin Club. He announces, there are more than fifty dead, women and children among them. He is weeping. He says, "Let us weep for those citizens who have perished: let us weep even for those citizens who, in good faith, were the instruments of their death." Who were "in good faith, instruments of their death" if not Robespierre, Camille, and Danton? But Camille feels sure that in the coming days Robespierre will blame Brissot. Camille hopes Robespierre will not blame him or Danton. Robespierre continues, "Let us, in any case, try to find one ground of consolation in this great disaster: let us hope that all our citizens, armed as well as unarmed, will take warning from this dire example, and hasten to swear peace and concord by the side of these newly dug graves."

All at once Camille is aware of a commotion outside, in the courtyard. In the hall, panic ensues. Danton takes hold of Camille's arm. National Guardsmen have arrived to make arrests, he says. They have warrants for the arrest of Camille and Danton among others, no doubt. Danton leads Camille out of the hall. They know passages for escaping undetected the erstwhile convent. Camille remembers Danton's words, *I can't ask others to risk what I myself would not suffer.* He feels that he himself is responsible for the deaths of more than fifty innocent French citizens this day. His breast aches. He weeps with sorrow and rage. When again he emerges in public, he will see to it that Lafayette and Capet are remembered as the perpetrators of this crime.

CHAPTER 4

CAMILLE ESCAPES TO THE Duplessises' country house in Bourg-la-Reine. Alone and on his way there by foot, he anticipates arriving. The white façade and black shutters gleaming in the light of the full moon that now illuminates the vacant road. He carries in his knapsack a bottle of cognac, and plans to fill up a tumbler once he arrives. There is a fine hearth and a captivating view of the countryside. Paris is only two leagues away from the house, and as a hiding place the house is imperfect, for it belongs to Lucile's family and therefore is traceable to him. Yet he plans to go no further. He does not expect to be hunted. For now, the king's apologists just want him gone and to cease writing, he supposes. Their loyalty is conflicted and they do not fear him if his pen is quiet. But alas, Lucile has remained in Paris, with her parents, which they all agreed is the safest place for her.

He feels as if a part of his soul was torn away at the Champ-de-Mars field. Images of the innocent people dropping, laying in pools of blood, or the stupefaction or screeching or convulsions of the wounded, the dead or bewildered children, the horror of the corpses on the dais, the crack! of the guns, and that he might have have been cut down and never lived again to see Lucile or have a son or daughter with her, press on him relentlessly. At times he is engulfed in grief and anxiety. Yet the walk and the loveliness of this night bring relief. He is again beneath that remarkable night sky. Sparkling white pinpoints so profuse that the dome's blackness is but foil and background—except where that moon's effulgence resides, also casting bluish shadows from roadside trees and gardens. He remembers in past summers this same sky, when returning to Paris with the Duplessis family in their rough country cart. The cart quiet; everyone sleepy, or absorbed in thoughts. The Duplessises are the father, Claude, a prosperous financier, the mother, Annette, and their two daughters—Adèle, the first-born, now already a widow, and Lucile. It was they who taught him love, only they whom he has loved, he tells himself now. It is on these nights, in close quarters with them, beneath that marvelous sky, that Camille has most profoundly experienced mystery's bewitching quality. Outside, the ceaseless clop-clop of horses' hooves striking stone, and a symphony of cricket songs.

He is already missing Lucile and longing for her. He will not allow himself to think that she may be at risk in Paris because of his involvement with Robespierre and Danton. As he walks, he grows increasingly wistful and reflects on the miracle of his membership in the Duplessis family. Before he knew the Duplessises, for many weeks Camille would see Annette, on sunny days in the gardens of the Palais du Luxembourg. She had long blonde hair and striking blue eyes, and she would wear a casual style of dress that had become more fashionable in the early 1780s. Always she was with her two young daughters. Finally, there arrived a pretext to engage Annette and the girls: one day he was with a former schoolmate, who knew them and introduced Camille to them. Subsequently, their pleasantries progressed to genuine friendship. Annette is twelve years older than him, but Camille wanted to become her lover, and he believed the desire was mutual. They embraced on a deep emotional level; there were long heartfelt talks over glasses of wine and as they walked the Seine. She attracted him with all of the qualities that he values in a lover—exceptional beauty, intelligence, charm, and her charity.

Yet it was not meant to be. For one thing, inevitably she introduced him to Claude, and Camille was disarmed by the husband's show of friendship and generosity. And he became attached to the girls. Once, when he and Annette were both drunk, he put his

45

hand on hers, and she moved it away and gently and affectionately chided him. She saw to it that the incident passed with not a hint of awkwardness, and he was too attached to them all to sever the relationship on account of his own humiliation.

Then on one of those sleepy summer nights as they were returning from Bourg-la-Reine (his current destination) to Paris, Camille began watching Lucile, petite and graceful, her fair hair alight even in darkness and falling around a serene, smiling face, with her father's black eyes; it is a face such as Greuze might have painted. This image of Lucile woke a response in him. Camille, then aged twenty-seven, began to see Lucile, then aged seventeen, with new eyes: "Is that Lucile?" he asked himself. He smiled. Yes, it is her, different but still Lucile, he thought, looking more and more at her face.

A few days later, he found himself standing in the doorway of her bedroom. She was seated at her writing table, scribbling in a little exercise book. The table was littered with miniatures and books and papers. The untidiness of her room was in contrast to the order of the rest of the house. She looked up and saw him there. He averted his eyes. Rising, she handed him the little book. Opening it, he glimpsed the contents. He handed it back.

"I can't," he said. "It's your diary; your private thoughts."

"I want you to read it. I want to be a writer like you. I have more of these journals. I want you to know my thoughts. Tell me what you think of my writing. Please read them."

Reading her journals—alone in his shabby apartment—affirmed his love for her. She was no longer a child, he saw; a subtle disquiet came through the pages of her journal. He saw that she assiduously read everything he published. She wrote: Rousseau is her idol. She thinks she will never marry, doubting her capacity for love. She is a stone, cold as ice. She feels that possibly she hates men, that she is a being set apart.

Camille was weary of his mean little apartment, but the redeeming quality was its proximity to the Duplessis house. Sometimes he could see Lucile in the garden out front from the garret window.

Finished reading another of Lucile's journals, he would get up and gaze at the house from the window, hoping to catch a glimpse of her.

As Lucille was now seventeen, she was able to escape the house for assignations. The first time he kissed her, she kissed back. At first they kissed gently, but then harder. Her lips parted, and so did his. Her tongue came a little ways into his mouth, which surprised him, and, he thinks, perhaps she surprised herself. They avoided the temptation of the Pont Neuf, so romantic, for lack of privacy. Paris is full of hiding places: alleys, groves, hedges, and alcoves, even an obscure café. They kissed, he reached up inside her bodice, fondled her, and in time she caressed him. His desire was fierce, but with Lucile his desire remained unsatisfied. He would not violate her. He was determined that she would be his wife.

Christmas holiday, 1787. Never had he felt love in the air as he did then, there in the Duplessis home. He must seize the moment, he had decided—he wanted to be loved as he loves them. This is the only thing that matters in the world, he thought, as he had so many times before.

For the evening's meeting, Claude was "Monsieur Duplessis." The spacious study was full of objects, some essential and others in evident disuse. On the large writing table was a book of accountancy and ledgers. There were glass-fronted bookcases with keys in the locks. On the windowsill, for decoration, were blacksmith's tools—tongs of various shapes and sizes for specialized uses and a chisel. In the corner on the floor was an anvil and a forged axe, as though they were sculptures.

Monsieur Duplessis is the son of a village blacksmith who holds the distinguished position of First Clerk in the Office of the General Control of Finance. He has not forgotten his roots.

Camille got right down to business. "Monsieur Duplessis, I want to marry your daughter."

"Adèle?"

"No. Lucile." He explained to Claude that he was in love with Lucile. He had known her since she was a child, and had regarded her affectionately as such, yet all at once was overtaken by a most irresistible love for her. He praised the beauty, grace, and intellect of his beloved, and expressed his devotion to her, and to the Duplessis family, which he wanted with all his heart to be his own family.

Claude was impassive. Listening intently. At last he replied, "She is too young."

"She will be eighteen in a few weeks."

"You are too immature."

He was twenty-seven, but by "you are too immature" Camille understood Claude to mean that Camille was too poor, and he was a philanderer. His ears were burning. He felt a crushing weight of disappointment. But Claude was smiling warmly. And he did, with kindness, ease Camille's humiliation. There was reason for hope, for optimism. Camille told himself that his deficiencies were still transient conditions. He would change, he told himself. But now Lucile took extra care when she came to him, not to be followed.

CHAPTER 5

PAINE ARRIVED AT LONDON Tavern early and stands outside waiting for Danton. He doesn't want his guest to walk through the door unescorted. He is anxious that the French Revolution's new de facto headman has not received a hero's welcome in London, and at this hour, the Tavern is full of conservative bankers. Nor is Paine a hero here, and he is thinking that he should not have selected this place for them to meet. The expected backlash to the initial popularity of his writings with the working class that brought him back to London has come. It has not been the easy triumph Mary Wollstonecraft predicted when she wrote him that *The Rights of Man* was sweeping the country. Soon after arriving in London, he was charged with violating the Royal Proclamation against seditious writings issued by Parliament—a proclamation, it seemed, aimed squarely at Paine.

He sees Danton's unmistakable, colossal proportions coming toward him down the west side of Bishopsgate Street. On his arm is a young blond-haired beauty in a casual, low-cut dress and a head piece with extravagant flower arrangement. She leans on his arm. As they approach, Paine sees her dress only need be simple, for the long blond hair adorned by braid strands, smooth bare shoulder and exquisite neck require no enhancement of lace or necklace. Upon reaching Paine, they stop, Danton kisses her on both cheeks and she turns, ignoring Paine, and goes back up Bishopsgate, wobbling a little. The two men shake hands and introduce themselves. This is their first meeting.

The place is full, dominated by the British bankers, now seemingly to a man staring at the two radicals. Paine is again wondering if he erred in selecting this place to meet, but Danton seems unperturbed. This is as much his milieu, Paine sees, as mixing with the *sans-culottes* in Paris streets. A waiter is making his way toward them. The waiter escorts them to a private room.

"Thank you, Brandon," says Paine. "Brandon, meet Georges. Georges, meet Brandon. What would you like to drink?" They both want cognac. The waiter turns and re-enters the noise and smoke and closes the door behind him.

Paine sips his cognac, keeps the tumbler aloft, and, gazing over the rim, he says, "Your conscience very nearly had to bear the violent extinguishment of my life. June 21, the day Capet escaped, I was viciously attacked by *sans-culottes* not twenty yards from where you stood, whipping the people into a frenzy. That is, if you have a conscience."

Danton ignores the bait. "Yet you were rescued, for here we are. Who was your savior?"

Paine is surprised that Danton has not heard the story. Has he really not heard the story? He has been lodging with Thomas Christie. Well, Danton has larger preoccupations. Yet now Paine does not want to bring Bonneville and Marguerite into this conversation. Paine does not trust Danton. He decides not to oblige Danton's manipulation, if that's what this is.

"I did not meet my savior. A calming voice from the crowd informed my attackers that I was an American. It did not take much to dissuade them. Most *sans-culottes* know that Americans are not soft on kings. The whole misunderstanding was rather ironic, and comic, in retrospect. Here the English consider me a regicide. What I need now is another miracle to deliver me from Pitt's assassins." William Pitt is the Prime Minister, appointed by King George, albeit with the support of the elected Parliament, and Paine believes that he is determined to redefine and establish the Prime Minister as dictator of Great Britain. Pitt's ambition has led him to purge British radicals who desire to eradicate the monarchy and any state church; there is, Paine believes, an unholy alliance between Pitt and the king.

"Perhaps you should return with me to Paris. We will keep you safe from Pitt."

Paine decides to ignore the overture, takes a drink and asks, "So what brought you to London, Danton?"

"I left France when it became clear that Lafayette had attained absolute power following the massacre at Champ-de-Mars, while the National Assembly remained under control of monarchist and bourgeois elements. It will not last. It is only for the moment. The streets are implacably and virulently against them, and only partially because the people cannot forgive the massacre. This seemed all the more reason for me to leave France and recalibrate. I first escaped to my father-in-law's at Rosny-sur-Bois, and then to Arcis, with my mother. I realized I was being watched. The townspeople would not have allowed the surveillants to take me, but it was only a matter of time before a sufficient force would come to arrest me. So I came to London."

"So what is your plan now?"

"It is time for us to declare war on our enemies within."

"France needs a constitution like the American one. Not more bloodshed."

"Those are just words. Come Paine. It was by arms that your United States won its independence from British tyranny. And words have not freed the slaves. What you have there is an aristocracy of landowners and rich merchants. Republicans revere Jefferson. Yet when he dined at Mirabeau's table and they worked on the *Declaration of the Rights of Man and of the Citizen*, Jefferson brought his concubine. Camille was there. He told me she was so beautiful, it was painful to meet her eye. And her skin is lighter than Camille's. Two consecutive generations before her had white plantation owners, and she was the half-sister of Jefferson's deceased wife. Yet she is Jefferson's slave though his lover too, as everyone knows."

Paine did not come here to debate the flawed American system or gossip about Jefferson, whom he regards a friend. He says, "Words have served you well. The Revolution has made much progress, by words alone. You have your revolutionary legislature. That is progress, notwithstanding that the Assembly has settled for a constitutional monarchy—at least for now. As we see here in Britain, that must not be the destination, but it is progress."

"We have our senate," Danton says, "and the king is in Paris, a prisoner in his own palace. But now the Assembly and Lafayette are the primary obstacles of republicanism, after they were once regarded its leading exponents. That is as far as our revolution has progressed."

"Through incremental reforms you can erode their authority," Paine says. "There is no reason for an armed revolt that will surely lead to civil war, making things much worse. You have made much progress so far by firmness and the mandate of the people."

Danton replies, "The French Revolution began on June 23, 1789. We are now two years past that event. The people gained their legislature, and yes, no blood was spilled. Yet was it mere words that wrought this momentous event? Necker persuaded the king to convene the three estates of the realm in Versailles to deliberate the financial crisis. The nobility and the clergy offered no help, so Necker persuaded the king to go over their heads, to the commoners. And so the Estates General was convened for the first time in one hundred and seventy-five years, so intractable was the monarchy before Louis Capet."

"Ah, you were there? Tell me what you saw. I have never heard a first hand account."

"I was not there. At the time, the prospect of a republican France seemed a small thing to me. I was grieving the death of my infant son François. Nor had I stood for election to the Estates General. Yet while grieving my dead son, what I learned from the gazettes had transpired at Versailles drew me out of my torpor."

Danton's disclosure about his dead son and his grief have touched Paine. He is starting to like the man and is curious to know more of his story. He says, "So how did you react to what you read in the gazettes."

"The proceedings began on May 5, and seven weeks later, still nothing was solved. More taxes for the commoners was the only solution that the first two estates would consider. Then on June 23, the king lost his nerve, and suddenly he purported to adjourn the proceedings. 'No remonstrance,' he told them, and he departed. The commoners refused to disburse. Comte de Mirabeau was presiding. He wore a great bejeweled sword on his hip, signaling both his nobility and rebellion against his class; he had chosen to be elected as a commoner. 'The king,' said Mirabeau, 'can cause us to be killed; tell him that we all wait death; but that he need not hope that we shall separate until we have made the constitution.' They ordained themselves an independent legislature called the National Assembly. They announced that the door of the National Assembly should always be open to all the nation. They were resolved to seal France's liberties with their blood. They cried: 'Long live the Republic!' And thus began the French Revolution."

Suddenly Danton's voice is a little strained and his eyes are misty. He is visibly moved by reciting these events. Evidently in his mind he has replayed them many times. Now composed, he continues. "The course of my professional life has been to press reform from outside France's institutions, so long as monarchist and bourgeois elements control them. I do not want to be a part of the problem. But after June 23, 1789, I became more engaged. I regret my absence there, and since then, the revolution has meant everything to me. I do not intend to let this moment in history pass."

"Well said," says Paine. "And so, the French Revolution was born, as a political revolution, and Mirabeau's force of argument and bravado wrought the achievement. And there was no bloodshed. You can now be what Mirabeau was then."

Danton barks a short laugh. "Camille says I resemble Mirabeau. It is true! Both of us shaggy monsters, our long black hair emanating power like Sampson, and faces marred by the smallpox. Such fearsome ugliness requires cultivation of an attractive and magnetic personality, and a sense of humor, to compensate." He laughs again, at his own quip. "In a sense, one man deserves all the credit for that progress. But was it really one man? No. Picture the scene. The Hall of Menus: it is vast, lined on the sides by columns in Doric order, and with lavish frieze-like reliefs and colossal draperies. Mirabeau standing defiant, the great sword on his hip. The delegates who remained, the commoners and a few clergy, each were seated on a chair richly upholstered in crimson and decorated by golden tassels and fleurs-de-lys. So too many of the royalty's soldiers menaced from amid the columns. When came Mirabeau's provocation, the troops did not move. For they themselves were commoners. It was a victory by and for the people. Mirabeau was but an expression of the people's will."

"Nor did the king or his henchmen order the soldiers to attack," says Paine.

"True. Yet, it was not Mirabeau's oratory that stayed their hand. They feared awakening the beast, the masses of the people, which now Lafayette has done. It is now only a matter of time before the beast will tear apart Lafayette and then the king." Danton's eyes shine defiant.

"I hope you are giving me a metaphor. Danton, you and your allies who wield great power in the streets must not allow France to descend to lawlessness and savagery. Blood will ever beget more blood."

Danton replies, "Lafayette should have considered that truism. Mirabeau's direction is now obsolete. While once I was under his spell, had he not suffered from an ailing heart and died so soon, I now realize, he almost certainly would have become a part of the problem. His not so secret wish was to be prime minister, to be France's Pitt, with Louis reduced to the status of a King George. Unlike Mirabeau, I have no sentimental or pragmatic attachment to the old order. I escaped the misfortune of being born a member of one of the classes privileged under our historic institutions, which for that very reason are almost always degenerate, and thus I have preserved all my native vigor, making a place for myself in the nation by my own efforts alone, without ceasing for an instant, either in my private life or in the profession I have embraced, to prove that I was capable of a combination of intellectual detachment, warmth of spirit, and firmness of character. Forever existing outside the old order, I do not hesitate to prosecute its total destruction."

The waiter returns with newly filled tumblers of cognac. Danton sips and then continues. "The course of the revolution is not up to me in any event. It is out of my control. Revolutions unchain all passions. A great nation in the process of revolution is like metal boiling in the crucible: the statue of liberty has not yet been cast; the metal is still in flux; the people are the furnace, yet no individual started the fire or can extinguish it; yes, we must try to lead the people; but if you do not give the furnace outlet, you will be unable to control it, and it will devour you. Whatever we have achieved in the revolution, it has only been by mandate from the people's demonstrated will. Three weeks after the National Assembly was formed, came the destruction of the Bastille, by the people. There was a little bloodshed. And then the king barricaded himself in the Versailles palace, like his ancestors. He reinforced the royal body-guard with the Flanders regiment. We heard stories. At the king's table, lavish feasts, the subalterns and nobles alike raising toasts to the royalty and stamping on the cockade. Lafayette would do nothing about this deplorable situation. The *sans-culottes* wanted the king in Paris, to keep an eye on him, and the peoples' will must be done. We knew it must and would be done by a spontaneous act of the people, and so it was. Yes, we placarded the city, and rang the tocsin on October fifth, yet the people's reaction was spontaneous. First came the women."

Paine says, "I have heard that it was a mob of women who provoked the king's transfer to the Tuileries Palace. How so was it women who achieved this? Not by arms, certainly?"

"This was spontaneous, and also by design. For the king's guard would not fire on women. Who wants to murder women? Ha! Tell that to Lafayette! The women came from all quarters. Then men joined the women in gathering and proceeding, men and women alike beating on kettles and pans, till they formed a multitude; a diverse, inexorably growing and roaring river of a multitude. 'To Versailles! Allons; à Versailles!' Camille was in Versailles covering the Assembly for his gazette, and he returned to Paris on a fast horse to record in his gazette what had transpired there. He told me how Lafayette and his National Guards had come and rescued the besieged royal family. Yet the people would not disperse until Lafayette announced that the king's entire household would relocate to Paris. On that day, Lafayette did not order the National Guards to fire on the people. He stayed his hand, as he did not want to rouse the beast. I witnessed the procession coming from Versailles on October 6. In Paris, the people, still buffeting, late at night at the Tulieres Palace, awaited the king, till finally he appeared on an upper balcony, and wearing a hat with huge tricolor. Henceforth Lafayette was in command of the king's guard. Yet who could know then that because of Lafayette's duplicity, or incompetence, the royal family would attempt to escape to Austria and return with an army from the Holy Roman Empire to crush the Revolution?!"

Danton drinks the last of his cognac and sets down his empty tumbler and continues. "So here we are, now. We have our senate, and the king is in Paris, a prisoner in his Tuileries Palace, actually. But the legislature remains filled with bourgeois and monarchist elements. We need more than words. We need a true coup d'état. The people are ready. They await our signal, our leadership. It would be an historic crime to let this moment in history pass, to fail the people." Danton has gotten to the point of his oration.

"Do you yet dare to return to Paris?" Paine asks.

"It is safe for me to return now. I should never have left. I should have remained in Paris as Robespierre and Marat have done. Once surrounded by my people, my enemies cannot touch me. Come with me, Paine. Let's go back to Paris together. You will lend the movement more credibility. Are you with us? We plan to grant honorary citizenship to distinguished foreigners who are devoted to the French Revolution such as yourself. We will reform the legislature and oust the royalists. You can be a delegate in the new legislature!"

Paine feels the tug of his attraction to Margurite, stretched all the way from Paris. Yet he responds, "I cannot participate in the violent overthrow of the monarchy."

"We will keep you safe, I promise."

"That is not the point. I am not afraid. I suffer plenty of risk here. I believe France is on the threshold of becoming a true republic, and this can be accomplished by political, non-violent means."

"The people will not abide incremental reforms. Nor will the king willingly cede the throne. He has no choice but to resist—"

"I do not believe this will be a long process," Paine interrupts. "The movement to republicanism is like the natural tides, and will sweep across Europe. Yet nor am I a politician, I don't speak French, and I am needed here in London." These are good reasons to remain in London, yet his memory of Marguerite intrudes. Each morning when he wakes, his first thought is of her, and daily, as now, she intrudes. He tries to suppress it, as he has done countless times since he left Paris. This source of a tug toward Paris cannot be denied; the joyous agitation he felt last he saw her still burns bright.

"Paine, you will always be welcome in Paris, even after we have done the dirty work. I think the English will disappoint you. In France, I agree it won't take long."

CHAPTER 6

ALL ALONE, CAMILLE IS struck by the quietude in the dead of night compared to the eternal human sounds of tormented Paris. Within the seclusion of this place and the surrounding forest of oak and pine trees he feels perfectly safe. He gets bored. And so, to stave off madness and make sleep possible, daily he takes very long walks in the countryside. The Duplessises' elderly gardener, who kindly brings him baskets of peaches and grapes, and dotes on him, frets about the walks he takes amid vagabonds and brigands hidden in the woods. Camille is amused by the concern, and undeterred. Eventually, he makes it all the way to the Palace of Versailles, a six-league round trip.

He is surprised to gain entry without question or resistance from the occasional guard stationed around the exterior. Inside, the palace is completely deserted. How silent is Versailles! He mounts the broad and sumptuous staircase, and then, upon the landing, is drawn forward by a train of Louises—he feels surrounded by ghosts, painting after painting covering the nakedness of vast walls, gazing in solemn sadness at the vacuous grandeur, the gloominess of the atmosphere giving a deeper shade to the gigantic fading figures, lost in the embrace of death. Warily he enters the endless apartments, deserted; the Hall of Mirrors, the War Salon, the Hercules Room, the queen's chambers: In the long looking glasses he catches fleeting glimpses of himself. There are once lascivious pictures, no longer seductive, that strike notes of sadness in his bosom, depressed at the dissipation of youth, beauty, and life.

He moves to the garden, traversing groves by the wide, neglected royal walkway; but even here, are ghosts. The flower-beds are choked by weeds. All is fearfully still. Within the trees, alleys run parallel or perpendicular to the main way he walks. At four intersections stand the four fountains dedicated to the four seasons; they are now all dry, the only water sounds the trickling in gathering moss amid the trees.

This, the deserted palace of France's kings! Also, a place of important events for Camille and the revolution. It was at Versailles that Camille and Robespierre were reunited. After Robespierre graduated from Louis-le-Grand, he returned to Arras, his ancestral village, to the surprise of everyone, while Camille remained in Paris. Apparently, Robespierre's virtues are not false. He told Camille that he wanted to return to Arras to help those who were less fortunate than he had been. Robespierre, the oldest of four children, was an orphan who came from poverty. But by age eleven, he had shown sufficient promise that the two aunts who raised him were able to secure for him a scholarship to Louis-le-Grand. As a lawyer, he represented indigent and criminal defendants. He and Camille both remained poor. They were reunited here in Versailles around the time the Estates General convened on May 5, 1789. Camille was not surprised that his highly strung and charmless friend, hyper-conscious of his own virtues, and at thirty still quite unknown (and unmarried), successfully made the hugely ambitious leap of election to the Estates General as one of the deputies for Artois province. Robespierre's return to his remote hometown after obtaining his law degree now appeared inspired.

Camille's father, Jean Benoît Nicolas Desmoulins, an attorney, was elected deputy to the third estate from Guise. Poor health prevented him from taking his seat. Camille hoped to take his place, but it did not come to pass, as the father would not endorse the son because he disagreed with Camille's radical politics. So, Camille came as a journalist.

Now Camille stands beneath the royal balcony. October 5,

1789, Camille stood here in this same spot, near midnight, amid the turbulent multitude laying siege to the Versailles palace beneath weeping skies. There were casualties upon this tempestuous sea of human beings, but the storm had yet to reach its climax. Two among the king's guard had perished—their heads bobbed on pikes high above the crowd, and their corpses lay mutilated. Fourteen bodyguards were wounded. Oh, the people!

Suddenly lights blazed upon the hilltop, and a roll of drums ensued. Lafayette and his National Guards from Paris! The roll of drums approached, down the Avenue de Versailles. The column halted, and Lafayette, at the front, dismounted and moved through the people as Moses parting waters. The multitude and palace guards alike allowed him passage through locked and unlocked and relocked gates. He passed by sentries and ushers until he gained the Royal Halls.

———

Finally, three weeks into Camille's exile in Bourg-la-Reine, his father-in-law brings Lucile. This first night together, she cooks for him, they drink wine to near drunkenness, and enjoy strawberries left by the gardener.

"Has Danton returned to Paris?" he asks.

"Danton is in London. I saw Dillon and he told me."

"Oh? Really."

"Danton felt he had to leave the country after Lafayette had taken charge of Paris."

"They are implacable enemies," says Camille.

"Yes. Dillon says Danton fled to England and has been hiding in London's Soho neighborhood, living with that Scot, Christie. Yet I have some news that will surprise you. Rumor has it that Robespierre is besotted with a lover."

"I don't believe you."

"Dillon says it's true. Robespierre has found refuge in the home of a fellow Jacobin, Maurice Duplay, a carpenter. Duplay's wife and three grown daughters also reside in the house, but Robespierre has his own apartment—a tiny room accessed from an external stairway. It is said that Robespierre is involved with the oldest Duplay daughter, Eleonore. She is the gatekeeper authorized to admit or refuse anyone who wants to climb the outer staircase to visit Robespierre's tiny quarters."

"How strange," says Camille. "I have always belived that, like St. Paul, Max would live all his life as an ascetic, absent the pleasures of women. Have he and this woman been seen anywhere about Paris?

"No. But it is rumored that she spends nights with Robespierre in that little hovel."

"So what has happened to Charlotte?" Camille is referring to Robespierre's beloved sister. They had been living together as though platonic husband and wife.

"She still lives in that little house. Not far from the Duplays, actually. Dillon says she is unhappy that Robespierre has left her."

"Where is Marat?"

"Marat has disappeared underground, presumably somewhere in Paris. His usual haunts. Nobody knows where he is."

"And what about our royalist friend Dillon. How is he?"

"Dillon is fine in the flesh, but he is anxious, full of dread. He said it is only a matter of time before the regicides return to Paris, they will be more fearsome, and the rabble will rule with vengeance. Lafayette is back at the war front, and he is struggling with discipline. There really isn't much reason left for you or Danton to stay away."

"Lafayette is sowing the bitter fruits of his transgression."

"Yes, he is everywhere loathed. There is no longer much to fear from him." She looks down, a shadow on her countenance. Camille lifts her chin. She continues, "I have not missed being in society, the parties to attend, the hosts and hostesses, I hate people. I really do. It's so nice to be here, this quiet, no mobs and shouting in the squares. Do you ever wonder whether we'd be more content with a more sedate, bourgeois existence?"

He gives her a look to suggest comprehension. The look is warming and knowing, he is sure.

Camille is agonizingly alert to his desire for Lucile. At last they find themselves in the bed, and they make love. After the first time she is crying, and he looks at her with sympathy and concern, and asks, "Why so sad?" She tells him that she is not sad; on the contrary, he has taken her to a place she knew existed but did not realize she knew about, and she has found that place, for now he has taken her there, to a place where she finally has a life. The second time he repeats the refrain that he loves her.

He nearly lost her, was at the brink of annihilation, and now he is inside her, her silken warmth; then it is he who is sobbing, into her ear, and grunting, and letting loose his seed inside her. He now gushes tears. And now after the third time, they have lain together naked for hours, and he wonders if the explanation for his tears may be simpler than hers, that this lovely woman is his wife and lover and tonight he made love to her three times, and all three times he brought her to completion—only that.

He wakes in the night as she lies next to him sleeping soundly. He hears the sound of whispering voices. He gets up and looks out the window and sees pines leaning to the wind. He imagines a faint lamentation that might be those perished at the Champ-de-Mars crying at their separation from the world. He feels fresh sorrow for these strangers, and now Lucile's desire for a quiet life outside politics has aggravated in him anxiety that his adventures could put her at risk. That she could be anxious or ever injured because of his actions is unbearable to him.

So strange how they might never have been married at all. It was only thanks to Mirabeau that Camille was able to clear the final obstacle to marrying Lucile. December 29, 1790. At last, Camille presented himself before the curé of St. Sulpice for certification that he was worthy to be married. For this interview he was alone, except the cleric and the notary.

"Are you a Catholic?" the curé asked.

"Why do you ask me?"

"Because if you be not, I cannot confer upon you a Sacrament of the Catholic religion."

"Well then, yes, I am a Catholic."

"I cannot believe a man who has said in one of his published pieces that the religion of Muhammad is quite as much proven to his mind as the religion of Jesus Christ."

Camille was prepared. He produced a written opinion of Mirabeau in which he maintained that "the only evidence of belief is the external profession of faith, and that marriage cannot be refused to the person who demands it, since he has stated that he is a Catholic."

"Since when has Mirabeau been a father of the Church?" the curé asked. Clearly he was not amused. The piece of paper had had its desired effect, Camille could see: he was pleased at the tremor, the note of alarm he detected in the curé's voice.

Camille laughed out loud. He could not help it. "Ha! Mirabeau a father of the Church! I will tell him that; he will be amused!"

"But the opinion itself condemns you, if you are to be judged by your external profession of faith, because that profession is in print. Before I marry you, I must exact a retraction." The curé had regained his poise, for now.

"I do not intend to write any more articles before my marriage."

"Then I must exact from you that you fulfill all the duties prescribed by the Church to those about to marry, and that you make your confession."

"I will be pleased to do so to yourself, Monsieur le Curé." Camille as a child perfected the art of the credible confession that reveals next to nothing. He made use of it now. He had no regrets, no wounded conscience.

Thus the wedding at last occurred on New Year's Eve, 1790, in St. Sulpice. Finally, Camille was at peace. For this interval the chronic rage was completely dissolved; he felt radiant and transfigured by happiness, wearing a white waistcoat, decorated with flowers. Lucile passed up the aisle on her father's arm, wearing a satin dress and a wedding veil trailing, with narrow sleeves and little basques and a silk garter embroidered with forget-me-nots and joined hands, surrounding the motto *Unisson-nous-pour-la-vie*.

There were two witnesses: Jérôme Pétion de Villeneuve; handsome, charming, eloquent in his advocacy of republicanism, he was admired by the king's sister Elizabeth, and, everyone felt, soon to be mayor of Paris. The other was Robespierre; his costume was the same as always. In that moment he had the anxious but rather gentle look of the domestic cat.

Though he promised to attend, throughout the day there was no sign of Mirabeau.

Standing beneath the bridal canopy, Camille felt he was about to cry. Robespierre was helping to hold the bridal canopy over the bridal pair, and he whispered, "Cry if you want to cry." Camille and Lucile both wept, which caused others (not Robespierre) to do the same.

Later, a few special guests joined Camille and Lucile about a large mahogany table in Camille's apartments, at the third floor of No. 1 Rue de Theatre Frangais, where the wedding breakfast was served. Among the attendees besides Camille and Lucile and Monsieur and Madame Duplessis, Lucile's sister Adèle (with whom Camille believed—vainly hoped—that Robespierre was besotted), there were Robespierre, Pétion, and Camille's good friend Jacques Pierre Brissot de Warville. Brissot was, as usual in an intimate social setting, hideously ill at ease. His nickname is "the Quaker", after all—for his Quaker's hat, the simplicity of his appearance, and the severity of his republican morals. Even then, he and Robespierre did not like one another.

———

August 20, 1791: It has become clear that the real power emanates from the streets, not the Assembly. A rising tide of protest demanded that the rabble's chiefs return. Marat, Camille, Danton, and Robespierre are returned to the Jacobin Club, and it is full. Camille stands at the tribune, he is speaking, and there is no stammer. He cries, "The king has put a pistol to the Republic's head; the gun has misfired, and now it is our turn."

PART II

CHAPTER 7

AUGUST 9, 1792. FRANCE has been ruled by royalty for over one thousand three hundred years. Before it was a kingdom, there was no France. Yet, Danton perceives that the people are ready to extinguish the monarchy. "An armed insurrection is inevitable," he tells Camille, "and the time for it is fully ripe. We did not create this mass movement. It is impossible to control the people. But we must try to lead them. They are beseeching us to draw power from them. To fail to do so, would be an historical crime." He is nearly frantic not to miss this opportunity.

Robespierre completely lacks this sense. He has disappeared from society. Last time Camille visited him, they met in the Duplays' cellar, not in the upstairs apartment as had become his habit. He is paranoid, claiming a royalist conspiracy is a foot to assassinate him.

It is at least true that nothing is settled, for better or worse. For over a year "the king" has been but a figurehead and a prisoner in his own palace. "What is the French government?" says Danton. "It is a puppet king and the Assembly, which is a diaphanous screen for the landowners and merchants and British capital. Here you see the manifestation of counter-revolution, and the people do not abide it." Blood flows in the streets; shootings continue. Nightly the skies are lit by conflagrations all across Paris. The nobility have been fleeing their estates and taking asylum at Coblentz.

Some see Robespierre as the seer. He laments that the Brissotins' war has destroyed the revolution, indeed destroyed France.

(The "Brissotins" are now the dominant block in the Assembly, for that tireless firebrand Brissot and his allies are its constituents.) The poetry of Robespierre's words resisting the Assembly's declaration of war against Austria is hard to resist: "Ah! I can see a great crowd of people dancing in an open plain covered with grass and flowers, making play with their weapons, and filling the air with shouts of joy and songs of war. Suddenly the ground sinks beneath their feet, the flowers, the men, the weapons disappear; and I can see nothing but a gaping chasm filled with victims. Ah! Fly! Fly, while there is still time, before the ground on which you stand opens beneath its covering of flowers."

Now, indeed, following repeated battlefield reversals, the offensive has failed. France is on the defensive. The army is in disarray. Lafayette repeatedly underestimated the widespread antipathy for him: in vainly attempting to mold Jacobin sympathizers masquerading as troops and National Guardsmen into a cohesive fighting force against the Austrians and Prussians; in writing to the Assembly from his field post and demanding the radical clubs to be "closed down by force"; in subsequently addressing the Assembly and denouncing the Jacobins and demanding that the radical clubs be abolished; and in calling for volunteers to help him forcibly crush the radical clubs. Since the Champ-de-Mars massacre, Lafayette has become the symbol for the government's historic oppression — what irony, not only because of his service to the United States, for Antoinette has always loathed him, and royalists everywhere blame him for inciting the French Revolution. When nobody paid him any heed, and Danton called him a traitor and a deserter of his troops, he fled Paris. Lafayette is gone, and it seems he can never come back and retain his head.

Danton has said, "Actually, whether or not intended, the Brissotins' war has delivered the coup de grâce to the monarchy. Everything is breaking our way, chiefly this misbegotten war. The people perceive that the émigrés deployed the Austrian army to save the king and stab their fatherland to the heart. It is in the name of the king that liberty is being attacked." The king did try to stop France's declaration of war, exercising the royal veto. But the Brissotins brow-beat him into withdrawing it.

Speaking only to Camille and lowering his voice, Danton said, "After the king was granted a constitutional monarchy, it was France who started the war. We know not, but the Austrians would have been content with this status quo. The king's veto may not have been motivated by perfidy but desire for stability and contentment with the status quo. It may have been well advised."

The Brunswick Manifesto, issued on July 25 by the Duke of Brunswick, commander of the Austro-Prussian Army, warned that Paris would be destroyed by the Austrians and the Prussians if the king is harmed. When Danton learned of it on August 1, he said, "Now this will be the last straw for the people." The Brunswick Manifesto enraged the people, from bourgeois gentlemen to common citizens of every working class, hair-dressers, harness-makers, carpenters, joiners, house-painters, tailors, hatters, boot-makers, locksmiths, laundry-men, and domestic servants. Camille has seen them all en masse, even women and children, armed with cutters, cudgels, and pikes.

And so Danton's prophecy has proceeded to self-fulfillment. Danton has been feverishly networking among the one hundred and forty-four delegates representing the forty-eight sections of the Paris Commune. Danton says that the delegates have mobilized the enraged citizenry and the Commune will direct the insurrection. Meanwhile—another break—six hundred conscripts from Marseilles have fallen under Danton's spell and are bivouacked at the Cordeliers Club—uniformed soldiers, ruffians, street rowdies, and cut-throats alike. Danton had persuaded the Assembly to invite to Paris the National Guards from the provinces on their way to the front, to celebrate July 17 and boost their morale. Following the celebration, their morale still foundering, and bad news coming daily from the front, they remain ostensibly to defend the capital and the revolution. Since the Brunswick Manifesto, they are now here to stay, and coordinating with the Paris Commune and Danton. The Marseilles contingent sing a war song they call "La

Marseillaise," which the *sans-culottes* have picked up and turned into the revolution's anthem. In the square outside the Cordeliers convent are crowded all kinds of vehicles—baggage and ammunition wagons, carriages, some of them requisitioned from the nobility, lacquered, gilt or silvered. Liberated mounted guardsmen gallop here and there. Bands of *sans-culottes* swing rifles and stream street to street, shouting, "*Vive la nation!*"

Tonight, a hot nightfall, a grand fecal odor is heavy in the air, and men decked in carmagnole, cap of liberty, and cockade are beating drums at dusky corners—enhancing the surreal disembodiment that Camille now feels. He feels his own individual life, and those of his collective countrymen, on the verge of a pivot, for better or worse.

Yet now, on August 9, when all plans are laid, has Danton lost his nerve? He has been gone for three days. Still, Camille has, as has been planned, in his short speech delivered in the crowded Cordeliers chapel, revealed the signal to announce the uprising. He cries, "So soon as the Cordeliers' tocsin is sounded let all the nation assemble; let each man, as in Rome, be invested with the right to punish known conspirators with death; and one single day of anarchy will do more for the security of liberty and the salvation of the country than four years of a National Assembly!"

Just then Danton appears as if from nowhere, leaps onto the tribune, and turns to face the crowd, an arm embracing Camille. He wears a red frock coat, purchased and saved specially for this occasion. He shouts, "Tomorrow the people will triumph, or we die!"

Pandemonium ensues. The people shout over and over, "*Vive Danton!*" (Robespierre is nowhere to be seen.)

When Camille and Danton step down from the tribune, for a moment they stand side by side amid the boisterous crowd. "Well said," says Danton. "Except the part about 'the right to punish known conspirators with death.' You may regret introducing the ethos of lawless executions. I wish to accomplish our aims without more bloodshed."

"I would prefer you had omitted any possibility of our deaths."

"We may be killed. I advise you to arm yourself."

"Good of you to come," says Camille. "I was expecting to do this on my own."

"I told you I went to Arcis. I visited my mother."

"For three days?"

"There is a good chance I won't see her again. When we last embraced, I tried to be low-key. But I own her home. I had to track down the notary. I transferred residence rights to her and my step-father for as long as they will live. I walked each acre of my land, bidding farewell to it too, every copse and riverbank."

True it is, their lives are in danger. Camille understands that the insurrection will be difficult, the outcome is uncertain. It depends on countless contingencies, the nerve of countless indi-viduals, each of whom is uncertain of the one beside him, totally uncertain of the distant individuals upon which the insurrection depends. The enterprise depends on the unity of all these individ-uals, and no one of them can be certain of what strength is with him or against them. The only certainty is that if they fail, their destination will be the gallows.

Commandant Marquis Jean-Antoine de Mandat is in charge of the king's guard, and he has warned that his National Guardsmen will repel force with force. A cannon on the Pont Neuf stands between Danton's Marseilles, who will lead the entire Left Bank uprising, and the Tuileries Palace. Mandat's mounted squadrons stand ready to charge, at insurrection, and descend on the Hôtel de Ville, the Palais-Royal, in the Place Vendôme. But Danton says that Marat, ever ubiquitous among the National Guardsmen and the Paris sections, though never seen, assures him that the National Guard will not fire on French citizens. But Commandant Mandat remains a problem, as do his nine hundred Swiss mercenaries sta-tioned in the Tuileries Palace. Tonight, Mandat's mounted gendar-merie and blue-clad National Guards march, clattering, tramping; his cannoneers rumble.

Later, Camille is with Danton at the Hôtel de Ville, and the Commune is in permanent session. Danton does the work of networking the anterooms, moving among the ward leaders. Camille marvels that they have come this far. Danton is huddling longest with those from the poor and crowded Saint-Antoine and Saint-Marcel sections. He steps out and tells Camille they will meet at Camille's house with the leaders of the Marseilles contingent, as planned.

"Go on," says Danton. "I'll see you there. And give your family some love." Yes, Camille thinks, he must see Lucile and Horace, his newborn son, maybe for the last time.

When Danton arrives near midnight, everyone is in good spirits. Camille and Lucile have wined and dined the Marseilles. Lucile is acting drunk, giggling, but has not drunk a drop. She must have an outlet if she must not weep. All are merry, if only from unbearable stress, except Danton's wife, Gabrielle, who weeps. Her two baby boys are at home and in the charge of their nanny, the girl Louise.

"Come with me," says Danton to the entire group, and the party moves to his place nearby. "The time has come," Danton reveals to the Marseilles. "When the Cordeliers' tocsin sounds, bring the Left Bank masses across the Pont Neuf. The cannon will not fire on you." He answers their questions, and finally says, "Now rest. I must get some sleep too."

All disburse. Camille hears Danton's heavy frame fall on his bed, before enough time to disrobe. At home Camille, too, sleeps fully dressed, his head resting on Lucile's shoulder. He sleeps an hour, and a pounding at the door awakes him. It is Danton. Time to return to the Hôtel de Ville. He hands Camille a rifle; Lucile is aghast. Camille thinks that this day he will not leave Danton's side.

At the city hall things are going to plan. The Commune has transmogrified into a new "Insurrectionary Commune." The mayor of Paris has yielded power without protest and is under house arrest. Out front, *sans-culottes* are smashing a statue of Lafayette. At first light, the tocsin at the Cordeliers convent begins to ring, and soon alarm bells peal from every parish tower. Armed citizens are appearing from everywhere. Among them are common citizens from every working class, even including women and children, all armed. En masse they are streaming to the palace. Still there are no shots, neither cannon nor gunfire.

The Commune sends messages demanding that Commandant Mandat appear at the Hôtel de Ville. At six in the morning, he arrives, unguarded. Danton confronts him in the vestibule.

Mandat: "I am responsible only to the genuine Commune, to honest men."

Danton: "Traitor! You will learn to obey the new Commune. It is we who save the people you betray. Put him under arrest."

Danton's new henchmen drag Mandat outside on to the steps. They are struggling through the crowd. *Bang!* Mandat lies motionless on the steps, dark blood pooling round his head. Someone has killed him, shot him in the head.

Danton cries, "Shit! I did not want that to happen! The people!"

The Assembly is in session, and it sends a message. The king has abdicated. Louis Capet became afraid, went with his family to the Assembly, and surrendered to the deputies. "Gentlemen," said Capet, "I come here to avoid a great crime; I think I cannot be safer than with you." Pierre Victurnien Vergniaud, who is presiding, said the Assembly will protect them, as it has sworn to die in defense of the properly constituted authorities.

"Come," says Danton to Camille, "we go to the Assembly. It is time to make our demands."

Three of them, Danton, Camille, and Louis Pierre Manuel, the Commune's chief executive, arrive at the Ménage. Still the only shot to be heard is the one that killed Mandat.

Capet and his family are separated from the Assembly in order not to interfere with freedom of debate. All of them are crowded into the small room called the shorthand-writers' box, adjacent and open to the main hall of the Manège. They are out of sight, and Camille does not want to see them.

Danton announces that the sovereign people, meeting in Sections, have named Commissioners, who will exercise all powers for Paris, and they have suspended the General Council of the old Commune.

In response, there is no remonstrance. Vergniaud replies that, after deliberations, the Assembly has suspended the monarchy.

It is done! The insurrection has succeeded.

Suddenly, the sound of musketry and cannon fire are heard from the direction of the palace. A stray ball flies through the open window of the hall and all duck.

"I assure you," shouts Capet from his hovel, "that I have ordered the Swiss to be forbidden to fire!" The sounds of firing grow louder and more profuse.

Before day's end, after returning to the city hall, they learn what happened. The Swiss mercenaries threw cartridge casings from the windows and displayed the red cap. The citizens took these as signs of peace and fraternity and, fooled by appearances, entered, thinking to render themselves masters of the palace without firing a shot. They had barely climbed the first steps of the stairway before the Swiss fired on them at point blank range. The citizens retreated outside, pointed the cannon, and the combat began. A large number of citizens were killed or wounded, but also among the dead are most of the nine hundred young men who were wearing the Swiss uniform. The citizens have taken the palace.

Yet France still needs executive power.

At three o'clock in the morning on August 11, Camille bursts into Danton's bedroom.

"You're the Minister of Justice!" cries Camille. Only two hundred and eighty-five voters were present in the Assembly out of seven hundred and forty-five members; all of the royalists, with a few exceptions, were absent. Danton was elected Minister of Justice, receiving two hundred and twenty-two votes. By the Assembly's decree he is entrusted, as Minister of Justice, "with all the functions of the executive power."

Danton takes hold of Camille's velvet lapels. "You're sure? You're quite sure I am named?"

"Yes. Minister of justice," repeats Camille.

"And you shall be my secretary!" says Danton.

CHAPTER 8

AUGUST 17, 1792. FOR Camille, there is no celebrating the success of August 10. The king is held in the Temple (the Knights Templar's ancient fortress is now the royalty's prison), while the Brunswick Manifesto stands, and Brunswick's forces advance toward Paris. The people's rage and excitement have reached new heights—the genie that can't be put back in the bottle. That a person be an "aristocrat" is sufficient crime to cost him his life. Everything which identifies an aristocrat, and which attracts the mob—a ring, a watch chain, a handsome pair of buckles, a new coat, or a good pair of boots—is punishable by death. The mob will kill a fellow man or woman as wanton boys would kill a cat. A ferocious mob forces the apartments of Antoinette's closest friend and waiting lady, the Princess de Lamballe, and decapitates her. They cut across her thighs and tear her bowels and heart from her corpse. They put her head on a pike and wave it in front of the windows of the Temple so that Antoinette can see it, and for two days her headless, mangled body is dragged through the streets.

As Minister of Justice, Danton proposes the formation of a special provisional tribunal to try the "criminals" who are charged with—what crime?—the crime of supporting Louis Capet and resisting the August 10 uprising. The Brissotins object that the real criminals are the mob. It is not a crime to have spoken on behalf of Capet, nor either to have discharged a sworn legal duty to defend the palace by force of arms. But there is nothing they can do to stop Danton's new dictatorial powers.

That night, Camille and Danton are walking, approaching the Pont Neuf. It is the hour of sunset, and the sun casts a glowing redness, illuminating the Seine, undulating and rippling, and shining bright red.

Danton tells Camille that his Revolutionary Tribunal will buffer the people's demands for blood, for retribution. The ordinary courts are inadequate for the emergency. He has to do this to slake the people's thirst for blood. He has to do this to halt the *sans-culottes'* mob violence.

Camille: "Some victims of the mob have been barely older than children and some were prostitutes, and how is it that our legitimate enemies could harm us while they are locked up or in exile?"

Danton: "I know all that. Eliminating the royalists is not the point."

"Then what is the point?" Camille whispers; he is choked by emotion, can hardly speak.

"The point is this: to mete out justice by the people in replacement of anarchy and general, uncontrolled slaughter in the streets."

"Justice—"

"I speak not of justice in the way that you suppose, man. The point is the terror, to monopolize it, to take the terror from the streets and the mob, to take it away from disorganized mobs, anarchic and blindly destructive, criminal elements and the dregs of the city population, bands of cruel ruffians and assassins, reeking with blood, all the unutterable abominations of the furies of hell!" Danton stops walking, takes hold of Camille's arm, and looks at him wide-eyed. "You know what I am talking about, for you have seen it. Let the justice of the courts begin, and the justice of the people will cease."

Thus, the tribunal is formed in just a few days. The forty-eight sections of the Paris Commune meet and choose the judges, accusers, and juries. (Robespierre is appointed one of the judges, yet he refuses to serve.) A beheading machine—a "guillotine," named after its inventor—is installed on the Place du Carrousel.

The provisional Revolutionary Tribunal sets to work with terrifying vigor. A man named d'Angremont is the first to succumb to the guillotine. He is convicted of being an agent of the king, and is beheaded on the Place du Carrousel. He is the first of the many victims of Danton's tribunal and the guillotine. But the machinery of Danton's inquistion, though serving up blood, cannot keep up with the people's demand for blood.

———————

August 31, 1792. News that Longwy has fallen to the invaders, and Verdun will soon fall, has stricken new terror in the populace.

There are just the two of them. Only two witnesses. At Camille's lovely office in the Place Vendôme that looks out onto the square. He is the Secretary to the Minister of Justice! Marat stands there at first, disdaining a seat. Now he slithers around Camille's desk and leans into Camille like a python, with his disgusting teeth and body odors. There are other witnesses, actually—the old portraits that line the walls—yet though Camille feels their judgmental eyes upon him, they are no better than him.

The Prussians, Marat says, will ravage the city. They will put the Capets back on the throne, reinstall the priests, and the royalists will avenge themselves mercilessly; they will take no prisoners. Paris will experience tyranny as never before—a bloodbath.

Marat says that the prisons are filled up with those who would avenge the royalty and now is the time to deal with them. He fears for the public safety. Something must be done with these aristocrats. They are traitors, counter-revolutionaries. They must be eliminated. Says Marat, in his sinister, pedantic way, "Let the justice of the courts begin, and the justice of the people will cease." Camille's blood runs cold, for he is quoting Danton; those were his very words.

———————

Camille tells Danton about the visit from Marat. Danton is ever the pragmatist, this time shrugging, tipping his head: *What else can we do, Camille?* This reaction, in relation to the gravity of the

79

matter at hand, sums up the character of the man, Camille now realizes. He has come to better know Danton. Danton despises the municipal populace on whose exclusive behalf the Jacobins purport to act, he dislikes as well Robespierre and Marat, and his principles are more in line with those of the Brissotins. But he has no confidence in the Brissotins, and they dismiss him as a vulgar profiteer and opportunist, because differing methods and conduct separate them entirely. Danton finds neither in their character, their principled opposition to the Jacobins, nor their methods, the energy or the resourcefulness requisite for saving the revolution, the grand enterprise which is the object of his love and devotion above all else. Danton, indifferent to personalities, sides only with those persons he regards most likely to ensure the survival of the revolution.

The point, he reiterates to Camille, is to take the terror from the mob and bring it into the institutions of the state. Indeed, to bring it into their physical places—the prisons, their courtyards, and immediate vicinities.

"My advice," says Danton to the heads of the Paris sections, "is that to paralyze our enemies, we must strike terror into the royalists." He need not say more.

———————

September 2–5, 1792. Verdun has fallen. Camille remains at home; he trembles, his breast aches; Lucile holds him, and he weeps into her neck—when he is not taking walks with Danton, that is. He learns from Danton that persons who are strangers to the *sans-culotte* milieu are appearing in the streets; they literally step from the shadows, and they stop the mob violence, the slaughters. They do not do it forcibly. For no power on Earth or in Hell could have done so. It appears miraculous; they are dark angels ascended from Hell itself. They absorb the terror, and so the mob violence ceases. Outside the penal institutions and inside the adjoining courtyards they install themselves behind a table and organize popular tribunals.

Who are they? Nobody knows. They claim no mandate, and there is none to be claimed. Yet, justice is improvised. Juries are formed, judges named, a prosecutor established, the prison records obtained. The prisoners are then brought before a tribunal one by one, their identities and the reasons for their institutional confinement verified. A short interrogation follows, after which the prisoner is declared innocent or guilty. If guilty, there is but one penalty. Yes, it is horrific: He or she is bludgeoned or hacked to death with whatever instruments are available. The bodies of victims are left to accumulate in a pile. A short while after the butchery ends, the authorities cart the bodies to the outskirts of Paris, where they are buried in pits and covered with chalk.

Danton is looking intently at Camille. He says, "Thus has the means of terror transferred from the mob to a means that looks like the state apparatus. And the mayhem in the streets has now suddenly ceased. And it turns out that I was right; no truer words were ever spoken."

During these four awful days, the homes of some of Camille's friends have been searched. Some of them like Brissot and Bonneville attended his wedding. None of them have been imprisoned or killed, fortunately.

What Mirabeau said to Camille on his death bed has proven prophetic. After the Estates General, Camille wrote to Mirabeau, to try to be put on the staff of the great man's famous gazette. He had heard that thousands were subscribing to it in Paris. Mirabeau made Camille his secretary. Camille wrote speeches and articles for Mirabeau, who called this initiating the young man into great affairs. Camille loved Mirabeau to idolatry; loved him like a mistress. Mirabeau mastered him by his genius and his egalitarianism, and he flattered Camille by his esteem. Frequently, Mirabeau took his hand, patted him on the back. Camille was touched by his friendship. But eventually, the great man's deepest wish became clear, at least to Camille—that the king and queen remain as such, though greatly reduced, and Mirabeau be their prime minister, as in Britain. Mirabeau's ambitions lay within that framework.

Camille's intuition was that Mirabeau's moderate philosophy would fail. The most extreme tip of the left wing was now mounting in favor among the people—not yet in the National Assembly, where bourgeois and aristocratic elements still held sway, but with the true public, especially in Paris. For the people do not well abide a universal panic of doubt, and all people will rally to the opinion that is sure of itself, so the crudest opinion inevitably is soonest most popular. Great is the power of belief, however crude it may be, and leads captive the doubting heart.

Marat said to Camille, "Mirabeau will corrupt you with luxury. I spend every waking moment thinking of the revolution. You should do the same, and we would respect you more." There was much truth in this. Mirabeau's burgundies and his maraschino had an attraction which Camille sought vainly to hide even from himself, and he had all the difficulty in the world to regain a republican austerity and to detest the aristocrats whose crime it is to enjoy such excellent dinners.

So after the wedding, Camille resolved to withdraw his services from Mirabeau (prompted by Lucile). Mirabeau wrote to Camille, *Well, poor Camille, has your head come right again? We have sulked with you, but we forgive you.* And thereafter, *Adieu, good boy, you deserve to be loved, notwithstanding your fiery flights.* He ought to have known that nothing could irritate Camille more than the phrases "poor Camille" and "good boy."

More than once Mirabeau sent his secretary from his office in Versailles, a distance of two leagues, to entreat Camille not to publish a page of what he had written (provided by Camille to learn the great man's reaction), to make this sacrifice to friendship, to his great past services, and to the hope of those in the future. Camille was gratified, discerning that Mirabeau dreaded Camille's censure, which was read by Marseilles and Paris alike, and which will be read by posterity.

March 27, 1791: Camille was watching from the galleries, Mirabeau presiding over the Assembly in the Salle du Manège. His neck was bandaged, wrapped in linen cloths to conceal marks left by leeches. Mirabeau spoke, loud and emphatic—five times he stood and spoke and sat, then left the hall. Camille stepped out also and found Mirabeau seated on a bench in the Tuileries Palace gardens, pressed by crowds. As usual, there were many people with applications and supplications and praising him. Camille pressed closer, hoping for something newsworthy. He heard the great man say to the friend with him, "Take me out of this!" Mortally ill, he had quit the tribune, not just for the day but forever.

April 2, 1791: Outside Mirabeau's house, Camille was at the gate, imploring entry—in honor of their former friendship, and to seek pardon. Unexpectedly, Camille was overtaken by grief, for the loss to France and to liberty of this genius. A message was returned that Mirabeau did not want to see him.

Camille persisted; the porter disappeared again. He returned. Mirabeau had relented. Camille entered Mirabeau's bedroom and saw his erstwhile mentor on his death bed. He retained the long black hair, but his face seemed to fall away, his head appeared diminished.

Amid the dying man's breathing, the gurgle and the rattle, there came a gleam in the eye; he recognized Camille. His breast sore, Camille leaned over and kissed Mirabeau, who embraced him with a tenderness and fervor as never before. He said, "I am dying, my friend; dying as by slow fire; we shall not meet again. Remember this, and write it. When I am gone, they will know what the value of me was. The miseries I have held back will burst from all sides on France. I carry in my heart the death-dirge of the French monarchy; the dead remains of it will now be the spoil of the factious." Camille remained with Mirabeau; his own grief was wholly unexpected. Seized by that same pain in the breast that he feels now.

On April 4, 1791, Camille was there among the onlookers who thronged all roofs, lamp irons, windows, and tree branches. The funeral procession extended four miles: all of Paris, with king's ministers, senators, national guards. Later, the night was lit up by torches afloat upon the undulating sea of the multitude. Sadness was painted on every countenance; many persons wept. There was the combined wail of mourners, trombones, and music. This was the mourning of a whole nation, even tears of men—no modern people had ever so grieved for one man.

But there was one who did not weep: Marat. On the very same day as the funeral, his paper, *The Friend of the People*, declared, "People, give thanks to the gods! Your most redoubtable enemy has fallen beneath the scythe of Fate. Mirabeau is no more; he dies victim of his numerous treasons, victim of his too tardy scruples, victim of the barbarous foresight of his atrocious accomplices."

And Camille joined Marat, for now Robespierre was his main muse. Camille and Marat, they were a duet! Camille wrote, "Go then, O corrupt nation, O stupid people, and prostrate yourself before the tomb of this honest man, the Mercury of his age, and the god of orators, liars, and thieves!"

Camille has not forgotten Marat's words on July 12, 1789 in the Palais Royale that impelled him to action so physically bold and out of character—"you are ever under the ascendency of others." This appears still to be true. He realizes now his ambition has led him to repeated betrayals of people who have mattered to him. First, his parents. They are estranged because his father would not support his election to the Esates General and then the Assembly as his father disapproved of his radical journalism. Then it was Mirabeau himself. Now the homes of some of Camille's erstwhile friends have been searched. The fulfillment of Mirabeau's death bed prophesy is coming to pass.

September 11, 1792: Paine opens a letter from Condorcet, dated August 20. It has been seemingly delayed by the censors in England or France, or both, for the envelope has been opened and resealed.

> *Thomas, my dear old friend,*
> *I send you greetings, as does our dear friend Brissot. The news that you are receiving of Paris ought to fill all who*

desire a republican France with hope and joy. By the time you receive this letter certainly you will have read newspaper reports of the extraordinary and momentous events of August 10 and thereafter. Meanwhile, the Assembly has bestowed you the honor of French citizenship. You share this honor with your countrymen Dr. Joseph Priestley, George Washington, Alexander Hamilton, and James Madison. Now all republicans are committed to winning next month a seat for Thomas Paine on our newly reformed national legislature—the core of a new government that omits a king! We look forward to seeing you in but a few weeks!

I do confess, mine was one of the 222 votes cast for Danton when he was elected Minister of Justice. There are those who have reproached me for giving my vote to Danton. Here are my reasons: It was necessary to have in this executive position a man who should enjoy the confidence of the people whose uprising had but then overthrown the monarchy; it was necessary to have a man who, by his ascendancy, could control the extremely untrustworthy instruments of a glorious, useful, and necessary revolution; and it was essential that this man, by his mind or character, should degrade neither his office nor the Assembly which would have dealings with him. Danton alone has these qualities. I chose him, and I shall not repent my choice.

No doubt you are concerned that he may exaggerate the maxims of popular constitutions in paying too great a deference to the ideas of the people; in making too great a use, in the conduct of affairs, of popular movements and opinions. I share your concern, but we had no alternative. The principle of acting only with the people and through the people, while directing the people, is the only principle which can safeguard the laws in a time of popular insurrection; and all parties that separate themselves from the people will end in destruction, and perhaps in destroying the people with themselves.

I hope you are consoled that Brissot himself supported

Danton's election. Brissot said to me: "This ought to be the seal of our reconciliation."

Louis was officially arrested on August 13, 1792, and by decree of the Assembly he was imprisoned in the Temple.

The Assembly that was a part of the French constitutional monarchy is now obsolete. So, the Assembly itself decided that it will be dissolved and a new legislature—the National Convention—will be established in its place, and that deputies must be newly elected to fill the new legislature. Elections will be held in the coming weeks, and we plan to campaign on your behalf. As a fully endowed French citizen you are eligible.

Paine has read in *The Times* about the awful events in Paris since August 20. He tosses the letter aside and mutters to himself, "So the dog returns to its vomit, indeed. The king is imprisoned in the Temple, yet they have traded a monarchy for a Danton dictatorship. I will not return to Paris to be a subject of Danton's tyranny!"

CHAPTER 9

THE MEAL IS SIMPLE: boiled cod, vegetables, and rice pudding. As host, Joseph Johnson is seated prominently at the head of the table. He is wearing a powdered wig—he is in his fifties and this is an accessory that is now in fashion mainly among older men—and, as usual, he keeps a tidy appearance in his habitual blue waistcoat. Paine has spent much time with Johnson, who is his publisher. But his host remains largely opaque, a lifelong bachelor living alone and quietly in this ample house.

It is September 12, 1792, and Paine is at Johnson's weekly dinner gathering, the "Johnson Circle," who regard themselves London's leading radical thinkers. They are people who come from divergent social circles and vary widely in age and personality, but they share a passion for common values including free exchange of ideas, support for full emancipation of women, eradication of monarchy, separation of church and state, and abolition of slavery.

The mood is somber. The group is unified in their distress at the latest news from France. Yet there is much disagreement among them, and as they discuss the current events in France, each guest expresses his or her distinct point of view.

As is his wont, Johnson has not expressed any opinion of his own, yet the press that he owns and operates on his ground floor issues works that captivate the Western world and seek to alter its course.

Joseph Priestley is reading from a letter from his son William about the ongoing events in France that are so disturbing for all to hear.

Mary Wollstonecraft is now pointing at Paine and, interrupting Priestley, she says, "It is your friend Lafayette whom I blame for this madness, these atrocities." Mary has over-drunk wine and she is animated. "Only he had the power and prestige and also knew better enough to himself have hewn and maintained a means to republican government. But he loved his office and his power more than he loved the people or correct principles. It is his ambition that got the best of him and made the conditions that enabled this barbarism."

Paine starts to speak but she interrupts, pointing again. "Don't tell me he is your friend, Thomas Paine. Don't try to defend him. You can no longer be that tyrant's friend and count me among your friends." Paine adores this woman's will, and her genius—yes, indeed, her genius. While other women tend to their needlepoint, Mary is issuing pamphlets—loosely sewn pages with no binding or cover transmogrified into ideological armies. Mary advocates that women must be transformed into rational and independent beings whose sense of worth comes, not from their appearance, but from education, and minds and bodies trained to self-discipline. Horace Walpole's rejoinder was to call her a hyena in petticoats. Yet in truth, she does attend to her appearance, as she is herself comely. Paine simply adores her.

She brandishes an edition of *The Times*, bringing it in front of his face. He recognizes the article and wants to groan, mortified. It reports that between September 2 and 5, Paris was "a scene of bloodshed and violence without intermission . . . twelve thousand persons fallen victims to the fury of the mob."

"Look! Read here," Mary says. Her thumb underscores a phrase near the end of the article, holding it out for all to see. She turns the paper around and reads aloud, "Are these 'the Rights of Man'?"

Here is Edmund Burke's most savage blow: Burke is not the author of the article, but Paine does not doubt that this rhetoric—"Are these 'the Rights of Man'?"—originated with Burke, and now he and his allies are rejoicing at the Paris bloodbath, for the discredit it has brought on the French Revolution and upon

Thomas Paine, laying at his feet the corpses of many thousands of French murdered in cold blood. Paine believes that every Englishman who reads this phrase will associate it with Paine's own *Rights of Man*. But Paine, like Rousseau, like Jesus, cannot be held responsible that he might be misread.

"Listen to me," Mary says, "these events have enabled Pitt to turn the great majority of English people against you; they are now hard set hard against you, and so Pitt feels the political will gives him licence to silence us by any means necessary. What will happen now to Louis Capet? If he is put to death, the public reaction here will be very negative."

"And I am supposed to leave England and never return?"

Mary has been urging him to flee Britain for France, for his own safety and for the good of the revolution. He has told her privately that he is now an honorary French citizen and has been elected to the newly formed National Convention. She also plans to migrate to France and wants to join him there.

"You will be tried here for treason in December!" she replies.

"If I flee, my enemies will have won, just as Socrates's executioners would have preferred that he flee Athens. If I leave, they will try me in absentia and convict me; I will have renounced my principles, and I will never be able to return to England. Nor will anyone regard me enough to give any credence to my works. I do not fear William Pitt's henchmen." The charge of treason against Paine—merely for his words—is, for Paine, enough sign that Pitt is actually a despot and concealing his true motives.

"You know that you can't stay here any longer, and the movement for liberty in France is in need of Thomas Paine," Mary says.

"If I remain, they will not kill me or imprison me. The people will not tolerate it. There would be an insurrection. I will not fly away like Louis Capet."

He does not tell them that he carries in his pocket a letter from Marguerite that he received only today. She pleads with him to return to France.

Marguerite reports that "all principles were abandoned" in

Paris at the beginning of September. People were slaughtered indiscriminately. She describes heaps of fresh corpses piled in the streets. Pools and rivulets of dark, clotting blood.

And it began with Danton's tribunal. His adjudications were completely arbitrary, and during the mass slaughters, the "triumvirate"—what she calls Danton, Robespierre, and Marat—willingly tolerated them. Brissot, Nicolas, Condorcet, and other Brissotins tried to halt the killings, but to no avail. The massacres are abated, for now.

Meanwhile, Robespierre openly rigged the process of elections to the National Convention, France's new legislature. Indeed, their very purpose in pandering to the *sans-culottes*, in empowering their bloody uprising, has been to ensure that Robespierre and his allies are elected as Paris representatives to the National Convention.

Robespierre insists that "ordinary men," "not men who write books," must lead France—except for Camille, who, she notes, Robespierre has also managed to get elected to the legislature as a delegate.

Now the Paris deputies, who are all Robespierre's allies, have organized to form an anti-Brissotin bloc. They allege that France is not yet ready for republican government, but this, Marguerite asserts, is but an excuse for despotism.

Vote rigging, however, has not prevented Paine's friends from securing election as Convention deputies elsewhere. Thanks to concerted campaigning by his friends, the Electoral Assembly in Pas-de-Calais has elected Paine to the Convention—and he must now return to France to fulfill this calling, Marguerite asserts.

Indeed, her letter was just today brought to him by a gentleman named Achille Audibert, of Calais, whom Nicolas and Marguerite deputized to go to London and bring Paine to Paris. Mr. Audibert entered the country surreptitiously and then slipped into London seemingly unnoticed by government officials, and is now sheltered at the residence of John Frost, where a number of other radical fugitives are hiding.

Mr. Frost, a barrister who is the secretary of the London Corresponding Society, which campaigns to increase the representation of working class people in parliament, is here at Johnson's dinner this very night. Audibert brought him two additional letters: from the electoral body of the department of Calais, containing the notification of Paine's being elected to the National Convention; and from the newly formed National Convention itself, also informing him of his being elected for the department of Calais.

What do Marguerite and his other friends in France and Mary expect him to do? He knows well. They expect him to turn the people against the despots, for in France the common people, the *sans-culottes*, are now the power. Indeed, exactly for his immense popularity, he has here in England been charged with treason. But in France he would join the National Convention, and truth be told, once the United States had won its independence, there was no place for him in public life there, because he is a radical writer and a philosopher, not a politician.

His role has been to be true to himself, and to browbeat and inspire the people toward social progress. Only against his better judgment would he enter politics in France, where the challenge of politics would be all the greater for his inability to speak their language, and the cultural divide between France and the English-speaking countries.

Yet he appreciates Mary's logic. The chain of causation leads directly from Lafayette's transgression to the current barbarism. "Lafayette is no longer my friend," Paine says, effecting a sadness in his voice. "Yet the tragedy of Lafayette is that the American republic may owe its very existence to his influence in the court of Louis Capet, and for that we all owe him our thanks. And what irony that the financial support that Lafayette helped to secure for the Americans was a cause of the economic distress in France that hastened the French Revolution."

Now Johnson at last speaks. "If Lafayette is a tyrant, I fear that by the time the current turmoil has taken its course, we may give new definition to the word. In any event, whether or not we regard

Lafayette's present condition as his just deserts, I don't expect that Thomas will be paying him social visits anytime soon."

Truly, Paine recognizes that indeed his long friendship with Lafayette is finished; for Paine now regards him a despot and he is now languishing in a Belgian prison, though at least he is safe from the Paris mobs. Just tonight John Frost brought news from Achille Audibert of what has most recently happened to Lafayette. On August 14, Danton put out a warrant for Lafayette's arrest. Lafayette fled—he planned to flee ultimately to the United States, and so he entered Belgium. But he was taken prisoner by the Austrians.

Poor Lafayette; both Mary and Burke, who loathe one another, regard this to be his just deserts. Everyone is against him—everyone in Europe, that is; he is still beloved in the United States. But there is no sympathy for him around this table tonight.

Priestley resumes reading aloud from and intermittently summarizing sections of his son William's letter. Like Marguerite, William asserts that the massacres have been planned and orchestrated.

Priestley pauses and looks up. "He says that I won election to the National Convention." "You will go to Paris?" says Paine.

"No. I will decline. I cannot speak French."

"I have thought perhaps I should do the same."

"I will not remain here," says Priestley. "I expect my new home will be your United States."

Joseph Priestley has suffered mightily for the cause of liberty in Britain and he is at the end of his rope. A mob incited by British government agents burned down his house and his farm, and his laboratory and library were destroyed.

William Blake shows up. A porter is at his side, and takes his coat with a solicitous murmur. Blake is seated and soon the cook arrives with a plate of food, and pours his wine.

Johnson employs Blake as a printer and an engraver of book illustrations. Of all of Johnson's regular guests, Blake is the only one who is not, at least in his own right, famous. But there is nothing commonplace about Blake; his remarkable hair and eyes are emblematic. His hair is of a light color, shaded with gold, resembling a lion's mane. His eyes are even more striking: very wide open, and almost too large for their sockets, unusually bright (radiance projected from his inner self?), piercing into those whom they now look upon. The very large pupils appear as though trying to enlarge themselves still more, as if to absorb all available light. The brilliance of his eyes seems to throw the rest of his face into shadow. Is it a madman's visage? Perhaps, Paine must concede, but he prefers to regard it a visionary's face; indeed, the image of a prophet.

"Where have you been this past week?" Paine asks kindly. "I have been calling on you, and your poor wife has had no information as to your whereabouts."

"I have been attending your trial; your trial and your execution. Traveling about by foot and by coach."

Paine feels a bit of unease. With Blake you never know if he is describing a vision or making a metaphor of a real event. What do Blake's visions mean? Perhaps it is madness, and Paine rejects superstition, yet he prefers that Blake's visions omit Paine's own martyrdom.

Blake has recounted to Paine his visions and their mysterious prophetic quality. When only four years old, he saw God's face at the window of his room. A few years later, he was beaten for saying that he had found the prophet Ezekiel sitting in the fields near his home. On another occasion, he beheld a tree filled with angels, who sang and waved their glittering wings in the branches. And once he saw a ghost, a human figure covered with metallic scales, standing at the top of a staircase. At fourteen, Blake refused to be apprenticed to an engraver named Ryland, on the ground that the man looked as if he would someday be hanged, as, indeed, some years later, he was. Before the death of his brother Robert, Blake saw his spirit flying away and clapping its hands for joy. And later, it was Robert's spirit which showed him the process by which Blake would engrave and print his books.

He has received visions all his life. He says that thinking and reading make the visions more frequent.

Suddenly Paine understands. He says, "I am being burned in effigy! It is flattering, actually."

Blake replies, "Don't make light of it, my dear Thomas. These are elaborate games, ceremonies such as I have not seen or heard of before—actually rehearsing, with exquisite formality and verisimilitude, the means and the realization of your annihilation."

"Where is this occurring?" Paine asks.

"Everywhere; all over the country. Marlborough, Leeds, Chagford, Dukinfield, Nettlebed, Bridport, Croydon, Box, Saddleworth, Chapel Milton, Cosham, Cross Street, Ellesmere. At Datchet, in Berkshire, you were hoisted on a nine-foot gibbet for the pleasure of the king as he passed from Windsor to Westminster."

"King George? He himself?" exclaims Paine.

"Yes, the actual king. He was not an actor. Yet, I am getting ahead of myself, for you were also accorded the formalities of a traitor's trial and execution. In towns in particular, you were formally convicted, placed in the local jail, sometimes in chains, and taken to the place of execution by sheriffs and javelin men." Blake pauses to eat and take a drink of his wine, while the table sits expectant.

"Tell me more, what else have you seen?" Paine says finally.

Blake swallows and continues. "In each place there were hundreds, sometimes thousands, of people watching. I was amazed! They dressed you in a hat, coat, breeches, stockings, and shoes. Always you were very handsomely dressed in black. I saw you dressed in mourning with a white cockade, a black coat, and holding your allegedly seditious writings in one hand, and a penitential scroll in the other; a wig flowing to your shoulders. They draped you in tricolor flags and had a devil accompany you to the gallows, singing 'a Ira.' I saw you eviscerated and chopped up, to emulate a drawing and quartering. Once, they filled you with fireworks, and you spit fire and were blown to pieces. Always they shouted out, calling you Monsieur Égalité de Orléans, a leveler, and a regicide."

"A regicide! I am against killing Louis Capet. I wish him banished to America. That is all."

"Once they had you with *The Rights of Man* in one hand and

a pair of stays in the other." The allusion is to Paine's trade as a staymaker, as his father had been.

"Ah yes, they mock my humble origins. No doubt it is the wealthy who are financing these elaborate farces."

"Indeed. Gentlemen, or perhaps, the government itself, are behind these events, for I saw Pitt's agents in attendance. The leading organizers are gentlemen of authority: magistrates, large property owners, prominent landlords; indeed, those who have been members of legitimate grand juries. At Bath-Easton, you were attended by several persons as official superintendents. There was a high sheriff, a clergyman, a clerk, javelin men, two high and petty constables, and an executioner with a large ax. Numerous freeholders enclosed the procession on horseback."

"No doubt, it is those who are most benefitting from the status quo," Paine says with some emotion.

"Yet these spectacles are leaving a deep impression upon the commoners. At a prominent hill, you were hoisted on a gibbet for several hours to allow the crowd an opportunity to pelt and whip you, and everyone participated. Only later did they burn you in a bonfire. At North Shields, you were attended by an ingenious mock-chaplain, who excited the laughter of the entire populace to immoderate degree. I have observed that here in England, hatred for you is widespread, and pervades all of the classes."

Paine grimaces. It is most painful to learn that he is the butt of laughter—worse yet, the laughter of commoners—in these ludicrous proceedings. "And no doubt there were clergy who volunteered to give me last rites and recite the Psalms!"

"I only saw chimney sweeps and the like substituting as clergymen."

Red-faced, Paine looks at Mary, and her face beams triumphant. He says, "So even lowly chimney sweeps are on the side of Burke and Pitt. What does this all mean?"

Blake turns to Paine. "What is the meaning of all this?" Blake's large eyes are glittering. "I have a strong feeling that you must not go home tonight, or you are a dead man."

"Really?" Though he is a supremely rational man, Paine is alarmed by Blake's premonition.

Suddenly Frost blurts, "You must go to France. You too have been elected to the National Convention, and the gentleman from Calais has come to fetch you, sent by your friends, who await you. He and I will escort you there. We can leave tonight."

"I will not flee to save my life! Then Burke and Pitt will have won, for I will have fled in cowardice."

He does not say that he is also quite satisfied with his place in the world presently, here in London. Here, life is good—one of philosophical leisure, friends, and enjoyment. He has no interest in making France's problems his own. He is a philosopher, not a politician.

Blake responds firmly, "Thomas, you must act quickly, and do what is necessary to save your life. Yours is no martyr's fate. A willing embrace of martyrdom would run contrary to your message. You elevate the individual; you affirm life and vitality and celebrate life's pleasures. Go to France, because that is the principled thing to do."

CHAPTER 10

FROST IS EVER THE conscientious and sagacious lawyer; he will accompany Paine and Audibert on the ferry from Dover to France. Before they depart, Frost examines the papers that Paine plans to bring with him. All even arguably seditious writings are purged.

Regrettably, Paine has already burned the letter he received from Marguerite, to conceal the most interesting parts to him, the final paragraphs:

> *Thomas, France needs a great man. As you see, there are none left. When can I expect to see you? France needs your experience, your intelligence, and your wisdom! Thomas, I miss you and I want to see you again. And thus do I turn this account now to myself, for I too have been affected by these calamitous and monumental events. The independent and self-sufficient mindset that I preached to you has begun to seem a little disingenuous, a little untrue to myself, for I am beginning to recognize that my deepest needs are unfulfilled. Deep within me there seems to be a changing of the season; I do not understand why, but it tilts toward you, Thomas. Do you mind that I am completely candid with you? Can you imagine with me a relationship that is a deeper and more intimate kind than to which is normally applied the label "friendship"?*
>
> *I do not mean love, for this word is burdened by expecta-tions and conventions that are intolerable to me and I reject*

*as unreal. I wish to find a person to whom I am willing to be
committed and faithful—not necessarily in the body, as the
Church demands, but in the ego. Perhaps this is not a longing you have ever experienced. At times I have felt the absurd
desire to come to you and offer my services as your protégé.
But it seems clear from your past that you do not really desire
or need a partner.*

*Since you left us, I have thought often of you and missed
you more than I ever expected I would. I cherish our intimate
friendship that overtook us so unexpectedly. The fear that I
will not again have the intensely satisfying pleasure of your
presence has been so painful that I could not bear even to
begin to write to you. I hope also that your memory of me
likewise evokes such tender sentiments. I know it is difficult to
express them in a letter.*

Watching the pages curl and blacken and disappear gave him a
pang because the intimate affections she has revealed went up in
smoke. And her failure to mention Nicolas—whom she has called
her lover—is noteworthy. Yet he destroyed the letter because he
must be careful about his associations with a young and desirable
woman such as Marguerite.

When Paine steps down from the carriage into the gray Dover
afternoon he feels grimy, disheveled, and groggy, having hardly
slept during the two-day journey from London. They did not stop
at an inn for fear of being apprehended by government agents.
Throughout the uncomfortable and tiresome trip, thoughts, insistently throbbing, of Marguerite, have sustained him. He hopes to
see her within a day.

But now having set foot in Dover, he is flooded with contradictory emotions and memories. There is sadness that after Dover,
he may never return to his native country, and torment that he is

deserting the cause of liberty here in England.

No day has passed absent some remembrance of Mary Lambert, his first wife, and the only love of his life. His mental image of her now is especially poignant, for it was here in Dover that they spent their happiest days together. And her grave is near Dover. She was an 'Orphan of Sandwich,' meaning she had no money or relatives to provide for her. Her father had been an excise officer.

She was an illiterate woman with a pretty face and a fine mind, whom he taught to read. He would have forever remained a master stay-maker to make a settled life with her. They married in 1759, and he will never forget the terrible night in 1760: Hour after hour passed and the babe would not come. How she perspired, and she held his hand, hers animal-like, like a claw. When the spasms came, she screamed. All at once blood burst from her womb and soaked the linens beneath her. She died, and the babe perished with her. His wife's dead face was a horror, unrecognizable to him; yet he held her tight and rocked her, and wept, till they both were blood soaked.

He was twenty-three, and a period of misery and misdirection ensued. He followed the example of his dead wife's dead father, and entered the excise service; was sacked from his job for "claiming to have inspected goods he did not inspect;" returned to stay-making only planning to exit the trade as soon as practicable; tried teaching schoolchildren but lacked the temperament for it; studied for the ministry but found it distasteful; and regained his job as an excise officer.

He never lacked friends, but was perpetually lonely. He was unloved; it was simple as that. He did not wholly lack female companions, but the relations were intermittent, ephemeral, inevitably brief, and sometimes transacted.

Then came his second marriage—to Elizabeth, daughter of Samuel Ollive; she now resides not far from Dover, in Cranbrook—the thought of which causes him regret, and shame. Elizabeth was educated, for her parents were Quakers, and her father, a tobacconist in Lewes who took him as a lodger above their shop, had been kind to him.

In 1769 the father died, and the tobacco shop foundered. Paine committed his own funds and saved the business, and in March, 1771, he married Elizabeth. Yet his interest was in London, not remote Lewes. His colleagues had united to petition parliament to raise their salaries. They needed a spokesman, and selected him, as much for his nerve as his superior command of words. The first pamphlet he ever issued was a petition to parliament concerning a plea for the excisemen, printed in 1773. The effort failed: a rebellion of the excisemen, who do not have the populace on their side, was not much feared by the elected parliament.

During Paine's sojourn in London, the tobacco mill was still, his groceries were unsold, and his wife and her mother were once again at the brink of destitution.

Paine was again sacked from the excise service, this time ostensibly for abandoning his post when he returned to Lewes to deal with his creditors. Worse, he could not face the confinement of domesticity in Lewes, and he did not love his wife (he had known love, and recognized that he lacked any for Elizabeth, however much he had hoped for it). And so he left his wife and what remained of funds raised from sale of the store. At thirty-seven, Paine found himself alone, homeless, and penniless.

Here in Dover they have no choice but to spend the night as the next ferry will not leave until seven the next morning. The inn that Frost has selected for them appears a cheerful place, with bright red shutters on the façade. Audibert cedes the two beds to Paine and Frost, and he retires to a feather mattress on the floor.

Paine wakes and realizes that someone is banging against the door. Frost is on his feet and opens the door. Soldiers are standing outside on the lamp-lit landing—they are dressed in the red coats of government agents. Paine is certain that they have come to arrest him, and he is afraid. His celebrated—or infamous—nerve has deserted him.

Frost, as the lawyer, takes charge of interactions with the redcoats. He steps onto the landing and for a few moments speaks to them in a low murmur.

Frost returns. "They want to search us," he says, "that is all. They are not bad chaps."

Paine says, "They are bad chaps, for they are here to search and to seize my private papers."

"They are not here to arrest you—so far—and that is what matters. We must cooperate with them, and then we can hope that we will be on our way."

"How do they know who we are?"

"The whole country is in an uproar since the Royal Proclamation, and your image is well known. They saw your name on the passenger list for tomorrow morning. They are with the customs office; their instructions are to be vigilant in uprooting treason. Come, you have nothing to hide. I must let them search your things. But, please, keep silent unless I direct you to speak to them or I ask you a question."

The chief officer is a young man; he appears younger than Frost, and is solicitous of the lawyer. A subordinate lifts Paine's trunk onto a bed; and it is with apologies to Frost and then to Paine that the young commander reaches in and begins riffling through Paine's papers. The first letter that he withdraws is from the President of the United States to Paine.

Frost lays his hand over the face of the letter, and says, "Do not read it." The young commander hands the letter to Frost and he gives it to Paine. Paine is impressed, for in Frost he sees a man with ideological rigor to match his own.

When the officer has taken what papers and letters he pleases out of the trunks, he takes them away to read. The hours pass. Sleep is now out of the question. Frost moves back and forth between the customs officials in their post, and the hotel room.

At daybreak Paine looks down at the docks. He sees the ferry, a modest-sized sailing ship.

Audibert leaves and now Paine is alone, as Frost is meeting with the customs officials. Audibert returns after maybe twenty minutes.

"The skipper will wait as long as he can for us," he says, "but he can't allow the boat to be marooned by the tide. He is a patriot, a friend of the revolution; a friend of mine."

"What is that crowd there?"

"They wish to bid the infamous Thomas Paine *adieu*. Word has spread around that you are here, spending your last day on English soil." The young man gives him a toothy smile. "Maybe we should make a run for it. The Brits left one guard on the landing outside the door. He's practically dozing. I can knock him headlong down the stairs before he realizes we're out the door. The sailors will save us from the crowd."

"No. Frost and I must abide by the rule of law. His aim is that we depart with leave of the British government, and my papers. I will leave England as Socrates left Athens—abiding the rule of law, and with my honor intact, whether dead or alive."

All at once Frost arrives; he has Paine's papers in hand. It is time to go. Frost replaces them in Paine's trunk. Audibert picks it up.

Once they are outside and nearing the docks, the people gathered there jeer and shout. Paine hears, "Here comes the atheist! Look at the atheist flying away to France. Coward!"

Yet the redcoats are now present, and they make a barrier with their bodies linked by staves. They are shouting, "Back! Back! Back!" A corridor appears amid the crowd; Frost, Paine, and Audibert bolt for the boat and finally up the gangway onto the vessel.

Soon afterward the sailors cast off. Paine sees the crowd, the redcoats, the receding shore, the village, and the white cliffs. Now suddenly more redcoats arrive, riding steeds that even from this distance Paine can see are lathered.

The foremost rider leaps from his horse and begins shouting furiously at the boat. Paine hears that they are shouting his name. He hears, "Return!" and the words "Order!" and "Arrest!"

Now muskets are drawn and aimed skyward. He sees puffs of smoke emitted and hears the crackle of their reports. It is too late. The ferry sails onward to France. He surmises that they left in the nick of time, just minutes before the order for his arrest arrived from London.

CHAPTER 11

THE WAY THE PASSENGERS gawk says that they know who he is. A group of them standing nearby are French, and they begin talking earnestly in their tongue, foreign to Paine, while openly glancing his way. One of the men speaks in his direction.

Audibert is beside him, and he translates: "He says the English have short memories, they are forgiving; for how else is it that you were able to return after your part in the American Revolution?" At this moment Paine appreciates fully that he has no desire whatsoever to return to England. He does not desire forgiveness from the English.

A steady breeze sustains their short journey; the winds are pleasant, not yet turned cold. The sea is gray and flat. This departure from England—with the foreboding that he will never return—brings to mind his own first meeting with a great man.

Paine learned the excise office had fired him after he returned to London from Lewes. He visited his good friend George Lewis Scott, the Commissioner of Excise, at home, and stood in his antechamber and wept—he felt betrayed.

Scott did not, as might be expected, defend himself for failing to protect his friend: an old man who was big and tall, he put his arm around Paine. The gesture surprised him.

Scott said, "Come now, with your formidable gifts you can do better than the excise office." Scott was a man of many resources—an extraordinary harpsichord player, a writer of science texts and encyclopedias, and with means. He was able to make use of Paine's skills, and employed him. Scott lent him a room.

One day Scott said to him, "I want you to meet a good friend of mine. He's an American: Benjamin Franklin. He may have some interesting work for you." Paine needed no explanation of Benjamin Franklin, the world-famous scientist and diplomat.

His appointment was the next morning at ten o'clock, at Franklin's residence, 36 Craven Street. When he arrived the porter admitted him. The house was silent. Paine was surprised that Franklin's antechamber was empty; he had expected a crowd awaiting access to the great man. Everything before in his life had been so hard; Paine was incredulous that this was so easy.

When he entered the study, Franklin was writing, and he looked up. He rose, and picked something up from his desk.

"Is this yours?" Franklin asked. He held the pamphlet before him in his right hand: the unfortunate pamphlet that Paine had written on behalf of the excisemen.

Franklin was not dressed as a gentleman. He wore a loose linen shirt, knee-breeches, high stockings, buckled shoes, and bifocals. There was not a stitch of embroidery, no front ruffle of lace, no silk, no gold or silver thread, and no wig. Paine was pleased, for neither did he, Paine, wear any such adornment or flourish, which had once been his habit. Franklin's gray hair hung lankly from his otherwise bald head.

"Yes. I wrote it."

"It is very good."

"It did not work. It failed to persuade anyone who mattered. I am capable of better work."

"It was not the pamphlet, it was not the quality of your argument, that failed your cause, but the corruption of your audience. I have experienced nothing but failure and humiliation here on behalf of the American colonies, before parliament and the king and the Prime Minister." He tipped his head and gave Paine a knowing smile; over the bifocals, his eyes themselves seemed to smile. "Yet I do wish that I could pamphleteer as well as you."

"I am no match for the intellect of Benjamin Franklin."

"It is not a matter of intellect. It is your poetry that gives the weight to your argument. Poetry's source is a mystery. I am a poor poet. What is your political affiliation?"

"I am a republican." Paine did not hesitate answering, though he had never before been asked such a question, and never identified himself as such before. In another setting he might have been afraid to call himself such a thing.

Franklin's face creased into a smile. He said, "Good. Good answer. Good man. We can make good use of your gifts."

"I will do my best. I write for the common man, and the parliament is not elected by commoners."

"We can no more alter that tide than the natural ones. I am resigned to war between the British and the American colonies. My sole aim here has been to avoid such a war. I have failed because I am absolutely committed to independence of the colonies. How many republicans do you suppose are in America?"

"I don't know. I suppose many more than here."

"There are more, though it would not take many to exceed the number in England. There are hardly any who recognize themselves as such among the great mass of common men, in England or in America. We cannot wage war against the British by decree or fiat. There has never been any place on earth such as America. We must win the commitment of the common men before we go to war with the British. You say you are republican. How deep is your commitment to this idea? You would need to be committed to this above all else."

"I do not fear the king or his agents. I hate them."

"You are an Englishman—"

"The cause of liberty and equality means more to me than my English birth."

Franklin raised his eyebrows. "Indeed, as it should. I am making you not only a proposal for possible employment. Here you can make your place forever in the history of men. The cause of America shall be the cause of all mankind. It is a cause that has been in the making since men habited the earth. My own son is the governor of New Jersey, and a monarchist; and I am prepared to disown him for this cause. I invite you to emigrate to America and we will employ you, writing on behalf of independence."

"Will we go together to America?"

"You will go before me. I am an old man and the journey is arduous. I wish to maximize my chances of surviving the trip and so I do not want to go in winter. I will go after winter."

Paine will arrive in Calais in a better condition than he arrived in America. He was so sick with a putrid fever that he and most of the passengers and the crew had contracted—and killed five of them—that they had to carry him onto shore on a chaise. So sick was he that he could not at that time turn in his bed without help.

He is convinced that the letters of introduction from Benjamin Franklin that he carried with him saved his life, as Franklin's friend Dr. Kersley, of Philadelphia, attended the ship on her arrival, and when he understood that Paine arrived with Franklin's recommendation, he instructed two of his men to bring Paine, and he provided him a lodging, where it took him six weeks to recover.

Now, gulls wheel in the colorless sky. He gazes hard at the occluded northwestern horizon, vainly seeking the British shore.

———————

When Paine arrives in Paris, the spires and towers of Notre Dame and Saint-Chapelle are dominant against a darkening sky. Lamps mark barges anchored in the Seine, and light the medieval maze of cobblestone streets through which their coach now passes. It is said that nine out of ten Parisians live crowded behind the walls they pass, mostly in boarding houses and tenements. Fishwives cluster in the central markets, and jewelers, goldsmiths, pastry-cooks, coffee-sellers, milkmen, and sellers of goods are at their stations along the quays or in the arcades.

The coach halts in front of White's Hotel, Paine's new residence. It is effectively a ghetto for Anglo-Saxon radicals expatriated to Paris in support of the French Revolution.

His lodgings are ample and clean—though, to his relief, shorn of any luxury.

CHAPTER 12

SEPTEMBER 21, 1792, AROUND noon, the Salle du Manège: There sit Paine and Etienne Goupilleau, his translator, side-by-side at the opening of the National Convention, amid the other seven hundred and forty-eight delegates. Each wears across his breast the tricolor ribbon of the representatives of the people.

Paine and Goupilleau are seated on the upper tier behind and to the right of Jérôme Pétion de Villeneuve, the Mayor of Paris who was just today duly elected President of the Convention, the first order of business. He is at the tribune, presiding.

The hall is ten times as long as it is wide, oblong and rounded at the ends, like the circus maximus. Beneath the vaulted ceilings and on both sides are six tiers of banquettes rising at a sharp angle from the floor, in which the deputies are seated, facing each other across a narrow aisle. On one side in the middle is the speaker's podium (called the tribune) and the bar of the Convention, where petitioners may stand to address the deputies. On the other side is the president's elevated chair, and just below him the secretaries' table. The galleries are at the far ends of the hall and in the above loge seats before the high windows, and they are immense. Goupilleau said they could seat fourteen hundred spectators, and now they are mostly filled.

To Paine the hall resembles a ship's hull, and the deputies are set sail amid a sea of French citizens, indeed, all Europeans. A voyage destined for where?

Danton's sonorous, proud voice is first heard as each issue

arises. It is all rehearsed, Paine sees—first, a motion is made, then Danton rises and speaks; and then each Danton crony rises and goes to the tribune to give a brief staccato oration echoing a part of Danton's advocacy.

In one such sequence the comedian and actor Collot d'Herbois rises; then the constitutional bishop, Curate Henri Gregoire rises, fully clad in his episcopal dress; and then Georges Couthon, who is crippled—Danton graciously helps him down from his seat in an upper row to the left of the tribune and guides him to the rostrum.

Robespierre and Marat remain seated and silent the entire session.

Danton's people propose an array of resolutions: that the cornerstone of our new constitution is sovereignty of the people; that our constitution shall be accepted by the people or be null; that the people ought to be avenged, and have right judges; that the imposts must continue; that landed and other property ownership be sacred forever. All are accepted in their turn. A motion is made and accepted that a new president of the Convention will be elected, or the sitting president must run for re-election, every fortnight, and the motion passes.

On this inaugural day of the Convention, Paine is already sick of Danton, of his arrogance and his ubiquity.

Finally, as the hour of adjournment nears, Collot d'Herbois moves that "Monarchy from this day is abolished in France." These are not mere words. Collot is a comedian and actor by profession—his exaggerated, sharp, grotesque features helping a comedic effect—but today his visage could not be more serious. "The people," he says, "have been declared sovereign, but they will not be so in reality till they are delivered from a rival authority, that of kings."

Danton and others rise to speak with climactic passion in support of the motion, Curate Gregoire most noteworthy for his zeal: "What need is there of discussion, where all are of one mind! The history of kings is nothing but the martyrology of nations. While we are all equally convinced of these truths, what need is there of discussing them?"

The Convention unanimously votes that the monarchy is

abolished in France and President Pétion in turn so declares. Paine is himself caught up in the cathartic enthusiasm and the emotion—notwithstanding Danton—and he joins the deputies; they are all on their feet, applauding and cheering, some of them weeping.

President Pétion orders that the decree be immediately published, making it an official act of the Convention, and that messengers deliver it to the armies and all the municipalities.

———————

Next day, Philippe Egalité mounts the tribune and petitions for the removal of all judges, to prevent their removal by popular violence.

Danton rises and speaks in favor of the motion: "Those who have made it their profession to act as judges of men are like priests; both of them have everlastingly deceived the people. Justice ought to be dispensed in accordance with the simple laws of reason. Let the people choose men of talent deserving to act as judges. Nor should it be required that a judge be a trained and certified lawyer. Thus we shall have removed all class distinctions among the people of France."

Paine is alarmed; he rises and asks leave to approach the tribune. Politicians elected by the *sans-culottes* will dispense justice, uphold the rule of law! It is impossible to abide.

Paine (through Goupilleau) moves for postponement of Philippe Egalité's motion for a more thorough discussion: "Having got rid of kings, France requires an independent, impersonal judiciary. For in a republic there is danger that the majority of citizens may be as oppressive as a wicked king."

The deputies react with loud disapproval.

Danton, still seated, remains silent.

The measure is passed by acclamation, and it is decreed that the judges will be removed and their offices filled by popular election. Further, the limitations on eligibility are abolished—the judge need not be a lawyer.

Following adjournment, Goupilleau explains to Paine that

there is no resisting Danton. To do so is to resist the revolution itself. Danton has been ever-present, undeterred, at the front of every event, beginning with May 1789 and even before that. Danton himself made the Cordeliers Club; he was at the storming of the Bastille; he was out front of those who confronted Lafayette at the Champ-de-Mars. Most important, the events of August 10 — the deposition of the Capets and the massacre of their Swiss guards — it was Danton who made that happen.

Paine says, "And he is responsible for what will surely be known as the September Massacres."

"Perhaps," says Goupilleau, "But if Danton is not a patriot, if he is not just, if he is a criminal, the revolution itself is a crime."

Later, in the evening of September 22, Paine and Goupilleau are walking the Seine. It has been raining constantly until a break came, about an hour ago. They are not speaking. That is fine with Paine. He has heard enough words today.

Suddenly they hear exuberant shouting. Victory at Valmy! The celebrants fly by, caps raised on bayonets. They shout, "*Vive la République!*"

In the coming hours the full story arrives in stages. La République is saved! The Prussians have abandoned the offensive and are in retreat. In the morning after Valmy, Field Marshal Brunswick and his men packed, lit any fires that were possible to light, and marched without tap of drum.

General Dumouriez's French army found ghastly symptoms in that camp: "latrines full of blood!" The Prussians are retreating fast as possible through Champagne, now trodden into a quagmire, the wild weather pouring on them–Dumouriez and his army in pursuit.

Next day, a man named Rebecqui, who has only just arrived at the Convention from the south, accuses Robespierre of conspiring to be dictator of France. A loud rumble of conversation ensues, and all eyes turn toward the accused. But Danton hurries to the tribune. He practically shouts, "That will be a happy day for the Republic, when a frank and fraternal explanation shall take place, and put an end to all suspicions—dictators and triumvirs are spoken of, but such accusations are vague and ought to be signed."

"And I will sign a statement," exclaims Rebecqui, rising toward the tribune.

"Do so. But we need specifics. Facts: places, names, who said what to whom, circumstances of the conspiracy. Can you provide any of these?"

Rebecqui does not answer.

Danton replies, "Let us quit all vague accusations of individuals. Yet let us affix the penalty of death to any who shall be proven to have proposed a dictatorship or triumvirate."

Robespierre, having been personally accused, comes forward and demands to be heard. He recites the support he has given to liberty.

"That is not the question," cries one of the deputies.

"He must be allowed to justify himself!" shouts Danton.

But before Robespierre can speak, Marat demands to be heard. He stands at the tribune amid a cascade of cries of "Down with Marat!" and murmurs of disgust. He stands silent until the noise abates.

"In this assembly I have a great number of enemies," rasps Marat, smiling.

"All, all!" exclaim what seems almost the whole Convention, rising from the benches.

"I have in this assembly a great number of enemies," repeats Marat, and he pauses. Now there is silence. "I recall them to a sense of shame. I declare that my colleagues, especially Robespierre and Danton, have constantly disapproved the idea of a triumvirate, or of a dictatorship. If anyone be guilty of having thrown out this idea, it is I!"

Now the deputies begin to shout again and boo and hiss. Marat stands there calmly, not speaking, until the noise abates before he continues to talk. "This accusation can only apply to me. Call down the vengeance of the nation upon myself, but before I cause opprobrium or the sword to fall upon my head, hear me. Am I accused of ambition? Behold and judge."

He points to the dirty handkerchief which envelops his head, and takes hold of and shakes the tattered waistcoat which covers his naked breast.

Marat continues, "Had I wished to affix a price on my silence, had I wished for such a place, I might have been the object of court favors. Well, what has been my life? I have been shut up in subterraneous cellars. I have condemned myself to penury and every danger. The steel of twenty thousand assassins was suspended above me, and I preached truth with my head upon the block. My ideas, however revolting they may appear to you, tend only to the public good. If you are not enlightened enough to understand me, so much the worse for you! Such is my opinion, written, signed, and publicly defended!"

He finishes and now an astonished silence prevails, then interrupted by bursts of laughter. Then a few partisans of Marat applaud him. He returns to his seat without much applause, but having quelled the expressions of anger that were thrown at him, and the accusations against Robespierre.

———

In the coming days a fixed seating arrangement materializes in the Salle du Manège. To the left of Pétion and at the highest elevation is the faction comprised of mostly Paris deputies including those whom the Brissotins hold responsible for the September Massacres. These deputies comprise what has become known as a party associated with Robespierre: the Montagne—or, in English, the Mountain—the individuals known as the Montagnards. Among them are Danton and Marat and other Jacobins. Camille Desmoulins is with them.

With the Mountain to the left of the President, the Brissotins are to the right. (Brissot prefers to call his circle the alternate name, "the Girondins." If he hears the word "Brissotin," he says, "What is a Brissotin? I am not one. I do not know such an organization. I don't think such an organization exists.") In between lays the area called the Plain, not only for the lower elevation of these seats. In the Plain are seated the deputies too timid to side with either the Montagnards or the Girondins. In this configuration, the split dividing the primary factions has become open and notorious, absent discretion or restraint.

Like the Montagne, the Girondins are not formally a party or club; they are all Jacobins. Brissot told Paine the epithet "Girondin" was awarded by their opponents, who tell the people in the streets that the Brissotins are from the department of Gironde. Yet they are not ashamed to be called Girondins. It appears clear to Paine that the Girondins control the Convention, as the numbers of delegates associated with their views are more numerous than the Montagne. This is evident from the fact that Pétion, the president, is a Girondin. And there is no prospect that a Montagnard will be elected to be president. Yet the Girondin control of this chamber derives from the fact that a majority of delegates represent departments outside Paris. It appears likewise clear to Paine that the Montagne control the Paris streets, for the Montagne are firmly in control of the Paris Jacobin Club and the Paris Commune. Which constituency is the more potent source of political power in this chamber, as a practical matter? Time will tell.

Paine does not call himself a Girondin, but he is seated among them, for his friends are here. But he is not pleased with the new seating arrangement and the factionalism that it connotes.

CHAPTER 13

ONLY PAINE AND MARGUERITE have come down to the Palais-Royal; Nicolas wanted to go to bed. And this time just the two of them are seated at the Café des Aveugles, drinking more cognac. They are near the sculpture in the center of the Palais, "la belle Zulima" — a wax statue of a naked woman done in realistic flesh color.

Marguerite sits smiling brightly, seeming interested in Paine's monologue about politics. He holds forth about triumphs in a time and place across a vast shining sea, that has (for now) lost its vital relevance to Europe, to live on here only in the intricacy of his robust imagination.

He pauses and looks around. All around them and the sculpture, along the promenade that fronts the boutiques and galleries, prostitutes are making contacts and assignations with their customers. They are breathtakingly elegant, like a flock of exotic birds. Arms uncovered to the shoulder blade. They wear plumes and headdresses, and chains around their long narrow necks and intricately trinketed bracelets on their javelin-like arms. Their dress is made of a tricot material that reproduces the statuesque effect of clinging drapery—you can mark their every lineament, all their secret charms. Stockings and shoes are abandoned in favor of sandals. Their voices are as fresh and melodious as running water. What a contrast they offer to their male clientele.

"Why is it that in the market for sex, only men are the consumers?" he asks.

"Two reasons: First, women will not pay for sex because to

do so would be an intolerable admission. Second, men have all the money."

"That is all? Surely sexual desire is different for men than for women."

"That expression is a crucial element of society's prejudice that so oppresses women. Women are no different from men when it comes to sex, like most else."

"Tell me, then. How does a woman feel when she desires a man carnally?"

"It burns, in the genitals—we become engorged, and wet, like your penis. We are no different from you."

"Here the sex trade is so open."

"There ought to be no dishonor in what these women are doing. It is the men who would be dishonorable, should they be violating a covenant that they have made with their wives and are now deceiving them."

"This flesh trade, it seems an abuse of these women."

"You would deprive a woman of the best available means to support herself?"

"No; I agree with you, actually. I hope to be instrumental in winning liberties for women that will expand the well-paying work that is available to them beyond this. Do you suppose that these women enjoy their work?"

"I think it tends to be tedious."

"Do they sometimes fall in love with their clients?"

"Perhaps. They would fall in love only by rare and pure accident. How excited would you be for sex with women you did not choose? In the service professions, the providers do not choose their clients. What is this 'love' of which you speak, anyway?"

"Upstairs, tonight, I first realized that I love you."

"Aha! Please, don't use that word in reference to me. It's like that word 'providence' you use in your writings." She is ablaze; her whole countenance is smiling.

"How so?"

"Poetic nonsense."

"Okay. Let's start with providence. What's wrong with that?"

"You know very well there is no God pulling at us as by strings here. Things will happen as they will by the doings of nature and human beings, and by chance."

"I agree with you. What I believe is that our movement will prevail because of natural laws. The power of truth resides with our side, within each of us. I call this power 'providence.' It is the same force that makes the sun rise."

"As an atheist, I understood." He is taken aback at her easy self-reference as an atheist. She is looking closely at him. "You are surprised to hear me call myself that? I see no difference that means anything between your deism and my atheism other than how you choose to define yourself to society. Regardless, I think your use of 'providence' as such misleads, and may be off-putting to the readers you are trying to reach."

"My aim is to reach the widest possible audience. I expect those of your intellect to understand what I mean. Those who maintain their faith in the story-book God of the Bible may interpret the baser meaning; yet they may thereby be persuaded to join our cause. Now, how do you analogize 'love' to 'providence'?"

"Love is a poetic emblem, a shorthand, for a process that is wholly natural; a process within our bodies. Nature wants us to mate and procreate. So we are drawn to one another, and our sexual engagement brings us still closer together. Our sex may be so satisfying, so intense and so frequent, that physical exigency ensues, like hunger. We become absorbed in one another. We call it love. Ah, come, Thomas. I have read and know well your rumination on the misery of marriage."

He well remembers the passage:

As ecstasy abates, coolness succeeds, which often makes way for indifference, and that for neglect: Sure of each other by the nuptial band, they no longer take any pains to be mutually agreeable; careless if they displease; and yet angry if reproached; with so little relish for each other's company, that

*anybody's else is welcome, and more entertaining. Their union
thus broke, they pursue separate pleasures; never meet but to
wrangle, or part but to find comfort in other society. When
fresh objects of love step in to their relief on either side, and
mutual infidelity makes way for mutual complaisance, that
each may be the better able to deceive the other.*

He says, "You are a fine student of my writings." Now he is
feeling more at ease.

"I am. And your writings on marriage are fine and memorable
lines, though sobering."

He watches her hands, their suppleness and shapeliness as she
holds the glass, brings it to her lips, and then holds them clasped
before her on the table. She is so beautiful. She evinces education
that is the envy of such as de Gouges and empowers her to con-
struct an independent life. And thus she has not fallen prey to the
pitfalls of marriage. She denies she is subject to (or denies herself)
the advantages or strictures of family ties.

––––––––––––

The names among the most recognized of the cafés—Café du
Caveau, Café des Aveugles, and Café du Sauvage—suggest the
pungent air, occult darkness, and sensual abandon that charac-
terize the subterranean retreat to which she now leads him by the
hand following their alcoholic preliminaries. He sees that in every
way the Palais-Royal is the underground of Paris. The Café des
Aveugles offers twenty separate "caves" for the sexual and narcotic
delectations of its customers.

On the bed they rifle one another's clothes until he finds her
sex and she has his—she wet as a sun-kissed autumn peach. He
pulls down her dress, and he kisses her bare breasts.

Later, he says, "I am so bad the first time." She turns and kisses
him. "I was nervous," he says. "What about Nicolas?"

"Nicolas knows where I am right now."

"He doesn't care?"

"He doesn't own me. He would never try to keep me to himself. Neither of us believes in that. I want you to regard me as the person that I am, absent reference to you or Nicolas or anyone else. This is the way it is with Nicolas."

She moves to the vanity, still naked, and is seated before the mirror brushing her thick, red hair, and smoking. Set aglow by candle light, her pale arms look like bronze—the rosy cheeks and neck are burnished. She pouts her lips, examining her profile. It is incomprehensible to him that another man has beheld this same scene that is to him holy.

Paine has gotten himself into a fine fix. He is in love with a woman half his age, and societal and natural structures prevent him from ever completely possessing her. Would nature permit him to live even until she is the age at which he arrived in America, when his own life really only began?

He is beset by a sensation he has not felt for a long time: mutual love of this kind is ever complicated, leaves him anxious, literally nauseated. He is unable to savor its pleasure apart from fear of its responsibility, and loss.

CHAPTER 14

OCTOBER 7, 1792. DANTON seizes the bottle and pours himself another drink, then tops off Paine's unfinished glass. The two of them have been seated at the ample table in Danton's spacious apartment, dining and talking for more than two hours. They have consumed large quantities of roast duck, stewed vegetables, cheeses, and nearly two bottles of strong red wine—and they are just getting down to talking business.

Danton says, "Robespierre doesn't want to be dictator; he doesn't want a dictatorship. But, he has told me"—here Danton raises his right index finger together with his robust, shaggy right eyebrow—"he is resigned . . . he is resigned that the people of France will return to a king, or they will install a dictator, which is essentially the same thing, because that's all they know, and they crave stability above all else. He is anguished over our predicament, but maybe he figures the inevitable dictator might as well be him." He laughs out loud.

This ought to alarm and infuriate Paine, but now he appreciates the contradictions and the brutal candor to be the source of this man's attraction. And tonight it is a relief to be conversing in English so easily with another person that he has found—to his surprise—that he likes so much. Paine can now see that Danton is a man whose natural warmth, wit, bonhomie, and force of personality draw you irresistibly into his orbit, yet you are left wanting more. He is a young man—thirty-three. Yet there is about him a kind of ageless wisdom, even as Paine's instinct tells him that

Danton is beset by dark personal secrets. He is indeed undeniably ugly, yet his charming personality—together with associated facial cues—render him nevertheless visually appealing.

They banter about Robespierre. Danton pokes fun at his pretentious and ugly clothes that never change, his archaic hairdo, his fastidiousness, his humorlessness, his self-importance, his adoration of Rousseau, always keeping his Rousseau bible, *Treatise on the Social Compact,* close at hand, whether the full-sized book on his desk or the tiny volume that he habitually carries about in his breast pocket. Danton tells of the portrait of himself that is the only decoration Robespierre keeps in his stifling little apartment, and the unappealing qualities of the women who love him. Says Danton, "He would be pleased to receive you in his little hovel. He keeps his virtue and poverty on exhibition as he pens the epistles of St. Robespierre. I'm sure that his gargoyle, his protector, that awful Eleonore Duplay woman, would let Thomas Paine pass and proceed up the stairs, to her holy man's mountaintop. As you approach the external staircase to access the little apartment, she will appear like a sentinel. Yet he would be pleased to explain Rousseau to Thomas Paine, as a good Christian missionary explains the Gospel to worldly men."

"Yet I am not interested in being sermonized."

Danton calls Robespierre a tight ass and laughs. "A man like that as dictator: It is impossible to imagine. He has no charisma, no magnetism. No real respect from anyone but all those women in the galleries at the Jacobin Club, really. Leave Robespierre to me. I can handle him."

Suddenly there erupts a cacophony of babies crying. Danton's wife, Gabrielle, appears at the table, carrying one in each arm—two brothers, as Danton has disclosed. She has been serving her husband and Paine, as though she were a waitress (she was trained in her father's café, where she met Danton when he was a new ambitious lawyer), more than once declining Paine's invitation to please join them at the table. Now the two sons have taken her measure.

With a kind of pained smile—she has an unadorned and

exhausted though well-proportioned face—she hands her husband the oldest child. The oldest is in his second year. The father stands, revealing his own enormous physique. He is burly if not obese. He wears a billowing linen shirt and trousers like the *sans-culottes* wear—Paine himself has taken to wearing the same outfit. He turns the child to face Paine and holds him in the crook of his arm.

The child is looking intently at Paine with big blue eyes, and Paine cannot help but return his gaze. Danton, perceiving the intensity of the interaction, says, "Would you like to hold my son?" Paine wants to decline; he has not done this in memory, if ever. But Danton is moving toward him and holding out the child for him to take.

The child passes into his arms easily, absent any look back or remonstrance, and turns and looks up at Paine and reaches up and touches a cheek and the nose. The sensation Paine feels is remarkable. It is pleasurable and potent and cascading through his inner self. For a few seconds he is oblivious of all else; he cannot hear Danton's words and he is choked with emotion. The child seems not of this world, miraculous.

The child suddenly shouts, "*Lumière! Lumière!*" which jars Paine out of his reverie, and the child is pointing at the nearest lamp. Paine regains his bearings—he is delighted to hear the child speak.

"He likes you, and he wants you to marvel at the light as he does," says Danton, clearly pleased. "He detects a good soul." He and Danton chat about the children.

A few minutes later he hands the child back to Danton and the two men sit down. The child sits on his father's lap, now quiet, looking here and there, bright-eyed and at ease.

Danton says, "The Girondins have been in charge. They have not done such a great job if you ask me. Where is our constitution? The people are still hungry and afraid. The war and the resources it has drained is a big part of the reason. I blame the Girondins for all that. They started the war. Indeed, the massacres would not have occurred but for the Brunswick Manifesto and the panic it caused, combined with the desperate physical conditions, which the war has amplified."

Paine is impressed that Danton is the first to bring up the September Massacres, but he ignores the comment for the moment. He replies, "Condorcet says that he and I will be on the committee charged with drafting the constitution. I'm sure you will be, too, if you want. Will you join us?"

"Yes. Of course. I would not pass up a chance to write my country's constitution with Thomas Paine."

"Brissot says that if France had not preemptively declared war, the Prussians and Austrians would have done so anyway. The Austrian monarchies are Antoinette's family and all of the European monarchies are alarmed by what has happened in France and therefore would like to restore Louis Capet to the throne. Europe is arrayed against us."

"Perhaps. But I have been directly involved in this, as Minister of Justice, and I am not so sure."

"The tide of the war has turned in our favor since Valmy. No?"

"Perhaps. We shall see. Brunswick's army has been rolled back east beyond all the strongholds captured from France—beyond Verdun, beyond Longwy, finally beyond the Rhine. They are gone for now." Standing with the child, Danton says, "We've sat here long enough. I need to stretch my legs."

In the other room the baby is now fed and quiet. Danton sets his son on the floor and tells him to go to his mother. The child runs off stiff-legged, and Danton follows him into the room. He returns with only his greatcoat in hand. "Let's go for a walk," he says.

They step through the front door onto his porch and then into the carrefour de l'Odéon, amid Danton's splendid neighborhood. It is late at night and the street is deserted, but it is lit up by lamps and brightly shining windows. The atmosphere is damp and rainwater is aglow.

They walk. Danton says, "Listen, I agree with you that this factionalism is pointless and it is very destructive. It must stop. In that regard, I want you to do something for me."

"What do you need?"

"See if you can get that Roland woman to leave me alone. She hates me. I am an open book; and I know I'm distasteful to her. I have tried to fuck her, but it has only made matters worse."

Paine well remembers "Manon"—what Madame Roland is called by her intimate friends. How could he forget: Marguerite introduced him to Manon at her salon not long after Paine met Marguerite—in the Rolands' apartment in the Britannique Hotel in the Rue Guenegaud; it was small and unpretentious. The Rolands are from Lyon, and had come to Paris because the husband, Jean-Marie, was an officer in the municipal council in Lyon and he was sent to negotiate a loan to the municipality from the National Assembly. Yet the salon is known to be hers, not the husband's, and it is popular. He remembers the husband, perhaps twenty years older than his wife: He was dressed simply, a man of the provinces—a plain black coat, with a round hat, and dusty shoes fastened with ribbons instead of buckles. He was wholly lacking in panache or charisma. There was about her a pleasing intensity and an eloquence that Paine could discern even though he understood hardly a word of what she said. When they did speak—privately, though only briefly with Marguerite translating—she had said that when Robespierre had visited he "spoke little" and "sneered a great deal." This had elicited much laughter from Marguerite, who had a kind of fawning approach to Madame Roland—for Manon, along with Olympe de Gouges and Etta Palm d'Aelders, the Dutch radical, are her three role models.

"Did you succeed?"

"Did I fuck her? Ha! I wish. No. I was rebuffed. There is no shame in it. Others have tried and failed as well."

"What has she done to you?" Paine asks.

"She is behind these continuous ad hominem attacks on me and Robespierre in the Convention. She is a sorceress; she lures men to her salon with sumptuous banquets. She plants ideas in the minds of our enemies at the Convention; it is not in the nature of these men otherwise to be so predatory. If you want harmony in the Convention, speak to her; she is behind all the acrimony.

She is the source of it. She is the one who continuously fires the ardor against me of those who have actual power and influence. I have always gotten along fine with Jean-Marie, but she has ruined our relationship."

"You may have offended her by trying to sleep with her. Perhaps that is what ruined your relationship with her husband."

"No. She regarded herself my enemy long before that, and her husband would approve of me fucking her for the good of the Republic. She is not so chaste herself, you know. But I don't judge her; not me, of all people. She's not so bad-looking notwithstanding her age"—she is four years older than Danton—"and her needs are no different than yours or mine—women are not so different from us as you might think. Her husband is an old man, so much older than she is. The libido is robust in anyone as ambitious as she is."

Paine is not much younger than her husband, but he is not offended, as he regards himself as in a much better physical condition—much younger than his own age in years. Paine considers that he ought to be offended just by the vulgarity of Danton's language, but he is not, as he himself is charmed by the brutal candor.

He decides to turn the conversation to a more sensitive and serious subject. Paine says, "I think she is upset by the massacres. Many of us feel we must purge from the Convention those guilty of such a monstrous crime."

Danton halts and turns to look directly at Paine. "I'm going to tell you the whole truth about the massacres. And then, as a further show of good faith, I'll tell you something else that I've never told anyone, and that must remain locked inside your mind's vault as well as mine."

"What if I told you I don't want to know any of this?"

"You have no choice. Now listen to me. It was Marat."

"How do you know this?"

"Marat revealed his plan to Camille, who told me. There was nothing I could do to stop it."

"So, you yourself were involved. You are one of the monstrous

criminals. And you, as Minister of Justice, may be the most culpable."
Paine feels his face twisted with hatred and pain, almost inhuman.

"I was not involved!" Danton says, nearly shouting. "I am guilty
of knowing beforehand what would occur, and of doing nothing to
stop it—just as, I wager, you will now do nothing to bring the perpetrators to justice. We are all afraid of the terror, aren't we? And were
you inclined to seek justice against the perpetrators, what could
you be telling the deputies that they don't really already know?"

"You might have saved your reputation by protesting. Now
you will be forever remembered by history as among the most
terrible despots."

"Perhaps. But I do not care about my reputation! I would
rather be known for my honesty. No power on earth could have
stopped the national vengeance from spilling over. There could
not be a revolution without blood, and no single man could hold
up his hand and say, 'Enough.'" He raises his eyebrows. "I have
no regrets. Had I tried to stop it, I would not have saved a single
life—even though I was Minster of Justice—and in consequence
the revolution was saved." Danton's eyes shine defiant.

"The massacres saved the revolution? Because your internal
enemies were liquidated, though they were safely behind bars?"

"No. Not because of that. There emerged a new authority to
replace the old, to replace the monarchy. After the massacres, men
volunteered in droves to fight the Prussians. The ranks of our army
swelled. What is justice anyway, if it is not of the people, if it is not
the people's justice?"

Paine does not know what to say. He feels nauseated, as though
he is about to expel all of that wine and food. He feels exhausted.

"Justice must be above the people," he finally says, more meekly
than he intends.

"You are speaking of monarchy."

"No, I am speaking of a judiciary that obeys the rule of law. I
had enjoyed this evening with you, but I see now that my original
supposition was correct—we have nothing in common. I think it
is time for me to return to America."

"The Girondins, the Jacobins, we were all to blame. The Girondins unleashed the terror when they plunged us into all-out war with Europe."

"So you are all blood-soaked. That's all the more reason for me to leave."

"Don't be ridiculous. You came here for a reason. You are now part of the enterprise. You can't run away; you must finish what you started. And you are our best hope. You must stay. I want you to do something else for me. Will you sit next to me in the Convention? What better way could there be to convey disapproval of the factionalism? What better way is there to bring about its end?"

"I am implacably opposed to penalty of death."

"In this, Robespierre will be your powerful ally. I am opposed to it as well. But our guillotine is a most humane device for administering an execution, if it must be done."

"Please. There is nothing humane about it. I need to return to my hotel. You have given me much to think about."

"No, let me tell you about Valmy. This is the great secret. Surely you would like to learn a great secret from me." He again raises his eyebrows. "You will see that your methods do not work so well here. As a gesture of friendship, I'll give you an example of what works here. I have told no one else, other than my own partners in crime." He laughs. "We Jacobins, we are committed, implacable republicans, but above all, we are pragmatic. You have heard that on August 10 the Bourbon crown jewels were stolen from the royal storehouse next to the Tuileries Palace? It was done at my direction. And I gave them to Brunswick to induce his capitulation at Valmy and subsequent retreat."

"I don't believe you."

"Suit yourself. Instead, you would believe in General Dumouriez's victory over the Duke of Brunswick? That Dumouriez's ragtag soldiers—albeit greatly increased as a result of the massacres—stood up to eighty thousand of the best soldiers of the age? I had thought you were a man of reason. I guess not."

"You are saying that we were victorious at Valmy because you bribed Brunswick?"

"It wasn't a bribe. It was an inducement; actually more of a consolation, really. Brunswick already had plenty of reason to abandon the campaign. After all, France started this war. Brunswick is a great soldier but he is a mercenary and, in his heart of hearts, he is one of us. He is resentful of his own masters. And he couldn't care less about the Capets. He signed the Brunswick Manifesto out of professional obligation, pure and simple. And he did not want his forces bogged down in France. Likewise, as a Prussian, he did not want to be outplayed by Austria in central Europe. Though united against France, the Prussians and the Austrians are truly rivals. Brunswick feared that holding fast in Champagne would cut him off from his rear. We informed Brunswick that Dumouriez's main force, once free to move, would invade Austria's possessions in the Low Countries. So, Brunswick already had good reason to abandon the campaign."

"So, he had good reason to turn traitor."

"Yes. But did you also know that he collects diamonds? And the Capets have taught us the extent that diamonds can corrupt." Danton stops and turns to face Paine.

Paine says, "So, how did you do it?"

"Knowing all this, I instructed Dumouriez to open up secret negotiations with Brunswick, and they were successful. The diamonds were delivered, and in return Brunswick's forces fled. As a result, the Republic is saved—from our external enemies at least."

"And what now will happen to the Capets?"

"You are a philosopher, Thomas Paine. Leave the politics to those of us who understand politics. In politics, you give the people what they want."

"What do you want from me?"

"I told you. I want you to sit by me in the Convention."

"First, you must resign as Minister of Justice. You yourself recognize that it is not right to retain both the office of Minister of Justice and a seat in the Convention."

"I agree. I will resign."

"Yes, you have promised to do so, and you have not followed through. You must do it now. Or I'll have nothing to do with you at the Convention. You must satisfy everyone that you renounce any prospect of a Danton dictatorship."

"After our victory at Valmy, Marat came to me and said that I should seize the dictatorship. The military would support it, and he guaranteed to deploy the terror in its execution. He said that as Minister of Justice, I possessed the essential platform. I declined. That should be assurance enough for you."

"You must resign as Minister of Justice, to prove your good faith."

"Very well. I agree. I will do it tomorrow!" he shouts out, the famous Danton roar engaged.

———————

Next day, October 8, 1792, Paine is seated beside Danton and the president has called the Convention to order. He cedes the floor to Danton by prior arrangement and the latter moves gravely to the tribune. He promptly announces his resignation as Minister of Justice, effective immediately. The deputies all stand and the hall erupts in applause.

CHAPTER 15

NOTWITHSTANDING THE USUAL TAVERN smells, Paine detects the scent of eau de cologne on his dining companion. Paine and Henri Bancal des Issarts, his good friend and fellow Convention deputy, are dining and drinking at White's Hotel. Bancal is elegant and impeccable in his personal style, even in speaking his near-perfect English, word by well-chosen word. They are seated at a small table amid the crowded din of exuberant talking and laughing.

The dining space is a sort of English tavern, implanted in the center of Paris—indeed the hotel is named after its English owner, Christopher White. Here, as in many of the actual English taverns, there occurs the networking among radicals with a public agenda. And so White's Hotel has become a ghetto of English-speaking expatriates (such as Paine) who came to France to escape arrest on account of their sympathy for the French Revolution or to put into practice their support for the cause. But Bancal is a Frenchman, and he is here as Paine's guest.

The two men are careful to speak in low voices so as not to be overheard, as they are discussing matters of mixed private and public qualities. Bancal is a lifelong bachelor and mostly reputed to be a smooth-talking charmer who has mastered the art of seducing beautiful women. He is fifteen years younger than Paine, handsome and still in his prime. Yet Paine perceives that silently Bancal grieves his youth's passing.

Tonight, Bancal has bent his ear expressing his fervent desire—for the first time ever in his life—to marry. He wants to marry the current love of his life, the young, radical English writer Helen Maria Williams. He is simultaneously exuberant and anguished—he is in the throes of the affair, which is still raging, but so far, she has declined his proposals, as she has no desire to marry anyone.

In addition to being brilliant and spectacularly successful as a writer, she is beautiful and lusty, the object of many desirable suitors. Bancal is well aware that he is not her only lover.

Like Paine, she fled to France as she was virulently denounced in Britain as a traitor, and worse, a harlot who violated conventional female propriety. And their social circles have repeatedly overlapped, at Joseph Johnson's and now here at White's Hotel.

At last, the conversation turns to the subject that presently interests Paine—Madame Roland; he did not arrange this meeting to hear about Bancal's affair with Helen Maria. Bancal knows Manon well, as they were lovers before he moved on to Helen Maria and they are still close friends. Paine wants Bancal to help him get Madame Roland to bury her hatred for Danton and help eliminate the rift between the Jacobins and the Girondins. If this requires him to hear more about Bancal's love life and gossip about her, then so be it.

"Danton is absolutely right," says Bancal. "She is the brains and the heart of the Girondins." He laughs. Then a pained look crosses Bancal's face, and he says, "I am surprised and a little ashamed to say it, but I am still grieving our breakup; there is a stab to my heart that will not go away. She is not among the most beautiful women in Paris. It is her conversation that draws you to her and leads you inexorably to love her. What a pity that you don't speak French, or you might take your turn with her. But our relationship had nowhere to go. She will never leave her husband; she refused my efforts to get her to be honest with him about us, and I grew tired of meeting her only in snatches of stolen time. She does believe that love is its own justification and that any civil or religious tie which prevents one following the dictates of the heart is unnatural and wrong. But she is not prepared to risk damage to her reputation, nor did she want to distress or quarrel with her husband.

So she adheres to our practice in France that so long as marriage remains a matter of business—of keeping marriage ties for the sake of society—satisfaction of the affections may be found in liaisons of which nobody complains so long as they are discreet."

"If she is so intelligent, so skilled a politician, why does she refuse the only relation that will enable the Gironde to keep the direction of the new government. We must make peace with the Jacobins, and only Danton can provide the bridge."

"Thomas, look at me, look at her husband. That will tell you all you need to know about why she hates Danton. We are in every way Danton's opposite—we are refined, reserved, dignified, well-mannered, and impeccably honest in our financial dealings."

Paine acknowledges the point that Bancal is making and says, "So, what can we do about her and Danton?"

"I don't think there's anything we can do. She knows exactly the kind of country she wants France to be, which is right, exactly what we want. And therefore, she is further from reconciling with Danton than she ever has been."

———————

Paine, Madame Roland, and Bancal are seated in her study in the Necker Palace, her husband's official residence as Minister of the Interior. Bancal translates, and Paine knows enough French to appreciate that the translation is smooth and assiduous. Bancal is deadly serious, and as such he is coldly, bloodlessly disingenuous.

Perhaps as a result of Bancal's example, Madame Roland herself is impelled to pretense: she is indifferent to the translator, pretends he does not exist. She is in her mid-thirties; a proud and serious face that inspires confidence and interest; the mouth rather large, though graced by a lovely and winning smile; the eyes, on the other hand, smallish and prominent, and well-moulded eyebrows of auburn, the same color as the hair.

"We need to make peace with the Jacobins, and Danton is the key," Paine says.

"I am not interested."

"And what if this is the only way to save the Republic?"

"You would call such a thing a republic? Why do you think I would want such a thing? You must not think much of me."

"Madame Roland, we need your cooperation and help. I am appealing to your pragmatism. France, like the United States, may have to remain a work in progress for quite some time."

"Here is my pragmatic response to you, Mr. Paine: The first principle of republican government must be restrictions on the ability of government officials to oppress and murder their political enemies. The next is that government must be vigilant against its own corruption. For these are the twin evils of authoritarianism. And Danton is their very personification—their embodiment."

"Please, call me Thomas. I do believe that Danton's objective with his tribunals has been to quell the *sans-culottes'* mayhem. All of us in the Convention are civilized and educated. This is a political divide we are addressing here—the republican system itself at work."

"There was a part of the September Massacres that was not the work of the *sans-culottes*—it was organized, efficient, and implemented a regime of systematized mass murder under a façade and pretense of judicial process. You do realize that during the September Massacres my own home was searched by the Paris Commune; some of us, such as my husband and I, Brissot, and Condorcet, were in terror of arrest; your own Marguerite Brazier and Nicolas Bonneville experienced the same."

Your own Marguerite Brazier. What can she mean by that?

He replies, "I am sure that Danton can be persuaded to support giving women the right to vote."

"I don't want that. Most women have been infantilized, they have been made imbeciles by our society—they are kept from education and physically abused. Just as children, they are unqualified to vote. They will vote as their men do. Thomas, you cannot persuade me; you may see that I myself am prepared to make the ultimate sacrifice, to suffer murder at the hand of my government for the kind of leadership to which we must aspire."

"I am sure you would. I do not doubt it."

"We may all have to make that choice."

CHAPTER 16

PAINE IS RETURNED TO the Necker Palace; Bancal brought him here, and they are not in Madame Roland's small, modest study, but in a huge drawing room, as needed to fit so many visitors. It is October 13, it is late, and everyone is in an uproar. Paine cannot understand anything that is being said except for snatches here and there and some that Bancal translates. Bancal informed him that the purpose of the meeting is to plan a retaliation—for last night Robespierre orchestrated Brissot's expulsion from the Jacobin Club!

All of the leading Girondins and their foremost allies are here—Manon, her husband, Brissot, Pétion, Condorcet, among many others.

The husband appears rejuvenated; there is a lively color in his face. He is reading aloud from a letter—from an anonymous, private individual seemingly unknown to anyone present, that was addressed to a magistrate. It recounts the bloody events of September 2; everyone is acquainted with most of this information. But a single phrase causes an uproar: "The conspirators talked of no one but Robespierre."

The Convention has charged Roland, as Minister of the Interior, with the task of providing an exact account of the state of Paris. He will use the occasion as an opportunity to expose Robespierre's complicity in the September Massacres, and the discovery of this letter will justify this action at the time.

Manon, the only woman in the room, sits at her work table, her fingers busy with her needle, while she hardly participates in the conversation.

Practically reduced to an uncomprehending spectator, Paine is admiring the furniture—the seriousness, the straight lines and right angles, the logical design, the fluted columns, carved friezes, oak and laurel leaf, wreaths, the Greek band—that imitate the designs of the Romans and Greeks—and the repudiation of the curves of the Rococo. It is all very much to his liking—very much in line with their age. What a pity that with the fall of Louis Capet, this style is suddenly very much out of style.

At last, the shouting stops: Manon has laid aside her needle-point and she is dictating. Her husband and Jean Baptiste Louvet, editor of the republican paper *La Sentinelle*, are seated near to her at the long table, taking down what she says, as at times she will turn to one or the other and dictate, seemingly composing two addresses at once. Louvet's narrow face is pale, lit up by lamps.

It seems that Louvet will be the spokesman who will formally charge Robespierre for his direction of the September massacres. But Manon's husband has risen to the occasion, reasserted himself as the master of this house and sage of the Girondins, and it seems that he has insisted that he will set the stage for Louvet.

The meeting has hardly concluded when a very peculiar-looking young man walks over and stands before Paine and Bancal. He is so thin that his body is almost but a rod. His face is narrow, angular and bony; the nose is long and sharp. He says in English, "Why do we allow this man in our midst here—he who sits beside Danton at the Convention?"

And it seems evident that the comment is not made in jest. His thin lips are pursed with such ferocity that they are a white line. His hair hangs unkempt, in rat tails. His eyebrows are mere lines, hardly visible.

Paine recognizes a Convention deputy but he does not know his name; he has caught glimpses of this strange man before but they have never been introduced or spoken to one another. He has never addressed the Convention.

Paine is determined to ignore the rude interruption, but Bancal stammers, "This is Thomas Paine; he sits where he pleases at the Convention, for he abhors the factionalism. Yet it was he who taught us the values that we espouse—not Rousseau! It is beyond peradventure—"

"Yes, of course, I was joking," says the thin man. "I have waited and hoped for a long time to meet the great Thomas Paine." He fixes his raptor-like gaze on Paine. "I am so pleased to meet you!" Still neither Bancal nor their interlocutor has had the social grace to tell Paine the man's name.

"Ah, my friends!" Condorcet's wide girth now also stands before them. "Thomas, have you before met my good friend here, Joseph Fouché?"

"I believe not."

"Ah! So let me introduce you. Fouché represents Nantes. It is the place of his birth and upbringing, so he is very much devoted and sympathetic to the interests of the prosperous merchants there who are as well our good friends and whose main interest is that business should thrive. Yet not so long ago he threw off a cassock. He is an apostatized cleric!"

"That is not entirely accurate," Fouché says.

"Tell Paine about yourself, Fouché!" says Condorcet.

"I was educated in the college of the Oratorians in Nantes. I did wear clerical dress and I had a tonsure and I shared the monastic life with the so-called 'holy fathers.' But I never took priestly vows and I never became ordained. I deliberately disqualified myself from ever becoming a reverend father. I was content, employed by the Oratorians as seminary teacher of mathematics and physics. For this was the vocation for which I was best suited at that time and place, and I learned as I taught my pupils. I have ever been a skeptic and was pleased when, after ten years, politics provided me a means of escape to the greater world."

"Each of us has arrived here by his own unlikely path," says Paine, now beginning to like Fouché. "Especially those of us born into humble means." Paine is impressed by the young man's biography.

"Where did you teach?" asks Bancal. Paine detects that his

136

friend is wary of this Fouché. How so?

"In Nort, Saumur, Vendome, Juilly, and Paris. Finally in Arras and then I returned to Nantes."

"So how was it that you entered politics?"

"I persuaded the holy fathers to transfer me to the sister institution in Nantes, where I was brought up. This enabled me to become even more meaningfully involved in the revolution, as I took up conversation with the leading residents of Nantes. We founded a club and within a few weeks it was reinvented as the 'Amis de la Constitution'—"

"The Jacobin Club!" exclaims Condorcet, clearly delighted.

"Yes, 'Amis de la Constitution' was its original name there, as here, before being rechristened the Jacobin Club. But we were a very different institution then from the current Paris Jacobin Club. In Nantes they want only a government that protects commerce and property ownership and defends the existing laws. So, when writs were issued for election to the National Convention, I presented myself as a candidate."

Fouché stops talking and an awkward moment passes between them. Suddenly Fouché excuses himself, and Paine and Bancal are left with Condorcet, who takes a seat beside them.

"I don't like him," says Bancal. "He is the one who wrote to the Convention opposing the abolition of slavery."

"Which earned him a fine wigging from Brissot," says Condorcet. "He was a politician speaking for his constituents, who maintain investments in the colonies, but he no longer supports slavery, mind you. Nor do Robespierre or Danton, for that matter."

"He seems an opportunist," says Bancal.

Condorcet ignores this and says, "We are waiting for the right moment to unleash him on the Convention. Listen to this: Fouché met Robespierre in Arras when he was still an obscure lawyer, and they became fast friends. Robespierre introduced Fouché to his sister Charlotte and he courted her. They became secretly engaged. But Fouché broke it off. That and Fouché's loyalty to his constituents in Nantes are now at the root of a terrible enmity that

Robespierre holds for our friend, which makes him completely irrational. So you see, Fouché belongs to us."

Condorcet laughs, then continues. "But you know, Henri, you may have a point about his opportunism. The woman he married is very ugly; while the lovely Charlotte Robespierre had no dowry, Fouché's wife is from one of the richest families in Nantes. But you will see that he has a fine mind and a talent for oratory. And the merchants in Nantes are good and important supporters of our cause. So let's deploy Fouché's ambition to our advantage."

CHAPTER 17

CAMILLE, MARGUERITE, AND OLYMPE de Gouges are seated around a table in the Palais-Royal, drinking cognac. Olympe is interrogating Camille. There is a palpable tension, but Camille is enjoying himself, here in the Palais-Royal with these two women he adores. He has with each of them that rarest and most rewarding of friendships—evolved from an intimacy that leaves no trace of hurt or rancor.

"So where is Robespierre?" she says. It is the evening of November 11, and Robespierre has not been seen at the Convention or at the Jacobin Club—he has not been seen at all in public—since November 5, the day he responded to Louvet's charges.

"The night after he responded to Louvet's accusations at the Convention, he left the Jacobin Club and he went home and collapsed. He has been in bed, sick, ever since."

"So what happened at the Convention? Why did Robespierre carry the day?"

"The accusations were very general, and the only specific evidence was an anonymous accuser. Danton adjourned and gave Robespierre some days to prepare a response. Then the immensity of popular support that showed up for Robespierre when he gave his response could not be denied by those in the Plain, or many of the Girondins. And now, because of their failed charges against Robespierre, the Girondins' conduct has made any reconciliation between themselves and the Jacobins impossible. They have only aggravated the animosity and fury of their adversaries, without obtaining a single advantage. They have strengthened Robespierre."

"What happened at the Jacobin Club?"

"Just what you would expect: There was a celebration, great rejoicings, and Robespierre was received as a conquering hero—the moment he appeared in the hall there was thunderous applause and all manner of hooting and whistling. He was urged to recount the particulars of his victory; he demurred, and then a member declared that such an undertaking would be contrary to his essential modesty. All the while he remained silent, and so others commenced to adore him. They called him Aristides and highly praised his simple and masculine eloquence."

"And, of course, these extravagant praises demonstrate that those adoring him, who know him best, appreciate his taste for just this species of flattery."

"No doubt."

"So what is the matter with Robespierre?"

"More of the same; he is sickly in the best of times. It seems his body is unusually vulnerable to disease. Here the stress associated with responding to Louvet's charges made him especially susceptible."

"The mind drives the mass. Thusly does Saint Robespierre self-flagellate."

"Actually, he has explained to me that the nervous strain of defending himself in the Convention took its toll. He has been overworked and winter approaches. His sister Charlotte and the Duplays endlessly quarrel, and I have observed that this has weighed on him."

"You have seen him?"

"I visit him, and we talk almost every day; as we have since before we were men, after all, except while he was returned to Arras."

"And so he is recuperating in his apartment at the Duplays'?"

"He is back there now. For a time he was not at the Duplay house, but with Charlotte, and she cared for him. She had made him move in with her."

"Where does Charlotte live?"

"Her place is around the corner from the Duplays, in the Rue Saint-Florentin."

"Why did he leave his sister's place?"

"Charlotte made the mistake of concealing Robespierre's illness from Madame Duplay. I think she gave him the care he needed, but when his condition did not improve, and he did not appear in public, Madame Duplay was furious. She demanded Robespierre's immediate return. Charlotte says he resisted at first but soon gave in because he did not want to hurt the Duplays' feelings. Now Charlotte is deeply resentful. She says he told her"—here Camille's voice becomes a falsetto—"'They love me so, they have such consideration, such kindness for me, that it could only be ingratitude on my part to reject them.'"

The women laugh at Camille's imitation of Charlotte's manner of speaking. Camille can hardly keep a straight face.

He continues, "Charlotte is very angry and I doubt she will ever forgive the Duplays or even her brother. She and her brother are a lot alike."

"Yes," says Olympe, "They are each of them equally susceptible to lasting personal offense, though of course he operates in a grander environment than her domestic concerns."

"That is one way to put it."

"And he left his lover behind with her family, so he could move in with his sister? Are the lovers finished?"

"His relationship with Eleonore is as much a mystery to me as it is to you. He seems to lack the usual male proclivities for women."

"And Louvet, Brissot, Roland, and the rest of the Girondins have been expelled permanently from the Jacobin Club?"

"Yes."

"On what grounds, other than their disagreeable words?"

"You mean, other than the fact that they tried to charge Robespierre in the Convention for mass murder and treason against the Republic? They are generally insufferable. They think the revolution belongs to them, that they are the ones who made it. They are the new aristocrats. Theirs is an aristocracy of education, of accumulated capital, and of hypocritical ministers."

Olympe says, "So what now, Camille? More trials? To take aim at the Girondins?"

"Robespierre seeks only what is best for the revolution, for the Republic. He is certainly not out for revenge against his accusers. He is not like the Girondins."

"What a sudden metamorphosis!" Olympe replies. "Robespierre, disinterested; Robespierre, philosopher; Robespierre, a friend to all his fellow citizens, even to his political rivals? It reminds me of the maxim: when a wicked man does good, he is preparing great wrongs."

"Robespierre is but one man, and he is very poor."

Olympe leans forward, in Camille's direction. Her cheeks are suddenly red. "You say he has no money, Camille. But he has friends who financially support his clandestine activities and who would give more to share with him a dictatorship! Chief among them, and their agent, is that miserable Marat. We have all heard that it was Marat who directed the September Massacres. I see that he has once again come out of his cavern in triumph, yet he is still covered with general ignominy. Again he shakes his pestilential papers, the firebrands of the furies; yet none of us will bow to him. All who love liberty throw stones at him, everyone curses him. He fancies himself a modern Nostradamus. But he will be forced back into his hole, obliged to squat in his subterranean den. I have made a proposal to Robespierre; when will I hear from him?"

"Oh, Olympe," says Marguerite, "will you stop that!" She turns to Camille, appearing distressed and helpless. "This is why I asked you to come here and speak to us. Tell her to stop this nonsense. She is making a fool of herself." She turns back to Olympe. "You are putting yourself among those harebrained women in the galleries. Everyone supposes that you must be in love with the man."

"Hush!" says Olympe, "I asked Camille to come here to make sure that Robespierre has my proposal."

"What is this about?" says Camille.

"I have written on a placard," says Olympe, "proposing that

together we take a bath, Robespierre and I, in order to wash away all the bloodstains he has accumulated since August 10. We will attach cannonballs to our feet; then, together, we will rush headlong into the Seine where the current is strongest. Of course, I am still useful to my country and I value my life. I don't expect him to accept. But if he does, I am ready to demonstrate that my patriotism is as great as his."

"Nobody understands irony any more in France," says Marguerite. "Voltaire is dead."

"I will make sure he is aware of your proposal," says Camille. "But I doubt Robespierre is capable of comprehending your irony."

"I have not seen Danton," says Olympe. "Where is he?"

"D-Danton does not matter much anymore," says Camille. "He has found it necessary to visit General Dumouriez at the front in Belgium and has remained there."

———

In the deepest part of the Paris night—the velvet cave—she writhes upon him. Suddenly Paine perceives someone else is in the room. He is afraid, momentarily, and she whispers, "I know. I know." She kisses his mouth with ardor, thrusting her tongue. He catches in the mirror—like the still water of a fountain, flashing the gold and scarlet candlelight—a human face—Nicolas's. His back to them, he is watching them in the mirror.

Then Nicolas is gone. Is this the first time he has watched?

Later, as they are laying together naked in the cave, Paine's eyes are brimmed with unshed tears. A shadow hangs over his joy. "What is happening to Nicolas?" he asks. From the café above he hears festive din, noisy human beings.

"I don't know. We make a pledge to one another of complete honesty, and it just forces us to wear different masks than were we concealing things from one another." Nicolas is the same man— the same generous, thoughtful friend, and lover—on the surface. But in a sickening sense, he has become a different man. "We've become strangers to each other," she says, pressing herself more forcefully against him. She says, in hardly more than a whisper, "Manon says the revolution has turned bloody and desperate, and will end badly, in the worst possible way. The factions are out to kill one another. You should leave. There is nothing more you can do here to help us."

His joy is turned suddenly to intolerable distress.

"What does Nicolas say?"

"Shhhh!"

"Where would I go?"

"Back to America."

"I won't leave you."

"Stop it."

"I can't leave Louis Capet."

She sighs; does not answer.

PART III

CHAPTER 18

NOVEMBER 13, 1792: PAINE wakes from a sound sleep. Somebody is pounding on the door of his room at White's Hotel. He gets up and he lights a candle and sees the time is just past four in the morning. He opens the door, still in his nightshirt. It is Camille Desmoulins.

Camille is dressed down in comparison to his usual attire, but he is one of those rare men who in a disheveled state appears adorable.

"What are you doing here, Camille? At this hour."

"I am your friend."

"No doubt. Have you just come from the Palais-Royal?"

"Indeed."

"You'd better go home and get some sleep before the Convention convenes."

"Surely you are used to receiving friends here."

Something is up, it is obvious. "Come in."

Paine is seated on the bed, and Camille on the only chair in the room.

"Who sent you?" says Paine.

"W-why do you ask that? C-can't I have good enough reason to be here on my own accord?"

"Danton?"

"Danton is at the front." Camille is having some difficulty speaking because of the stammer. Finally, the words spill out. "L-l-listen to me, Paine. I am here because there are those among my circle who care for your wellbeing. Why else would I be here at this hour? D-do you think that I am here to solicit your alliance?"

"So, what did you come to tell me? Go on, out with it."

"I'm here to talk about the matter of Louis Capet."

Paine gazes at him and does not answer.

Camille continues, "T-today, deliberations will begin on Capet's fate; there will be a push that he be prosecuted and tried."

"From the Montagne?"

"The *sans-culottes* are now in charge. Through the Paris Commune."

"I hope you are wrong about that. He is entitled to his day in court. Just as any citizen, just as you or I would be. What charges will be brought against him?"

"Treason; perhaps no more than the crime of having been the king of France."

"Get to your point, Camille."

"There has been an important development. Evidence of a conspiracy against the revolution has been discovered. It is far-reaching, even implicating some who have been thought to be heroes of the revolution. W-we now have conclusive evidence that when he tried to abdicate, Capet planned to join the Holy Roman Emperor and invade France."

"What are you talking about? Are there witnesses?"

"Y-yes, there are. And we have documents, which are conclusive. A cache of documents has been discovered in the Tuileries Palace. A locksmith named Gamain approached Roland. He had been a complete unknown to any of us. He told about an *armoire de fer*—how do I say it?—a safe, a secret safe that the king kept in his private room. Last May, Gamain was smuggled into the palace to install the *armoire de fer*. He finished his contract and they paid him, and when he got home he got very sick and nearly died. So he says. He says they poisoned him; maybe so. I think he is trying hard to save his head. So, yesterday, he contacted Roland and told him the story. Roland went to the vacant palace with the locksmith and found more than six hundred pages of private papers."

"What do they contain?"

"Plans and scenarios for the king's flight; correspondence

between William Pitt and émigrés. Comte de Mirabeau is conclusively exposed as a traitor." Camille says this with a tremor, and his eyes are suddenly shining. "He was on a retainer from the king. The royalty paid his debts!"

"What did Mirabeau do for them?"

"There are letters from Mirabeau imparting advice: stir up trouble, make Paris ungovernable so that power might, by default, be returned to the throne. The king promised Mirabeau an additional million francs once the Assembly was disbanded. All along . . . Marat judged him rightly."

"Who else is exposed?"

"The only one that matters to us right now is Louis Capet."

"Anything about Danton?"

Camille smiles knowingly. "Nothing that I know of."

"How do you think the Convention will react? Have you talked to Robespierre about this?"

"I have not spoken to Robespierre. He is still very sick. I came to tell you first. Now there will be a strong movement to charge and try the king and to punish him for these crimes, for this treason."

"Why are you telling me this?"

"I have heard that you would try to defend Capet. I have come to warn you that the sentiments against him are so strong because of this, that it would be unwise to do so. I wanted to speak with you before the Convention begins its deliberations on this topic today."

"If what you say is true, and I do not doubt you, I believe he should be charged. How did you learn this?"

"Manon told Marguerite, and asked her to tell me. Marguerite insisted that I come here first."

"You were just now with her?"

"Yes."

Paine is taken aback by this disclosure. He hopes that Camille does not notice his reaction. "Will there be an announcement today?" Paine says.

"No. Not for a few days. First, there will be deliberations in back rooms, to agree on what to be made public and how. Roland has begun sharing the information informally. It is too difficult for him to bear alone." Camille chuckles. "But I expect that by the time you arrive at the Convention this morning, most of the deputies will know."

"I intend to say that he should be charged and tried. I will not support penalty of death, and I assume that Robespierre will oppose this as well."

"If he survives this illness. He is not well. Yes, you are right. He has not gotten over his revulsion for the death penalty." Camille is standing. "I will see you at the Convention."

Later that day, Paine is listening rapt to Goupilleau's translation, as the delegates debate the fate of their deposed king. A deputy soon to be forgotten has just spoken zealously for the king's immunity from prosecution, legalistically citing exchanges of contractual consideration inducing Capet to submit to the Constitution. There is a restless interlude, and suddenly a sleek and somber Louis-Antoine-Léon de Saint-Just is at the tribune. Hardly the legal age for deputies—twenty-five years old, the youngest—deputed by Aisne in the north, this is the first time he has ever spoken to the Convention.

Paine nonetheless recognizes him for his smooth and youthful countenance and slight stature—he appears more a student than a senator—with olive complexion and long black hair. Yet he has written books and served with distinction in the National Guard, rising to the rank of lieutenant-colonel. He has seemed mild natured, but now the words he speaks burst into flame and blaze, his voice rich and resonant.

"What?!" says he. "You, the Convention, his adversaries, are laboriously seeking a due process for the purpose of trying the 'Citizen King'! You are striving to make a citizen of him, to raise him to that quality, that you may find laws which are applicable to him! And I, on the contrary, I say that the king is not a citizen, that he ought to be tried as an enemy. Try a king like a citizen! That word will astonish detached and cool posterity. To try is to apply the law; a law is a relation of justice; what relation of justice is there then between humanity and kings? To reign is, of itself, a crime. It is impossible to reign innocently. The madness of the thing is too great."

By now several hundred of those gathered in the Salle du Manège, deputies and overflowing galleries alike, are on their feet shouting "Hurrah!" For never have such brazen words been spoken so eloquently in this hall before these senators. And the elegant simplicity of Saint-Just's brief against the king is powerfully seductive: That the king be a king is sufficient reason to charge him. For to be a king is itself an act of violence and oppression against his alleged subjects. Paine himself cannot help but feel a shiver of excitement at the poetry and the subversive quality of Saint-Just's words.

The noise abates and Saint-Just exclaims, "Due process for a king is but hypocrisy. It is not the mode of procedure which has justified all the recorded vengeance of nations against kings; but the right of force against force."

Upon concluding his speech, there is pandemonium. Paine, regaining his wits, thinks, can it be that the name of this man is really Saint-Just? The name is perfectly attuned to the spectacular piety of the man who bears it; can this be by accident? Yet what irony in that name, for what he preaches is not justice.

CHAPTER 19

NOVEMBER 18, 1792: PAINE is beset by the drone of many people talking in the lobby and adjoining rooms of White's Hotel—a party hosted by the salon known as the British Club. He feels quite alone, though he stands amid the tenants and guests of the hotel as they, like bees in spring, bob and wander about, come together in clusters for conversation, and disperse again—each of them bearing his or her preferred alcoholic drink, and Paine has his habitual cognac. Hotel employees are moving about with silver trays serving fancy canapés to the guests.

The men are dressed in clothes as varied as the trousers and shirts of the *sans-culottes* and traditional gentlemanly attire. The women, however, are less variable, outfitted in the simpler, more revealing gowns that Paine is used to seeing at the Palais-Royal. Paine, on Marguerite's orders, has let his hair hang long and undressed, and he is wearing trousers and a loose-fitting cotton shirt—the attire of revolutionary politicians.

Among those more than one hundred people present, there are distinguished British, American, and Irish intellectuals, poets, and authors who are in France because of their support of the revolution. The greater part of them are quite willing and well equipped to hold forth on the current events with ease and self-confidence.

Except for Paine, the most famous revolutionaries and intellectuals are at the centers of the conversational groups, surrounded by old friends and strangers alike who are eager to listen to them lecture about their celebrated opinions and experiences. There are many here who have been prominent in revolutionary politics for many years in America and Europe, and therefore are Paine's old acquaintances and friends.

Were he willing to do so, Paine could be at the center of one of these circles. Usually at such events, he is constantly surrounded by people who treat him with respect, deference, and even flattery because of the fame he has gained for his decisive role as a writer and a philosopher supporting the American and European revolutions, and now because he is an honorary French citizen and a Convention deputy.

Yet really he is in no mood for idle talk about politics or the drama unfolding in the Convention; tonight he walks about the party feeling anxious and full of dread for the future. Most unsettling is his inability to affect in any way the politics here in France. He has been reduced to complete uselessness, he now recognizes; he is hardly more than a bystander. Tonight it is all Paine can do to be cordial and not dismiss with absentminded disdain those who greet him.

The largest crowd is formed around John Hurford Stone, the president of the club, and the young woman who, as everyone knows, is his lover, Helen Maria Williams (who is also Bancal's lover), standing close by him. Amid the crowd they are both dazzlingly young and prominent. Together they preside over the club, and they are together hosting this party. (Stone is married, but his wife is nowhere to be seen, as is usual at British Club functions.)

Paine knows Helen Maria well, has been with her repeatedly in social settings in Paris and London. The curly black hair, bare shoulders and arms, and the elegant gown, the smiling painted lips and eyes that gaze both defiantly and tenderly, are not all that hold her interlocutors' attention. She speaks naturally but cleverly and with wit, and there is her towering literary reputation. Paine can hear the throaty timbre of her voice, denouncing Robespierre, Danton, Marat, and Saint-Just.

Paine's American friend, the poet Joel Barlow, is himself at the center of one of the more populous circles. There are other poets, including an intense and attractive very young man reputed to be a prodigy, named William Wordsworth, whom Paine has only just met tonight.

Suddenly he sees Gouverneur Morris, the American ambassador to France who (lamentably) replaced Jefferson, also standing alone; he is dressed as an aristocrat. Morris waves to him, but Paine looks away, pretending not to have seen the greeting. Paine does not like Morris, and apparently the feeling has been mutual. And in Paine's present state, Morris is the last person Paine would like to talk with tonight.

Yet Morris ambles over, adroitly maneuvering his pegged leg (he lost his right leg a few years back, from a carriage accident, but the amputation has not deterred him); he appears genial, rakishly handsome. Morris's character is such that he claims to be the author of the Constitution of the United States, a document that its true authors could only appreciate that—in popular mythology—must transcend any individual claim of authorship, if it is to fulfill its intended purpose. He claims he wrote the constitution even though he advocated that the nation's president and the senators be granted lifetime appointments, and failed in doing so.

Though he signed the American Constitution and had a hand in founding the United States, Morris has been a close confidant and advocate of the king, and before Louis Capet was arrested on August 10, spent many a night at the Tuileries Palace.

"Just the man," says Morris. "Thomas Paine. Just the man I want to see. Still playing senator for this accursed country, I see. You and your comrades are doing a fine job of governing, in the midst of all these confusions, what with the confiscating of church property, selling the domains, curtailing pensions, destroying offices, but especially by the great liquidator of public debt, paper money." Morris is such a hidebound conservative that he is infamously opposed to paper money under any circumstance, especially revolutionary France's counterfeit—for all practical purposes—assignat.

"*Guerre, famine et peste,*" Morris continues, "that is the lot of these inconstant people. This nation is working its way back to the stone ages. And yet you are the same revolutionary as ever, I see. I see you have your usual comfort in hand." Morris nods, indicating the drink in Paine's hand, then looks up and down, examining his hair and attire.

Paine strains to keep cool. He says, "What is a high flying monarchy-man like you doing here, Morris? This is not your crowd."

"Oh, I make it my business to keep track of this crowd. It's my job. But I don't intend to stay for the dinner and the toasts, rest assured."

"And so you are, as usual, shutting your eyes and opinion to every fact against your predisposition, believing everything you desire to be true. I am sure you have kept President Washington's mind constantly poisoned with your forebodings."

"It is true, Paine. I am filled with sinister forebodings. And it is but my calling to share them with the president. Tell me, what is the Convention up to with the king?"

"He will be tried, as he must be, in order that his removal from the throne is formalized, and pursuant to the rule of law."

"The rule of law, of course; the rule of law must ever rule. What is his crime? This callow youth Saint-Just, who seems to have attained momentum for his cause, says that it is just that he was born a king, does he not?"

"He conspired with the Holy Roman Empire, and he is responsible for the massacres of innocent civilians, at the Champ-de-Mars, and on August 10."

"He conspired with the queen's family because he was born the king, and to save his office, as was his duty. When I heard that the crowd had amassed at the Champ-de-Mars, I walked to the Heights of Chaillot to observe what passed below. At length, I heard the militia had fired on the mob, and killed a few of them. The crowd scampered away as fast as they could. This affair, I thought, would lay the foundation for tranquility. I was wrong. A more serious response was needed to restrain the abominable populace. As for August 10, the king was not at the palace when the massacres occurred. He had fled to the Assembly and surrendered. So how can he be blamed for the bloodshed? And who will be held to account for the September Massacres?"

"The Girondins are preoccupied with seeing justice for the September Massacres, but it is easier said than done. Presently the business before the Convention is the king's trial."

"And he will not be replaced?"

"There will be no more kings."

"Will there be an executive office?"

"We are working that out. In the new constitution."

"A good constitution should ensure the rights of a nation under the government of a good king. I am told that there is a majority in the Convention who think a king is still necessary."

"That is not true. So you would deny the blessings of liberty enjoyed by our country to the people of France?"

"How different was our situation in America. Everyone performed cheerfully his part; nor had we anything to apprehend but from the British, the common enemy. Such is the immense difference between a country which has morals, and one which is corrupted. The former has everything to hope, and the latter everything to fear. The French are not yet reformed enough in their morals and their habits to form a democracy. They fail to reflect that they have not American citizens to support a constitution. France needs to restore the king to his office at once. A popular government is good for nothing in France. Equality is the great deceit that has entrapped the French Revolution in its own destruction. Here, liberty can be insured only by existence of a monarch. It may as well be Louis XVI. I believe the king to be an honest and good man."

"Liberty insured only by existence of a monarch? And you call yourself the author of the American Constitution!"

"Paine, what does liberty consist of other than opposite of the violence and despotism of revolutions? Unquestionably, there has been more crime acted within the last three years on French soil than is usually to be found in the records of history; and, as

unquestionably, the systems reared on such abominable foundations must soon crumble into ruin. Such is the unalterable law of
God, attested by the undeviating experience of past ages."

"We will set the nation on the right path, and God will have
nothing to do with it. Here, as in America, God relies upon the
works of men. France needs a legitimate constitution establishing
truly democratic institutions."

"I am skeptical of what you say. I expect you to fail. But don't
worry that I would blame you entirely. The progress of this nation
seems to be much greater in the fine arts than in the useful arts.
The whole of society here is dissolute; pleasure is the great business, utter prostration of morals, the extreme rottenness of every
member, a perfect indifference to the violation of all engagements;
the great mass of the people have no religion but their wants, no
law but their interests. A sick body with a weak head is what they
are. And while bread is wanting, while the economy is bankrupt,
and anger swells up from the provinces and the streets of Paris
together, while there is no certainty whose command a regiment
will obey, yet, dinners, parties, and balls are held as usual, and the
opera and the theaters are thronged with larger audiences than
before. These are the modern Athenians—alone learned, alone
polite, and the rest of mankind barbarians!"

"It is easy to sit on your ambassador's perch and pass judgment
on the participants and contestants in this moment of history. You
cast stones at those of us grappling with despotism."

"So, Paine, what will become of the king? What after the trial?
The scaffold? Will the Convention murder him?"

"No. There will be no killing the king. Robespierre opposes penalty of death in principle. And the king is too valuable to destroy.
Danton also opposes his execution. I believe he should be exiled
to England or the United States, with his family, and ultimately
he will be. At worst, he will remain in the Temple indefinitely."

"History informs us that the passage of dethroned monarchs is
short from the prison to the grave."

Paine feels himself out of patience. "Morris, you are yourself corrupt; you are compromised. You are in no position to analyze these events objectively. Everyone knows the source of your allegiance: your cosseted upbringing and Madame de Flahaut."

Morris was himself born into aristocracy in New York City, and he is a trained lawyer who has always habituated lofty circles; but the crux of his devotion to the king is that his lover has been Adélaïde de Flahaut. She is a very desirable creature of Parisian society who once maintained a well-known salon of her own that was a gathering place for royalists. Still just twenty-eight years old, she is married to the sixty-three-year-old Alexandre-Sébastien de Flahaut de la Billarderie, the Keeper of the King's Gardens.

"And you are not similarly compromised? I hear you are besotted morning till night with, in addition to your cognac, a courtesan who dwells with Nicolas de Bonneville in the Palais-Royal."

Paine is enraged. He hisses, "If you were not an invalid, I would strike you."

"Were we not in polite company, I would invite you to do it. I am nimble enough with my peg leg, whether as a lover or a fighter."

"And so you are a hypocrite, preaching Christian morality while carrying on with another man's wife."

"Paine, I tell you truly, I am at heart a republican and I always have been, and France is a natural ally, and so we are interested in her prosperity. So, too, I love France and the French people. Yet here, in this nation, I preach respect for the king, attention to the rights of the nobility, and moderation. France is not ready for democracy or republican government. There is no universally true political system. Good institutions depend on the country. Since I have been in this country, I have seen the worship of many idols, and but little of the true God; I have seen many of those idols broken, and some of them beaten to dust. I have seen the late constitution, in one short year, admired as a stupendous monument of human wisdom and ridiculed as an egregious production of folly and vice."

At last, a male voice cries out, "Dinner is served!" The doors to the dining space open, and inside a German band is playing enthusiastically.

"I must go to my table," says Paine, relieved. "Goodbye."

"Enjoy yourself, Paine. So long. Will you come visit us at the embassy? Our dinners are simple but well prepared, good and nourishing."

Paine does not answer and turns and heads toward the dining room.

The dining room is spacious and beautiful, now decorated by countless place settings. There are many tables, and the alcoves and irregular shapes that comprise the space easily make room for the over one hundred guests who are now seated as directed by butlers and maids and as, Paine presumes, has been pre-determined by Helen Maria and Stone. Purportedly there is no effort to seat anyone by rank or importance, but Paine finds himself seated between the hosts and Sir Robert Smyth and his wife, Lady Charlotte Smyth—certainly it is the two wealthy husbands who have financed this lavish celebration.

Lady Smyth is seated directly to the right of Paine, and Helen Maria to his left. He regards Charlotte's husband a good friend, but has never before met the wife. Robert Smyth is a committed revolutionary, but unavoidably, he has acquired that venerable look of nobility, with the broad, self-confident face and gestures, heavy physique, and fat fingers. He is a good deal older than his wife, though her hair has turned nearly completely gray, and she has a vaguely beleaguered yet pleasing look.

John Hurford Stone and Helen Maria are busy projecting their brilliance as the hosts; Helen Maria is not much interested in Paine, and Robert Smyth is making his way around the hall, still chatting. Paine is left to make small talk with Lady Smyth.

Her countenance is bright, gazing at Paine. He realizes that she is awestruck by his fame. She looks vulnerable, and is a little breathless. He discerns in her features that she was once a great beauty; yet—he now appreciates—she is still lovely: soft-featured, with eyes that are a dazzling blue.

She puts a hand on his forearm. "I was just last week in London, and I spoke with a very good friend of yours: Mary Wollstonecraft."

Paine's heart skips a beat. He is ever reminded of how fond he is of Mary. "Oh, where did you see her?"

"Robert and I attended one of Joseph Johnson's dinners."

"Wonderful! I adore those people and miss them so. I especially miss Mary." He feels, all at once, a pang of yearning for those old friends. Suddenly he feels as if he is about to weep, recognizing that he will likely never return to their midst.

Charlotte says, "Well, the good news, if you have not heard, is that it looks like you will be seeing Mary again soon, and perhaps for good. She is migrating to Paris next month."

He says, "She has not written me. I had been wondering what happened to her."

"She said she had not heard from you."

"Yes, I have been busy with my new life, my new challenges here. Frankly, I have been overwhelmed. I expected her to come sooner."

"She has been melancholy, and somewhat paralyzed. But she is over it now, and ready to join us here." She reveals, now in a discreet, lowered voice, that Mary has confided in her about an entanglement with the painter Henry Fuseli. They gossip a bit about it. Paine now learns that the affair ended disastrously for Mary.

They discuss some of the others of Johnson's circle. Paine is glad to hear that William Blake, eccentric as ever, is still engrossed in his startling poetry and engravings, some of which he shared with Charlotte and her husband. "He is ignored today," says Paine, "but his works are for the ages," and Charlotte enthusiastically agrees.

He relates his extraordinary last night in London, how Blake's visions and warning catalyzed his decision to leave for France. Hardly before he knows it, he finds himself confiding the terrible disappointments and loss of self-confidence he has experienced here in France. Yet finally he is enjoying himself tonight, and eating and drinking with relish.

She is listening with evident heartfelt sincerity, gazing earnestly with those dazzling blue eyes. She says, "Thomas, clearly you can't control all of the events here. Your inability to speak French and your limited history here in France are difficult handicaps. What, in the course of this history that you are involved in making here, matters most to you, to which you could direct your most energetic efforts, and you could possibly change? Where can you make a difference? Something that will be remembered for the ages, and that would be emblematic of your life's most important work and your reputation."

He is at a loss for words, and there is silence, though actually it is not in the least bit awkward. Finally he says, "To help write a proper constitution for France, and to save the life of Louis Capet."

"Those achievements would be worth a lifetime. Would they not?"

Her husband returns to the table and soon the three of them are enjoying a discussion about the Johnson circle and British politics. Paine wants to ask about the status of the indictment against him, but he fears that the news would not be good, and he wants to retain this positive mood.

During the second course, Paine hears the dry pop of champagne corks, and bottles are passed and poured. He hears Stone announce, "It's time to begin the toasts!" And Stone is on his feet, followed by everyone else in the room. Stone raises his glass, the rest of the room follows, and he shouts the first toast: "To the French republic that is founded upon the Rights of Man!" Everyone shouts, "Hurrah!" and takes a drink, and the trumpets of the German band begin playing *Ça Ira*, a famous revolutionary tune. When the band quits, Stone raises his glass and shouts the second toast: "To the armies of France; may the example of her citizen soldiers be followed by all enslaved nations until all tyranny and all tyrants are destroyed!"

Now everyone again shouts, "Hurrah!" while the German band plays "La Marseillaise." Paine tells Charlotte and her husband that it will soon be proclaimed by the Convention to be the Republic's official national anthem.

Stone's third toast is "to the achievements of the French National

Convention!" Everyone turns to look at Paine while shouting their hurrahs; amid the cheering, he smiles miserably. Yet Charlotte beams as she stands beside him, and pats him on his shoulder.

Paine seizes a toast. He announces it with emotion and misty eyes: "To the perpetual union of the peoples of Britain, France, America, and the Netherlands: may these soon bring other emancipated nations into their democratic alliance!" The room explodes in ovation.

Helen Maria proposes a toast: "To the women of France!" And one of the military men intones, "Especially those bearing arms to defend liberty's cause, such as Mademoiselles Anselme and Fernig!" These are female officers in General Dumouriez's entourage in Belgium.

Another toast, proposed by John Hurford Stone, is to "Tom Paine and his novel method of making good books known to the public through royal prohibitions and prosecution of authors!"

Paine bows humbly. He is thinking that he should have stayed a writer and kept out of politics.

CHAPTER 20

TODAY, NOVEMBER 21, ROLAND has disclosed to the Convention the *armoire de fer* found in the Tuileries Palace, and he has filed with the Convention the cache of documents, their contents already widely known among the deputies. Already there are rumors that the documents were pre-selected and there are gaps. To protect Danton? Paine thinks how that would be ironic given Manon's loathing for him, yet perhaps the Rolands have come to appreciate Danton's importance as a liberal and a bridge between the factions.

Mirabeau's bust in the Manège is covered with a black veil.

On December 3, Robespierre returns to the Convention, finally recovered from his illness. He stands at the tribune, delivering his speech addressing the king's fate.

"Regretfully then I speak this fatal truth—Louis must die because the nation must live. I propose to you an immediate legal action on the fate of Louis XVI. I ask that the National Convention declare him, from this moment on, a traitor to the French nation, a criminal toward humanity."

Paine is stunned by Robespierre's declaration that the king must die. Even more, Robespierre has proposed an immediate death sentence for the king.

When Robespierre finishes, the Convention is thrown into disorder. One motion after another is thrown out of the tumult. But the secretaries cannot hear them.

Somehow, Paine is able to hear Marat, his distinctive voice from atop the Mountain. He moves for an immediate vote on Louis's punishment and demands that the vote be published.

Finally, Pétion, at the tribune, is able to get a motion heard and recognized: "That Louis will be tried and judged by the National Convention." The motion carries by a wide majority.

Paine can see that Robespierre is stunned by the defeat.

December 11, 1792: "I announce to the Assembly," says the current president, Bertrand Barère, "that Louis is at the door. Representatives of the people, you are about to exercise the right of national justice. The dignity of your session ought to correspond to the majesty of the French people. Let us give a great lesson to kings, and a useful example for the emancipation of nations."

From the Mountain, another man speaks loudly, "It is necessary that the silence of a tomb terrify the guilty man." He is the former butcher, Louis Legendre.

Many throats murmur displeasure at the gratuitous cruelty of the remark.

Barère gives a signal and Louis is led in. Paine has not seen him up close before. He had expected that he would see a king, albeit a king who has been deposed. Instead he sees but a man. Whatever else may be said of this man, he carries himself with dignity.

He is simply dressed in a plain walnut-colored silk coat, and his hair is natural; he does not appear in any way regal, or a powdered and pampered courtier. Louis has been continuously described in public as being ugly, fat, smelly, and stupid. But now Paine sees that he is reasonably handsome and well groomed. He has an aquiline nose, deep-set eyes, and a full sensual mouth. If there was a time when he was obese, the strains and perhaps deprivations of his confinement have left him reasonably well proportioned.

It is yet to be seen whether he is in actuality stupid. Today's appearance will be a test, as he is here alone, unaided by any counselor.

A profound silence descends within the chamber. Louis stands before the Convention, surrounded by Generals Santerre and Wittinghof, the mayor, and two municipal officers.

He is facing Barère, who finally says, "Louis, the French nation accuses you. The National Convention decreed, on December 3, that you would be judged by it. On December 6, it decreed that you would be brought before the bar. We are going to read to you the declaration of the crimes imputed to you. You may sit down."

He is shown a hard-backed chair, where he sits straight-backed, seemingly unperturbed. Now Barère begins the interrogation. Louis is perfectly composed, sitting silently as he listens to the reading and then responds in turn.

"Louis, the French people accuse you of having committed a multitude of crimes in order to establish your tyranny by destroying their liberty. You suspended the meetings of the Estates General, then dictated laws to the nation, and posted armed guards to intimidate the delegates. What do you have to say?"

"There did not exist any laws concerning these things," he says clearly.

"In the days before the fall of the Bastille, you ordered troops to march on Paris and you spoke as a tyrant."

"I was then the master of whether or not the troops marched; but I have never had the intention of shedding blood."

"You persisted in actions against national liberty by delaying the decrees abolishing personal servitude and delaying recognition of the *Declaration of the Rights of Man and of the Citizen*, at the same time doubling your bodyguard and summoning troops to Versailles. You encouraged these troops to insult the national cockade and the nation."

"I admit to the first two actions that you identified, because I believed them to be just. The size of my bodyguard and any summoning of troops was the responsibility of my ministers. As to the cockade, that is false."

"You violated your oath and attempted to corrupt Mirabeau."

"I don't recall what happened at that time; but all of it occurred before my acceptance of the constitution."

"You spent public money for the purposes of corruption."

"I had no greater pleasure than to give money to those who needed it."

"Who are those in the Assembly to whom you promised or gave money?"

"None."

"You tried to flee the kingdom by going to Varennes and thereby aligning with the Holy Roman Empire in a planned invasion of France."

"That accusation is absurd. It was a trip, a vacation, as I explained to the Assembly."

"You directed the massacres in the Champ-de-Mars."

"That event can in no way be attributed to me." Here Paine detects a tremor in his voice.

"You are responsible for shedding French blood on August 10."

"No, monsieur, it was not I." And now his voice breaks, he bows his head, and he appears about to weep.

Barère waits a moment, perhaps anticipating that the king will break down, or giving him time to compose himself. In any case, the king recovers, and Barère continues.

"You have worked to impede the revolution and the establishment of a constitution."

"If impediments have been placed, that is the responsibility of my ministers."

As the interrogation proceeds over the coming minutes and hours, Louis repeats the same refrain: He is innocent, and the blame, if any, lies with his ministers: "Never did the idea of counter-revolution enter my head." "I executed all the orders proposed to me by the ministers." "I forbade the sending of money to émigrés in exile." "I disavowed the actions of all émigrés to raise money and troops in my name." "All encouragement of the enemy's aggressions, and the failure to prepare the French military, were the fault of the ministers." "All the correspondence passed through the ministers." "I ceded all authority to give such orders to the ministry."

At last, after three hours, the interrogation appears to be over, and Barère says, "Do you have anything to add?"

"I ask to see the pieces of evidence that allegedly support these accusations."

The legal scholar Charles Éléonor Dufriche-Valazé undertakes the task of showing Louis the documents and interrogating him on them. Contemptuously, Valazé refuses to stand in the king's presence or to face him. He pulls up a chair to the bar of the Convention and sits with his back to the king; he disdainfully passes documents one by one over his shoulder to the king.

Louis responds without the least hesitation; his responses are always essentially the same. "I don't know." " I don't recognize it." "I don't know about it." "I don't recognize it any more than the others." "I disown it." "I disown it as much as the others." "I have not the smallest knowledge of them." "I know nothing about it." "This I own, but it consists of charitable donations which I have made." "I have no knowledge of it whatever." "I disown it likewise."

Valazé: "Do you recognize this as your handwriting?"

"No."

"Did you build a safe in the Tuileries?"

"I have no knowledge of it."

"Do you acknowledge your writing and your signet?"

"I do not. I know nothing of these pieces."

Louis refuses to recognize his signature on any of the documents. He turns to Barère and explains to him that the presence of the Seal of France on a document does not mean that the king affixed it.

At last the documents are exhausted and once again Barère asks him if he has anything to add.

Louis says at once, "I want a lawyer."

The request is met with silence—the silence of a tomb. The deputies have not expected this. Paine has seen that Louis is actually not stupid. In reality, Louis is confronted with three options:

Repudiate the authority of the Convention, refusing to participate meaningfully in the trial; beg for mercy; or take up the deputies' challenge, hold them to their implicit promise of due process, and thereby try to win his liberty and his life. In the course of his responses to the interrogations, and in requesting a lawyer, he appears to have chosen the third option, which nobody expected.

By insisting on a fair trial, Louis is compelling his accusers to live up to the principles for which they claim the revolution stands—even as the trial pits the king against the revolution itself, for the consensus now is that the king and the revolution cannot live side by side.

Paine sees that here is a man who comes determined to fight for his life.

Presently, Barère recovers; he ignores the request, and Louis does not repeat it. Barère says, "I invite you to withdraw to the Hall of the Conferences. The Assembly must deliberate."

Louis is escorted out.

As soon as he disappears, Marat is at the tribune. He shouts, "This is not an ordinary trial! We don't have to concern ourselves with the chicaneries of courts. There is no need to allow him a lawyer."

A free-for-all of shouting ensues, and more delegates rush the tribune, where there is a physical scuffle.

Eventually, after much shouting by Barère, order is restored. And the Convention issues a vote, by voice, that Louis should have a lawyer of his choice.

CHAPTER 21

PAINE STANDS IN THE vestibule of a modest house in the Paris suburbs—the king's lawyer's temporary home. The resident, Lamoignon de Malesherbes, arrives promptly to open the door; he is gray, in his seventy-third year, and he is a fine-looking old man. He is expecting Paine, as the two have exchanged letters.

His greeting: "Ah! Thomas Paine; at last I meet the infamous Thomas Paine, he who has brought all of this calamity upon us." Malesherbes has left retirement and his château in Fontainebleau for this modest house, in order to defend the king.

The old man has touched a spot where Paine is sensitive, where he is presently most insecure. He is sensitive about his legacy, his place in history, appreciating as he does that he is this day in fact living history, and he does not wish to be held responsible for all that may come to pass in the French Revolution, or because of it. Yet, Paine can see, from old Malesherbes's smile and his lively eyes, that he is teasing. And Paine brings nothing but overwhelming affection and admiration for this king's lawyer.

When they are seated in the drawing room, Paine says, "I want to thank you for your courage and dedication in undertaking the king's defense. Even Marat expressed his admiration."

After the king was removed from the Convention, and it was resolved that he would be tried and allowed counsel of his choice, Barère produced and read aloud to the deputies a letter just that day received from Malesherbes, in which he volunteered to represent the king: "I want Louis XVI to know that if he chooses me for

169

this function, I am ready to devote myself to it. I have been called to be counsel of he who was my master during the time that this function was sought after by everyone. I owe him the same service now that so many men find it dangerous."

Malesherbes is a celebrated lawyer; and though he was of the king's court, as the king's lawyer he brings immense credibility. He was a reforming minister and a friend of the revolution, and during the years of royal censorship he made himself a protector of many of the *philosophes*.

Meanwhile, the Convention learned that the king's choice of counsel was Guy Jean Target, and if he declined, Francois Denis Tronchet. Both of these were renowned lawyers. Target immediately declined to represent the king, stating that he was too old at fifty-four. Advocate Tronchet, however, agreed, despite being twelve years older than Target.

Thus it came to pass that the king accepted Malesherbes's offer and he and Tronchet became the king's counsel.

Malesherbes replies, "What else could I do? He must receive the ablest defense, which I regard myself capable of providing."

"What can I do to help?" asks Paine.

"I cannot tell whether you are judge or prosecutor or both. You are not part of the defense, that much is clear. I understand that you urged that he be tried."

"It was either that or punishment without trial."

"You denied that he is immune from prosecution as king. You allege the possibility that he conspired with the Holy Roman Empire, and thus you encouraged the indictment."

"That I admit. Yet I wish him a long life and that he regain his liberty whatever the outcome of the trial. He did not choose to be king, and his alleged crimes amount to that he has been a king, and behaved as such. It is, after all, a political trial. How is the king?"

"When I first saw Louis in the Temple, he ran forward to meet me. I sank to my knees and burst into tears. He raised me, and we remained long clasped in one another's embrace." Malesherbes's voice is unsteady but he continues. "He said, 'Ah, is it you, my friend? You fear not to endanger your life to save mine. But all will be useless. They will bring me to the scaffold. But no matter; I will gain my cause if I leave an unspotted record behind me.'"

Malesherbes stops talking. His emotion has gotten the better of him. He wipes away a tear and continues. "I did not try to dissuade him. The outcome seems foreordained, and I will not deliberately give a client false hope. Yet we went right to work on his defense. The Convention has given us woefully inadequate time to prepare. We must present the defense on December 26! It seems his truest hope is to set the record right for posterity."

Paine shudders, beset by a wave of emotion. These words have moved him nearly to tears.

Malesherbes describes their work on the defense. Commissioners of the Convention bring the documents supporting the indictment every day to the Temple and return the same day to fetch them. The king peruses them with great attention that impresses everyone; he is in good spirits. They have engaged a third lawyer, Raymond Desèze, a younger man who will present the oral argument to the Convention, and the team is well functioning.

"Yet," says Malesherbes, "the arguments have been developed in conformity with the king's wishes. I see now that the kingship brought out the worst in Louis, for I see now in him a character that he scarcely ever revealed at Versailles. Now stripped of his advisers, his ministers, his courtiers, he is completely bereft of power, and he is forced to make his own decisions. And I see emerging a man of tough character and of dignity. When Desèze read his argument to Louis, Tronchet, and myself, I had never heard anything as moving as his peroration. Tronchet and I were touched to tears. Louis too was moved, but he insisted that the peroration be revised and suppressed, for, he said, he did not want to play on feelings."

Malesherbes pauses for a moment, as he is again beset by emotion. He continues, "Yet the king has not been allowed to see his family, notwithstanding the decree of the Convention that it be permitted. His keepers have refused the favor, and they inform him that the Commune denies the request." The Paris Commune is in practical charge of the king's incarceration. For they control the superintendence of the police, hence the police force of Paris, and therefore also the guard of the Temple. And thus it is to the Commune's resentful, vindictive, and overbearing authority that the royal family has been subjected. "He has been told that the Commune has ordered the separation during the proceedings. They deny him the only consolation he has requested."

"And the Jacobins are in charge of the Commune," says Paine. "But Robespierre, who is in practical effect their master, will do nothing on behalf of the king?"

Malesherbes nods his head.

Paine says, "He will be reunited with his family. He must be tried, and if convicted, there will be a consequence, but he will not be put to death. I believe the Convention will expel him from France and allow him to emigrate to the United States. I will accompany him there, and see to his and his family's good treatment."

"He can live with that, if needs be. What makes you so sure that will be the outcome?"

"The Girondins and their allies—I am among them—are firmly in control of the Convention, and we will not allow that he be put to death."

"I think rather that Louis's fate depends on the will of the people, and there is nothing that you, as an Englishman—"

"I am an American."

"There is nothing, as an *American*, that you can do about that. The fate of the king is a matter between Frenchmen. The real Convention is in the streets. And the Jacobins are ever at work persuading those who will be the real judges. I want to show you something." He stands and leaves the room and returns with a document, which he hands to Paine. "Have you seen this?" says Malesherbes.

Paine has not seen it. And he is surprised. It is a pamphlet. As it is in French, he cannot read most of it. He does understand the title to be "Opinion upon the Judgment of Louis XVI," and the author is Camille Desmoulins.

"I have not read it," says Paine.

Malesherbes takes the pamphlet from him, and reads, translating, "'Louis Capet deserves death. He ought to be punished as an outlaw, and as one more culpable than the lowest brigand or robber, for one still finds honor amongst thieves.'"

"We will see what I can do about this," says Paine.

CHAPTER 22

PAINE KNOCKS; THE DOOR opens and he bolts straight into the vestibule, demanding to see Camille. He hardly notices the pretty, slender young woman he passes. They have never met, but he hears her utter "Monsieur Paine" (he is used to being recognized by strangers), and in French she directs him to the drawing room on the right. He enters and finds Camille.

He cannot help but notice the room's fine furnishings and elegance.

Camille is wearing spectacles and is reading some kind of journal. On a table nearby is a bottle half filled with cognac and beside it a near-empty glass. Camille removes the spectacles, looks at Paine, and now his dark face, surrounded by the superb unruly long hair, is beaming.

He remains comfortably seated and his linen shirt is untucked. He loudly instructs "Lucile" to bring a glass for Paine. Paine immediately and insistently declines, and Camille shouts never mind.

"What is this?" says Paine, thrusting Camille's pamphlet at him like a dagger. It is the copy given him by Malesherbes.

"It is my pamphlet on the j-judgment of Louis Capet," Camille says calmly. He begins to explain the substantive arguments. Paine is resolved not to interrupt the monologue, to be polite, having disrupted the quiet enjoyment of this home.

Camille explains that the constitution of 1791 set it down that the person of the king is inviolable, and therefore, it is argued, he is immune from prosecution. But the primitive code of nations—that is unwritten, yet has always existed and still exists as the very foundation for all governments—decrees that no law is law until it is freely subscribed to by the people. The populace never agreed to this law of inviolability. In fact, they protested against it after the king's return from Varennes in the famous petition of the Champ-de-Mars, the signing of which was only prevented by the massacre of patriots—and this alleged term of inviolability thus came into being by duress, only by the terror let loose by the Champ-de-Mars massacres. Furthermore, Camille asserts, if there had been a contract between the king and the people guaranteeing his inviolability and hence his immunity from prosecution, this would have become null, owing to the repeated "treasons" of the king.

Camille speaks slowly and remains perfectly controlled. In contrast, Paine is himself beset by a rising tide of fury.

Finally, Paine can endure no more and he shouts, "I don't care about all that right now! I have said I support a trial of the king. As to the question, 'does the king deserve death?' you have already sentenced him to the scaffold, even before the Convention has heard his case or deliberated on whether to adjudge him guilty!"

Camille begins to describe the king's corruption of Mirabeau, the bribes. He is now less composed, his rancor rising to the surface, and the stammer asserting itself. Suddenly, he shouts condemnations in French of Mirabeau and the king. Paine notices that the young woman who greeted him has come into the room and is seated, listening to Camille. Paine appreciates that she is Lucile, Camille's wife. She has an ambiguous half smile on her face, though Paine can see from her eyes that she very much agrees with Camille. Paine wonders whether she can speak much English; no doubt she can, more than she lets on.

Says Paine, now trying to remain calm, "It does not mean he should be put to death, and you were wrong to condemn him before he is tried. You call yourself a republican. You fancy yourself one of his judges in the trial that is yet to come, yet you condemn him before the evidence is in."

Camille replies, "Alright. If you want to see the cards, here they are, on the table. It is him or us. We will kill or be killed. So long as he lives, he is a powerful element around which our enemies all across Europe can rally. This young Saint-Just fellow is hard to take, but he is right about the absurdity of trying a king whom you have, at least for now, vanquished by force. Is the revolution just or is it not? That is the question. You heard Robespierre: the king must die so that France can live. It is . . . it is evident that the people have sent us here to judge the king not as a citizen, but as a king, an enemy of the people, and to give them a constitution."

Camille is once again calm, yet now his look and something in his voice bespeaks insolence and defiance.

Paine says, "Ah! So now we get to what is really going on here. The crux of it. Kill or be killed, as you say. And, ultimately, this rationalization can apply to any one of us, can it not, Camille? Where is Danton? He told me he could handle Robespierre. I should be speaking to him."

Still sounding insolent, Camille replies, "He is still at the front on official business, conveniently. But he will return in time to cast a vote on the fate of the king."

"And now Robespierre is your principal. Mirabeau, Danton, Robespierre, your pen is ever the agent of ambitious men. Why don't you be your own man, for once."

Camille appears momentarily surprised and then thoughtful, as though Paine has said some things that have given him a fresh perspective to consider. Then all at once the color rises in his face, and he says, "Paine, I have told you before, think carefully about which side you choose in this trial of Capet. This split will be final and irrevocable. Yet this is a contest among Frenchmen, and you should stay out of it. Don't say you weren't warned. Why don't you ask your good friend at the Palais-Royal what she thinks you should do?"

The last comment pricks Paine like a long stiff needle, and he is dismayed by his reaction that must appear evident to Camille.

Paine stands, and says, "I must be going."

176

The cool clear evening aggravates Paine's highly sensitized condition, consumed as he is by disturbing and contradictory thoughts and emotions. He realizes that in England, even in the United States, he will be condemned by many as a regicide. "I will be unfairly blamed for bringing this to pass," he says aloud to himself. "Brissot and the rest of the Girondins are convinced that they control the Convention majority, and they will stop the execution. Yet the Jacobins seem better able than the Girondins to achieve their objectives." And in the back of his mind there is an irritation, a lingering question about the connection between Camille and the woman he loves, Marguerite. It seems that in his interactions with Camille she always comes up in some way; she is forever associated with that other man.

Paine goes straight to Bonneville's apartment. He is aware that Bonneville himself is in Germany, meeting with his Illuminati friends. He won't return until next week. When Paine violently knocks and the door opens, Marguerite is standing there, and he is alarmed by her appearance. She has been crying and appears afraid.

She says sharply, "You did not need to beat on the door that way."

He is taken aback. She is annoyed at him; until now their relations have been nothing but cordial.

She invites him in and seats him in the drawing room. Still on her feet, she hands him a piece of paper. It purports to be a facsimile of a letter from Olympe de Gouges to the National Convention.

"Have you seen this?" she asks emphatically.

"No." He has not seen it.

"They did not read it at the Convention?"

"I have never seen or heard of such a thing." It is true, even though it bears yesterday's date.

She reads him the key phrases, translating them into English as she goes, and he patiently listens. Flushed, clearly upset by what she is reading, she is perhaps more beautiful than ever. "'I offer myself, after the courageous Malesherbes, to be Louis's defender.

Let not my sex be an objection: that heroism and liberty may be possessed by women, the revolution has shown by more than one example. I am a frank and loyal republican without blame and without reproach; no one can doubt it, not even those who have disagreed with me. I may therefore undertake this case . . . Beheading a king does not kill him. He lives long after his death; he is only really dead when he survives his fall from grace.'"

When she pauses, he exclaims, "Good grief! She is offering to assist Malesherbes in defending the king! That is absurd!"

"Yes! It is. She has lost her mind. Or, she believes it a clever means to publicize her new play. In which case, she is all the more deranged. The letter also mentions one of her plays, which will soon be acted."

"It has not been read to the Convention. Perhaps there is no harm."

"She has placarded it all over the city. And when she was leaving her apartment today, a bunch of ruffians attacked her. I just returned from her place; I went there at once when I heard what happened to her. She has shaved her head, for what reason I know not. And when her bonnet fell off, they all saw her bald head. One of the men yelled, 'Who will give twenty-four sous for the head of Madame de Gouges?' And she replied, 'Friend, I bid thirty.' She is immensely proud of that response. The crowd laughed and she was released. Yet still she is covered with cuts and bruises; an eye has turned black." Marguerite's voice begins to falter. "I think that eventually she will antagonize these vulgar men into killing her!"

"You have done all you can do for her."

"I have not done enough, and I must do more. She is my mother—"

"She is your mother?!"

"She is not my natural mother, but she took me in as a child, an orphan. My mother was a courtesan and died giving birth to me. They were colleagues. She raised me alongside her own son and saw to my education, primarily financed by Jacques Biétrix de Rozières; my own surname, Brazier, is a fiction and a modification of his, much as she fashioned her own name. Almost since she came to Paris, Monsieur de Rozières has been her favorite lover, but now he has terminated their relationship. He is afraid of her. He is afraid that her conduct might lead to his ruin, or his annihilation. The coward! He has been somewhat as a father to me, but I am done with him, as he has now deserted her."

She comes and sits on Paine's lap. She puts her arms around his neck and rests her forehead on his shoulder. They sit quietly for a few moments then she raises her head and forcefully kisses him on the mouth. Her eyes are moist and their noses briefly touch. He wants to make love to her. They will forget their problems, in one another's arms. But he cannot resist the question, even knowing it may spoil the mood.

"Is Camille your lover?"

She is extraordinarily self-possessed, there is no color in her face, and the emotion is gone from her voice, as she says, "He has been my lover for a very long time. But we are finished now."

"Before Nicolas?" Paine croaks. He is hardly able to form the words, and is greatly annoyed at the sound of his voice.

"Yes, and then he lived with Nicolas and me. We had an understanding. But all of that is in the past." Now Paine notes a tremor in her voice, and her cheeks are reddened.

"Before and after he was married, then?"

"He would not have married a woman of my class. The illegitimate daughter of a prostitute. I am a prostitute myself! I have no income except for the support that I receive from my lovers." She laughs, joylessly. "Lucile has made him financially secure. But he has kept coming back to me." Again, he notes a tremor. Her eyes are shining.

He is angry, and hurt. He says, "Actually, I do see, as you have said, that you don't love anyone. You continued your relationship with Camille after he and Nicolas had their falling out. I assume the 'understanding'—as you put it—ended at that point. I saw tonight that Nicolas has come to loathe Camille for the most noble reasons. Least of all you love Nicolas, it seems. Yet how can I possibly regard your affection for me as anything other than a manipulation?" He eases her off his lap and rises. "I think I should go."

"Wait!" she says. "I told you Camille and I are finished. Your reaction doesn't dignify you, and it's unnecessary. I don't know what love is, but whatever it is, this thing of mine we call love belongs to you. I don't know why you are bringing Nicolas into this. He has nothing at all to do with us."

"How long ago did you end it with Camille?"

"Yesterday. His article was the last straw. I told him so. It is horrible. I knew it would upset you and Olympe very much."

"Only yesterday? It is hardly over."

"Believe me; we are finished." Now she kisses him again and begins to unbutton his shirt. He returns the kiss.

They make love in the bed that she shares with Nicolas. This time they truly make love—they are naked and breast to breast, joined together and kissing deeply, he embraced by her arms and legs; he upon her then she on him.

Later, she lies naked, not yet bothering to get up and wash herself.

"Did you mean it when you said that you love me?" she says.

"Yes." He says it without hesitation. Yet does he really love her? He has not for a long time considered the cost of love. At this moment it occurs to him that perhaps it was the terrible death of the love of his life, and their child, that had kept him from love all these years.

"Take me and Olympe to America with you." He plays along. "When would you like to leave for America?"

"Tomorrow. I want us to leave tomorrow."

"I am expected at the Convention."

"You will have to resign your office, if we are to leave for America."

He understands. The point is not to leave tomorrow. There may not be an available ship bound for America for a while. She wants to know if he is more devoted to her than to his calling, than to France, even than to the king or republicanism.

He did not expect the discussion to take this turn. He did not expect any discussion with her ever to take this turn. His reaction is a feeling of pity for her. He appreciates that notwithstanding her culture, her education, her abilities, every one of her actions is in reaction to her status as a woman. She has no means to support herself, to take herself to America, because she is a woman — unless by means of resources obtained from a man who loves her. All of her lovers give her money, except him, but he does not pay anyone for anything. Because he is Thomas Paine. The whole situation feels degrading, and he does not feel that he is about to make a courageous decision.

"I will take you to America, but not now. I have to finish what I started here. You and I, Olympe, Capet and his family, we will all go to America together, after the Convention tries him and exiles him to America." He gets up. "I must go."

"So soon?" she says. "You can spend the night."

"I can't," he says. "I must meet with Brissot; we are planning my address to the Convention on the fate of Louis Capet." He is lying. There will be no meeting with Brissot, and there are no plans that he speak.

"Very well," she says, rising to clean herself. "Suit yourself."

He dresses rapidly and does not look at her. When he leaves and after the door closes behind him, he thinks that he hears her crying. He cannot be sure, but he turns over in his mind that what he heard must have been the sound of her sobs.

CHAPTER 23

DECEMBER 26, 1792: THE first day of the king's defense has arrived, and Paine hangs on Etienne Goupilleau's every translated word. The president, Defermon, had to shout out several times and ring his bell to gain the Convention's and spectators' attention to demand their silence. And now the hall is absolutely silent. The president announces, "Louis and his defenders are ready to appear at the bar. I forbid the members or spectators to make any noise or show any kind of partisanship."

Accompanied by his three lawyers, Chambon the mayor, and Antoine Joseph Santerre, the commandant general of the police, Louis walks slowly to the bar. Evidently, again he is here as Louis the man, not as a king. His dress is understated. He has exchanged the walnut-colored greatcoat for a dark blue one.

"Louis," says the president, "the Convention has decreed that you would be heard definitively today."

"My counsel," says Louis gesturing toward Desèze, "will read you my defense."

Desèze stands tall and erect—his presence seeming to occupy an outsized presence in the hall—with a large head, thick eyebrows, a full head of natural hair. Louis is seated behind him at the bar, attentive and composed.

"Citizen representatives of the nation," the lawyer begins, "the moment has come when Louis, accused in the name of the French people, can make himself listened to in the midst of the people themselves."

He begins with the first line of argument, which Camille anticipated: Louis's immunity from prosecution because he acceded to the constitution of 1791—a bargain struck with the French people. As the lawyer speaks, his gestures are emphatic yet restrained and dignified, and his sonorous voice comes in appealing tonal variations.

He now turns to the procedural defects in this trial. He lowers his gaze and fixes it upon the delegates. "Citizens," he says, "I will speak to you here with the frankness of a free man. I search among you for judges, and I see only accusers. You want to pronounce on Louis's fate, and it is you yourselves who accuse him! You want to pronounce on Louis's fate, and you have already declared your views! You want to pronounce on Louis's fate, and your opinions are disseminated throughout Europe! Among Frenchmen, only Louis has no law and no procedures! He has neither the rights of a citizen nor the prerogatives of a king! He has the rights neither of his former state nor of his new state."

Desèze then substantively addresses the charges against Louis, point by point. "First, consider the alleged improprieties that must be attributed to Louis himself and not to his ministers. When Louis in 1791 accepted the constitution, he no longer had the means to become the all-powerful tyrant alleged in the charges against him. Do not condemn Louis because he vetoed many pieces of legislation desired by representatives of the nation—for example, many of the decrees having to do with the Church—as it was the constitution that gave him this very veto power. If Louis at times made mistakes, or exercised bad judgment, he did so with the best intentions, and always conforming to the law of the land. At no time did he violate the constitution or his own deeply held principles."

Unavoidably, Desèze must address the events of the Champ-de-Mars massacre and August 10. He has the good sense not to argue that Champ-de-Mars occurred before the constitution was operative and therefore Louis is immune from prosecution for that atrocity. Instead, he blames the ministers, Lafayette, and Mayor

Bailly. Louis was not there, and he did not direct and explicitly disapproved of their actions.

August 10 led to Louis's arrest and imprisonment, and the extinction of the monarchy. Yet Desèze cannot challenge the legitimacy of August 10, for the Convention will not find Louis innocent if it must mean that the revolution is guilty. Yet he must defend his client against charges that he is responsible for the violent deaths of many Frenchmen by the Swiss Guards. If Louis had directed an attack on French citizens on August 10, then he is guilty of treason as charged.

"Citizens," the lawyer says, "he was only defending himself, his family, and the monarchy from attack. And in any event, at the time of the bloodshed he had fled and submitted himself to the Assembly. Before Louis left the Tuileries, there had been no bloodshed. After he left, he had no responsibility for what happened; he was the prisoner of the Assembly."

He pauses only momentarily, then he continues, "Louis ascended the throne at the age of twenty, and at that age he gave an example of morality. He carried to it no culpable weakness, no corrupting passion. In that station he was economical, just, and severe, and proved himself the constant friend of the people. The people wished for the abolition of a disastrous impost which oppressed them—he abolished it. The people demanded the abolition of servitude—he began by abolishing it himself in his domains. The people solicited reforms in the criminal legislation to alleviate the condition of accused persons—he made those reforms. The people desired that thousands of Frenchmen, whom the rigor of our customs had till then deprived of the rights belonging to the citizens, might either acquire or be restored to those rights—he extended that benefit to them by his laws. The people wanted liberty; and he conferred it."

Here there erupt murmurs, nearly coalescing into uproar. The lawyer pauses until the noise abates, then he continues, "He even anticipated their wishes by his sacrifices; and yet it is in the name of this very people that men are now demanding . . . Citizens, I shall not finish—I pause before history. Consider that it will judge your judgment, and that its judgment will be that of ages!"

Suddenly Desèze is finished, having talked for over three hours. His shirt has become drenched in the fetid air. Silence reigns in the hall, until Louis asks to say a few words on his own behalf, and the president grants him leave.

Louis reads his statement: He is innocent. "I declare that my conscience reproaches me with nothing, and that my defenders have told you the truth."

Paine is profoundly shaken by the power of Desèze's argument, and the king's reserved dignity. He fully appreciates that the king's trial is not fair (of course!) and is sick at heart about it.

As soon as the king has left the hall, a violent tumult arises. Goupilleau is trying as best he can to capture the statements for Paine. Some want further discussion before a vote is taken.

CHAPTER 24

GOUVERNEUR MORRIS'S SPACIOUS ANTECHAMBER is crowded, and it is only half past seven. Paine had hoped to be the first to arrive and gain quick access to the ambassador. But here in Paris, within specific segments of the population, America has become a popular destination, and émigrés to the United States must gain leave from this embassy.

He looks around and sees grim looks, here and there a gleam of desperation. He is well aware that they are from among the more prosperous of Paris, and mostly devout Catholics; the laborers who serve them, such as chefs, seamstresses, and hairdressers; and priests. But here they are all outfitted such that he cannot tell one class or occupation from the other.

He is greeted by a man he recognizes as Morris's valet; a man such as Morris must have a valet. Paine is immediately recognized, so he need not give his name; he explains that Morris has had delivered to him a letter asking that Paine come and see him immediately.

Across the antechamber, directly in front of Paine, there are double doors which are ajar. Suddenly, he hears a voice boom from beyond the doors. "Tom Paine; I hear Tom Paine. Bring him in, George, I must see him at once! Come in, Paine."

The office is large and luxuriously appointed, with book-filled shelves, paintings, and windows that look out onto the streets of Paris. Morris rises energetically and, notwithstanding the peg leg, moves briskly around the desk to greet Paine and seat him; then he returns to his side of the desk. Morris picks up a sheaf of papers that he flourishes like a banner.

"Paine," he says, "you lost your trial in London. A jury at Guild-hall convicted you of sedition and sentenced you to death, in absentia. I'm so sorry."

"The jury was handpicked by Pitt's henchmen."

"No doubt. Yet it is my duty to inform you that if you ever again set foot on British soil, or are captured by English forces when traveling by sail, you will be summarily imprisoned and hanged."

Clearly, Morris is enjoying himself. Paine feels a crushing weight; he is crestfallen and cannot conceal his reaction. Morris's response is a look of unrestrained self-satisfaction.

Paine says, "The trial must have been a one-sided affair, with me absent."

"You received the ablest defense possible, though your advocates received no fee; indeed, they have paid a heavy price." Morris examines the papers in his hand. "Erskine vigorously defended you." Thomas Erskine, attorney general to the Prince of Wales, is Britain's most famous and most successful criminal lawyer.

Still looking at the papers in his hand, Morris says, "The prince notified Erskine that he would dismiss him from the royal sine-cure if he represented you; Erskine ignored the threat, and the prince did what he promised. The English papers have accused Erskine of treason, conspiring with you, and they have called him a Jacobin. Erskine argued for four hours, even fainting in the midst of his oration.

"Listen to this, these fine words spoken by your lawyer on your behalf: 'Government, in its own estimation, has been at all times a system of perfection; but a free press has examined and detected government's errors, and the people have from time to time reformed them. This freedom has alone made our government what it is; this freedom alone can preserve it; and therefore, under the banners of that freedom, today I stand up to defend Thomas Paine.' You received the ablest defense available."

Paine is overcome. He says, hardly able to speak, "No truer

words were ever spoken than these by Erskine. Such words will outlive the memory of William Pitt."

Morris continues reading aloud from the report set forth in the papers he holds. "'Yet when the prosecution stood to reply, foreman Campbell interrupted, telling the judge, "My Lord, I am authorized by the jury here to inform the Attorney General that a reply is not necessary for them, unless the Attorney General wishes to make it, or your Lordship." Mr. Paine's trial was this instant over. The instant Erskine closed his speech, the jury, without waiting for any answer, or any summing up by the Judge, pronounced him guilty.'"

"I was well defended, but nevertheless the trial's outcome was foreordained; the trial was rigged," Paine says. "The venal jury did not even consider my case. They were Pitt's agents, pure and simple; and I am sure that Edmund Burke is taking no small satisfaction from this, hypocrite that he is. This is what William Blake foresaw, which is the very reason I am here. He saved my life. I left because of his advice, not to flee the charge of sedition. Certainly, I would have been lynched, murdered before the trial occurred had I not heeded his advice."

"Who is William Blake?"

"He is a good friend of mine. A very good friend, an artist with a brilliant, visionary mind. His poems and engravings will outlive the memory of William Pitt or Edmund Burke. I owe him my life. I should have known. I was introduced to English justice growing up in Thetford. When I was a child, I could see the gallows from my house. So I am condemned to die merely because of what I have written and said. Even for an unabashed monarchist such as yourself, Morris, this must be tragic and unjust."

Now it is Morris's turn to look vexed. "Paine, my commitment to unrestrained free speech is beyond question. This has happened to you because the British nobility are in a panic. They look across the Channel and see what is going on here in France, and they see a fight for their own very existence. They feel they must prevent a tide of bloodlust and madness that is rising up on the European continent from inundating Britain. They fear for their very lives. First the September Massacres; and now the guillotine is busy here. It is going to get worse here, and there, mark my words. Pitt is cracking down all over Britain."

"I understand. And they have roused the common man against me, and now the nobility will betray them. There is no liberty in Britain, nor equality. It is for this reason that I rejected it as my homeland; and when I departed for France, I knew I would not return."

Morris is leafing through the papers, not looking at Paine. He says, "Your publisher James Ridgeway was taken off to prison in chains. Erskine's horses were released from their harnesses and his carriage was pulled through the streets by a cheering mob."

"Morris, stop. I've had enough." Paine is about to flee.

"You do realize, Paine, that it is no coincidence that the English staged your trial at the same time as this travesty here in Paris that will decide the king's fate? Thesis and antithesis. Or is it that?"

"What do you mean?"

"The English regard you as bearing no small blame for what is happening here in France, not only the king's so-called trial, but other atrocities begat by the revolution. Your trial is in retribution for what is going on here at this moment, and your trial was as fair as the one of the king in which you are participating. Perhaps that is the whole point of it."

Paine is taken aback; he is black with rage. "Very well, I must be going. I am indifferent to the British judgment upon my character, but I don't have to sit here and take it from you." He stands.

"Paine, sit down. We have more to discuss. You are correct that it is the British judgment that has been declared upon you, and not my own. You are the object of their vilification, and now their legal judgments and armed forces and police, because you are their most prominent countryman in the French Revolution. Your writings have been enormously popular in Europe and fomented the revolutionaries, and you are now a French citizen and elected to their legislature. In British eyes, you are a traitor, and the most famous British traitor."

He stops, raises and levels his gaze at Paine, and continues, "Yet the British are attacking you, but not you alone. There is a broader program. Pitt's agents have sent government spies to infiltrate republican clubs. Informants are bribed with cash to give testimony against progressives. Prosecutions have been commenced all over England against printers, publishers, even for offenses committed many months ago. The printer of the *Manchester Herald* has had seven different indictments issued against him for seven paragraphs in his paper; and six different indictments for selling or disposing of six different copies of your books. These actions are bringing the targets to ruin, whether or not they are imprisoned. It will get worse once the British and French are formally at war, which will inevitably happen. Mark my words. Then God save all British subjects who remain in France, such as yourself."

Paine sits, and says, "I am no longer a British subject. I am as American as you are. I could have chosen to be one of President Washington's ministers, as you have. I know very well the power of my writings to move the masses, and your opinion of me, Morris, and I am as indifferent to it as the British one. I am no more to blame for the evil that men do in reaction to my writings than is Rousseau or St. Paul. I hope my friends in London are well. How is Joseph Johnson and his circle? Have you heard?"

"I have heard nothing. What is your impression of developments at the Convention? What will happen to the king? That is now the question that most urgently affects your own fate."

"His appearance at the Convention threw it into disarray. The king's lawyer gave a magnificent argument; sympathy for the king was only enhanced by the rumor that the lawyer had not slept for four days when he addressed the Convention. But sympathy for the king is due not so much because of his lawyer's advocacy. Many deputies, and even many in the galleries, were impressed by the king's dignity, his self-possession, and his respect for the proceedings even as his lawyer condemned them as illegitimate and unfair. I was among those so impressed, actually. He behaved as Socrates, honoring the rule of law, though the law be an ass. And had Louis refused the Convention's power to try him, a trap would have been sprung. His denial of the people's sovereignty would have been the final proof of his tyranny. But since his trial began, Louis has presented himself as just a man who expects to be treated the same as any citizen. And now it seems that this tactic aggravated the division of the Convention. So since the king's appearance and his lawyer's argument, speeches have gone on for days, beginning with Saint-Just: Montagne and Gironde, one after another, debating the king's fate so fiercely it would seem their own lives depend upon the outcome. Now, in the midst of this gridlock, the Gironde are arguing that the fate of the king should be determined by an a 'appeal to the people,' by plebiscite."

"Indeed," says Morris, "the losing side will have made this trial determine not just the guilt or innocence of the king, but also the legitimacy of their own cause."

Morris reaches for a newspaper lying on his desk, examines it, and reads aloud: "'Defenders of the king, what would you require of us? If he is innocent, the nation is guilty. We must finish answering, for the very act of deliberating accuses the People.'" He looks at Paine. "Thus spake Saint-Just, and thusly the deputies have tethered their own fates to that of the king. The winning side will have quite shrewdly played the loser."

Paine considers the remark and does not respond. He has always felt that the Jacobins are better at this political game than the Girondins.

"And you can't be sure of the vote's outcome, can you?" says Morris.

"That's true. No, I can't. There are seven hundred and forty-nine deputies, and perhaps one-third have spoken at the Convention or published their positions. I cannot be sure how the silent majority will vote. And some delegates have even expressed shifting positions. But as always, I am convinced of the justice of my cause, perhaps to a fault."

"Yes, Paine, you always have evinced a kind of religious fervor, even as you mock the faith of others. Paine, I have followed these developments, and here is my assessment: The Gironde have over-played their hand. The debates over the appeal to the people only highlight that the king must be erased. And, unfortunately, I think the Jacobins will prevail."

"But I do not believe they will vote for his execution. I plan to oppose the death sentence, and couple this with a proposal to send the king to exile in America."

"Paine, stay out of this. It's not really your fight. If you defend the king, you will be at risk if Robespierre and his allies carry the day. And you can't leave. You are trapped. The British navy patrols the Atlantic shipping lanes, their ships are outfitted for war, and the British may board any French or American vessel with no prov-ocation. An officer would eagerly bring you to London in chains for your execution. It would make his celebrity and career."

"Would President Washington be interested in paying a ransom for the king?"

"He does not want to be drawn into this. I'm sure he would offer the king asylum, but he would not offer any ransom. He does not wish to negotiate for the king's life with America's most important ally. Trust me. Since August 10, I have been involved in every scheme to save the king, and there have been many. I want to save him at least as badly as you do."

"What about Pitt? As much as it galls me to utter his name, if he would bargain for the king, I would support negotiations with him if it could save the king's life."

"My informants tell me that Danton already made such an overture. He sent the Abbé Noel to London to make a proposal to Pitt. I think Danton wanted a bribe, a brokerage fee."

"Danton? He is at the front, with the army."

"Yes, but his friends have kept him informed. Pitt would not see Noel, stating that the British desire to remain neutral in the internal affairs of France."

"What makes you think Danton wanted a bribe?"

"Danton has been receiving illicit funds from émigrés and Pitt since he was in London during 1791. He is no better than Mira-beau. I know you won't expose him, because compared to the rest of his party, he is a voice of moderation."

"If the French kill their king, it will be a signal for my departure, regardless of the risks, for I will not abide among such sanguinary men. But first, I will attempt to persuade them to send the king to America, and I will offer to accompany him and his family."

"Paine, stay out of this contest. I warn you—do not speak in his defense. As you see, I've had an uncanny ability to predict the course of events here. I know these people. They are depraved. If you don't follow my advice, and get yourself into trouble, don't bother to ask for my assistance on behalf of the United States. You will have gotten yourself into a predicament that I will be unable to redress, and I will disappoint you."

CHAPTER 25

January 15, 1793: Paine is at the tribune, and Goupilleau stands beside him. The Salle du Manège is filled up to bursting with delegates and spectators in the gallery. The noisy and reeking multitude spills outside, flooding the palace grounds like swells buffeting the hull of a great ship. This turbulent and expectant sea stretches yonder far beyond eyesight—for all Europe, even all nations, anticipate the fate of Louis XVI. Yet inside, presently, the hall is silent, attentive.

Goupilleau is reading aloud Paine's (translated) proposal for the disposition of Louis Capet. No motion is made for adoption of Paine's proposal that the king be sent to America, and there is no direct response. Paine is stunned. After day upon day of uproar and tumultuous indecision in this hall, his solution to the problem of Capet, which has meant so much to him, just dies quickly and quietly.

Next, Bertrand Barère, the immediate past president, is at the tribune. He says, addressing the deputies, "It is for you to vote, before the legacy of Brutus, before your country, before the whole world. It is by judging the last king of the French that the National Convention will enter into the fields of fame!" The Convention and the galleries explode in raucous approval.

Now Vergniaud, the current president, is at the tribune. Vergniaud is the Girondin who argued most eloquently and persuasively for an appeal to the people. Now he reads the three successive questions, in form and order precisely as agreed to by the Convention factions, which the delegates will now adjudicate.

The hall is hushed, otherwise completely silent, as he reads aloud, deploying the full force of his resonant, sonorous voice. "Is Louis Capet guilty of conspiring against Liberty? Shall our Sentence be itself final, or need ratifying by Appeal to the People? If Guilty, what Punishment?"

Goupilleau does not bother to translate for Paine. For in the course of the exchanged fury and pontificating, and negotiations, these questions have become as familiar to him as they would be if inscribed and studiously committed to his memory in English. With Danton's absence, while he is at France's military front, Paine has migrated back to the Girondin side of the hall. Now, just in time, Danton has materialized and is seated beside his comrades on the Mountain.

The president instructs that deputy after deputy must answer to his name: "*Couplable*," or, "*Non couplable*." As to guilty or not guilty, the outcome is never in doubt. The verdict is unanimous, except for a feeble twenty-eight still in the swamp who refuse to vote at all.

Paine himself shouts out, "*Couplable!*" followed by "Guilty!" in his native tongue, in case there be any doubt about his conviction—which in turn elicits a satisfied rumble in the hall.

Likewise, the verdict on the second question is never in doubt. A majority of two to one, including Paine, answers that there shall be no appeal to the people, and there will be none.

Now it is ten o'clock at night, and the Convention adjourns. The first two questions settled, a calm lies over the delegates. Yet a calm that is tense; a calm before the storm. Tomorrow the deputies will decide the third question. What punishment? Paine or any other delegate with whom he speaks is completely unable to predict the outcome. He is not even sure how Danton or many Girondins will vote. On the morrow will come the epic struggle.

Paine returns to his room at White's Hotel. He is utterly alone, and painfully aware of that fact. Tonight he has no friends or colleagues. Most painful is the recognition that he has become completely irrelevant in the Convention. He has no speech to prepare. Many of the deputies will give an oration before voting, but everyone urges him to remain silent. Condorcet and Brissot will speak against death. No doubt so will Vergniaud.

Condorcet told him that his young acolyte Fouché will finally speak, and he will deliver fine words that Condorcet helped him fashion on behalf of sparing the king. Condorcet hopes that as Fouché is from Nantes, the former cleric's advocacy will secure essential votes from the more conservative provinces.

Paine thinks about Louis, also alone in his room at the Temple, separated from his family, also bereft of friends or colleagues. Certainly, like Paine, he can't stop thoughts flowing, reflecting upon how he arrived at this terrible fix. Paine hardly sleeps, and when he does, he sleeps fitfully, skittering on the surface, breaking in and out of unconsciousness.

Most of the next day is taken up by debates over public order and procedural matters. The Paris Commune has closed all roads entering Paris. The mayor and his ministers are summoned and questioned about the measures. The Convention decrees that Paris including all public spaces and establishments should remain open to all French citizens and visitors from abroad.

Now Comte Lanjuinais is at the tribune—tall, erect, and with eyes blazing, this noble is displaying fearless opposition to the Mountain. He moves that the number of votes by which the king's sentence should be passed be fixed at two-thirds, as in the criminal courts.

Danton bellows in strong opposition—no longer is there any doubt about how he intends to vote—contending that the standard must be by bare majority.

Undeterred, Lanjuinais exclaims, "After the king has in every other way been denied procedural due process, we should at least observe the rule which demands two-thirds of the votes. We vote under the daggers and the cannon of the factions."

At these words, delegates are on their feet and fresh storms of protest are bursting forth. At last, Danton's motion for a bare majority carries, the Convention declaring that "the form of its decrees is unique, and according to this form they are all passed by a bare majority."

Danton moves that this session of the Convention shall be "*sans désemparer*"—that is, "shall be permanent till we have done"; shall continue until the voting on the king's punishment is over and the verdict is rendered. And the Convention so decrees.

Robespierre moves that there shall be no secret ballot: each delegate must mount the tribune and announce his vote in the presence of all the delegates and citizens in the galleries; and the Convention so decrees.

The voting does not begin until eight o'clock in the evening. The voting proceeds by roll call—ushers shrilly shouting each deputy's name and department, and each one so summoned rising and mounting the tribune to cast his vote. Deputy after deputy is mounting those steps, pausing at the tribune, where lamplight is most intensely cast, casting his fateful vote. Some just say, "Death;" others declare support for continued imprisonment until France is at peace.

Paine imagines that he must be witnessing an event like none other in the history of nations and kingdoms. Never before has any senate thusly adjudicated a king's life, and thereby determined so much else that depends upon the king's fate, which now hangs trembling in the balance. And never have a nation's fate and absurdity been so juxtaposed as now.

Expectant throngs still flood all corridors, the galleries, and the palace grounds, now dusky in the dim lamplight. Among the people, what is taking place resembles spectators drawn by bloodlust to gladiatorial games in ancient Rome. The ushers are become as box-keepers, opening and shutting the galleries for privileged persons connected to the Mountain region—for example, D'Orléans Égalité's mistresses, or other dressed-up women bearing the tricolor and rustling laces.

Within the galleries the crowd is consuming snacks and ices, and drinking wine and brandy and placing wagers. While in truth what unfolds before them in this hall is history of gravest possible consequence, not games, gallant deputies come and go from the best seats in the gallery, treating the well-dressed ladies with refreshments and small talk; elegantly coiffed heads nod responsively, while some have in hand card and pin, keeping score as though at thoroughbred races.

Higher up, battalions of unrouged and unpainted Amazons roar and shriek approval at votes for death, and issue "Haha" heckles and hiss at votes for mercy.

Paine hears from outside a festive din and the telltale sounds of wagering; he imagines betting going on in all the taverns and coffee houses of the neighborhood.

Amid the tumult, as each deputy ascends the tribune, deputies and spectators alike observe silence in order that he might be heard; but once he has announced his vote, loud expressions of approval or disapproval immediately burst forth. Disapproval is strongest and increases in response to votes cast not for death. Sometimes the deputy immediately dives back into the human sea again. Others turn and make threatening gestures and hurl abusive epithets at those delegates who are issuing the jeers.

Paine observes that these dreadful scenes have left many Girondins seated around him appearing shaken. Accompanying many a death-vote there emerge numerous other carefully wrought provisos, conditions, explanations, and suggestions for mercy.

Suddenly, Vergniaud, the Convention president—he who has appeared so deeply affected by the fate of Louis XVI, and who has declared to his friends that he shall never pronounce sentence of death on the unfortunate king—Vergniaud himself, now utters, "Death!" At this moment, Paine appreciates that he will never forget, as surely as he will never forget the moment he first laid eyes on the kindly visage of Benjamin Franklin, the moment when he heard this deputy from Bordeaux drop from his lips the unexpected and terrible word, "death."

Surely Vergniaud's prosperous and conservative wine-producing constituents at Bordeaux would not approve. No doubt Vergniaud will give them the all-purpose excuse: he will say that he voted thusly to avoid civil war. Paine knows the true reason: it is because some deputies are beguiled by the fraudulent bargain: kill or be killed!

Now ensuing Girondin deputies are following Vergniaud's death vote. One of them is Joseph Fouché, deputy of Nantes, the man who yesterday assured his friends and allies that he would make the moving speech on behalf of Louis prepared by his mentor Condorcet. As he is from Nantes, surely his conservative merchant constituents would want him to spare Louis, but swiftly he mounts the tribune and with downcast eyes and pallid lips mutters, "*La mort.*"

Still, Condorcet and Brissot are true to their word, voting no to death.

Philippe Égalité resolutely votes death. His perch is on the Mountain, he is the king's estranged cousin, proprietor of the Palais-Royal, and the revolution's financier during its early days, but the sound of his pronouncement of death upon his cousin Louis is greeted initially with awed silence, then murmuring through the hall.

Predictably, incorruptible Robespierre, who was once implacably against capital punishment, emphatically votes death, as do, also predictably, Marat, Saint-Just, Danton, and Camille. Among these, Robespierre gives the longest speech.

Now spectral and respected Abbé Sieyès ascends the tribune. Abbé Sieyès, heterodox man of God whose 1789 pamphlet *What is the Third Estate?* incited transformation of the Estates General into the National Assembly. Abbé Sieyès, who received more votes than any other for his appointment to the committee to draft the new constitution. Hardly pausing upon reaching the summit, this monumental figure says, "*La mort sans phrase.*" Goupilleau whispers the translation: "Death, without provisos." As the abbé vanishes from the tribune as fast as he ascended it, the Mountain and the galleries break out in pandemonium.

It is not until next day, January 17, at midday, that Paine's name is called. Exhausted, he swims to consciousness, and then climbs through fog to the tribune, and there stands, pausing, hands clasped behind his back. His heart thumps as though he is afflicted by stage fright, and perhaps he is. At length he says, speaking slowly in practiced French, "I vote no to death, and for the confinement of Louis until the end of the war, and for his perpetual banishment after the war."

Once returned to his seat amid the usual heckling, he perceives a shift in momentum. Bancal declares that his vote is likewise for the confinement and banishment of Capet, not death, "because it is that of Thomas Paine, the most deadly enemy of kings and royalty, whose vote is for me the anticipation of posterity." Another deputy elaborates: "By the example of Thomas Paine, whose vote is not suspect, by the example of that illustrious stranger, friend of the people, enemy of kings and royalty, and zealous defender of republican liberty, I vote for imprisonment during the war, and banishment at the peace." And another: "I rely on the opinion of Thomas Paine, and I vote like him for imprisonment."

Now nearly forty-eight hours have passed since the voting began and has continued without adjournment; it is early evening, January 18.

"Citizens," says Vergniaud, "I am about to proclaim the result of the deliberations. You will observe, I hope, profound silence. When justice has spoken, humanity ought to have its turn." The hall is indeed silent, as Vergniaud reports that there are seven hundred and forty-nine members of the Convention, but fifteen are absent on commissions, eight from illness, and five have refused to vote, which means that a bare majority would be three hundred and sixty-one votes.

The president now discloses that two hundred and eighty-six have, with varying conditions, voted for detention or banishment; two have voted for imprisonment. Forty-six have voted for death with reprieve either till peace, or till the ratification of the constitution; twenty-six have voted for death, but with stay of execution. Vergniaud states that these seventy-two votes were dependent on a latter clause and therefore will be counted as against death votes.

Precisely three hundred and sixty-one therefore voted for death unconditionally; so, by margin of a single vote, Louis Capet is sentenced to death!

In a sorrowful tone the president now declares, in the name of the Convention, that the punishment pronounced against Louis Capet is, "Death!"

Suddenly Malesherbes is at the tribune; he is weeping, sobbing, pleading for the king's life. But he pleads in vain.

CHAPTER 26

GOUPILLEAU AND PAINE HAVE found a secluded place in the palace grounds to talk, enough removed from the celebratory din to hear one another, though they speak in whispers. Paine is resolved to speak to the Convention tomorrow and make a final plea that Louis's life be spared. He has asked that Goupilleau remain available, in order that he may translate and then read the speech to the delegates.

Goupilleau is furious. He says, "Find someone else. I am finished with this fool's errand. Don't you see? Your cause is lost."

"The margin was one vote. And you heard those deputies who voted against death and cited me as their example."

"It may as well have been by five hundred votes. The Jacobins have prevented their defeat by any means necessary. And surely they will see to it that they retain today's victory. Most of all, this is what frustrates me: you and your friends, with your high-flown ideals, your education and your books, and your humanity, are no match for the Jacobins, who know how to win at this political game. So your sophistication and your goodness are for naught, even as supposed Girondins still outnumber Jacobins. As you saw, it was Girondins who provided the final necessary votes, because the people are firmly against you, and now the Girondins are terrified."

"I will give the people a lesson about humanity and liberty."

"That is precisely my point. You are ever ready to lecture the French about humanity and liberty. You have such a high opinion of your morals and wisdom about liberty. Yet you can't speak their language, you need an interpreter, you are uneducated in French history and culture. You should not even be here. What are you doing here, Paine? You should have stayed in America and stuck with philosophy and writing. You are no politician. I know I am not the first to give this advice: stay off the tribune while the Convention adjudicates Capet's fate!"

"Are you saying you refuse to translate my speech for me?"

"Indeed! And I resign as your interpreter. I'm done with this catastrophe. I am going home, to bed."

"I understand. You are spent, exhausted; you are not yourself. I hope that after you get some rest you will rethink this decision. Go on, get your sleep. I'll get someone else to help me tomorrow."

"Be careful, Paine, or you may find yourself mounting the scaffold."

The final comment takes him by surprise. He feels the blood rise to his face, and he gives his translator an inquiring look. Goupilleau turns on his heel and walks briskly away.

Paine arrives panting at Bonneville's door and knocks, mindful of the chiding he received from Marguerite last time he was here (he has not seen her since then, and he has not attempted to contact her, nor she him). There is no answer. He calls out to them. Still no answer. He looks in the keyhole, and imagines that he sees light, but when he knocks again and calls, there is no answer.

He has nothing to translate, anyway. First, produce the work requiring translation, he decides; that is essential. Then find a translator.

Back at White's Hotel, he commences to write. He has hardly slept in three days. But exhausted though he may be, his mind is immediately engaged, he is energized as a beast about to fight for its life, and he pours into this work all of what drives him, from the unexpected personal triumph of his American experience, and the surprising failure and frustration that has characterized this adventure in France.

Above all, his instinct tells him, he must be true to himself—that is, to the aspirations and principles that brought him here; he writes for his legacy as much as to save Louis Capet. Still, the message is not easily developed and refined. He works until nearly three in the morning, writing and rewriting. At last, he is satisfied. The concluding sentence captures the essence of his message: *Do not, I beseech you, bestow upon the English tyrant the satisfaction of learning that the man who helped America, the land of my love, to burst her fetters, has died on the scaffold.*

When he finishes, work in hand he rises and descends into the early morning. Having nowhere else to go, he arrives at Bancal's apartment and knocks hard. The door opens and Bancal stands in his nightshirt.

"Paine! What brings you here at this hour? And after our ordeal . . . You should be sleeping."

"Henri, I am so relieved to see you. I need your help. I plan to plead for Capet's life. I've written my speech, and I need someone to translate it and read it to the delegates."

"Thomas, are you sure?"

"Henri, is that Tom Paine?" It is a woman's voice. Helen Maria Williams emerges in the corridor, her only clothing a bare white sheet that she wears like a toga, gripping it at her midriff—she is supple and firm as a tightly sheathed dagger. Her hair hangs loose and uncombed and he sees the wreckage of make-up that still only enhances the beauty of her face. She is a woman who would be beautiful as ever emerging from manual labor at a slaughterhouse, and he has never seen a more attractive image than hers at this moment. The longing and envy he feels is a contradictory and dynamic ingredient to his tempestuous feelings.

Bancal says, "Yes, it is. Come in, Thomas."

"Will you do this for me, Henri? I have no one else to help me."

There is a long pause. Finally, Helen Maria says, "He certainly will. It is just the sort of thing that a man I love would do. Paine, leave the papers and Henri will meet you at the Convention at eight thirty with the translation. Thank you for doing this, Thomas."

"Thank you, both of you. Henri, I must tell you, Goupilleau believes we are risking our lives. That is why he abandoned me."

Bancal appears thoughtful.

"Ha!" barks Helen Maria. "Henri is too adroit to wind up on the scaffold. The Jacobins will not get the best of him. And that is the real reason that I love him."

When the Convention is called to order, Paine sits anxiously anticipating Bancal's delivery of his speech. First, Joseph Fouché gives his first speech there, which he shouts from the tribune. Paine can only gather the gist of it—a harangue against the king, demanding his prompt killing, to avoid the retribution of assassins. Paine understands his concluding sentence: "History is on our side and is against that of all the kings of this world."

Later, Bancal is at the tribune and is his usual self; perfectly elegant, amiable, absent malice. Paine is with the deputies on the Girondin side; they have decided that Bancal, a Frenchman, should be alone at the tribune. Bancal's stoicism is in contrast to Fouché's outburst, and Paine's internal tempest. He begins to read Paine's speech. "'The decision come to in the Convention yesterday in favor of death has filled me with genuine sorrow—'"

Suddenly Marat is on his feet, loudly interrupting; he shouts, "I submit that Thomas Paine is incompetent to vote on this question; being a Quaker, his religious principles are opposed to the death penalty!" (These words and the ensuing shouts are well within Paine's comprehension of French.) Bancal dutifully continues reading.

Someone from the Mountain: "The words you are reading are not those of Thomas Paine!"

Marat: "I denounce the translator. Such opinions are not Thomas Paine's. The translation is incorrect."

Another deputy, Garran, to whom Bancal showed the translation as well as Paine's original writing, anticipating just such an accusation, yells, "It is a correct translation of the original, which I have read."

Marat descends to the floor, shouting, "Paine's reason for voting against the death penalty is that he is a Quaker!" He is pacing about, limping and stooped in his usual way and dressed in the dirty clothes, with hideous, festering face. And the galleries and the Mountain are whipped into frenzy; Bancal's words are being lost in the din.

Paine can no longer remain seated. He winds up at the tribune, standing beside poor Bancal, who is still reading, appearing unperturbed. The French words suddenly come to Paine, and he shouts, "I have been influenced in my vote by public policy as well as by moral reasons!"

Derisive yells deluge Paine's words, and those of any Capet defender. Paine is humiliated, overmatched, overwhelmed. He is drowning, consumed by a violent and brackish sea. The last thing he sees is Camille's twisted sneer. He thinks he hears the words, "I told you, Paine, stay out of this."

He is nugatory, and Louis Capet will die.

He has done more harm than good, he sees. Later, a final vote is taken. Vergniaud instructs the deputies that no conditions or provisos are allowed. The final tally: three hundred and eighty for death, three hundred and ten for reprieve.

CHAPTER 27

THE CONVENTION IS IN sitting, and Camille is supposed to be there. But he has no intention of missing this momentous event—what he regards as his handiwork. He is, after all, first a journalist. And but for him, he tells himself, this would not be happening. He belongs here, at the Place de la Révolution, once the Place de Louis Quinze, not at the Convention. Everyone recognizes him, and the National Guard has facilitated his gaining the best place to stand and watch.

Before him rises the scaffold, and upon it the guillotine, near the old pedestal where once stood the statuette of Louis XVI himself. Irony of ironies! Though no accidental irony, to be sure. A wide berth around the scaffold bristles with cannons and armed men—except for Camille, in his elect place, and D'Orléans Égalité nearby in a cabriolet (the king's cousin is also playing hooky from the Convention, as for him too this spectacle is not to be missed). Spectators, mostly women, crowd and continue gathering at the rear. Inside the carriage, Louis is praying, reading prayers for the dying, it is said.

The carriage opens and out comes Louis, impassive, dressed in a maroon coat, gray breeches, and white stockings. The drums are beating. Suddenly the king cries, "Silence!" in a terrible voice; and, obediently, the drums stop.

Camille is vexed that the drummers should obey the king. Yet Louis does what is required and mounts the scaffold, then strips off his coat and drops it, and stands exposed in a sleeved waistcoat.

Charles-Henri Sanson, former Royal Executioner of France during Louis's reign, and now High Executioner of the First French Republic, greets his former employer; an awkward interaction. Sanson's assistants, his son among them, approach to bind Louis. At first he resists, and Abbé Edgeworth makes a sign to the executioners and takes Louis aside. After they speak privately, the king submits. What did the abbé say? It can only have been that since the Savior himself submitted to be bound, so too must the king submit.

Next the executioners cut his hair to expose the neck. His hands tied, and neck bare, the king now advances to the edge of the scaffold and looks upon the crowd. His face seems very red.

He shouts, "Frenchmen, I die innocent: it is from the scaffold and near appearing before God that I tell you so! I pardon my enemies; I desire that France—" Nearby there is an officer on horseback; the horse leaps forward, spurred, and with hand uplifted, the officer shouts, "Drums!" The drums recommence and Louis cannot be heard above the din. "Executioners, do your duty!" commands the officer.

Now, with alacrity that bespeaks fear, all six executioners take hold of Louis and tie their plank to his body. Together, and at a mutual nod, they lift the board and set it down on the assembly, align the neck inside the lunette, and swing it shut with a clang. Abbé Edgeworth, stooping to the king, says loud enough for Camille to hear, "Son of Saint Louis, ascend to Heaven!"

Absent further ceremony, promptly Sanson pulls the string and down comes the axe. The *bang!* signals that the king is dead. Camille is surprised at the blood, the amount of blood. The guillotine is drenched; a lake of blood upon the scaffold; down the steps flow cataracts of blood; and, suspended above, a pink mist.

Sanson lifts Louis's head—the face now hideous—and shows it to the crowd. The crowd roars, again and again, growing louder, finally howling, "*Vive la République!*"

The king is dead! The king is dead! Camille keeps thinking in near disbelief. He is giddy. Nightfall, Camille, still alone, is back at the Palais-Royal, the place where he truly first made his name. It is full of Jacobins. And tonight Jacobins are more than ever before cordial with Jacobins, and even with those few Girondins who may be here.

"It is done, it is done," is the refrain. Round upon round is hoisted in honor of their achievement. At last, they are all brothers! No?

Camille does not dwell in any single establishment. He is too energized to sit still. He feels a solid sense of achievement. He is joyful. Finally! The revolution has accomplished something real, he tells himself. His body's reaction is a mystery—he hums with sexual desire that sets a new high even for him.

He should go home to Lucile—and the baby—he realizes. She'd be glad to share this moment with him, in bed. But he finds himself at the door of Bonneville's apartment, reckless, taking a chance that he is gone. Camille knocks mightily on the door and shouts, and Marguerite opens it and lets him in. She is wearing only a short loose linen shift; her breasts are almost entirely exposed and her legs and arms are bare.

He believes that she has been waiting for him only. She opens her mouth to speak, but Camille takes hold of her and pushes her back against the wall, kissing her open mouth. Her tongue tastes of cognac. She has been drinking, alone.

She gasps, "No, Camille, no."

"Yes!" he breathes in her ear. He kisses her again, and when she kisses him back, her no is now yes.

He lifts the shift roughly over her head, revealing, as he imagined, that she is completely naked. Inside the bedroom, she shoves him to the bed with such force that he feels nearly under attack. She mounts him and when he enters her, such is her wetness and warmth that he does so instantaneously to the hilt, and the sensation will remain with him as long as he lives.

Later, when he gets up to leave, dressing, she seems to be sleeping. He reaches into his pockets and empties them of the assignats he carries, placing them on the bureau. Suddenly she is sitting up on the bed.

"Take your money," she says. He does not respond and leaves, going home to Lucile.

PART IV

CHAPTER 28

DANTON HAD SAID, "I am lost. I am finished." These were terrifying words to Camille, who feared the consequences for the revolution if there were no Danton. Poor Gabrielle; Gabrielle is dead; on February 11, she died giving birth to Danton's fourth child, a son, born dead; both she and the babe perished. Danton was at the front.

Yet scarcely a month has passed and Danton has found solace in the arms and bosom of Louise Gély, his erstwhile house maid, sixteen years old. And he has returned to the Convention, albeit he is not the same Danton as once was.

It is now March 10, in the Manège, and Camille watches his friend closely with mixed joy and anxiety: Danton stands upon the tribune, and so profoundly does the grimness of his aspect affect the deputies that they are silenced. All of the famous charm and bonhomie are gone. He looks older, the jaw is clenched; never before have his cheekbones been as prominent as they are now. His face is hollowed. He looks exhausted.

The mood is grim because of perils that confront the nation. So many armies are advancing toward France; penetrating through mountain passes, navigating the seas, marching over plains and highways: All across Europe resounds a call to arms in retribution against this country that has murdered its king!

Two hundred and sixty thousand Dutch Austrian combatants are advancing against France from the Upper Rhine and Holland, and to swell their ranks, come from still further north, are forty thousand English, Hanoverians, and Dutch; there are fifty-six thousand Prussians, and twenty-five thousand Hessians, Saxons, and Bavarians bristling alongside the Rhine at points from Basle to Mayence to Coblentz and to the Meuse; thirty thousand men are gathered at Luxembourg; and sixty thousand Austrians and ten thousand Prussians march alongside the Meuse to challenge French sieges of Maestricht and Venloo.

Yet more terrifying are France's enemies among Frenchmen, inside France itself. The fanatical provincials of the Vendée have exploded in open insurrection, indeed civil war, incited by the king's death. Their chieftains, Cathelineaus, Stofflets, Charettes— erstwhile merchants—are shrewd and well spoken, with great influence over their fellow men. From hiding places, mere peas- ants, with crude arms, rustic uniforms, and fanatic Gaelic fury, swarm the best-disciplined National Guards, howling battle cries of God and the king.

Such tidings have in Paris provoked great tumult, with fresh outcries against traitors and counter-revolutionists. Shortages of grain have substantially worsened since December, exacerbated by the merchants' fear of theft and pillage, price controls, and the farmers' disinclination to take paper money—this fictitious money, the assignats, so abundant, their real value declining daily with the consequence being hyper-inflation.

Bread is not the only article the price of which has enormously increased; also that of sugar, coffee, candles, and soap. The laun- dresses have come to the Convention to complain that they were obliged to pay thirty sous for soap, which had formerly cost them but fourteen.

Thus it was in this context that Marat, writing in *The Friend of the People*, declared:

> *In every country where the rights of the people are not empty titles, ostentatiously recorded in a mere declaration, the plun- der of a few shops, and the hanging of the forestalled at their doors, would soon put a stop to these malversations, which are driving five millions of men to despair, and causing thousands*

to perish for want. Will then the deputies of the people never do anything but chatter about their distresses, without proposing any remedy for them?

Thereafter rioters gathered in the streets and began insisting that the prices of all articles should be reduced one-half; soap to sixteen sous, lump-sugar to twenty-five, moist sugar to fifteen, candles to thirteen. They commenced to pillage and took great quantities of goods; initially, they paid the half prices, the goods being forcibly taken at this rate. Before long, the rabble refused to pay at all.

Yet still worse, could it be that General Dumouriez himself is perhaps secretly turning traitor? At the Convention arrived a letter from the general scathingly critical in tone and content, and the Convention itself was the primary object of his wrath. There are shortages of cartridges and clothing; shoes are soled with wood and pasteboard. In managing the war effort the Convention has done nothing right, he says.

Consternation abounds at what true ambition this egotistical yet physically diminutive general may harbor. Duke of Belgium? And, say, his aide-de-camp Égalité the younger king of France? That would be a fine end to the revolution!

So who is there now, thinks Camille, but Danton to navigate the Convention through this valley of the shadow of death? The hour is late; his gaunt face ghostly, lit by candlelight. The deputies, exhausted, having sat on the benches hour upon hour listening to the harangues from Danton. Now the denouement arrives. A deputy shouts that he should finish, that they may soon adjourn.

Danton roars, "Let us create terror to save the people from doing so. Let us organize a tribunal—it cannot be a perfect one, that is impossible, but the least bad we can make it—and put the sword of justice to the heads of our enemies. I demand that this revolutionary tribunal be set up forthwith, at this session, to give government the means of action and the energy it needs. After this tribunal, you must organize an energetic executive power, which shall be in immediate contact with you and be able to set in motion all your means in men and in money."

Deputies on the right react, grumbling, interrupting Danton. He bellows above the din, "All your arguing is miserable! I know only the enemy. Let us beat the enemy. Today, then, the extraordinary tribunal, tomorrow the executive power, and the next day the departure of your commissioners for the departments to enforce by iron fist the rule of law on the provincials. People may calumniate me if they please; but, let my memory perish, so the Republic be saved."

Shrieks and howls of approval burst from the public galleries, also thumping the balustrades in celebration and support.

CHAPTER 29

MARCH 28, 1793: PAINE is walking amid the usual street smells of dung and sweat and (lately) blood (his imagination?)—he is thoroughly beset by gnawing disquiet, stricken by a kind of disease. He hears gasps and shouts; faces are turned upward. He looks up and sees a burst of fat raindrops descending the night sky and then striking all around and upon him, and now he smells the sharp tang of wetted stone. People are taking cover under awnings and in doorways.

He lengthens his stride, walking hurriedly in the intensifying rain to the tavern associated with White's Hotel. Inside, he shivers and shakes like a wet dog, removing his hat. He looks up, and the landlord is there to greet him bearing in each hand a tumbler of cognac. Paine nods and smiles in thanks, and takes one in each hand, not the least bit shamed that his need has become so regular, so predictable, so public.

Glasses in hand he walks through the tavern, into the hotel, and straight up the staircase to his room. Once inside, he re-locks the door. The small room is cluttered—papers and books piled high on the desk and strewn across the floor and on the bed—and the bed is unmade.

He opens a drawer in the desk and takes out a stoppered bottle partially filled with a dark liquid, then sits on the bed, still in dark except for a yellow gaseous light emanating from outside the window. His back against the bedhead, he places one glass on the window sill, grips and uncorks the bottle as he still holds the other glass

217

in his palm, and from the bottle pours a portion of the dark liquid into the glass he holds, swirls the mixture, and then commences to sip. He leans his head against the bedhead, looks obliquely out the rain-spattered window, and waits for the elixir to take effect.

He lifts the glass and tilts it, gazing at and through the luscious bronze-colored translucent liquid; against the glass it leaves a fine, longitudinally patterned, dissipating veneer. Yet it is the unseen constituents of the glass and its contents that captivate him now: the atoms; minute, irreducible, and practically infinite. Like the liquor/laudanum mixture and the glass, he is himself but the sum of atoms—indeed, everything is but atoms reacting one upon the another.

Now imagining the atoms, he chides himself for his predicament, for his hubris. I was not; I was; I am not; I do not care. The Epicurean mantra. This reassurance, and the atoms of the drink in combination with his own, the constituents of Thomas Paine, make him feel better. Some men have sought to become famous and renowned, thinking that thus they would make themselves secure against their fellow men. Live unknown, admonished Epicurus. Paine has called himself an Epicurean. So what is he doing here?

He thinks of all that has befallen him since his early days in Thetford. He should have stuck to writing, like Epicurus. Except for his writing, his life has been nothing but failure and sadness. He recalls his arrival in France. He had set out from Calais in superb spirits, flush with excitement. Now he is continuously gripped by dread and anxiety. His life has never been settled, but it is now in disequilibrium as never before. Never has he felt so alone and adrift. At least he is free. He has not been arrested, and must avoid arrest by any means necessary. The thought of imprisonment makes his stomach churn. But is he actually free now? He feels imprisoned in this tiny room.

Yet, he suddenly realizes, he regrets none of what he has tried and failed at here in France; single-minded pursuit of pleasure requires an indifference to the suffering of others. He regrets none of it—except for Marguerite, that is. He cherishes the memory of her, their shared pleasures, and regrets terribly that they are finished. For she has broken off the relationship; steadfastly she ignores his inquiries and entreaties. He thinks about his farm in New Rochelle, all that he left. They might have settled there. More than anything right now, Paine misses the company of a woman.

Both glasses are drained, he realizes. He considers going and getting another. That would require walking, and descending and then ascending the steps. Perhaps that could be managed, but could he talk? His tongue feels alien, wooden.

He hears a knocking. Someone is knocking on his door, he realizes. He would ignore it, were the knocking not so tentative, were it more brazen and insistent. He senses a woman's knock.

He rises and, with a tremendous force of will, unlocks and opens the door. Lady Smyth stands before him. He does not know what to say. He remembers meeting her last November; he has not seen her since. He notices that beneath her wool jacket she wears a dark blue cotton gown that is striking for the richness of the blue and small white spots that make it look like the firmament. Her hair hangs loose and wet beneath a brimmed hat.

"Charlotte," he says. He does not know what else to say, though he is pleased to see her.

"I was at Helen Maria's salon just now," she says, "and she is beside herself that Henri Bancal is going to the front. She is inconsolable; beset by terrible premonitions. I know you and Bancal are friends. She told me you are allies in the Convention. So I decided to come."

"Come in, please," he says. Neither he nor his room is in any condition to receive visitors, but he does not know what else to do; this conversation cannot occur in the hallway, and he does not want to take her to the tavern. Neither of them speaks as he takes her wet coat and drapes it over the chair, and offers her a seat on the bed, which she accepts.

He feels that he wants to touch her in some way, and, as if sensing this, she reaches out and momentarily grips his forearm as she moves to the bed. He lights two candles, apologizes for the mess.

She gracefully dismisses the apology; then he offers to fetch her a drink. To his surprise, she accepts the offer.

He is sufficiently excited that gaining access to the drinks and returning to his room poses no challenge. When he enters, she is still seated on the unmade, cluttered bed, patiently waiting. He closes the door behind him and sits down beside her and relinquishes the drink he got for her. He is a little out of breath.

"Why can't Danton go to the front, as before?" she asks.

"No, Danton will not go," says Paine. "The Convention has lost confidence in him."

On March 14, the Convention received another letter from Dumouriez, only the latest one, that was filled with insolence and blaming the government for his failures. Danton persuaded the deputies to let him make yet another trip to the front to talk sense to his friend. But Dumouriez refused to withdraw his letter, and Danton returned to Paris a failure.

"How did Bancal get mixed up in this?" Charlotte asks.

"The Minister of War, Pierre Riel de Beurnonville, has asked for volunteers to go with him. Henri volunteered. Ironically, I think he must have done it to show Helen Maria he is a man of action, willing to take risks for the Republic. Camus, Quinette, and Lamarque will go as well. They will inquire into Dumouriez's intentions and they hope to secure his loyalty."

"Is there something you can do for him?"

"Not a thing," Paine says. "I have tried to dissuade him, and he will have none of it. He has made up his mind. And I fear that if he backed out now, the consequences would not be good for him. He would fall under suspicion of disloyalty."

Now it is as though their prior conversation picks up where it left off. He relates his abject failure and crushing disappointment for having failed to save the king. Then, to make matters worse, the constitution that he and Condorcet proposed to the Convention was roundly rejected; yet he disparages the document, blaming Condorcet for writing it all himself and indulging his high-flown rhetoric. He describes the terrible work of the Revolutionary

Tribunal that was conceived by Danton.

He pauses; they sit quietly; rain beats against the window. Those magnificent bright blue eyes are fixed upon him. She places a hand on his forearm, and with the other sips the drink. In the dusky light her features appear just as they must have when she was the dazzling young beauty that married Sir Robert Smyth. She is still striking, fine featured, her skin supple. The blue dress and her stunning blue eyes make a fine match.

"How have you been?" he finally asks.

"Oh, well enough," she says. "This is all quite disturbing to those of us who left our homelands and staked our lives and well-being on the fortunes of the French Revolution."

"Indeed. How is Robert reacting to this?"

"Robert? I don't know."

He looks at her surprised, inquiringly.

She takes her hand away. Suddenly she is blushing, and then she laughs. She looks vulnerable, and blushing still, touches her lips. He nods slightly and tries his best to give a look of sincerity, inviting her to speak.

She giggles and says, "Robert; I'm not seeing much of him lately. I am quite sure that he is with his new friend. She is a ballerina. It's all well and good. We are fine. We are revolutionaries now, and we have a tacit understanding. This goes with the program. Doesn't it? You should know. We can be libertines now. I am just as free, but haven't been able to bring myself to . . . I feel like the revolution is passing me by. Someday we'll all go back to being proper again, I'm sure of it." She laughs again and bites her lip.

He places his hand on hers, and she does not seem as surprised as he is by what happens next. She is upon him and in his embrace; they are kissing open-mouthed, he vaguely aware of her scent, subtly perfumed, pleasant. He realizes she is now crying, so he pauses and moves his head back—their lips are apart. She moves forward, again upon him and kissing forcefully, grabs his hand and guides it to her breast. She is wearing a corset, and she reaches underneath and struggles momentarily to unhook it. When she is free, he begins to caress the breast and is amazed at how lively and heavy it feels. He gets onto his feet and madly swipes and claws at the books and papers cluttering the bed, sending them scattering.

Later, he lies on top of her and watches as rain strikes and streams flat against the window; she is still embracing him. He hears the flow and gurgle of water cascading over the eaves and down drainpipes. He looks around at the messy, cluttered room.

He says, "I have to get out of here."

"I can arrange for you to live in a house in Saint-Denis with some Englishmen." The timbre of her voice is low, almost a rasp. "It is one of our investments. It's a very large house and has been operated as a hotel. We can get you your own apartment, with a personal entrance."

He nearly weeps. "Thank you. I need to get out of Paris. Would you visit me there?"

"Yes," she says. "You may visit me as well."

"Thank you." He lowers his head into the silken hollow of her neck and shoulder.

CHAPTER 30

APRIL 6, 1793: CAMILLE imagines that the young aide-de-camp will someday make a fine leader of men—that is, if he survives the Revolutionary Tribunal. Louis Lazare Hoche stands at the tribune caked with mud accumulated in his frantic dash from General Dumouriez's bivouac in Belgium, destroying three horses. He says he came here straight away. Yet the deputies are rancorous as they grill him.

He stands erect in filthy uniform and, notwithstanding his evident fatigue, is calm and poised, patiently fielding each question. Hoche discloses that two days ago Dumouriez defected, with a small staff of escorts, vaulting over ditches and into morasses, plunging for their lives amid volleys of musket shot and even grapeshot and curses. Several servants were killed, but the general and his loyalists escaped to the Austrian general's headquarters.

Deputies ask, who has followed Dumouriez? Hoch identifies General Égalité—Louis-Philippe, the duke's son. Dumouriez also took at gunpoint the four deputies who were the Convention's authorized commissioners, including Henri Bancal.

Amid howls and loud grumbling, Hoche assures the deputies that his commander, General le Veneur, who sent him, remains loyal. Indeed, it is because most of Dumouriez's general staff, le Veneur among them, refused his order that the army march on Paris—ostensibly to restore order and the rule of law—that Dumouriez defected, while the army remains loyal to the Convention. It was for this reason that his master sent him, to reassure the Convention.

The interview concludes, and Hoche is arrested and taken away. A flurry of urgent motions and resolutions ensue: A reward is offered for the head of Dumouriez; and all the relatives of the officers of his army are to be apprehended to serve as hostages. Forty thousand men shall be raised in Paris and the neighboring towns, for the purpose of defending the capital, and Marquis de Dampierre is invested with the chief command of the Army of the North and the Armée des Ardennes (the army in Belgium).

The army must be answerable to the people. But a great army cannot be directed, nor can the nation's security be overseen, by a legislature. After various speeches, a committee is adopted. This committee, composed of nine members, is to deliberate in private. The Convention charges it to consolidate and to increase the function and the action of executive power; the Convention even authorizes it to suspend the Convention's own resolutions when the committee deems them contrary to the general interest, and to be responsible for addressing all urgent matters and events and to take all necessary actions and measures to ensure the internal security and external defense of the Republic. The Convention decrees that all resolutions signed by the majority of the committee's members shall constitute the proper and lawful exercise of executive power. The committee is authorized to issue orders of arrest.

And now Camille begins to see that that his friend Danton, returned to the tribune, is speaking with a kind of joy, as this is what he has been advocating. All at once he is demanding such measures that only a dictatorship can produce: a calling of all the people to the defense, and fixing a maximum price upon bread. Now the Convention seems filled with the energy and spirit such as is the aspiration of an army, the certitude that with discipline and authority all things can be done.

Near midnight Danton states, with great satisfaction, "This committee is precisely what we want, a hand to grasp the weapon of the Revolutionary Tribunal."

Yet in naming the committee they deliberately eschew reference to executive function; it shall be known by the banal "Committee of Public Safety," and its term shall be one month and one day.

Who will comprise the Committee of Public Safety? The consensus, it seems, is that the Convention needs men of action. And thus the names that Camille hears read out after midnight are all Jacobins, Danton among them.

It is resolved that the Committee of Public Safety will act in coordination with the Committee of General Security (commonly called the Police Committee). The Convention formed the latter in October 1792 for the purpose of ensuring the internal security of France and to protect the Republic from both external and internal enemies—but up to now its presence has been occult, and its activities have not made much difference.

Finally, before adjournment, Danton rises a final time. He shouts, "People may condemn me as they please. I do not care. I care that the Republic be saved, not to be loved by the benighted people!"

April 7, 1793: The hall falls silent. Why? Marat is ascending to the tribune. His skin disease has progressed and his health has grown worse. Shirtless beneath his ragged waistcoat, he now appears nearly as a walking corpse just climbed out of its grave. Where once the majority of the Convention would have heckled and shouted vitriol at him, they all now sit silent, waiting for him to speak. For pity? No. It is because Marat has best foreseen and foretold France's perils, both within and from without; and the authoritarian regime that is now coalescing here is the regime that Marat all along has prescribed. Among the deputies, only he has preached the truth. The question now is: who will prevail, Girondins or Mountaineers? Upon reaching the tribune, he straightens his back, stands erect, and with his right hand firmly grips the right edge.

Straight away he gets to his purpose; he says, in a rasping, singsong voice, "I move that the Convention revoke the deputies' immunity from prosecution; that the Convention may prosecute any of its members against whom there are strong presumptions of complicity with the enemies of freedom, of equality, and of the republican government." The imprecise, malleable description of the offenses targeted can only mean that Marat intends not a means for prosecuting enemies of the state, but a weapon aimed at political enemies of the Mountain. Yet the motion carries, supported on right and left; Camille votes yes. Kill or be killed, indeed!

Next Robespierre returns to the tribune, announcing the practical, predictable application of the decree just issued. "I demand that every one of the whole Orléans family, known as Égalité, be brought before the Revolutionary Tribunal. I further move that the tribunal be made responsible for investigating and prosecuting all of Dumouriez's accomplices." The motions carry (Camille votes yes), and thus the apprehension and transfer to the prison of Marseilles of Philip of Orléans and all his family is decreed. Camille looks at Philippe Égalité; he can only pity him, though his own treachery for his cousin Capet is being visited upon him now. He is suspected by the Jacobins and the Girondins alike, and accused of conspiring with everybody because he conspired with nobody, notwithstanding his demonstrable and important support for the revolution, and his voluntary abasement, relinquishing the very title Duke of Orléans. Nobody can do anything to save him.

CHAPTER 31

WHEN HE HEARS LUCILE greet Robespierre at the front door, Camille gets up and hides his glass of cognac in a cupboard. A visit from Robespierre is not unusual, and Camille often drops in on his old friend's apartment. But whenever Max calls on them, it is for a purpose, and Camille and Lucile are anxious to present a tidy appearance and avoid distractions.

Usually, Lucile will take the baby to Danton's place. Horace is Robespierre's godson, but how much patience does he have for a bawling baby? Who could know? For not even Camille can say. But today, Horace is sound asleep. So, Lucile joins the men in the fine and impeccable drawing room financed by her dowry. She will only listen, intently.

These past few months, Robespierre has turned paler and thinner. His usual formal and proper (almost ridiculously so) costume hangs still more loosely on his frame, and dark shades are embedded about his now deeper-set eyes. A true revolutionary must neither eat nor sleep, it seems.

Robespierre greets Camille and is seated. He spends almost no time on pleasantries. "There can be no doubt now," he says, "Marat has been right all along. But some of us always knew that he was right. We couldn't say so and achieve what we've now accomplished, so we let him say what had to be said, even if it required us to pretend to be disapproving. Now he's the people's hero. So be it. I did not enter politics to be a hero, and now we have gotten the Convention to a place where we can do good things for the people. We must ask ourselves, Camille, what have been our ultimate objectives? What did we set out to accomplish? It seems that not everyone who called themselves patriots have been of the same mind. I am talking about true patriots like the two of us, not the likes of Mirabeau. What has been our objective? Our undertaking has been for the greatest part of the people, for the poor; those who have been most oppressed. But what we have learned is that the revolution itself has attracted enemies of the people, those who wish to elevate themselves on the backs of the people, merely replacing the royalty and the old nobility with a new aristocracy. Well, you and I have not sacrificed everything—indeed, perhaps ultimately our very lives—to replace the royalty and the nobles with wealthy merchants and landowners."

Camille winces at this mention that they may give their lives for the revolution. He has never intended to die for the revolution, and would avoid doing so at all costs. It is disconcerting that lately Robespierre has been obsessed with death, to the point of apparent madness. He has told Camille that he is convinced he will soon be assassinated, and in his speeches at the Jacobin Club he has repeatedly offered himself for martyrdom.

Recently, Camille heard him shout, "We know how to die, and we will all die!" ("All! All!" everyone shouted around the hall. But Marat stood up and said, "No! We are not going to die; we will give death to our enemies, we will erase them!" For the first time, Camille felt actual affection for Marat.) In a subsequent speech Robespierre declared, "One republican who knows how to die can exterminate all the despots!" Camille is skeptical that his or Robespierre's death would solve any of the revolution's daunting problems.

Now, Robespierre continues, "It is more of the same tyranny. That is what has happened in Britain, in America. What have the so-called revolutions in those places accomplished? Nothing. They have replaced one tyranny with another. All the ambitious persons who have until now appeared in the theater of revolution have had this in common: they defend the rights of the people for only as long as seems necessary. All have regarded the people as a stupid herd, destined to be led by the most able or the strongest. As in America and Britain, here they have regarded that the true power ought to lie with those who own property. Before, the power was hereditary; now it lies with the wealthy, those who have become rich by whatever means. It is no less oppressive. To them, the first social law is the right of property ownership. They have cared nothing for the rest of the people, they have cared only for themselves, and they have been wrong. It is not true that property can ever be held by a man in opposition to another man's subsistence. The first social law is that which guarantees the means of existence to all members of society; all other laws are subordinate to this one; property is only instituted or guaranteed to affirm it."

Camille has heard all of this before, in Robespierre's speeches especially to the Jacobin Club and also in the Convention. This was the rationale for the law of price control for wheat and flour, *le maximum*. The Convention has decreed that each département is required to fix the prices for these goods at a fraction of market prices, and then to police the system: every farmer and trader is required to declare the inventory of cereals in his possession, and the local police force is empowered to inspect his premises without warning to verify the accuracy of the disclosures. Anyone convicted of misrepresenting his inventory, or hiding cereals, will face a possible sentence to the guillotine.

Camille wonders what will happen to supplies without the market to establish a price that justifies production. These measures enacted ostensibly to benefit the poor have ensured that the Jacobins are backed by the *sans-culottes*, which was their overriding motivation, not per se to help the poor. The Jacobins themselves have personally sacrificed nothing for the poor, and nobody can predict the long-term consequences of the price controls.

Camille would very much like to say such things to Robespierre right now, and to Saint-Just, Marat, and the *sans-culottes* in the Convention and the Jacobin Club. But he does not intend to die for the revolution—the safer course is to go along, even though he is quite sure that Robespierre would protect him simply because of their shared history.

"Naturally," continues Robespierre, "those who hold the property will not willingly part with it. Property required for sustenance of all the people must be forcibly redistributed. This is the crux of Marat's message, which we have known all along is right."

Yes. Camille has recently heard Robespierre begin to echo Marat's exhortations; he, Robespierre, now urging the *sans-culottes* to rise up against those who claim property as established by the old regime, or by even their own superior efforts, which by universal justice belongs to all of society: "You have aristocrats in the Sections; drive them out! You have your freedom to preserve; proclaim the rights of your freedom, and make use of all your energy. You have an immense people of *sans-culottes*, so pure, so vigorous; they cannot get away from their work, so let them be paid for by the rich!"

"We have come a long way," says Robespierre, "and we are rightfully proud of our progress. But there is much more to do, as the people continue to suffer. And what grieves me is that under the current system we have done all that we can do. There is nothing more that we can accomplish in a divided Convention. We need to control fully the passage of laws in order to accomplish our ambitious objectives, which we pursue only on behalf of the people. We've tried hard to get everyone to follow our program, but there still are those who have regarded representative assemblies as bodies composed of men either greedy or credulous, who can be corrupted or tricked into serving their criminal projects. We cannot allow such pursuit of corrupt personal interests to defeat the revolution. We must put a stop to their criminal projects by any means necessary."

Yes, the Girondins' "criminal projects." Camille has heard Robespierre elucidate the Girondins' treasons. For weeks, Robespierre has been repeatedly accusing them of disloyalty. Camille remembers everything, how this came to pass: Robespierre himself had joined Danton in declaring full confidence in Dumouriez and his conduct of the war. But when the general turned traitor,

Robespierre, recognizing he was exposed, went on the offensive, and accused Brissot and his allies of complicity with the treachery of Dumouriez.

He spoke of plots and hidden enemies: "If you wish, I will raise a corner of the veil." "Raise it all!" came cries in response. He described a web of conspiracy against France that linked Pitt, Dumouriez, the Girondins, property owners, and merchants in France bent on retaining their assets, and the émigré nobility working to recover their *ancien régime* status.

Here Camille cannot contain himself. "Max, I would be surprised if Brissot and Pétion are conspiring with Pitt, or Dumouriez, or our other enemies. I agree with you that their purpose is to protect the rich and property rights. But I can't picture them being disloyal. We have all known one another for a very long time. You and they were witnesses at my wedding. Do you have proof that they are traitors?"

Robespierre's eyes open wide, his brows a high-arch. "What more proof do I need? You have seen it. Their own actions in the Convention have betrayed them. Their actions and objectives are in concert with the endeavors of France's enemies. Their aims are the same—to restore the *ancien régime*. Dumouriez and Brissot were the first apostles of the war, a war that has only put the revolution at risk, nearly destroyed it. Not only that, you have heard them say they intend to pursue us to death, to have our heads, literally."

Yes, Camille remembers, in the Convention: Pétion: "It is time at last to end all this infamy; it is time that traitors and perpetrators of calumny carried their heads to the scaffold; and here I take it upon myself to pursue them to death." Robespierre: "Stick to the facts." Pétion: "It is you whom I will pursue." Uproar ensued and then the painter David rushed to the middle of the Manége, ripped opened his shirt and, pointing to his bare breast, cried, "Strike here! I propose my own assassination! I, too, am a man of virtue! Liberty will win in the end!"

Alas, Pétion's great weakness has always been his quick temper and his wrath. But Camille can empathize; Robespierre has sorely tried the patience of his political opponents. The Convention is going insane, thinks Camille. Now among the deputies themselves, it is kill or be killed.

"Our most dangerous enemies," says Robespierre, "are among us, not on the front lines." Robespierre pauses and, now looking eye to eye with Camille, he says, "Camille, we need your pen again. Like last time, with the king."

"Max, what could I add? You have exposed the Girondin conspiracy better than I ever could."

Lucile gives him an imploring look.

"Camille, you are smarter than any of us. We need to take our complaint against the Girondins to the next level, to the masses. We need a pamphlet. We need a published document that the *sans-culottes* will take to their homes and to the tavern. We need to mobilize the great mass of the people against our political enemies. And we need you to explain the evidence thoroughly and systematically. Use your mastery of the pen and your legal training."

"I don't know if there is proof that the Girondins are disloyal."

Lucile has been holding the imploring look, and here her look turns dark and disapproving.

"Camille, you are France's most gifted journalist. I'm not going to tell you how it's done. You will weave a narrative with specific reference to events, and documentation that I will provide, that will be credible to the masses, like you did with the king. The object here is to persuade, and, after all, the people believe what they want to believe. What is truth, after all? The object of free speech is that in politics there be winners and losers. As we have seen, the written word is our most potent weapon. Your stammer keeps you silent in the Convention and at the Jacobin Club, but it is your special gift for writing that enables you to contribute to our movement in the most meaningful way."

Camille feels himself blushing hotly, and Lucile is looking at him incredulously.

"I must go," says Robespierre, standing. "I am sure your pamphlet will be marvelous. If you see Danton, give him my best."

Camille is seated at his desk, blank pages and an inkwell before him, and pen in hand. Near at hand are Roland's personal papers confiscated by the Jacobins after he resigned as Minister of the Interior, two days after the king was executed. Morning light pours into the study through the oblong window beside him. Outside, the clattering of horse hooves and wheels creaking; human sounds; a sudden flight of birds.

He must get himself into a frame of mind to undertake this task—with zeal—that Robespierre has assigned him, and to produce a document that is effective, that will achieve the desired result.

Lucile has impressed upon him that he must do this. He has no choice; he must do it for her and for their son Horace. His first duty is to keep himself safe and free, in order to keep them safe. Could he return to the practice of law? What does that even entail in this age? He was never a dedicated or even really competent lawyer. Indeed, could he even just walk away from the revolution now, spurning Robespierre? Surely that would not be possible.

He spoke to Danton about this, but Georges is self-absorbed; absorbed with his own Committee of Public Safety; absorbed with sweet young Louise, his new lover. Danton is ever the pragmatist: once again, this time shrugging, tipping his head, hands splayed, meaning, *What else can you do, Camille?* This reaction, in relation to the gravity of the matter at hand, sums up the character of the man.

Pen in hand, Camille begins to write, filling the blank pages before him. He develops a new narrative of the French Revolution, one that recasts and interprets the words and actions of the Girondins as naturally intended to undermine the Republic, cause its collapse, and replace it with a new edifice of privileged classes and even royalty aligned with France's enemies in Europe and Britain—that will rest on the backs of the *sans-culottes*.

While claiming to be motivated by love and virtue, the Girondins' true objectives have been to spare the king from the guillotine in order that he may be restored to the throne, and they have supported merchants, private property, and free markets in order to restore the old aristocracy and expand it with new elements. This explains their approach to politics, which so closely resembles the clandestine politics of the royalty's regimes: they conduct their politics in private; they use their positions of power to promote their own interests and those of other elites; they regard themselves as superior to the *sans-culottes* because of education and wealth, thereby justifying the dispensing of patronage to their friends, and their use of resources that belong to the public to support their nefarious activities which are motivated only by corruption, ambition, and egoism.

He makes good use of Roland's papers, citing many instances of secret meetings and plans for hidden political campaigns in their and their friends' interests, and against the wellbeing of the *sans-culottes*. It was Girondins, after all, who plunged France into the wars that are now the means by which its enemies seek to crush the revolution, annihilate the Republic, and restore the *ancien régime*. Indeed, the Girondins themselves have vowed to pursue their enemies, who are the true patriots, to the death.

Step by step, Camille develops the narrative, finally arriving naturally at the charge that the Girondins are traitors against France who have secretly been in league with the king, the Holy Roman Empire, Britain, Pitt, and Dumouriez. How else to explain their actions?

He sits back and reads his work, reaching with his pen and refining it here and there. He sighs, recognizing that there is not a shred of evidence to support the conclusion. He must rationalize the lack of evidence, which he can do, for failure of proof is in the very nature of a conspiracy, is it not? He writes, *It is absurd to ask for hard evidence and judicial proofs that one has never had. Not even in the conspiracy of Catiline, for conspirators have never been in the habit of letting evidence against themselves be open to discovery.*

He admires these lines. He cannot resist the allusion to Catiline, who conspired against the Roman Republic in the first century B.C., though none of the *sans-culottes* will know whereof he speaks.

Now reminding himself that his pen has the power, by its artistry, to bring his words into being, into reality, he writes:

> *I bring to light that the party of the right in the Convention, and principally the leaders, are nearly all partisans of royalty, accomplices in the treason of Dumouriez, directed by the agents of Pitt, of d'Orléans, and of Prussia, and of having wanted to divide France into twenty or thirty federalist republics, or rather to overturn it, for never in history has there been a conspiracy for which there is more proof, and with a host of still more violent presumptions, than this conspiracy, which I call that of the Brissotins because Brissot has been at the heart of it.*

He rereads the entire text, feeling an internal throb of satisfaction upon each word. He is trembling with pleasure and excitement. The text finished, he adds the title, a sudden inspiration: *Fragment of the Secret History of the Revolution.*

CHAPTER 32

CAMILLE IS SEIZED BY a condition of egotism that recurs, supposing that he himself has been the cause of the unprecedented scene before him and events developing outside the Convention's chamber. No legislature has ever met in the conditions that the National Convention does now: A mob of insurrectionists, each wearing his red cap and carmagnole, crowd the floor below them; outside, the Tuileries complex and the gardens are filled and surrounded by a great crowd, roughly estimated at one hundred thousand strong, mostly also decked in red cap and carmagnole.

From outside, the tocsin peals and drums beat incessantly. Today, June 2, 1793, the deputies sit facing the president in a tiered semi-circle. The Convention is meeting at its new home—the refurbished theater for the Tuileries Palace. Gone are the velvet curtains and drapes at the stage and windows, chandeliers, gold leaf, flowery frescos, and the curves of artfully detailed boxes. Now every surface and edge is plain: right angles and straight lines and planes. Upon the stage there stands an immense rectangular tribune draped with tricolor. Behind the president now standing at the tribune hang vertically three gigantic tricolor flags. Also upon the stage there are plaster statues of Brutus, of Rousseau, and of the martyred Jacobin Lepelletier, assassinated on January 20, the eve of the king's execution, at a restaurant in the Palais-Royal.

It is being murmured around the hall that Marat, who is absent ostensibly while stricken by a flare-up of his skin disease, has climbed the tower of the Hôtel de Ville and rings the tocsin with

236

his own hand. Paris is barricaded all around; all of Paris is under arms and watchful.

Upon the tribune are papers from which the president—Jean Hérault de Séchelles, the young, rich, and popular deputy who has just been appointed to the governing Committee of Public Safety—is reading aloud the text of a demand that the Convention hand over, to the forces laying siege to it outside, twenty-two traitorous Girondins—the leaders and most popular ones, namely Brissot, Buzot, Louvet, Barbaroux, Guadet, Condorcet, Pétion, Rabaut St. Etienne and others. These are the same purportedly conspirators identified in Camille's pamphlet, *Fragment of the Secret History of the Revolution.*

Indeed, examining the recent timeline and links in the chain of causation reveals that it is not without reason that Camille credits himself for what is transpiring; or blames himself—for Camille is, himself, in terror at what today transpires.

On May 17, the Jacobin Club published Camille's pamphlet and distributed it to all of the sections of the Paris Commune. Next day, the Convention was in a tumult, the galleries filled with protestors brandishing Camille's pamphlet and shouting, demanding justice for Brissot and the other "traitors."

Thusly goaded, the Girondin Isnard, drunk as usual, seized the tribune and, amid violent interruptions, purported to lay down a Girondin ultimatum, recklessly indifferent to his party's means to follow through: "If ever the Convention were physically threatened, if ever by one of those insurrections that have been so unceasingly repeated—if by these incessant insurrections—any violent attack should be made on the national representatives, I tell you, in the name of all France that Paris would be annihilated—the traveler will seek along the shores of the Seine whether Paris had ever existed!" Howls and catcalls ensued from the galleries and the Mountain, inviting Girondins to proceed and try to do to Paris as the Roman Republic did to Carthage.

Emboldened, and enraged, the Girondins—still perceiving themselves in the majority within the Convention, whether or not in control of the streets—arrested Jean-Francois Varlet, the so-called Apostle of Liberty and a Paris section president. He was torn from his warm bed at midnight, his alleged crime the making of declarations and patriotic songs to insult the Convention.

They arrested Jacques Hébert, his alleged crime being an offensive article in his paper *Le Père Duchesne*, named after his alter ego, a fictional *sans-culotte*. Hébert is not just a radical and vulgar journalist posing as a *sans-culotte*; he is also the deputy procureur of the Paris Commune. His arresters came to the Hôtel de Ville to seize him; quick to obey the rule of law, though the law be unjust, like Socrates he acquiesced, taking leave of his colleagues while bearing a martyr's mien of high solemnity.

Then demands from section upon section of the Paris Commune came hurtling forth for the prisoners' prompt release, and the Convention promptly obliged.

Still, on May 26, Robespierre stood before the Jacobin Club: "When the people are oppressed," he roared, "when it has nothing left except itself, then only a coward would not tell it to rise up. When all the laws are broken, when despotism is at its peak, when good faith and modesty are trampled underfoot, that is the time when the people should rise up. That time has arrived!" Women and men raged from all the galleries, in the Jacobin Club, and in the Convention.

Meanwhile, a "Central Committee" of all the forty-eight sections of revolutionary Paris coalesced in dreadful deliberation within l'Évêché, the former Archbishop's Palace, looming huge and ominous, presaging a new August 10. In these occult proceedings, the Central Committee commenced to send resolutions to the Paris Commune at the Hôtel de Ville, while in turn receiving resolutions from the forty-eight satellite sections.

On May 31, around noon, the Convention was in session, and suddenly the deputies heard a report of the alarm-gun, and the tocsin began to peal; mingled with these were the tempest-sounds of a multitude arriving outside the hall. The alarm-gun is placed on the Pont Neuf, and whoever fired it without a decree from the Convention granting leave committed a crime carrying penalty of death.

Scarcely had the alarm-gun sounded than red-capped, official-looking men, accompanied by a regiment of ninety-six red-capped men bearing arms, arrived and proceeded to the tribune, introducing themselves as Commissioners from the Insurrectionary Administration of the Department of the Seine. They were also Paris Mayor Jean-Nicholas Pache with other Municipality or Commune officials. It is well known in the Convention that the mayor is a friend of Marat's, and holds great enmity for the Girondins. He brought shocking and bizarre news.

The mayor described how early that morning, while he sat in deliberations with his staff, there entered the same ninety-six armed men, previously unknown to the mayor and his staff. They declared themselves to be plenipotentiary commissioners acting as representatives of the forty-eight revolutionary sections of Paris; that the sections and their constituents were all in a state of insurrection; and that they were here on behalf of the Sovereign in Insurrection to dismiss from office the entire municipal government.

The mayor and his staff removed their sashes, which constituted the official part of their dress, and withdrew into an adjacent salon. Yet hardly a moment passed before the ninety-six called them back, and reinstated them, informing the mayor and his staff that the Sovereign had deliberated and decided that they were worthy and qualified to hold a new and improved office, Insurrectionary Magistrates, and so the insurrectionaries administered a new oath of office.

The mayor now therefore declared himself and his companions to be Insurrectionary Magistrates in combination with the Committee of Ninety-six. The mayor read out threatening demands to the Convention: A charge sheet against twenty-two named traitorous Girondin deputies; expansion of the Revolutionary Tribunal; the creation of a revolutionary army of *sans-culottes* in every town of France, including twenty thousand men in Paris; the establishment of workshops for the manufacture of arms for the *sans-culottes*;

bread to cost no more than three sous per pound; the purging of all administrations; the disarmament, arrest, and condemnation of all suspected traitors; voting rights to be restricted to *sans-culottes*; the establishment of workshops for the old and infirm; the exaction of forced loans from the rich; and the immediate payment of bonuses to defenders of the country.

They added that armed forces were peaceably traversing the city and arriving at the Tuileries grounds; and that all the insurrectionary authorities would come in a body in the course of the day to make known to the Convention their convictions and their demands. Strictest order was being observed, they said, and every soldier had sworn to respect and to enforce respect for persons and property.

Also, the mayor read a note from the provisional commandant of the post at the Pont Neuf. The deputies learned that a new Provisional Commandant-General was appointed: one Hanriot, devoted to the Commune, and previously commandant of a battalion of *sans-culottes*. Hanriot gave orders to fire the alarm-gun; but the commanding officer of the post refused his order, demanding a decree from the Convention. Hanriot sent his emissaries back in force, they overcame the resistance of the post, and fired the alarm-gun.

Exclaimed Vergniaud, "Whatever be the issue of the conflict which may this day take place, it would lead to the loss of liberty. Let us swear then to adhere firmly to our duty and to die at our posts rather than desert the public cause."

A large majority of the delegates then immediately rose with acclamations, and took the oath proposed by Vergniaud. Camille was not among them.

Someone shouted a demand that a search should be made for the commandant-general who had had the impudence to order the firing of the alarm-gun, and that he be summoned here, to the bar.

Practically the entire hall silenced him with shouts to shut up.

Then Danton appeared at the tribune and immediately the hall fell silent. No doubt every Girondin and many a Mountaineer alike were wondering about his role in the events of the day. After all, the Committee of Public Safety, also known as the Danton Committee, now ostensibly the supreme governing authority in France, had done nothing in reaction to the insurrection.

"I address myself," cried Danton, "to those men only who have some notion of our situation, and not to those stupid creatures who, in these great movements, can listen to nothing but their passions. Hesitate not then to satisfy the people!"

"What people?" asked a member on the right.

"That people," cried Danton, "that immense people, which is our advanced sentry for progress, which bears a bitter hatred for tyranny and to that base conservatism which would bring it back. Hasten to satisfy it; save it from the aristocrats, save it from its own fury; and if, when, it shall be satisfied, perverse men, no matter to what party they belong, shall strive to prolong a movement that is become useless, Paris itself will reduce them to their original nothingness."

Then Robespierre, risen from yet another sickbed, stepped up to the tribune. Wracked by whatever it was that now ailed him—his cheeks and eyes were darkened hollow, the feverish eyes burning within the sockets, his whole countenance otherwise pale to whiteness—he paused, and wavered.

"Conclude then!" shouted Vergniaud impatiently.

Replied Robespierre, "Yes, I shall conclude, and do so against you. Against you who, after the revolution of August 10 wanted to bring to the scaffold those who had accomplished it, against you who have never ceased to provoke the destruction of Paris, against you who wanted to save the tyrant, against you who conspired with Dumouriez, against you who have rabidly pursued the same patriots whose heads Dumouriez demanded, against you whose criminal vengeance has provoked the same cries of indignation that you want to proscribe in those who are your victims. Ah yes! My conclusion is the decree of accusation against all the accomplices of Dumouriez and all those whom the petitioners have designated," referring to the twenty-two traitorous Girondins identified by Camille in his *Secret History*.

After this, Robespierre returned to his seat and collapsed heavily and with great ceremony.

After long and contentious debate, it was ten o'clock at night, and now the past two nights the Convention has gone home while remaining deadlocked over the demand for the twenty-two Girondin deputies alleged to be traitors.

Now, today, June 2, the deputies are prisoners in the hall, surrounded by the one hundred thousand led by Hanriot and his army, who won't let them leave. At the tribune stands the Girondin Lanjuinais, who is defiant. "I come," he says, "to submit to you the means of quelling the new commotions with which you are threatened!"

From the Mountain come shouts: "Down! Down! He wants to produce a civil war."

"Thus far," resumes Lanjuinais, "you have done nothing, you have suffered everything; you have sanctioned all that was required of you. An insurrectional assembly meets, it appoints a committee charged to prepare a revolt, a provisional commandant charged to head the revolters: and all this you suffer!"

The hall is in such an uproar, deputies from the Mountain howling so loudly, and Girondins shouting in support, that Camille cannot hear what else he has to say. Suddenly several deputies of the Mountain—Drouet, Robespierre's younger brother Augustin, Julien, and Legendre—storm the tribune. They take hold of Lanjuinas and try to drag him away, but he clings to it tenaciously.

At last the president, Hérault Séchelles, gains the tribune and is able to command the attention of the hall. "The scene which has just taken place," he says, "is most afflicting. Liberty will perish, if you continue to behave thusly. I call you to order, you who have made such an attack on that tribune!"

Some degree of order is restored, and Lanjuinais moves that the revolutionary authorities of Paris be dissolved—meaning, that the unarmed Convention should take control of the armed one hundred thousand.

Yet before the Convention can address this superfluous motion, the mayor and his entourage appear again. This time they speak calmly and resolutely: "The citizens of Paris have been under arms for these four days. For four days past they have been claiming of their representatives their rights, unworthily violated; and for four days past their representatives have been laughing at their calmness and their inaction. It is necessary to put the conspirators in a state of provisional arrest: it is necessary to save the people forthwith, or the people will save themselves!"

There ensues a lively debate, culminating in a vote that within three days the Paris Commune will present their recommendations to the Convention.

"You do not have three days!" the mayor cries, now losing his calm and shouting. "If you do not hand them over, you will all be forcibly put under arrest!" Upon which they withdraw from the hall.

Now Isnard and three other deputies among the twenty-two who have lost their nerve mount the tribune and tender their resignations. Each says that the Convention is no longer free to rule in any event, and expresses hope that his resignation will be enough to mollify the insurrectionists.

Then President Hérault-Séchelles rises. He is unusually somber, though resolute. "We cannot leave this place whether openly or in stealth," he says. "Neither through the doors or the windows; the guns are leveled at us as we deliberate here; we cannot freely express our positions or beliefs. It is our duty to assert our authority that we are granted by all the people in France to govern. I propose that the whole Convention go forth out of this place as a body, to show our unity, even in defiance of the armed forces, to show we are determined to retain our authority, and to satisfy ourselves that we have nothing to fear and that our authority is still recognized and respected."

Now the whole right side rises, shouting agreement, and the Plain follows suit. Camille remains seated; he has no intention of following them. The Mountaineers around him also remain seated and Camille intends to retain his life. The lone exception is Danton, who rises and then joins President Hérault-Séchelles, who is now declaring himself the head of the procession. Seemingly they are alike aware that this day history is being made, and of their place in that history.

Those gathering behind him are issuing jeers at the Mountain. "Cowards!" one shouts. "Now the people will see who are the real patriots, who is prepared to die for the Republic!"

The Montagne, overcome by the others' goading, and shame for remaining behind, yet still unmoving, are finally drawn from their perch, when Danton calls to them, "Come with us, comrades. It is necessary that we all follow the president. None must be seen to cower here. All of us must confront the power and resolve of the sovereign people, whatever our persuasion."

Reluctantly they rise and join the rear of the procession, Camille and even Robespierre among them. Camille understands. No one can be sure what meaning will be taken if anyone remains behind.

Meanwhile, Paine is not at the Convention. He is in Saint-Denis, where he has found a refuge from the tempest he was enduring practically alone. He lives here with like-minded expatriates, all English, and has ceased attending the Convention sessions altogether. The house is large enough that it has operated as a hotel. His personal living space, which he has all to himself, is comprised of three rooms—one for wood, water, cleanliness; another is the bedroom, and beyond it there is a sitting room which looks into the garden through a glass door.

On the other side of this door is a small landing surrounded by a railing. This is where he and Charlotte Smyth are now seated in wrought-iron chairs, a similarly constituted table before them. Nearby, a staircase descends, nearly hidden by vines. Here he may descend to the garden and then to the street without going down the stairs inside and through the house.

Charlotte already has often come to visit him, and he has by this route escorted her to his apartment undetected. The Smyths being among the financiers of his current living arrangement, she is well familiar with these premises. The house and its courtyard are enclosed from the street by a wall and gateway, and Charlotte has a key, so she is able to let herself in and out through the gate as needed. They have spent the nights in sleeping together, her coach parked a discreet distance from the house.

Now, on this June 2, when Paine hears news of what is transpiring at the Convention, he takes leave of Charlotte immediately. His lover bids him farewell in tears, pleading that he not risk his life, or better yet, that he stay with her. News of the insurrection has reached the outskirts of Paris, and now more news: Madame Roland is under arrest, by some mischief called a Central Insurrection Committee, and her husband has fled to the provinces to exactly where no one knows. She is imprisoned in the prison de l'Abbéy.

Paine is now coming to the Convention in a cab. He is enraged, and rage is the surest counteractant to fear. He arrives at the Tuileries Palace grounds mid-afternoon. Approaching the palace precincts, he sees a great crowd far as the eye can see. Departing the cab, he makes his way through *sans-culotte* men and women, mean and mostly armed. He is handed a red cap, which he takes gratefully and puts on his head.

He sees everywhere that they have been encamped here for days. Because of all the tightly packed bodies, camp gear, and weapons, he makes his way with difficulty. He sees that the municipality has been well prepared for this siege of the Convention—camp furnaces are liberally distributed, and prevalent food carts are the source of victuals circulating everywhere unbidden to ensure that none of the one hundred thousand strong need go home to eat. There are temporary outhouses. Among the crowd are female patriots, whom the Girondins call Megaeras—with disorderly serpent hair, who have exchanged the distaff for the dagger. They are of "the Society called Brotherly," which meets at the Jacobin Club.

Paine reaches the front of the crowd, nearest the Convention, and here National Guardsmen and armed volunteers bristle, with fixed bayonets and cannon. They should be resisting invasion at the Austrian front or quelling uprisings in La Vendée, but they will not go or stay there, and the government is powerless to punish real treason or desertion.

Their commander is visible above the ranks, sitting atop a war-horse prancing among the ranks, amid a plumed and mounted cadre. Paine has heard of the commander before. His name is François Hanriot, and this is the summit of his life's ambition. Hanriot was born to poor parents in Paris, servants to aristocrats; he was once a peddler and a shopkeeper and then a soldier in America under Lafayette; returning to Paris, he was eventually an orator for a local section of *sans-culottes*. He was a section leader in the September Massacres and his involvement in those mass murders gained him his place as a soldier in the National Guard in Paris, rising to the rank of captain.

Rage drives Paine, and he has every intention of accessing the Convention, to address the Convention and the galleries, to demand a stop to what he has heard is going on within the hall. He has heard that the Convention is being held prisoner in its own hall until it acquiesces to the insurrectionaries' demands for the arrests of twenty-two allegedly traitorous Girondins. Yet he has hardly formulated in his mind what he will say. Arriving at the east-side door, his entry is blocked by two sentries from the National Guard.

"Halt! Who goes there?" The voice is from behind. He turns, and a plumed Hanriot is there, sitting on his warhorse and silhouetted by the slanting sun.

"I am Thomas Paine," he says in French.

"I know you," says Hanriot in English.

Paine brandishes the document bearing his credentials. "I am a delegate to the National Convention," he says, "I am entitled to enter."

"You may as well use it as curlpaper in your hair."

Paine is turned facing Hanriot and all at once Danton is at his side. Danton says in English, "Paine, you must do as he says. Do not try to enter. Leave this place. Or you will find yourself among the twenty-two."

"You did this. Dictator! And what has your Danton Committee done to stop it?"

"It is the people, and there is nothing I can do. Revolutions cannot be made with rosewater, after all."

"Revolutions are like Saturn; they devour their own children."

Now Paine sees that more delegates are pouring forth from the hall, led by valiant Hérault-Séchelles; he is wearing a red cap of liberty, but the others are bare headed. They are moving as a body toward Hanriot and the other plumed horsemen, who are barricading their way.

Shouts the president, "In the name of the National Convention, make way!" Addressing the soldiers, he shouts, "Seize the rebel!" He is ordering Hanriot's men to seize their commander!

Hanriot does not make way. "I receive no orders," he barks, "till the sovereign people have been obeyed. You shall not leave this place till you have delivered up the twenty-two."

Still the Conventioneers press on, nearly reaching Hanriot. He pulls the bridles, and his horse steps back some fifteen paces, and he draws his flashing sword; the other cavalry do the same.

"To arms! Cannoneers, to your guns!" Hanriot shouts. The infantry level their rifles, readying to fire, the cannoneers stand at attention, lit torches brandished and poised, ready for the order to fire.

Danton takes hold of Hérault-Séchelles firmly by the arm and draws him another way. The Convention proceeds to the garden, and Paine sees their way is similarly obstructed. He hears shouts, "The nation forever!" "The Convention forever!" "Marat forever!" "Down with the right side!" The Convention changes course and is now advancing with purpose to the Pont Tournant. Here another battalion blocks its egress from the garden.

Suddenly Marat materializes with his own entourage, some one hundred red-capped boys, following, crying, "Marat forever!" and approaching the president. He shouts, "I summon the deputies who have quitted their post, to return to it." And the delegates, except for Paine, yielding to his survival instinct and a sharp look from Danton, obey. Paine returns to Saint-Denis feeling still lonelier and more ashamed.

———————

When the deputies return to their seats, they are to a man badly shaken. Couthon is on the stage, seated on his wheelchair by the tribune, having been carried there by two of Marat's acolytes.

"Does not the Convention," says Couthon, his face sober and severe, and voice resonant, "see that it is free. As you see, we are surrounded by friends."

More than anything, Camille hates mendacity. He wants to cover his face so he can hide his expression, whatever it may be. A fine outlet would be a bitter laugh, but he cannot laugh at this moment and place.

Thus the Convention, the hall overflowing with armed red-capped friends, and surrounded by friends on warhorse, at cannon, and bearing rifles, and yonder more friends brandishing daggers, clubs, and pistols, proceeds to vote as browbeaten. The Mountain is unanimous; some of the others issue brief protests; many remain in silent protest. When votes are counted, the outcome is that the denounced twenty-two—plus ex-ministers Clavière and Lebrun and others, and less three deputies exonerated by Marat for having been led astray—shall be under "arrestment in their own houses."

Brissot, Barbaroux, Vergniaud, Louvet, and others, thirty-two in all—for Marat has added and subtracted from the original demand, and there is a net gain of ten—all of them known as Girondins, are now escorted peaceably away by two armed police-friends each, all their other friends watching silently.

Camille sighs quietly. Now Robespierre has his wish; a Convention undivided, with singular purpose. No?

When Camille departs the Convention, he does so alone. Today he has had quite enough of Danton and Robespierre; one or the other is his usual companion as he makes his way home by cab or on foot, but not tonight. It is ten o'clock, and the night is starlit. No moon has risen. The hundred thousand are returning to their homes, their calling ended, and quiet is returning to the city and the palace grounds. But Camille is not at peace, his innards turbulent and he is troubled by a seed of secret shame.

CHAPTER 33

July 14, 1793: Robespierre has returned to Camille's drawing room, where he declines the cognac offered by Camille.

Marat is dead, slain by a woman. Everyone in Paris is talking about it. The assassin's name is Charlotte Corday. Yesterday, Corday insinuated herself into Marat's apartments, past his terrible sentinels, his women—his wife, her sister, and the cook. They told Corday to go away. Marat sat soaking in a medicinal bath to soothe his diseased skin. Then from the front door she cried out that she had information about an uprising against the Republic originating in Caen, her hometown. Hearing this, Marat ordered his women to let Corday come and see him.

Then she stabbed him through the heart while he sat in his bath.

"She is from Caen," says Robespierre. "It is no coincidence that she is from Caen. The Committee of General Security has learned that fugitive Girondins are gathering in Caen, planning an insurrection. Pétion and Barbaroux are there, defying the warrants for their arrests, staying in the hotel Mansion de l'Intendance. This barbarous act was the poisonous fruit of a Girondin conspiracy."

Camille can read the scheming in Robespierre's mind. Marat's assassination, and by the hand of a woman from Caen, gives rise to the opportunity to cast the Girondins not only as traitors, but also murderers of Marat, the beloved friend of the people! For this crime, as well as for their treasons, the Girondins must be dealt the most extreme punishment.

"Of course, that must be right," says Camille. Hard as it is to believe that Corday, a woman, acted alone, actually Camille is skeptical that the Girondins are behind this. Nothing could be more violently contrary to their character. They have been as defenseless and accepting of their lost liberty as sheep. For that matter, he is also skeptical that any real insurrection is brewing in Caen, just as he does not really believe that the Gironde are traitors.

"What does the assassin say?" says Camille. Charlotte Corday was apprehended at Marat's place and transported to the prison de l'Abbéy.

"She maintains that she acted alone. That is unbelievable. I want you to interview her, Camille. Use your journalist's technique, your legal training and your charms, your way with women. Get her story. We need the truth from her. Then you will expose her accomplices in one of your articles. You will introduce the story to the public, and your reputation will grow greater still."

"She will soon be tried. Then maybe we'll find out the real story."

"Yes. She'll soon be tried, so we don't have much time. I'm sorry, but I don't have great confidence that your cousin will expose her accomplices in the trial." The public prosecutor Fouquier-Tinville is a cousin of Camille's and obtained his job by nepotism; he is beholden to the Jacobins. "She is sticking to her story that she acted alone," Robespierre continues, "and I don't think he's up to getting her to confess the real story. We need you to get it from her. We can't put a woman to the torture, after all."

Actually, Camille can tell, Robespierre wants him to report a confession that incriminates the Girondins, whatever may transpire in the interview.

———————

Next morning, Camille arrives at the prison de l'Abbéy and is escorted to Charlotte Corday's cell. They are seated on the narrow bed inside her cell.

She is dressed to receive visitors—a tall, beautiful woman with pale skin and long chestnut-colored hair pleasingly decorated with blue ribbons. The forehead is beautifully shaped; the eyes a grayish blue, like the sky of Normandy; the painted lips are rich in curves, and ample; the chin square, appropriate for the boldness of her infamous act. She wears a fine gown—a loose white Indian muslin with blue spots and a low neckline. What he sees before him is in contrast to a popular myth that is developing.

Camille has seen that the Jacobins have posted across the city a text portraying a great ugliness:

> *This woman being called pretty is not pretty at all; she is a virago, chubby rather than fresh, slovenly, as female philosophers and sharp thinkers almost always are. It is generally true that any pretty woman who enjoys being pretty clings to life and fears death. Her head is stuffed with all sorts of books; she declared, or rather she confessed with an affectation bordering on the ridiculous, that she has read everything from Tacitus to the Portier des Chartreux. All these things mean that this woman has hurled herself completely outside of her sex.*

"I am Camille Desmoulins," he says. "I am a journalist and a delegate in the National Convention. I am happy to meet you." She is twenty-five, not so much younger than he is, and he hopes his comparable youth and his reputation will appeal to her.

But she does not react to his name, to seem to care or recognize it, or pay him much attention. She is impassive. He decides to begin with flattery, and he remarks on her beauty and tells her that she does not appear as the Jacobins have led him to expect.

This elicits a response. Her eyes widen, and darken. She says, "There is a movement in Paris that has tried to dispossess Charlotte Corday of her act, by stripping all of her feminine qualities: Hers is a monstrous and unnatural femininity that dares engage the greatness of Marat. And so they reaffirm the righteousness of my deed! The Jacobins cannot bear that I—Charlotte Corday, a woman—is the first of their enemies to have responded to their monstrous acts with a deed, not high-flown words. To Marat's appeals for blood,

I have responded with bloodshed. Though certainly it was not he himself who Marat had meant be killed! It is for this reason that my act is fully justified; only I, a woman, have in kind responded to their revolutionary ideology of deed over speech."

He is taken aback by the grandiosity of her speech, referring to herself in the third-person, and, most of all, the fluency and vigor of her words. Nor is this what he came for. Momentarily he is at a loss, but he does not take the bait. He asks her how she has been treated.

She says that she has, for three days, enjoyed a most delightful peace. Everyone has been wonderful. Her jailers have been kind enough to bring her every available newspaper; she has devoured the copious words that have been written about her—Charlotte Corday. They brought her needles and thread so she could repair her favorite dress which she wore to Marat's place—and which she is now wearing—and combs, dressings, ribbons, and a mirror, so she could fashion a decent coiffure. They have let her take baths.

She is talking a lot, and saying it well. She is indeed an educated woman. She notes the differing reactions of men and women. Among the women, she has been the object of fury presaged by the wailing and screaming of Marat's women the night that she slew him.

The Society of Revolutionary Republican Women have declared:

We will people the land of liberty with as many Marats as children borne by the Revolutionary Republican Women, we will raise these children in the cult of Marat, and swear to put in their hands no gospel other than Marat's works, with verses in his memory, and curse the infernal fury brought forth by the race of Caen.

"Marat as object of worship, as Christ figure, is amusing and reaffirming to me," she says. "If only these women understood the irony. Yet I forgive the women. They are frightened that I have aroused rampant male hatred of women, and it is their general lack of education and their ignorance, the outcome of male oppression, which explains their idolatry of Marat."

Camille has heard enough of this; she is not moving in a direction that will serve the object of his visit.

He says, "You killed Marat?"

"Yes, it is I who killed him."

"No pity, regret, no remorse?"

"I feel none."

He asks her to tell him what happened, to start at the beginning of what led her to Marat's place. But she begins with when she first laid eyes on Marat in his bath. Half of him was under the dirty water, and she was unable in any way to see the rest of him except for the torso, shins and feet, for lying across the bath's rim before him was a plank that he was using for a desk—upon it were papers, a pen, and a bottle of ink.

He bid her come near him, purring words to put her at ease, for this was his "office." She began to tell him about the Girondins in Caen. Her hand was then inside her bag; she felt for the bare blade and gripped the knife's handle. She moved toward him and, in a quick movement, slammed the knife into his chest, to the handle, and withdrew it—one swift movement. She dropped the weapon onto the makeshift desk, the blade glazed red. He must have cried out, for his wife, Simonne, returned, and she was screaming.

During the confusion immediately after she stabbed Marat, she thought briefly that she might escape. She moved quickly through his bedchamber and the corridor and made it to the vestibule, but two neighbors—men—coming in response to the screams, detained her. They knocked her to the floor, kicked her, and tore her favorite dress—finding her testament, tucked beside her bosom.

But they did not kill her; they did not even strike her. The men tied her hands behind her back with handkerchiefs, and she sat on the floor against the wall awaiting her fate. She did not expect to survive the night. It was then that she had to endure the agonized shrieks of Marat's women—Jeannette Maréchal, the cook, even brandishing at her the bloodied knife. The Commissioner of Police arrived, with some other police and a few soldiers of the

National Guard, and he formally put her under arrest.

The police interrogated first everyone else in the house, before questioning her. They took her into Marat's bedchamber, where the hideous corpse was laid, and she calmly confirmed that she had killed him.

It was past two in the morning when the police escorted her down the stairs. She heard the noisy crowd gathered outside in the hot night, and discerned from the sounds that they were mostly women. The doors were opened and the Commissioner of Police shouted that the crowd must yield, "in the name of the law!" And the crowd did as it was ordered and fell back. They loaded her into a waiting coach which took her straight to the prison de l'Abbéy. Realizing her destination, Charlotte was pleased, for here is where they keep Madame Roland.

"So, now will you tell me about how it was you came to Paris?" Camille asks.

She does not answer. He is aware that she came from Caen bearing a letter of introduction from the Girondin Charles Barbaroux, requesting that she be provided quick access to the Minister of the Interior. Ostensibly, she came to Paris on an errand for a friend from her school days, a nun who had emigrated to Switzerland and needed help restoring her pension that the Jacobins had cut off believing she was a royalist.

Camille thinks about dashing, young, devoted republican Barbaroux. He must be only a couple of years older than Corday, still in his twenties, and they would seem a well-matched couple. Involuntarily, he is aroused at the thought of Corday and Barbaroux as lovers, and Barbaroux with his worldly charms manipulating her into undertaking Marat's assassination. Perhaps she is so smitten with Barbaroux that she is pleased to die for his cause.

He continues, deciding to be more explicit, "Whom did you tell you planned to do this?"

"I told no one about my plan to kill Marat."

"No other person?"

"No."

"Who helped you make the plan?"

"Nobody. I carried out the entire enterprise alone, only on my own behalf."

"And for this deed you are prepared to die."

"I will die an honorable death, and for this, I am pleased to die."

"Then for what reason do you protect the men on whose behalf you killed Marat?"

"Nobody else was involved. There were no men. I acted alone."

"Y-you have confessed the crime. There are eyewitnesses. Y-y-your fate is sealed. Your accomplices should as well be pleased to die an honorable death. Just give us their names and perhaps you will receive some kind of a reprieve. I'm sure that the Revolutionary Tribunal will not be pleased to condemn a woman to death. But if you tell the whole truth, and still yourself cannot be spared, I will implore those who seek your death to let you die on your own terms." He is not sure what he means by that. It seems she is already dictating the terms of her death.

She meets his gaze and she stares; she has taken offense. "And thusly," she says at last, "do men such as yourself belittle me in the most profound way. You do not believe that I, Charlotte Corday—a woman—am capable of having planned and carried out Marat's killing without support and instruction from men. You are convinced that I was a mere instrument of men. I have reiterated that I acted alone, and there is no conspiracy, and I do so again—there was no Girondin plot to kill Marat.

"I have read the newspapers," she continues. "They claim I was backed by 'a faction of scoundrels,' 'enemies of the people.' No one is satisfied to have a mere woman of no consequence to offer to the spirit of a great man. I have now entered the Pantheon of history, and history will vindicate me. Because in truth, I did it alone. This is what you must put in your article. The night that I killed him I lay in here on my bed, and I heard from outside, '*Marat est mort! Assassiné par une femme du Caen!*' I smiled to myself at that."

He sees she is resolute and his mood has turned anxious. He hasn't the will to invent a conspiracy. And, in a sense, he is smitten by her. She is indeed beautiful, and she fixes him with triumphant eyes, lips swelled with anger. All at once he wants to kiss her here and now. He reaches out and takes a handful of her hair at the nape and, pulling her to him hard, he kisses her roughly.

She pulls back violently and spits in his face, from nearly point-blank range; he pulls her to him again, and they are cheek to cheek, wetted with spit and tears.

"Camille Desmoulins," she rasps, "I know who you are. I am a republican. I once thrilled to the storming of the Bastille. Philosopher, you have sold your soul to bestial men. You want to know why I killed him? I'll tell you, and give you a chance to redeem yourself. Then maybe you, too, can die an honorable death."

He lets go, and again she meets his gaze. Her eyes are now black. He wipes his face.

"I killed him to avenge my lover," she says.

"W-w-what happened to him?"

"A woman. She still lives. Her name is Eleonore de Faudoas."

"Where is she?"

"La Force Prison." Her head jerks suddenly, as though her own words hit her like a physical blow to the head.

"Why is she there?"

"She is a young woman. Her father, the Marquis de Faudoas, commanded a regiment of the Swiss on August 10. My aunt and I were their neighbors in Caen. He was retired and lived there with Eleonore, and his wife's sister. Eleonore's mother was the wife, who is deceased. When the situation for Louis XVI grew more dire, he returned to Paris and rejoined the king's guard."

"On August 10 the Swiss killed many citizens. It is the worst possible crime."

"Eleonore commanded no regiment! She is not a royalist! She believes as you do."

"The father is dead?"

"No. He survived the counter-attack and slaughter of the Swiss. He surrendered and was arrested. The three of them are at La Force. The father, the aunt, and Eleonore. The Revolutionary

Tribunal has yet to try them as there are a multitude awaiting trial."

"They now imprison entire families of the traitors, especially the worst ones. They are all charged as such. They are all regarded as subversive."

"You agree with this?" Charlotte asks.

"She should not be charged for her father's crimes."

"Yes. Can you save her?"

"I can't imagine how."

Suddenly, Camille is seized by an acute pain in his breast. He excuses himself and tells her he must go, as he has all at once fallen very ill. He leaves gasping, his chest aching. When outside the prison, he vomits in the street. The pain in his chest continues, and at home, he must lie in his bed, which brings some relief. When he has recovered somewhat, he writes to Robespierre, apologizing that he failed to get Corday to admit that anyone was involved other than herself, and now he is very ill, and in bed. Camille remains in bed and there is no response from Robespierre. (Of all people, he can empathize with Camille's condition, sickly as Robespierre is.)

Camille will not tell Robespierre about Corday's female lover. Nothing would come of that but to make the young lover's doom more certain. Camille feels that, in a profound way, Corday has taken his measure.

CHAPTER 34

NEXT DAY, CAMILLE FEELS better, though a dull ache remains, and he cannot keep himself from Charlotte Corday's trial. The new Paris Revolutionary Tribunal meets in the chamber that the parlement had used before 1789, inside the Palais de Justice and above the Conciergerie dungeon on the small island in the Seine at the center of Paris. But the room is changed. The king's throne and Dürer's painting of Christ are removed, the tapestries are stripped from the walls, and the royal fleurs-de-lys carpet is rolled up.

As Charlotte enters the courtroom and is escorted by guards to the box, complete silence prevails. Her calm is carrying the moment. Before the Revolutionary Tribunal—the magistrates decked in costumes meant to overawe—she appears deliberately indifferent. Camille regards the magistrates' garb a dark parody of the Classical age he so adores. They wear black habits, black mantles draped like togas, huge hats with brims upturned to expose the faces. The hats are decorated with plumes, ribbons, and a monstrous pair of cockades on either side, the size of saucers, one black, the other tricolor. White cravats render a sacerdotal air, and, on the bosom, each wears a medal suspended from a tricolor ribbon, bearing the head of Liberty in the Phrygian bonnet, and the emblem of the Roman fasces. Everyone else, except Corday, wears a red cap of liberty.

Once she is seated, the tribunal president asks her name. She tells him, and then he asks, "Do you have an advocate?"

"I chose one; he is a friend, but it seems he is afraid to accept my defense."

The president looks around and his gaze falls upon a man well-dressed and of about thirty-five near the front of the galleries—a lawyer, Claude-François Chauveau-Lagarde. The president orders him to undertake the prisoner's defense, and also appoints one Grenier to act as his clerk. This lawyer and the clerk take seats in the prisoner's box near to Charlotte. Corday ignores them.

The trial is simple. The witnesses are examined and the evidence presented. The wife, Simonne, is weeping. "I denounce to the universe," she cries, "the crime of Charlotte Corday. The memory of Marat is the only property left to me. I wish to consecrate to its defense the final days of a languishing life."

Still, Corday is impassive.

There is a family resemblance between Camille and his cousin, the public prosecutor, though the prosecutor is older. The complexion is dark, he is slightly built, attractive, and well groomed, his long black hair well combed and tied into a pony's tail, and his mannerisms are refined. Unlike Camille, his emotional tenor is generally controlled and cool. But Camille sees that today his cousin is vexed at the particulars of the evidence: Corday slew Marat alone, without accomplice or support.

Now she is testifying.

"You killed Marat?" asks the prosecutor.

"Yes, I killed him."

He shows her the knife. "Did you kill him with this?"

"Yes."

"Please tell us, who trained you where to place and thrust this knife to make it most lethal?"

She replies calmly, "I am no assassin. Nobody trained me how to kill. I have studied human physiology, on my own. I am self-educated for the most part. That is how I knew."

Now the prosecutor tries vainly to induce her to give names of accomplices and instigators.

Camille sees that a young man who is seated alone in a place not far from her is sketching her picture. Now it is the interaction between these two that most interests him. Camille can see that, aware of the young artist, she has turned so that her profile is at the angle that she imagines is most alluring to him. His picture will be history's testament of her true self.

The prosecutor tries a new approach. "The Girondins you got to know in Caen, they hated Marat, correct?"

"No doubt. They had to flee for their lives, for mere words, because of Marat."

"And this fed your own fury against Marat."

"I had reason enough to kill him on my own account. I had no need of others' hatreds."

"Why did you kill him?"

"I am a republican. You have my testament. May I read it aloud now? Republicanism may be an impossible dream in any epoch or place. But somebody must decide between liberty or death. Or else the people know nothing else but oppression. Their impulse is to submit to authority, however much it may oppress them." Here she nearly loses her composure, but holds on.

"The Girondins, they converted you to this ideology."

"I was a republican before the revolution, and I have never lacked conviction for republicanism, for as long as I can remember."

The prosecutor produces the two short letters that she wrote to Marat the day she killed him—seeking an audience. He reads them aloud to her. "You wrote these words?"

"Yes."

"You said there is a conspiracy."

"There was no conspiracy to kill Marat."

"You are so self-righteous about your deed. And yet you deceived Marat's wife, and Marat himself. You got close to him by lying to his wife and deceiving your victim, gaining his trust."

She is unperturbed. "I think the end has justified the means. The architect and chief of anarchy is dead. You have peace. I killed Marat to save one hundred thousand lives."

"Have you confessed to a priest?"

"No."

He leans toward her and says, "How many children do you have?"

She looks disconcerted, blushing. "You know I have never been married. I have no children."

And just when finally the prosecutor has gotten her a little angry, he terminates the examination. The prosecutor sits, and Camille detects a slight shake of the head. His victory is assured in the sense that legally she is guilty of murdering Marat, but not according to the narrative that he and his constituents undertook. The evidence shows only that she did it herself, with no accomplice or support.

Her lawyer, Chauveau-Lagarde, stands. He gives her a reassuring glance, moves before the jury, and says only this: "My client admits this murder; she premeditated it, and before the very prospect of her own death she shows no remorse; and I commend myself to the prudence of the jury." Then he takes his seat. Camille sees that she is pleased.

The jury retires at noon, and after ninety minutes the court is reconvened and solemnly the president announces that a verdict has been reached. One word: "Guilty." And then the president reads the sentence of death by guillotine. It will occur that very night, at a time to be announced.

———————

Likewise, Camille cannot miss her final act. She is at the Place de la Révolution, standing on the scaffold. Drums are beating so loudly as to be unpleasant. She must feel the crowd, the spectators, but will not face them.

Above the din, a bark: "Executioners, do your duty!"

Four executioners take hold of her and, with practiced speed, tie her to a plank. Two of them lift the board and set it down on the assembly, align the neck inside the lunette, and swing it shut with a clang. An unfrocked priest, the abbé Lothringer, is there. He stoops and cries, "Charlotte Corday, ascend to Heaven!" There is above her the great blade suspended, about to drop. Seconds move like minutes. The blade glints; the sun is setting, and in clear blue sky there is in silhouette a great bird circling.

Later, Camille learns that her final request was to see the man who was sketching the picture of her, and her jailers obliged. Camille has heard that she was joyous when the painter arrived. She asked him to do a portrait of herself. She spent as much time before the picture as posing for him; the process was more collaboration than interaction between painter and subject. At last, she stepped back, examined her likeness, and was content; just then jailers arrived to take her to the guillotine.

CHAPTER 35

OCTOBER 16, 1793: PAINE sees that the tumbrel bearing Marie Antionette approaches, and silence prevails. Paine feels ashamed to be here, but he can't keep away. In good conscience, he can neither stay away nor be here. He will forever be associated with the French Revolution, and he must not shrink from what his enemies will say he helped bring about. But he is terrified, and nor can he do anything about this destruction of the revolution and his good name. His presence here is now a self-abasement.

Marie Antoinette, erstwhile Queen of France, has been taken from her cell in the Conciergerie, the fourteenth-century fortress on the Île de la Cité, to which she was transferred after the king's death, separated from her children. Paine attended the trial, a silent spectator, reduced as such by the terror. The king's trial, whatever may be said about fairness of the process, rent the Convention. In contrast, his wife's was but a brief show trial, for treason and moral turpitude—a written statement was presented; her eight-year-old son was induced to testify against her through these papers, and he said that she molested him. And the Revolutionary Tribunal issued her sentence with unanimity, absent discord or dissent. The king arrived at the scaffold in a fine carriage; his wife is being paraded with bound hands in an open oxcart, to the scaffold here in the Place de la Révolution—where Paine now stands at the foot of it.

He has been incredulous that they would actually execute a woman like this. Perhaps the disservice that Charlotte Corday did to the women now imprisoned, and who will be arrested in the future, is that the men on the Revolutionary Tribunal discovered that they have a taste for sentencing a woman to the scaffold. It seems that Charlotte Corday has roused rampant male hatred of women. The source of hatred everywhere for Marie Antoinette, though stripped of office and made a widow by the Jacobins and their guillotine and in prison—and now doomed—is her crime of being a woman. She led the king astray just as Eve did Adam.

Marie Antoinette mounts the scaffold alone; her outfit is spec-tacular—all in white, a pristine chemise, petticoat, morning dress, and bonnet. She is only thirty-seven, but her physique is thin and her hair, now cut short, is white as a crone's. Still, her spine is ramrod straight as she ascends to the platform. It appears she may have stepped on the toe of the primary executioner, Sanson, and seemingly utters an apology. He graciously nods acceptance. The executioners seize her, and Paine can no longer bear to watch, his gaze downward. There ensues a roll of drums, barked commands, and a priest's incantation. He hears the blade's awful *bang!* Then a cascade of blood issues from the platform, pouring down the steps; Paine's feet are flooded by the queen's blood. Then there is the executioner's triumphant roar, and he is brandishing the hideous head, held by the white hair strands. Paine's legs buckle; he regains his wits lying on the pavement, in the lake of the queen's blood.

Paine is alone in bed now, thanks to the kindness of strangers who helped him home. He cannot sleep, and is therefore miser-able, yet he dreads the inevitable dreams; the queen's dead head, her blood; his own blood, his head. He must burn his shoes and bloodied clothes. He will not write about what he has seen. He cannot write of it.

CHAPTER 36

CAMILLE, WITH A SOLEMN expression unusual for a visit to his cousin, the public prosecutor, steps into Fouquier's office at the Palais de Justice, above the prison and adjacent to the Revolutionary Tribunal. The office is pleasingly large, for it is the same space occupied by Fouquier's predecessor during the reign of Louis XVI, and commands a striking view of the Seine and the Parisian domes and spires. But the room feels strangely vacant; walls and floors are bare of picture, carpet, or ornament, and there is no other decoration. The paintings, mirrors, carpets, and sculptures have been removed.

Fouquier is standing with his hands clasped behind his back. Camille can see that he has been pacing, in contrast to his usual place, seated and carefully analyzing the papers on his desk, and scribbling notes, or composing a legal brief.

Fouquier is fourteen years older, and Camille has always looked up to him. As a lawyer, Fouquier has succeeded where Camille failed; as a journalist, Camille is a well-regarded advocate, but his legal career was short and undistinguished. Camille is amazed that the two of them are here as they are, and at this place and time.

"I hope I am not disturbing you." Camille is surprised at his deference, at his timidity in the presence of his cousin. They are both powerful politicians at this moment in history in Paris, but Camille is by far the better known and connected of the two, not only because of the artistry and boldness of his journalism, and he is a Convention delegate, but also for his close friendships and

266

alliances with Danton and Robespierre.

"No. Come in, Camille. Sit down. Let's have a cognac, to celebrate the big victory."

"I hardly think that winning a death sentence of the wretched widow of Capet is worth much celebration."

Fouquier smiles and shakes his head. "I am never sure what to expect from you these days. Nobody has hated her and vilified her more than you have." He is pouring Camille and himself a drink. He hands a glass to Camille, and the two of them sit on a sofa.

"I don't have much problem with killing the queen, per se, on the same grounds as we did her husband. N-nor have I much problem, per se . . . with executing women. They are as capable of treason as men. Desperate times require drastic measures. We are at war against all of Europe. A civil war is waging in our interior. These pressures have broken Danton himself. He once carried the revolution. He has taken his young bride and fled to his birthplace in the country at Arcis."

Weary of the Convention and the ceaseless conflicts, beaten down, Danton left Paris in mid-October. "I am sick of men!" he said. He wants to be far from Paris during whatever fate is to befall the Girondins, he told Camille.

Continues Camille, "Perhaps we can abandon the guillotine in the tranquility of a happier future time. Yet the way it was done to the queen degrades us all."

"What do you mean?"

"With the boy." Her eight-year-old son, Louis, had been seized as he clung to his mother's skirts. Custody of what remains of the king's family has been firmly in control of the *sans-culottes*, through Jacques Hébert. Hébert has been on a tear; he is now the spearhead of the terror. Hébert is the radical journalist posing as a *sans-culotte* who is also the deputy procureur of the Paris Commune and whose arrest on May 31 at the Hôtel de Ville as directed by the Gironde (followed by his nearly immediate release in response to the fierce *sans-culotte* backlash) had been among the events that catalyzed the reaction among the National Guard and the masses that led to the downfall of the Girondins on June 2. Hébert himself had been among those who whipped the revolutionary sections of Paris into a frenzy, and then helped to coordinate the siege of the National Convention.

Camille is dismayed that Hébert and his people have seized control of the Cordeliers Club, which he and Danton founded. They have used it as an instrument of their depravity.

As part of the "reeducation" of the king's son, Hébert and his henchmen repeatedly intoxicated him, then beat him, and taught him "La Marseillaise;" hearing the boy sing this, with childlike male swagger, and wearing a red cap of liberty, stirred terrible contradictions inside Camille.

In the queen's trial, Hébert authenticated a signed statement from the child. His guardians had caught him masturbating. "Where did you learn to do that?" they asked, disapprovingly. "Mama taught me," said the boy; he'd learned well what his captors wanted to hear.

The statement, signed in a child's hand that, to Camille, could only be disturbing, said that the queen took him into her bed and taught him to masturbate. After the statement was read, the queen in her testimony responded with dignified denials. She aroused Camille's sympathy, and he could tell that many others present had had the same reaction.

"I was not aware—" Fouquier begins.

"Robespierre is livid, for who could believe such a thing; and involving a child in his mother's trial this way is appalling to him."

Fouquier avoids his gaze. "I'm sorry you and Robespierre aren't happy about it. I play the hand I'm dealt," he says.

"Why call Hébert to testify? W-what did he have to do with the charges against the queen?"

"Do you think I had a choice? The revolution is not exclusively your and Robespierre's affair."

Yes, thinks Camille, not the Convention, nor Robespierre, nor Danton, is your master. I certainly am not. Hébert and the Paris Commune are now your masters. The Convention and the Paris

Commune have been rivals, and it seems inevitable that Robespierre and Hébert must eventually have a mortal reckoning. He hopes his cousin is not a casualty of the confrontation.

"Now the Girondins will be tried," says Camille. These are the thirty-two expelled from the Convention on June 2, less the ones such as Pétion and Barbaroux who are still at large.

"Yes."

"I think you will have a struggle there. Brissot will fight."

"As will the others, I'm sure."

"Brissot is the warrior among them. It's an ambitious case."

"Ah!" Here Fouquier gets up, walks to the desk, and from the neatly piled papers, seizes a document. He exclaims, "The case is already well prepared!" Camille is chagrined. It is his pamphlet, *Fragment of the Secret History of the Revolution.*

"I'll tell you a secret," Camille says, "Just between you and me. I don't believe any of that document. Not a word of it. They are guilty of disagreeable words, no more. It seems that today in France, an accusation is as good as a conviction. A bitter jest may lead men to the guillotine."

"Why did you write it?"

"Y-y-you know good and well why I wrote it . . . R-Robespierre made me do it." He finishes his drink, and his cousin refills his glass.

"Camille, if you are suffering from a wounded conscience, it is too late to do anything about it."

Camille is feeling in his breast that pressure combined with ache that has become chronic. It has kept him up nights; it flared up during the queen's trial and execution. Initially, he wondered if he was suffering a heart attack. He now has accepted that, indeed, it is his conscience. Nothing has surprised him so much as the realization that he has a conscience.

"Call it what you will," he says. "The truth is that the Girondins were my friends. We started the revolution side by side. The rationale for everything that the Jacobins have done has been that the end justifies the means. Everything has been done for the people, for the revolution. I have been insensitive . . . cavalier about grave matters, I now see. I underestimated the power of the printed word. I appreciated, all along, that I was being extremely ruthless, even cruel. I hoped to destroy political careers. I did not expect that my intangible arrows would kill. I was doing it for the people, I told myself. But the people are but an abstraction. And I agree with Danton that actually they are not so lovable, while Brissot and the others have been my friends. I dined with some of them the night of my wedding. Brissot was there, and Pétion and Robespierre were witnesses at my wedding—"

"Pétion is still at large. He won't be tried. Not now."

"So he is. I wish him well. He does not have to die." Camille pauses, then says, "Too late, I suppose. There is no turning back."

"Yes. It's too late, Camille. You made them traitors. As traitors, they must suffer the ultimate penalty."

"And what will happen to Olympe de Gouges?" She has been in prison nearly three months. She reacted to the fall of the Girondins by issuing written demands for their reinstatement in the Convention. Then she sent the Committee of Public Safety her poster, "The Three Urns, or The Salvation of the Fatherland, by an Aerial Traveller," which set forth her words: "An arbitrary law worthy of the Inquisition, that even the *ancien régime* would have blushed to implement, imprisons the esprit humain and has wrested my liberty from me in the midst of a free people."

She was unable to find a bill-poster willing to placard it, so "The Three Urns" never was disseminated; she only delivered it to the Committee of Public Safety. But its contents were intolerable insolence for being spot on the mark. As a result, she was arrested. She has no attorney. The presiding judge denied her a lawyer on the grounds that she is more than capable of representing herself, as is evident from her writings.

She remains defiant. Somehow, as a prisoner she has published two pamphlets: "Olympe de Gouges at the Revolutionary Tribunal," in which she describes her interrogations by the tribunal, and "A Female Patriot Persecuted," which condemns all of the proscriptions, the imprisonments, and the executions.

Her friends have made these publications possible. Camille is not one of them. He has lacked the courage even to visit her in her confinement. Nor has he had the nerve to visit Marguerite since Olympe was arrested.

"She will be tried immediately after the Girondins. As you said, women are as capable of treason as men."

"She is not a traitor. She has remonstrated at proscriptions for mere disagreeable words."

"The antagonism for her is stronger than for the men. I can't help her."

Camille wants to say something, but he can't; he can't speak, and he doesn't know what to say. The pain in his chest is so unbearable that he closes his eyes; he is about to cry out. He feels that he is about to faint.

His cousin says, "Camille, I have some advice for you. Stay away from the trials."

CHAPTER 37

CAMILLE APPRECIATES THAT HIS cousin has given him good advice. He should stay away from the trials of the Girondins. But he is drawn by a terrible fascination to witness the outcome, whatever it may be, of the monstrous deed he has done. Perhaps he feels that what he has done is evil and cowardly, and he must witness its consequences as obligation or penance.

Camille feels that what is happening to the Girondins here is also happening to him. His role in the cosmic drama of the French Revolution is clarifying, and he feels that there must be a reckoning, a price exacted, for the terrible thing he has done, as in a Greek tragedy.

First, the prosecution is allowed to put its case, then the defense will be allowed to respond. Fouquier portrays Brissot as guilty of atrocious treasons: He plotted against the people on behalf of a new aristocracy of property ownership and commercial prosperity; he "prostituted" his support to Lafayette, and then led the people into a trap at the Champ-de-Mars, where Lafayette massacred them; he wanted Louis XVI held in the Luxembourg prison after August 10 instead of the Temple where the Mountain confined him, as part of his plotting an escape by the royal family; he was involved in Marat's assassination; he incited and masterminded the Vendée and Marseille insurrections; even the uprisings in Calvados, Lyon, Avignon, Caen, and Nîmes, which occurred in response to the Girondins' arrest, are laid at his feet.

Fouquier contends that the true motivation for Brissot's support for black emancipation was to ruin the French colonies, and he betrayed Toulon, which the royalist city officials recently handed over to the British with its French naval base, arsenal, and forts. The rest of the Girondins conspired with Brissot in the commission of these egregious crimes, while they provoked the war against all Europe in which France is now engaged that presents the gravest danger to French liberty.

The "witnesses" who are called to develop this case are, in truth, nothing of the sort, for they could not have experienced that to which they attest. No one knows better than Camille, for it is he who originally spun these arguments. They are, yet again, Hébert and his gang of fanatics and scoundrels from the revolutionary sections.

Brissot acts as his own and the other Girondins' attorney. Though he has always been slender and hollowed in appearance, he is now remarkably gaunt and fatigued, seemingly wasting away before Camille's eyes. He is suffering. But he is relentless in his valiant defense of himself and the others. He undermines the competency of the witnesses to present the testimony they purport to offer, and effectively refutes every single point.

This all takes time, and during a recess Camille hears Hébert complain to the chief judge (indifferent that he might be overheard), "Need there be so much ceremony about shortening the lives of wretches already condemned by the people?"

Then, after two weeks and just when seemingly the tide is turning, the judges abruptly cut short the proceedings, and the hearings end on October 30. Still Camille is hopeful—secretly—that Brissot has left a strong enough impression that the jury will return an acquittal.

He is seated on a bench placed before the jury box, beside Joachim Vilate, an ex-priest and a Jacobin, when the jury returns from their deliberations (Robespierre is nowhere in sight). There is something in the expression of their faces that is alarming, and so when one of the last ones passes by, a man named Antonelle, Camille impulsively stands and says to him, "I pity you. Yours are terrible functions." He feels himself losing self-control.

He will ask himself over and over, Why did I do that? Perhaps it was a futile, last-ditch effort to alter the terrible course of events that he himself had set in motion and the dreadful outcome that he saw inscribed on the jurors' faces. The jury does not delay before issuing its declaration: All of the Girondins are guilty as charged.

Before he knows it, Camille shouts, "Oh, my God, my God! It is I who kill them! My *Secret History*! Oh my God, this has destroyed them!"

Without knowing, in a paroxysm of agony, he has thrown himself into Vilate's arms. Now there is a profound silence throughout the hall as the jury's sentence is read: Death. Camille feels the floor give way under his feet; he utters, "I am going, I am going, I must go out!" And he faints, and all is black.

At home he falls headlong into bed and doesn't emerge from it until morning, though he hardly sleeps. When Lucile comes to join him, he barks at her to go away, and commences to weep. He does not respond to her gentle prodding; he can hardly bear to face her; he remains silent and brooding in her presence.

Nor, of course, is Marguerite's comfort an option. Danton, now his only friend outside his marriage, has "retired" to Arcis with Louise, now his young bride. Danton cannot bear to participate in the terror. It has been Danton who provided him moorage and perspective, even eloquent rationalization amid the turbulent events of the revolution. Without him, Camille feels adrift, ungrounded.

All Camille had ever wanted was a life of meaning. He is no ascetic like Robespierre, but unlike Danton, for him the revolution was not mainly a better way to earn a living. Ingrained in his impulse to write is a desire for enduring contribution, lasting renown, and meaning.

His conscience is agonizing, and on top of this, he appreciates, his legacy is beyond repair, beyond vindication. Yet he is not powerless. The very predicament in which he finds himself has occurred because of the power of his pen. Perhaps he could save the Girondins, or at least, Olympe, who has not been tried, by writing something. But he cannot bring himself to do it. For he himself is paralyzed by the very terror that he helped to create.

He feels he must attend the executions the next morning, October 31. And so he does. Five carts take them by the usual route to the Place de la Révolution, and Camille pushes his way through the crowds, following it. The multitude is vast and, hampered by them, the procession takes two hours to reach its destination.

The atmosphere is clear, cool, and sunny, and houses on either side of the roadway and the procession are decorated as if for a festival—tricolor are flying from the windows. Colored placards bear the inscription that today resonates as never before: *Unity, liberty, equality, fraternity or death.* Everyone is trying to upstage for patriotism, for it has become dangerous to be considered less revolutionary than your neighbor.

The crowd is jeering, hurling abuse—what, thinks Camille, have the poor Girondins done to them?—yet all of them are facing the crowd and singing "La Marseillaise" as they pass by the gaily decorated windows in the five slowly moving carts.

All of them but one is singing, that is. Upon announcement of the sentence, and just after Camille had fainted, one of the condemned, Deputy Charles Valazé, a legal theorist and agriculturalist, stabbed himself through the heart with a concealed knife, falling instantly dead. Camille had regained consciousness amid the shouting and consternation as Valazé was still emitting a fountain of blood (the Valazé spectacle sufficiently distracted everyone present that Camille suffered no adverse personal repercussion for his own antics).

The corpse is being transported in the first cart with the others, who are singing. In time Camille notices that they are altering some words to mention the "bloody blade" of tyranny and shouting, "*Vive la République!*"

De Sillery, the oldest of them, is the first to die. He embraces his comrades in the first of the five carts, all of them shouting, "*Viva la République!*" He mounts the steps, bows to the spectators with grave courtesy, walks purposefully to the guillotine, and the executioners brusquely tie him to the board. Thus does the same ceremony ensue time after time, each condemned embracing others who are close by, and bowing, until the last to leave his cart.

Twenty times the blade falls, *Bam! Bam! Bam!* . . . A piercing, terrifying sound. Beheading them all, including the corpse. The scale of blood-flow off the guillotine expounds the horror. Vergniaud, who makes a show of throwing away the poison with which he had been provided the night before, so that he could die with his friends, is the last among the condemned to climb the steps. His head is cut off precisely thirty-one minutes after Sillery's.

CHAPTER 38

NOVEMBER 1, 1793: OLYMPE'S trial begins. Camille cannot face her, and of course does not. Yet he cannot stay away. He skulks about at the rear of the crowd, careful to avoid being seen by her, as she sits in the box of the accused. He has hardly slept for countless days; he feels the onset of the grippe, and fever, in addition to his aching chest.

What he sees happening before him is preposterous. His cousin is questioning Olympe—one of Camille's lovers and the former guardian of another of his lovers—as the accused before the Revolutionary Trubunal. He questions her about her name, surname, age, occupation, place of birth, and residence. She replies that her name is Marie Olympe de Gouges, age thirty-eight (actually, she is in her forties), *femme de lettres*, a native of Montauban, living in Paris, Rue du Harlay, Section Pont Neuf.

Referring to "The Three Urns," Fouquier charges her with publishing "a work contrary to the expressed desire of the entire nation." It "openly provoked civil war and sought to arm citizens against one another. There can be no mistaking the perfidious intentions of this criminal woman, and her hidden motives, when one observes her in all the works to which, at the very least, she lends her name."

It occurs to Camille that, in contrast to those who have been charged before, she is condemned by the tribunal strictly for her writings. She is the true martyr of the revolution, for all of the crimes alleged against her are comprised strictly of her words. Still, this time, for now, Camille says nothing, and his emotions are in check. The entire case against her is comprised of her writings attacking the Jacobins—their focus was Robespierre and Marat, for she has despised these two men most of all.

The public prosecutor reads from her writings: Marat was "a destroyer of laws, mortal enemy of the order, of humanity, and of his country," who was "living large in a society in which he was both a tyrant and a plague." Her invective against Robespierre was stronger still, declaring, "You tell yourself that you're the unique author of the revolution; you haven't been, you are not, you will never be anything other than disgrace and execration." The prosecutor reads her invitation that Robespierre meet her at the Seine River, that they may both drown and thereby rid France of them both.

Throughout this barrage, she sits quietly, her head held high. She makes no argument, nor examines witnesses. For in actuality she is not equipped to defend herself in this arena. She is smiling much of the time, sometimes she shrugs her shoulders; at times she clasps her hands and raises her eyes toward the ceiling of the room; then, suddenly, she makes a gesture showing astonishment; sometimes she gazes at the jury, the court, or the spectators.

Fouquier calls her a monarchist, for in her writings trying to spare the king's life, and offering to serve as his lawyer. Camille's cousin charges that her writings reveal that "monarchy seems to her to be the government most suited to the French spirit."

Next, Fouquier questions her. She testifies that she was motivated to write "The Three Urns" by the revolts in a large number of départements, notably Bordeaux, Lyons, and Marseilles. Her hope was to bring all of the parties together by enabling them to choose the kind of government which would be most suitable for them. Accordingly, her only desire was the happiness of her country.

Fouquier: "How is it that you believe yourself to be such a patriot for attempting last June to bring about a reconciliation with the rebellious départements, concerning a fact which could no longer be at issue because the people had formally adopted and implemented a republican government?"

Olympe: "This is the form of government that I have supported as the preferable one; I have professed only republican sentiments, as the jurors can convince themselves from reading my works. Even so, the handbill for which I am brought before the tribunal was never posted. To avoid compromising myself I decided to send twenty-four copies to the Committee of Public Safety, which, two days later, had me arrested."

Fouquier: "If 'The Three Urns' was not made public, it is because the bill-poster refused to post it."

Olympe: "That is true."

Fouquier's assistant, a man named Naulin, reads a few lines from a letter of Olympe's that Camille finds incomprehensible. He shakes the letter at her and shouts that here she is "advocating principles of federalism."

Olympe: "My intention was, as I have said already, pure, and I want only to be able to show my heart to the citizen jurors so that they might judge my love of liberty and my hatred of every kind of tyranny."

Fouquier asks her to declare whether she acknowledges authorship of a play manuscript found among her papers entitled, *France is Saved by the Tyrant Dethroned*, and she does so.

Fouquier: "Why did you place such injurious and perfidious declamations against the most ardent defenders of the rights of the people in the mouth of the person who in this work was supposed to represent the Capet woman?"

Olympe: "The Capet woman is saying things that are appropriate for her in this dramatic work."

Finally, Fouquier says, "Tell us precisely, madame, concerning the sentiments you have expressed with respect to the faithful representatives of the people whom you have insulted and calumniated in your writings, do you still hold such opinions?"

There is a long pause, then she answers, "I have not changed; I still hold the same opinions concerning them, and do not retract them. I look upon them as ambitious persons."

Fouquier asks, "Is there anything more you wish to say in your defense?"

"Just that I was the founder of the popular societies for my sex, yet now I have destroyed myself in order to propagate the principles of the revolution."

For Camille, these exchanges bring a crushing weight and agony on his chest. He is at the brink of crying out again. The horror is that she does not want to die; of course she does not want to die. He is filled with contradictory emotions; he is furious at her that she got herself into this predicament; he, Marguerite, and others begged her to stop inciting powerful men. Yet he is overwhelmed by pity for her, and he wants to take her in his arms and console her, for at last his glance has met hers, and he can see that now she finally looks distressed. Is it because she sees him here?

She has aged these past three months, and there are dark circles under her eyes. He is stricken by shame at his actions that have brought them to this fate. He is covered with cold sweat, he can hardly breathe, and now feels consumed by exhaustion and sickness. His nerves are shot. All at once Olympe is looking at him, and the prosecutor is looking at him. He feels bodies coming at him, that he is being crushed. As a hand seizes him firmly by the arm, he suddenly realizes that the court is in recess. He thinks, before all goes black, that he must have cried out something without knowing it.

The chief of police and his henchmen take Camille home. Lucile tucks him into bed and finally he sleeps; yet it is a fitful sleep, for there is no waking from this nightmare. Not until two days later does he emerge from his house and learn from the papers what befell her. She was condemned to die for "writings tending toward the reestablishment of a power attacking the sovereignty of the people," and guillotined.

Fouquier asked her if she had any final words to say concerning the application of the law, and she replied, "My enemies will not have the glory of seeing my blood flow. I am pregnant and will bear a citizen for the Republic." She was examined by a physician and found not to be pregnant. This last, pathetic effort to save herself hits his bruised and lacerated conscience so hard that for many seconds he is bent, on his knees, and unable to breath.

He reads the obituary:

Olympe de Gouges, born with an exalted imagination, believed her delusions were inspired by nature. She wanted to be a Statesman; it would seem that the law has punished this plotter for having forgotten the virtues suitable to her own sex.

Later, he reads, in a Jacobin paper:

Remember the shameless Olympe de Gouges, who was the first to set up women's clubs, who abandoned the cares of her household to involve herself in the Republic, and whose head fell under the avenging blade of the laws. It is shocking, it is contrary to all the laws of nature.

Yet he finds in a paper, published anonymously, still producing texts sympathetic to the Girondin point of view, these phrases:

The execution took place the day following the trial, towards 4p.m.; while mounting the scaffold, the condemned, looking at the people, cried out: "Children of the Fatherland, you will avenge my death." Cries of "Vive la République" were heard among the spectators waving hats in the air.

Is this what happened? It matters not. Enemies of the terror are at work on their own narrative, which as well roundly condemns Camille—what, he feels, he deserves. All witnesses are in accord about one thing, Olympe was calm and dignified in death.

———

The guillotine rises and falls, a relentless systole-diastole.

Ironically, Camille cannot stop imagining his own execution, his own conduct during the last few minutes of his life. This leads irresistibly to his attendance at every trial of his former friends and acquaintances, to observe their conduct. Yet now he does so in a numbed, perfectly controlled condition.

On November 6, Philippe Egalité, erstwhile Duc d'Orléans, is tried before and condemned by the Revolutionary Tribunal. Throughout, he is impassive, accepts the verdict without protest. Egalité attends his guillotining with no sign of fear. Camille thinks he discerns a smile on his lips.

On November 8, it is Madame Roland's turn; she is the one, charges Camille's cousin, who was the covert leader of the Girondins and orchestrated all of their traitorous pronouncements and actions. She, too, appears before the tribunal unrepresented by legal counsel; she is completely alone, for her husband has escaped and is at large. It is said that she has left her daughter, who wept as they parted when Madame Roland was arrested, at home alone.

Nobody is there to lament her—except Camille, in his secret shame.

She nevertheless retains the personal qualities that made her a pillar of the movement with which she has been associated. At her trial, Fouquier and his assistants bully her unmercifully. She bears her full testimony notwithstanding her inquisitors' repeated demands that she answer only yes or no, and tell her that she is "not here to be clever."

Finally, she weeps, but only when they probe her private life and her personal relations with Girondins other than her husband— bludgeoning her with sexual innuendo. Yet she never admits guilt or compromises her friends. She is adjudged guilty by the jury of all men and, when condemned to die, she declares defiantly, "You judge me worthy to share the fate of the great men whom you have assassinated. I shall endeavor to carry to the scaffold the courage they displayed."

As she stands upon the scaffold she raises her eyes and murmurs something that Camille does not catch. He consults the paper, published anonymously and still producing texts sympathetic to the Girondin point of view, which dutifully reports, "She looked up at the Statue of Liberty, and uttered, 'Oh Liberty, what crimes are committed in your name.'"

And so, day after day, the guillotinings continue—of fallen politicians, failed generals, defiant writers, deserters, and courtesans alike.

Robespierre is nowhere to be seen.

PART V

CHAPTER 39

DANTON IS BACK. HE did not defect to London or join traitorous émigrés in Geneva as rumored by his enemies, and as Robespierre himself has speculated. He has returned, and his presence is a palpable relief to Camille. Tonight the two of them are strolling alongside the Seine.

"Good as your vacation may have been for your health," says Camille, "it has not served our political convictions or the national interest. Nor your political career."

Danton was in Arcis until mid-November; then he went to his childhood home in Arcis-sur-Aube, a little town in Champagne. He told Camille that he had had every intention of remaining there, and cultivating his garden, like Candide. In the place where he grew up, he could finally breathe, and put into perspective the events since 1789.

He tried to forget the blood of the Gironde that was spilled on October 31. He became a new man, with his young wife and beside his mother and his old nurse, and he regained his humanity, his capacity for affection and tenderness. He told Camille that it was as if he had "passed from the atmosphere of a blacksmith's forge into the restful air of an oasis."

Yet he also regained the original aspirations that had drawn him to the center—indeed the pinnacle—of the French Revolution, and it was these that impelled him back to Paris.

They are approaching the Pont Neuf and it is the hour of sunset. The setting sun casts a glowing redness, illuminating the Seine, undulating and rippling, and shining bright red.

"Look at the Seine!" exclaims Danton. "It's filled up with blood. The Seine runs with blood."

"The civil wars," Camille says, "the internal threats, and our war with nearly all the rest of Europe have impelled Robespierre to embrace the terror. He rationalizes that it is necessary to destroy what remains of counter-revolution. I think he enjoys his power. From the Tuileries, you can watch the death carts en route." Camille pauses; both men stand silent, watching the crimson water.

The Committee of General Security, now called by everyone the Police Committee, works in close collaboration with the Committee of Public Safety, and is Robespierre's new instrument of terror. The more powerful Committee of Public Safety, effectively a dictatorship under Robespierre's control, sends direction to the Committee of General Security, which dispatches police to execute the arrests.

The Police Committee's headquarters are not just a meeting room, but the center of an intricate network covering the whole nation. Dispatches from the Convention, its various committees and envoyés en mission (commissioners to the revolutionary armies in the provinces to propagate the terror there), from the sections and municipality of Paris and other large cities, from administrators, clubs, and spies all over France, have kept the Police Committee well informed. The Police Committee is well supported by more than a hundred office employees in adjoining rooms who strain to keep up with processing the constant flow of information.

The Police Committee has questioned suspected counter-revolutionaries and also many public functionaries and private persons suspected of all manner of disloyalty. To the Police Committee have come masses of petitioners to denounce or to defend suspected enemies of the Republic. Friends, neighbors, even wives and husbands, parents and children denounce one another to the tribunal.

Camille has read that Mayor Bailly was beheaded upon a guillotine that was set up on the Champs-de-Mars specially for this occasion, where in 1791 as he had been beside Lafayette, the National Guard had fired on the people. Fair enough. A reckoning for the Champs-de-Mars massacre was in order. But what about others being slaughtered who themselves had condemned the Champs-de-Mars massacre?

Jean-Marie Roland is dead. He was hiding in Rouen. When he learned that the Convention had murdered his wife, he left a note condemning the "Reign of Terror," coining the term. His corpse was found three miles away, seated against an apple tree's trunk, having impaled himself through the heart with a cane-sword.

"I shall demand that we spare men's blood!" exclaims Danton suddenly, facing Camille. "That is why I returned to Paris. The Convention must be just to those who are not proven enemies of the people. The Revolutionary Tribunal, the Committee of Public Safety, Robespierre himself—all of this I conceived and brought into being! I am to blame. Now I must undo it all or it will destroy all of us, the whole country."

"Georges, everything you did was to channel and create outlet for the pent bloodlust engendered by generations of the royalty's and the Church's oppression. But now there is no point in making demands on the Convention unless you want yourself to be charged as a counter-revolutionary. Half of its members are gone—guillotined, imprisoned, in hiding, or sent away as envoyés en mission. Those who remain are but an ornament, like the senate in the Roman Empire. They are terrified. You relinquished leadership of the Committee of Public Safety, and now Robespierre is firmly in control of it. His tool, Saint-Just, has turned the committee into a dictatorship. There are no longer any elections. I think they mean to keep their power, don't you? Yet they delude themselves with sanctimony and piety that would make a priest blush. Virtue must be combined with terror, says Robespierre. Virtue without terror is impotent; terror without virtue is destructive."

At least Saint-Just is gone, for now. But he will return and, in his absence, his power only grows. He is in Alsace, working on shoring up the Army of the Rhine, directly overseeing military efforts, now in partnership with Philippe-François-Joseph Le Bas—a Convention delegate from Caen who is said to be a lover of Saint-Just's sister Henriette.

There seems to be nothing that Saint-Just is incapable of doing well. He has imposed harsh discipline and reorganized the troops, and reversed the prior losses. It is said that the common men adore him; among the measures, he has ordered shot incompetent officers, even a general. He will return to Paris a military hero, on top of his political triumphs. He was even the one who wrote the new constitution now under consideration.

Danton turns to Camille and says, smiling defiantly, "What is your virtue? There is no virtue firmer than what I show my wife in bed each night."

"Georges, this is no joke. For Robespierre, virtue is equality, love of the fatherland, devotion to the general welfare above private interests. It all sounds like high-minded nonsense, but it is how he justifies the terror. The aim for virtue is the source of the blood you see everywhere."

They stand in silence, Danton chastened, apparently, and then Camille says, "I have a plan. It is all that is left to us."

"Tell me about it."

"I am planning to start a new journal. A series of pamphlets, really, as I will be the only author. There is no one else but me who can or will do it. We will demand clemency for the two hundred thousand prisoners that remain. We will redeem ourselves for being accomplices in the murder of our friends by saving two hundred thousand."

"What good will that do, Camille? We'll be next on the scaffold and save no one."

"The people will end the terror, just as they have given it license. I believe that there are a majority of the people who have been silent and are as repelled by the terror as we are."

"I believe you; but what will Robespierre do to us before the people can demonstrate their support? The people are ignorant, confused, and they are disorganized, except by the perpetrators of the terror. And the people are afraid. They are terrified."

"I don't believe Robespierre will harm us. Our ties and our history are too strong."

"Maybe for you; not for me."

Camille is now surprised at Danton's timidity. He is not used to it. Camille never thought he'd see Danton afraid, but so he is. Danton appreciates, apparently, that his power is gone, and he does not want to die.

"Yes, Georges, of course . . . And nor would Robespierre protect me if it meant putting himself or even his power at risk. We mustn't let him fear for loss of his popularity and prestige, nor certainly for his personal safety. His power on the Committee of Public Safety is not absolute. We must proceed with caution and deliberately, even with Robespierre's support."

Danton raises his eyebrows and Camille continues.

"Yes, with his support. I'm serious. I myself have been Robespierre's mere tool, and now it is time to make him mine. My pamphlet's first number will attack the terror, but in guise of an attack on the 'ultras,' the 'enrages'—Hébert and his awful *Le Père Duchesne* newspaper and those thugs from the Paris sections who collaborate with him."

Camille is ready to do this; he hates Hébert for, among other reasons, his grotesque and cruel behavior in the trials of the Girondins and Olympe and even the queen.

Camille continues, "I will show Robespierre the proofs prior to publication. He will approve, because he hates Hébert and his henchmen as much as we do. He deplores their methods; their gratuitous cruelty and their coarseness. He regards them as deploying the terror absent virtue. He disapproves of their atheism, their Cult of Reason, and wishes to vanquish it to make room for his Cult of the Supreme Being. Only Robespierre is virtuous, the Incorruptible; he really believes that. And they are his rivals. He does not want to share power with them. Then Robespierre himself will own the pamphlet, and he will defend us. When we demand clemency for the imprisoned, he will have no choice but to support us."

"Come on, Camille, take up your pen! Write to demand clemency! I shall support you." Danton is raising his fist. "You see my hand. You know how strong it is."

CHAPTER 40

DECEMBER 4, 1793: CAMILLE arrives at the house situated in the Rue Saint-Honoré, nearly opposite the Rue Florentin. From the street, the interior looks inviting, with lamps ablaze. Camille discerns a shadow at the window as he passes by. Camille walks toward the house, though not to the front door, passing instead through the carriage entrance on the right. It is the most direct way to his destination.

He hopes to avoid dealing with Eleonore Duplay, and she has not materialized, though he senses her watchful gaze. She would not detain him; Camille is one of the few visitors as to whom she would not play gatekeeper. But he is agitated and not disposed to interact with anyone until he completes the purpose of his visit to Robespierre. He has come in early evening, and at this hour Robespierre is almost certainly alone and at his desk working on his next address; this is what he spends most of his life doing, outside of the Convention or the Jacobin Club. That Robespierre is alone is what Camille hopes for, in any event.

He knocks, and it is Robespierre who, from within, asks who it is. Camille replies, and he hears his friend stride to the door and open it.

He is dressed formally as ever, with his blue coat, embroidered shirt, and white breeches, and his narrow face is pale and gaunt and looks tired. Sure enough, Robespierre is alone. He sees the document in Camille's hand, his friend's severe expression, and seems to recognize that Camille has therefore come with a purpose.

"Come in, Camille. What is it you have there?"

"P-proofs for the first number of a new paper . . . A series of pamphlets, actually, as I'll be the only writer. I mentioned it to you a while ago. I thought you may like to read it before it is published."

"Ah, yes. Indeed I do. Thank you. Come over here."

Once inside, Camille hands him the proofs. In the bare little room the only decoration is Robespierre's own portrait on the wall behind him. There is a small mirror beside the window. On the desk, beside papers and a pen and inkwell, sits the Rousseau bible.

There are no chairs in the tiny apartment, and usually Robespierre prefers that his visitors stand. But he makes exception for Camille and other special friends, and his habit is to invite them to sit on the neatly made bed. They sit down and Robespierre begins to inspect the document.

Camille is nervous and happy to remain silent while Robespierre reads and develops his impression of the pamphlet. Camille wrote it virtually with Danton looking over his shoulder, the two of them anticipating this very moment, when Robespierre would be drawn into their scheme, or countermand it. This initial installment has been written primarily for his eyes.

It bears the name *The Old Cordelier*, which was Danton's idea, and Camille is indicated as the only author. He is described as "a Deputy of the National Convention" and "a founder of the Jacobins." There is a slogan beneath the title *The Old Cordelier*: "Live Free or Die!" And as an epigraph, there are the words of Machiavelli: "As soon as those who govern are hated, their rivals will begin to be admired." These, he anticipates, may be permanent features of each succeeding edition.

"I like the name," says Robespierre. "'The Old Cordelier'; the original ones, such as yourself. Not the new Cordeliers—Hébert and his people. The new Cordeliers have no principles, no soul. They only seek power and to tear down whatever stands in their way. They are despots."

For Camille, these initial comments have been extremely

pleasing to hear, and Robespierre is now reading with interest. As he reads, Camille's secret excitement is growing to almost unbearable pitch.

In this initial number, Camille's theme is that the real "counter-revolutionaries" are those alienating and disgusting the populace with their extreme, violent, and oppressive measures. He has not identified by name the objects of his condemnation. But his praise of Robespierre leaves no doubt that he aims his invective at Hébert and his party.

Camille and Danton hope to gain Robespierre's support and protection on account of the evident attack on Hébert and his people while separating them from Robespierre. Yet the pamphlet announces its purpose as no less ambitious than to restore freedom of the press in France; and it is here that it is truly bold, setting the stage for Camille and Danton's plan eventually to broadly attack the terror, and for their proposed program of clemency.

At last Robespierre looks up at him. He says, "Very well, Camille. I'm truly impressed. It's good to see you exercising some initiative. When is your next issue?"

"I plan to issue a new pamphlet every five days."

"Good. I want to contribute something to it. Under your name, of course. I want all the credit to go to you."

"Thank you."

"I like this, but I think it's possible for us to be more explicit in future issues."

Camille is relieved. More than that, he is awash with joy, but must retain a most serious expression. He cannot wait to tell Danton.

The printer and the booksellers are pleased, as is Robespierre, for the first number of *The Old Cordelier*, issued on December 5, the day after Camille's meeting with Robespierre, has sold out ten thousand copies.

The second number is ready for issue on December 10. Like the first, it assails Hébert and his party as counter-revolutionaries, for their fanaticism and extremism, but more explicitly, naming them. Camille compares Robespierre to Tiberius Gracchus, a Roman populist and reformist politician of the Roman Republic in the second century B.C. As a plebeian tribune, Tiberius Gracchus caused political turmoil by introducing legislation that would reform agrarian laws to transfer land from wealthy, predominantly patrician landowners to poorer citizens. Factions arose in the Senate who were covert instrumentalities of the wealthy, proposing legislation that was even more radical than Gracchus's reforms. Finally, with Gracchus's legitimate efforts to reform having been eclipsed by the fraudulent, extremist, and unrealistic proposals of the covert agents of his enemies, the people acquiesced when he was murdered, along with many of his supporters, by wealthy members of the Roman Senate and followers of the conservative factions. The movement for reform died with Gracchus.

Camille enjoys drawing allegory from ancient Greek or Roman history to reinforce a current political argument. But it is distasteful to him that in this second issue, Robespierre has interfered and aggressively deployed his pen to ardently condemn Anacharsis Clootz, himself a Jacobin, as a counter-revolutionary. Camille disapproved, but said nothing. Clootz, a German, is his own man, and Camille likes him for this, and his intelligence. Nevertheless, the first priority is to enmesh Robespierre in this scheme. So the second number goes to press with the marks of Robespierre's heavy pen. Like the first, it is a hit and sells out quickly.

CHAPTER 41

DECEMBER 12, 1793: THIS time it is Robespierre who arrives at Camille's house unannounced. Horace is playing at his feet, and on this occasion Camille again does not bother to put away the glass of cognac. He is feeling relaxed and confident. Lucile looks at him and nods at their son, meaning that she should remove him, but Camille waves her away.

"Horace," he says, "say hello to your godfather." Horace gazes at Robespierre intently, not uttering a sound.

Robespierre looks at the child, smiles, and says, in a ridiculous falsetto, "What a good boy. Your father needs to behave himself as well as you do." Horace crawls to Camille, who lifts the boy and balances him on a knee. Camille thinks that Robespierre would probably deprive his godson a father if he felt he had no other option.

Perhaps because of Camille's momentary change in countenance, Robespierre is suddenly all business. "I'm afraid I have some vexing news," he says. "From the Jacobin Club."

"What now?" All at once, Camille is ill at ease. "What I expected? Attempted retribution for my writings."

He looks at Lucile, who comes and takes the baby from him and disappears into the next room.

"No. Not that. Some at the Jacobin Club noticed your self-reproach, your antics at the trial of the Girondins and that de Gouges woman. Also, there's that published letter in defense of Dillon. They have demanded that you appear for a purification ceremony."

Camille's defense of his friend Dillon was published as "Letter to General Dillon," after Dillon implored him following his imprisonment. There was not much to say about any case against Dillon, except that there was no evidence of disloyalty to the Jacobins or treason whatsoever. On the contrary, he has served the Republic on the Belgian front at great personal risk. The name Camille Desmoulins coming to his defense was enough to save him, for a time, and Dillon was released.

The purification ceremony applies to those accused of slackness in their devotion or service to the Republic, or worse, of "incivism," the most intolerable sin. The accused must appear on his own in the hall before the assembled members of the Jacobin Club for examination and to purge the sins of which they are accused. If adjudged innocent, the defendant resumes a status as member in good standing of the club; if he fails to disprove the suspicions or accusations that led the Jacobin Club to summon him, he remains unclean, and his name is erased from the membership of the club.

That is what happened just yesterday to Anarcharsis Clootz; his name was erased from the club's membership after a violent speech delivered by Robespierre, who repeated verbatim the accusations he had written in the second number of *The Old Cordelier*. This is tantamount to a death sentence. For expulsion from the club leads inexorably to arrest and trial before the Revolutionary Tribunal. Now, Camille frets, he will have yet another innocent man's blood on his conscience.

Camille is indeed vexed. "I think th-that, in actuality, some want to condemn me for my words. We are returned to the Spanish Inquisition."

"Come, Camille. You can't be surprised that the club wants to get to the bottom of whatever possessed you to write that piece on behalf of Dillon. He has never concealed nor apologized for the fact that he is a monarchist. I know you aren't a fool; you know what you need to do. I'll be there, and my purpose will be to help you out of this. Just follow my lead; you'll know what to say; say what I invite from you, and all will be well."

"When am I required to appear?"

"Tomorrow afternoon, at two."

After Robespierre leaves, Camille visits Danton, who still lives nearby; trying to stay calm, he describes the ordeal that awaits him.

"Ha! Well done, Robespierre," says Danton. "He is behind this. This purification ceremony nonsense, this religious rite, his invention. He wants you to know that your life depends on him. Your life is in his hands. He doesn't trust you. There's that Dillon business. Now, of course, he's nervous that I'm back, and there's *The Old Cordelier*. He's giving you a chance to cross him; to rebel. Don't. We need to be smarter than he is. We'll live on and stop the terror. He's right. You need to speak from his text. Do what you have to do."

Now Camille must endure the torment of a sleepless night. The ultimate horror is this: yes, he can save himself, but it is his very humanity that makes him suspect to the Jacobins. He grieved at the death of his old Girondin friends; he was anguished that he was indubitably an agent in their annihilation and Olympe's death. Yes, they had become his political enemies, but he grieved for them as a human being, for their death and their suffering, because of their humanity and their past associations and friendships. He did what he did to save Dillon only because he is a friend; the time is long past that their relationship would be other than a problem for Camille.

The empathy between one human and another is the very essence of our humanity. So too, it seems, is our inhumanity to one another. Camille feels trapped. Robespierre has outmaneuvered him once again. He embarked on *The Old Cordelier* project to recover his humanity, to redeem himself. Yet to continue that course, he must reaffirm his very deeds that he has sought to expiate through *The Old Cordelier*.

Considering the price of rebellion, he imagines what it must feel like the moment that the guillotine makes contact with your flesh. He imagines his dripping head, held up by the executioner for the crowds to howl at. Would he suffer?

How would he conduct himself on the scaffold? He is haunted that he may not be able to maintain the dignity shown by Brissot,

Madame Roland, Olympe, and so many others. For him, life is still precious. Most troubling of all, he worries what will happen to Lucile and Horace if he dies. At last, he is reconciled; he must survive for them. This single thought gives him enough peace to sleep for a few hours. He will retain his humanity by prioritizing his love for his wife and his son.

Next day, before the Jacobin Club, he feels better, more in control; thoughts of Horace and Lucile are still ever present. He must survive this test for them. He must live for Lucile and Horace. The anticipation was worst of all. Now he feels that with Robespierre on his side, he can slip past his inquisitors.

Camille is seated before the club members in the spacious hall. The galleries are empty; this is a closed session. A man named Lefort stands at the rostrum, interrogating him.

"What is your connection with Dillon?"

"We had been friends, nothing more. One of my faults is that I am attracted to certain people even against my best interest, for reasons I do not well understand."

"That is why you defended him?"

"No. I believed Dillon to be brave and useful to the Republic, and therefore I defended him. I was deceived. He misled me. I regarded him a friend, so I defended him. I regret what I did. I have not seen him for three months."

Here Lefort pauses, as Camille's new condemnation of Dillon, his change of position, sinks in. Lefort is a skilled questioner.

Later, Lefort asks, "We have heard that at Brissot's trial you said that the Girondins were true Republicans and would die like Brutus."

Camille has been mentally rehearsing the speech he is about to give, and now is the time to deliver it. "That is not true. I did not say that. Yet, I was distressed at the trial of the Girondins and would like to explain why. I was in an extraordinary position with regard to the Girondins. I have always loved and served the Republic, but I have often been deceived respecting those who pretended to serve it. I adored Mirabeau; I confess it; but I sacrificed my friendship and my admiration as soon as I realized that he had ceased to be Jacobin. I was always the first to denounce my own friends. From the moment that I realized that they were conducting themselves badly, I resisted the most dazzling offers, and I stifled the choice of friendship that their great talents had inspired in me. I have done this because I cherish the Republic. And now, of the sixty revolutionaries who attended my wedding, only two friends remain to me now, Danton and Robespierre."

Here he is careful, exerting himself, to avoid even a hint of tremor in his voice. "All the others have emigrated or are guillotined. Of this number were seven of the twenty-two. A movement of emotion in me was surely very pardonable on this occasion. Notwithstanding, I swear that I did not say, 'They die as republicans, like Brutus.' I said, 'They die as republicans, but as federalist republicans,' because I do not believe that there were any royalists amongst them." He meant that they too were republicans, yet they would not subordinate the interests of their constituents in the provinces to the survival of the nation and the Republic.

"Camille has been unlucky in his choice of friends!" now cries one of the Jacobins present. "Let us prove to him that we know how to choose ours better, by welcoming him warmly."

Now at last Robespierre says something, his intonation pious. "Camille is easily led and over-confident," he says. "He has virtues and weaknesses. But he has always been a republican. He loved Mirabeau, Dillon; but he has himself broken his idols when he found that he had been deceived, sacrificing his friends on the altar he had raised to them, as soon as he understood their perfidy. I adjure him to pursue his career with confidence, but to be more reserved in the future, and to endeavor not to be deceived with regard to the men who play a great part upon the political stage."

Robespierre is himself the law. So Camille is adjudged by the club to be clean, and he leaves with his life saved. Yet he wrestles with a growing disquiet.

CHAPTER 42

TODAY CHARLOTTE SMYTH IS in tears. Her husband has been arrested. It seems that wealthy British merchants pose a greater risk to the Republic than a philosopher who tried to save the king's life, for Paine is still free. Yet having destroyed the Bastille, they must hold Robert in a beautiful edifice, the Scots College. The universities have now been abolished by the Convention, and this one is now a prison.

She tells Paine that she is unable to carry on their dalliance while her husband, whom she loves very much, is imprisoned by despots, his life in grave danger. She pleads with him to help her. But his intervention would only make matters worse for the Smyths. There is nothing he can do for them. He has not been to the Convention for many sessions.

Now he spends most of his days alone. He is the only lodger left in the Saint-Denis house. They took the last two English lodgers besides Paine. Awakened by loud banging at the gates, he saw the landlord going with the candle to the gate, which he opened, and police with muskets and fixed bayonets entered. Three weeks later, the police returned and took the English landlord off into the night. He does not understand why they have yet to come for him.

He is unable to write. Pen and ink are of no use to him: no good here can be done by writing, for no printer dares to publish what he writes. There is risk even in writing private anecdotes of the times, for these would be thoroughly examined, and tortured into any meaning. There are no personal subjects of which he can bring himself to write, for he grieves at the fate of his friends.

Once again, he finds solace only in cognac, and also some relief by walking alone in the garden and in the surrounding neighborhood. He curses the revolution he was once proud to defend. He expects, every day, the same fate as his friends — arrest and beheading by guillotine. He appears to himself to be on his death bed, for death is on every side of him.

Yet sometimes good things happen when least expected. Marguerite arrives suddenly in his room while he is lying on his bed; he has been drinking. She appears as the first time he laid eyes on her. A pretty face with a prominent nose and golden eyes, a cascade of curled bright red hair; petite, with bare arms; a simple unadorned blue dress cut low at the neckline; the dress highlighting her narrow waist and the supple lines of her body; her jaw line exquisite. Her lovely lips are parted. It is no hallucination.

She says, "I felt that I could not end what was between us as I had done. What we have had between us is genuine, it is real." Her voice is shaking. She takes a step forward and appears unsteady; she herself has been drinking.

He says feebly, "Oh, look at me; I'm in no condition to receive visitors, least of all you; my apartment is so messy. I have kept thinking of you."

Then all across this — the terrible memory of his dead friends and his ruined revolution — comes the magnificence of her naked body. She lies in the crook of his arm, both of them naked, their bodies pressed together, communicating nothing more than the warmth they exchange in that cold, darkening apartment.

They turn to face one another; there are passionate, spontaneous kisses, and it is as though he is enveloped, insulated by her bosom and caresses from the terror and grief that were in the atmosphere all around him before she came. They make love, and then while laying there once more together, he realizes that it is sadness as much as longing that has brought her here.

Disengaging herself, she says softly, "I must tell you about Nicolas and me."

She and Bonneville are now married. He is still continually in Germany at work on his clandestine Illuminati projects. She is lonely. So, not entirely content, she has returned to Paine's arms.

———————

Living thusly, at the brink of both death and ecstasy, inspires him to write again in earnest. He is now resolved to begin working again, for indeed, he has no time to lose. Yet in order to do so, he must put out of his mind the memories that bring him dread and grief.

He titles this new work *The Age of Reason*. In religion's former place, there must arise a new creed that gives meaning, for without meaning, it is impossible to maintain order. The new creed ought simply to be this: Humans must be free to seek meaning for themselves, and for all humans, through experience, which will lead finally to finding meaning within their inner selves. Human experience itself is the source of all meaning, not only the meaning of our own lives, but also the meaning of the entire universe. The power to find meaning through strictly human experience resides within each and every human, and thus all humans must be not only free but also regarded and treated as equals, and each life is precious to an equal degree, irrespective of wealth or social status or gender or race.

He contemplates the source of humans' rights to liberty and equality, but there is nothing to say that would not sound like resort to scriptural authority. He decides that it is impossible to discover any origin of rights other than in simply the origin of humans. He decides it is best just to presume that human rights attach to human existence, and so he does not address their source.

CHAPTER 43

SOMEONE STEPS BOLDLY ONTO the landing outside and knocks loudly, insistently. Paine rises from his desk and opens the door, his heart beating wildly. It is Camille Desmoulins. Camille is losing weight; he is a lean little man with an exaggerated jaw line and prominent cheekbones. His eyes are hollowed and tired-looking. The terror is exhausting everyone, it seems, though for distinct reasons. Camille enters. Paine returns to his desk, and Camille seats himself on a chair.

"What do you want, Camille? Are you here to arrest me? You won't be able to do it alone."

Camille's face darkens; a blood rush, whether from anger or shame, Paine cannot tell. He is certain that to kill does not come naturally to this young man.

Camille replies, "N-no. I am here to help you. The time . . . h-has come for you to leave France. I am aware that within a few days the Convention will issue a resolution for your arrest and imprisonment. I warned you not to try to save the king. N-now this is the consequence. Everyone knows where you are, of course. I even know how to access your secret back entrance."

"Did Marguerite send you?"

"No. She and I no longer speak. H-how can I help you elude arrest?"

"I cannot accept your help. You are possibly the person most responsible for the murders of my friends. Now Clootz is proscribed because of you. It is natural that they draw a connection between Clootz and the other foreigner who is a delegate to the Convention. You will be responsible for our end as well."

Camille's eyes flash, and he leans forward. "Paine, I plan to stop the terror. Danton and I believe that a majority of the people disapprove of the terror."

"I don't believe that a man such as yourself can stop the terror."

"H-have you seen my new paper, *The Old Cordelier?*"

"I have. It is the reason that Clootz is proscribed."

"R-Robespierre wrote those words. H-he is approving the proofs before they go to press. I have no other choice. Nonetheless, *The Old Cordelier* has criticized the terror, and it will eventually demand a stop to it. That is our plan."

"You have a potent pen. That much we have seen. But you are always under the dominance of others. There is always an over-lord. For now, your pen is Robespierre's primary instrument of terror. You will never be your own man. You will never act on your own account. And this will be your legacy for all eternity. Mine will be *Common Sense*, and that I tried to save the king. I prefer to go to the guillotine than bear a reputation such as yours."

"I would put my own life at risk if I rebelled against Robespierre. I have a family. A child and a w-wife."

"There you go—as I said, a man such as yourself cannot stop the terror. You will never be your own man. Leave, Camille; I want nothing to do with you."

Camille is rising from the chair. "Paine, I will do all I can to stop the terror before you fall victim to it. I promise."

"You killed the mother of your lover."

Camille stops in his tracks. He looks at Paine, stricken. He says, "Yes, I did. And I killed my lover too; Olympe was my lover also." He puts his hands to his face and flees Paine's apartments.

Camille has been a long time seated at his desk; the same place where he composed his *Secret History* and each edition of *The*

Old Cordelier. It is time to compose the third number of *The Old Cordelier*. Yet his pen is paralyzed. The purification rite was so distasteful, degrading; the foul taste of it still consumes him. Even alone, as he is now, his face is hot with shame. Robespierre's words to the Jacobin Club were impossible to bear, as were Paine's.

He has a throbbing headache. *You will never be your own man. You will never act on your own account. And this will be your legacy for all eternity.* These words are hitting him in the head like fists, ceaselessly.

Paine is right, he realizes. He must disengage from Robespierre and act on his own account, to stop the terror. That is the only way.

A book lies open nearby—*Tacitus*. He has an idea, but he is frozen by fear. He cannot execute it. Finally, he sighs, fixes his gaze on the book, and puts the pen he holds in contact with the blank page before him. He can write it without cost. *Just write it*, he tells himself. He'll write it and see what comes of it. He'll write it or try to; he'll see if what he writes is even any good. Whatever he thinks of it, he can then decide not to publish it.

He gazes at the printed page, the *Tacitus*. He begins to write, a contemporary satire of *Tacitus*. As satire, perhaps his words will less likely offend, and yet as satire, their impact may be more profound. Even better, his satire will deploy irony. Now the words flow, filling page upon page until he is finished.

Since the Republic and the Monarchy are even now engaged in a war to the death, which must inevitably end in a bloody victory for one or the other, who would deplore the triumph of the Republic after having read the description which history has left to us of the triumph of a Monarchy, after having thrown a glance upon the rough and unpolished copy of the picture given us by Tacitus which I am going to present to the honorable circle of my subscribers?

Augustus was the first to extend the law of lese-majeste, in which he identified writings which he called counter-revolutionary. As soon as words had become state crimes, it was only a step to transform into offenses mere glances, sorrow, compassion, sighs, silence even. Everything gave offense to the tyrants.

He writes much more than this, providing explicit examples, but these words are the crux of it. Now the satirical, the ironic turn: today the revolutionaries themselves, not the dead royalty, are the analogues of Augustus!

Yet the portrait of a tyrant, drawn by the hand of the greatest painter of antiquity, and by the historian of philosophers, is now become the portrait, taken from current events, of those today who liken themselves to Cato or to Brutus; and that which Tacitus called despotism and the worst of governments sixteen centuries ago, is today called liberty and the best of all possible worlds.

He is, perhaps, more explicit than he needs to be in connecting the regime which currently rules France—not the deposed royalty—with Augustus. He reiterates that he is shielded by the law of the liberty of the press, and he again dares any man to assert that one may not write as freely in France as in England.

When he is finished, he leans back and inspects his work, editing, making improvements. He is awash with joy, a sense of triumph and well-being. This, he is sure, is the finest thing he has ever written, and it will help rehabilitate his legacy. It is his destiny to have composed it; and only his sordid past could have led to this.

He must show it to Danton, then to Robespierre. He cannot bear to reveal it to either one of them. They will both, he is sure, impel him to alter it, or to scrap it altogether. Yet can't he just say it was merely a translation of *Tacitus*?

He resolves that neither will see it before publication. He must make this statement; he simply cannot do otherwise and continue to live with himself.

CHAPTER 44

CAMILLE AND DANTON HAVE been walking along the Seine, and now it is nearly the same hour as their previous meeting here when they first planned *The Old Cordelier* and resolved to stop the terror. But in this twilight now the sun is not blood red; a glowing orange ball descends behind the horizon. Their habit is now to speak out-of-doors. The true source of the regime's power is a vast number of collaborators, informants, and spies.

"You didn't show me your draft of the number three," says Danton. "It has drawn a great deal of displeasure from the Mountain."

"I didn't think I needed to; it was my best work ever. If . . . if it displeases those who would perpetuate the terror, so be it."

"The point isn't that you need me as editor. We agreed that we would collaborate and reach agreement on the content."

"I'm sorry. The truth is that I feared you would kill it. And I had to say what I said."

"It is very good." Danton turns to look at Camille. He grasps the stonework of the bridge as if he is unsteady on his feet. "Camille, I know how you feel. I share your craving for redemption. Remember, and history will not forget, that it was I who first proposed the Revolutionary Tribunal, and then the Committee of Public Safety. Then I could not save the Gironde." He is choked by emotion, and a great tear streams down the scarred and misshapen face of this once great tribune of the people.

"We sold out the number three printing in record time. F-fifty thousand copies."

"I'm surprised Robespierre approved it."

"I didn't show it to him either."

There is a silence. Finally, Danton says, "Have you heard from him since it appeared?"

"No. He has been ignoring me. Even at the Convention."

"Have you tried to see him?"

"Not yet."

"You should go to see him. Show him a great deal of affection." Danton pauses. "But wait; let's think about this. I wonder about Robespierre's reaction. Perhaps he is on his heels. When will your fourth number be ready for me to read?"

"Tomorrow."

"What is it going to say?"

"I think that now is the time to demand a Committee of Public Clemency."

"Very good. Let's do it! Then wait seeing him until after we issue that one. If you see him first, he may get you to show him it first, and then kill it."

———————

The Old Cordelier, number four, begins with an epigraph, from Robespierre's bible, Rousseau's *Social Contract*: "The strongest is never strong enough always to be master, unless he transforms strength into right, and obedience into duty."

Rousseau, Robespierre's Jesus. Camille's hope is not necessarily to avoid inciting Robespierre. It is to convert him. He understands perfectly well that this is hubris, yet this vain hope is all that he has left to give life meaning, and he reasons that certainly Robespierre must yield to what must be the true longing of the masses. Still, he remains confident that his lifelong friendship with Robespierre will save him, if not the power of the majority of the people whom he is sure are repelled—though terrorized—by the terror. His public, yet very personal appeal to Robespierre:

*O my dear Robespierre, my old college friend, you whose elo-
quent speeches posterity will read and reread, remember the
lessons of history and philosophy: that love is stronger, more
enduring than fear. Why would clemency be a crime in our
Republic? Open the prisons to the two hundred thousand citizens you call suspects, for in the declaration of rights there is
no house of suspicion. You wish to exterminate all your enemies by the guillotine! Was there ever any greater folly? For do
you send a single soul to the scaffold without making ten new
enemies for yourself among their families and friends? Do you
believe they are dangerous, these women, these old men, these
morons, these self-servers, these foot-draggers of the revolution
you are locking up? No, the strong and the brave among them
have emigrated. The rest do not merit your anger. Let us create
a Committee of Public Clemency and, believe me, liberty will
be strengthened and Europe will be vanquished.*

December 21, 1793: Early in the morning a long queue forms
at the door of the publisher bookseller, Dessense. Camille cannot
stay away; he is there to greet them and thank them for reading
his pamphlet. Soon they are fighting with one another to get the
fourth number of *The Old Cordelier.* By afternoon the printing is
sold out, and they are paying for it at second hand, at third hand,
the price rising always, until it reaches as much as a louis for one
copy. Impatient, the people read it in the streets; Camille sees that
some of the faces are streaked with tears.

That night, in the Jacobin Club, one Nicholas, a juror on the
Revolutionary Tribunal, mounts the tribune and shouts, "I rise, to
denounce Camille Desmoulins! I accuse him of having written a
libel with criminal and counter-revolutionary intentions. I appeal
to those who have read it. Camille Desmoulins has been within a
close shave of the guillotine for a long time! I demand the expulsion of Camille Desmoulins from the bosom of this society."

Loathsome Hébert stands and says he supports the measure. Yet there is no motion, and Robespierre gives Camille a sharp look, indicating he should remain seated and not speak. Indeed, everyone knows that because of his stammer Camille is not an effective speaker, he does not think well on his feet, and his practice is to respond in writing.

"So this how it is going to be," Camille says to himself. "This is, after all, not merely a journalistic feud. It is a fight to the death." He resolves to present his written brief on his own behalf in *The Old Cordelier* number five.

The sharp look that Robespierre gives him is nevertheless meaningful. Robespierre is still looking out for his interests. Robespierre has not spoken to him since publication of the third number, and Camille is hurt and angry at this silent treatment. They should have it out if Robespierre is unhappy.

But he cannot bring himself to visit Robespierre. And he does not want to show insecurity or weakness. Yet, the people, Camille feels, are on his side.

CHAPTER 45

EACH TIME THE NIGHTMARE has been the same. A loud knocking on the door as he sleeps and, waking, Paine cannot get up to answer the door. He is paralyzed. Shouting comes from outside, in French: "Open up! You are under arrest, by order of the Convention. Open the door!"

This time is different. Suddenly he is awake and able to move. The knocking continues. He realizes that he is awake, and this is no nightmare. He is in White's Hotel. It is December 28, and yesterday he came here to dine with friends and spend the night. It is about four in the morning, and he laid down to sleep not three hours ago, after a subdued night drinking with the poet Joel Barlow, Helen Maria Williams, and John Hurford Stone—the latter two of them imprisoned last October and newly released with the help of Helen Maria's sister's French fiancé. Mary Wollstonecraft was there—her pregnancy starting to show, while her counterfeit husband is away in La Havre pursuing some dubious business transaction. While in France she has found a new lover, the American Gilbert Imlay, and he has made her pregnant. But he has not agreed to marry her. Rather, Ambassador Morris is helping them carry on a pretense of marriage to protect Mary from arrest. As a British subject, she is at risk. Also present was Achille Audibert, the young man who escorted Paine from England to Paris.

The thumping at the door is getting louder, as are the shouts from the corridor. Still in his sleepwear, he unbolts and opens the door. Eight men stand near the doorway. Five uniformed policemen, two members of the Committee of Public Safety—he recognizes their faces, but cannot recall the names—and the hotel manager; seemingly he has just arrived, out of breath, bearing a duplicate key to his door.

"I asked them to knock first, as a courtesy," he says, breathless.

A document is handed to the hotel manager, and he is asked to read it aloud, translating it into English for Paine. The hotel manager reads, in English, "The Committee resolves that the persons named Thomas Paine and Anacharsis Clootz, formerly Deputies to the National Convention, be arrested and imprisoned, as a measure of general security; that an examination be made of their papers, and those found suspicious put under seal and brought to the Committee of General Security."

———————

The following evening, after a trip to Saint-Denis and the police's search of his papers there, Paine is newly arrived in the Luxembourg prison. With a kind of relief he settles exhausted on the paillasse inside the cell, his new home—measuring eight by ten, level with the earth outside, floored with brick. Close-fitting boards let in slivers of lamplight from outside a window. He is relieved that he was able to save *The Age of Reason*, leaving it with his friend Joel Barlow, who accompanied him to Saint-Denis. He sleeps, then wakes in pure darkness, feeling his heartbeat, feeling as though he were buried alive, with terrible clarity appreciating he could any time be dragged to a tumbrel. A whispered curse for getting himself into this predicament. Finally he falls back to sleep. He wakes to slivered sunshine and the scent of must, the walls damp. Inside the cell, the only furniture is the straw-stuffed mattress upon which he lies, a chair, and a box for his belongings.

CHAPTER 46

CAMILLE IS HUNCHED OVER the fifth number of *The Old Cordelier* when Lucile enters his study. She hands him papers, pages of a letter, just received from Louis Fréron, a commissioner in Toulon, which the revolutionary army has just recaptured from the British. Fréron is an old friend, as old a friend nearly as Robespierre. They attended the Lycée Louis-le-Grand together. He was the one who introduced Camille to Lucile and her mother, and he became one of Lucile's ardent admirers and would-be lovers. He was with Camille in the Palais-Royal on July 12, 1789. He has been on the Mountain with Camille, Robespierre, and Danton, but for many months now he has been in Toulon.

The letter swoons over Lucile, as is his custom. He "misses the thyme and wild herbs with which Madame Desmoulins' pretty, dimpled hands had fed me;" he recalls "the idylls, the willows, the graves, and the bursts of laughter of that Lucile who read Young and Grecourt at the same time;" in his mind's eye, he sees Lucile "trotting about in her room, gliding over the polished floor, sitting for a moment at her piano, and whole hours in an easy-chair, dreaming, giving the reins to her imagination, then making the coffee with a filtering-bag, behaving like a sprite and showing her teeth like a cat." He is charmed remembering her "melancholy mingled with her sweet laughter."

Then, about Camille, his attitude is, quite naturally, completely different. This letter addresses *The Old Cordelier*, fretting over the "denunciations" of Camille; he counsels that Camille "should bridle his imagination with regard to his Committee of Clemency."

He also tells Lucile about the joy he has experienced finding his sister and her family, who were residing in Toulon when it fell to the British, safe as ever in their residence now that it is once again in French control. It was his concern for them that impelled him to volunteer and press to be appointed the Convention's representative with the expedition to retake Toulon.

Camille casts the letter aside and bows back over his work. "What a lovely portrait he paints of you, Lucile," he says.

"Camille, speak to me. Look at me," she says emphatically. "What is happening to us? You and me? We are all we have. Yet you tell me so little any longer; I know more than you think I do. We have gotten ourselves into difficulties, I know, but if we are to solve our problems, it will be the two of us who do it, together. You confide only in Danton, but nobody listens to him anymore. He's lost his courage and vigor. Now, look at me." She grips his shoulder, demanding that he meet her eye. "I laugh no more; I never touch my piano; I dream no more: I am nothing but a machine now."

It is true. Ever since the Jacobins' murders of the Girondins and Olympe, everything has changed, for their relationship and for him, for their social circle, as much as for France. He does not speak to her as he used to; perhaps he blames her partially that he has killed their friends. Only during those bursts of energy as he is composing the latest number of *The Old Cordelier* is he a semblance of his old brash, charming self, and only then does he try to be warm and generous toward her. Yet, in truth, none of this is her fault; she did not ask to be here, with him, buffeted by the Reign of Terror. She cares mostly about their son, her family.

He tries to give her a look of empathy and infuse his voice with warmth. "I have been reproached enough at the Jacobin Club for the third and fourth number of *The Old Cordelier*. I cannot take any more reproach; from Fréron, least of all. He does not seem to have actually read them, though I know he is a subscriber. I won't accept chiding from one who has helped bring the terror to Toulon. Have you heard about the mass murders of suspected royalists there?"

"Didn't Robespierre approve the proofs?"

"He did." This is a half-truth, but he doesn't want to make her afraid. "And he is dealing with aggressors on all sides. Collot d'Herbois has just returned from Lyon, and Saint-Just and Le Bas have returned from Alsace to Robespierre's side. From places where they all supervised mass murder. These brutes can tell that I do not approve of them, and so they are my bitter enemies. The Cordeliers Club cast me out. You are right that Danton is no longer effective. Danton and I, we are hemmed in on every side, and only Robespierre and possibly the unreliable people—fickle and disposed to the herd—protect us." These last words he says with some bitterness.

He pauses, then tries to make his voice more upbeat. "Yet I am sure that my vanquishment of Hébert will finally reform Robespierre! I am sure of this. I will deliver Hébert's headless corpse to Robespierre." By now, Camille is shaking, nearly in tears. "But I'm afraid that Max now thinks that I have been too outspoken. My hope has been to force an end to the terror, and so while my explicit target has been Hébert, Max now sees that more broadly I attack the terror, and therefore his own deeds. He is afraid, as I am."

"What do you mean, 'afraid'?" She herself is suddenly looking afraid, and he feels his heart ripped from his bosom for it.

"W-we are afraid of losing our positions, our influence. Just that. Y-yet I must deal with the terror as I have decided to do, without regret; I must move forward with this project. Of what importance is success to me? Lucile, because of something I did, dozens of people I once called our friends are now dead. I cannot bear the sight of all this accumulated injustice, death, and wrong. The dead, too, have children; they have wives and mothers and fathers." He stops, choked, feeling again that he is about to cry. "And also Hébert is crude enough to attack me for marrying a rich woman." Innuendos concerning Camille's infidelities are the currency of *Le Père Duchesne*, with repeated insinuations that

Camille married Lucile for her money.

Her eyes flash. "Ah! Why do they talk about me at all? Let them ignore my existence, let me live in the midst of a desert. I have asked nothing from them; I will give them everything I own, provided we don't have to breathe the same air! The monsters." Her face is trembling, her eyes are filled with tears, but he sees that she will not let herself cry. "Camille, I know you are doing what you feel you have to do to save the revolution."

"It's not just that. I have to save my soul and yours, or there is nothing more to live for."

"If only we could just forget them, and all the misery they cause us. Camille, hold me."

He rises, and they embrace; it has been a long time, and it feels right, it feels good. She says, "Life has become such a heavy burden. There is nothing but horror around us. I can't even think—thinking, once such a pure and sweet pleasure—alas! I have shut such terrible sorrow in my heart, meeting you with such serene looks. I try to effect courage that you may not lose yours, but I can't take this anymore." They are both crying now. "Do what you have to do to save the revolution and to save us too." She covers his neck with kisses; they kiss on the mouth.

"Where is Horace?" he asks, his voice husky.

"Danton's; he is with Louise."

She takes his hand and leads him into the bedroom. They make love; a kind of pathetic, grasping, desperate love, wetting their cheeks with mutual tears.

Camille feels that in the fifth number of *The Old Cordelier* he is writing for his very life—his own and possibly Danton's and their families'. His instinct is to defend himself and his attacks on the terror, and to show no weakness. He can do that and avoid offending Robespierre by bringing the full force of his condemnation on Hébert, who is the ideal target for the fifth issue of *The Old*

Cordelier. Camille's memory of Hébert's cruelty and subversion of due process in the trials of the Girondins and Olympe fires his hatred for that man and hardens his aim to destroy him. But he must take care to avoid criticizing Robespierre.

> *Don't you know, Hébert, that when the tyrants of Europe wish to vilify the Republic, when they wish to cause it to be believed that France is covered with the darkness of barbarism, that Paris, so praised for its Attic glory and taste, is peopled by Vandals; don't you know, wretched man, that to gain their ends it is extracts from your writings that they insert in their gazettes?*

Now is the time to remind Parisians of his bona fides as a patriot, and so he recounts the events in the afternoon of July 12, 1789, when Camille climbed up on a table and cried out to the milling crowd, "To arms!"

Hébert is also loathsome to him because of his belittlement of Camille's marriage and Lucile. Now is the time to defend his wife and their marriage, while leveling at Hébert (as innuendo) a potentially lethal charge of financial chicanery.

He again involves the ancients as inspiration, hoping to elevate his message above petty political self-interest, to universal importance. He aligns himself with Brutus and Cicero.

Camille also defends Deputy Pierre Philippeaux, as he promised himself he would. Philippeaux, the commissioner returned to the Convention from the Vendée, is young, upright, proud, and naïve. He does not hide his anguish and guilt—his stricken conscience—at atrocities he has witnessed in the Vendée committed by the now victorious revolutionary army. On December 23, in the marshes of Savenay in Loire-Inférieure, not far from Saint-Nazaire, the revolutionary army finally crushed what remained of the rebel army, finishing the battle in a massacre. Then the Convention resolved that a policy of scorched earth must ensue. Philippeaux has inveighed against the cruelties of the Republican generals, whom he calls "the executioners of La Vendée," and, like

Camille, he demands clemency for the Vendeans and all others incarcerated as counter-revolutionaries. With terrible vehemence he has denounced "useless cruelties and senseless tactics." Farms have been destroyed, crops set afire, and even forests burned and villages razed. Killings have targeted residents of the Vendée regardless of whether they are civilians or soldiers, their politics, age, or gender. Women have been a special target, for they are carrying, or would carry, anti-revolutionary babies.

It is said that after the Convention adjourned following Philippeaux's address, a friend said to him, "What have you done, you unlucky fellow? You have let loose the War Office, the Committees, the Cordeliers, the Jacobins, and the Commune upon yourself!" Fearless, Philippeaux published a pamphlet that reiterated his accusations of treasons against the generals in the Vendée.

In *The Old Cordelier*, Camille extolls the courage and integrity of Philippeaux.

Finally he writes, *The condition of things, such as it is, is incomparably better than four years ago, because there is a hope of "amendment."*

Once he has completed the piece, Camille writes to his estranged father: *Farewell, I embrace you; take care of your health, so that I may press you to my heart if I am to outlive this revolution.*

CHAPTER 47

JANUARY 5, 1794: TONIGHT at the Jacobin Club, there is a special session; today the fifth issue of *The Old Cordelier* was released — again, every paper was sold within a few hours, and then resold and passed around. The hall is packed, and seats are being sold at high prices. Collot, the comedic actor returned from Lyon, is at the tribune.

He says, "I demand that the club examine further the conduct of Pierre Philippeaux and Camille Desmoulins."

Here it is, thinks Camille. *The reckoning. Once again I will be subject to the purification rite, as was bound to happen.*

Collot cries, "I accuse Philippeaux of conspiring against the revolution with other counter-revolutionaries!"

He then turns to Robespierre, who is now the Jacobin Club's president, after Marat's assassination. Collot pauses. Certainly, he will speak more gently of Camille than he did Philippeaux — after all, Camille is the public voice of the revolution and Robespierre's best friend. Indeed, Collot says, "I am convinced of Camille's genuine patriotism. But he has been misled by bad company." He turns to Camille. "Camille, be more careful in the future; I ask only that you be censured by this assembly."

The patronizing tone of voice and its content are exactly as Camille heard from Robespierre after the second number of *The Old Cordelier* was published. Apparently, they have been talking. Camille cannot help it; he is enraged. He has had enough of being treated with such disrespect. Camille stands and shouts, "Wait!

What do you mean? I demand that the last number of *The Old Cordelier* be read immediately! It contains my defense."

"I oppose the motion!" It is Hébert. "Camille wishes to turn the people's attention from himself, to complicate the discussion!" cries Hébert. "He accuses me of having robbed the treasury—it is an outrageous falsehood!"

"I have the proof of it!" Camille shouts back. He must not shrink from this duel with Hébert. Kill or be killed.

The exchange causes a great tumult in the hall. Now one of Robespierre's shills, his younger brother Augustine, advances to the tribune. The noise abates. In a tone that seems intended to be calming, he says, "These personal disputes should not be allowed. This society does not meet to protect personal reputations, nor is it responsible for the public finances. If Hébert is a thief, that is a matter for the Committee of General Security to investigate; but what does it matter to us? Such reproaches ought not to interrupt the general discussion here."

"I have nothing with which to reproach myself!" cries Hébert.

"You are responsible for stirring up dissent by attacking the liberty of dissent!" responds Augustine.

Hébert falls silent, and Robespierre rises to speak.

"Let's lay aside these personal quarrels," he says, "for the sake of the Republic." His voice is measured, dry, conciliatory. "Now is not the time to discuss Camille's attacks on the editor of *Le Père Duchesne*. Hébert's deeds are well known in any event. Let us confine our discussion to the scope of Collot's original motion—Philippeaux's conduct in attacking the leaders of the army in La Vendée."

Camille is relieved. Robespierre still protects him, while striking backhanded at Hébert, their mutual adversary.

Philippeaux's objective has been not just confession, but to shame. Yet Robespierre, Hébert, and their ilk will not be shamed. Charges fly against Philippeaux; he is not there to defend himself, as he is excluded. They allege that Philippeaux was a Vendée sympathizer. Philippeaux supported counter-revolution. Philippeaux is a traitor.

Three days later: Robespierre is calling his name. Camille received the invitation only last night—in actuality, a summons, to appear at the Jacobin Club and defend his conduct with respect to Philippeaux. Another closed session. He is vexed that Robespierre didn't warn him.

"Camille Desmoulins!" Robespierre calls again, as Camille approaches the hall. "Very well, the people will judge him in his absence."

"Wait! Here I am," says Camille, running in. He is breathless, and now doubly vexed at Robespierre.

When he is seated, Robespierre says, "We have summoned you to explain your dealings with Philippeaux."

Camille answers, "I scarcely know Philippeaux." This is true. And Camille has realized that he cannot save Philippeaux, that all his energy and resources must be devoted to saving himself and his family, and his honor. He cannot save Philippeaux, just as he was unable finally to be of much help to Dillon, who was rearrested yesterday. Yet he will not make matters worse for young Philippeaux.

Camille says, "I am neutral as to his claims. I have no opinion on the matter. I was carried away by his writings, and I confess I did not inquire into their truth. Nor yet have I investigated his claims. My praise was ill-considered, and I retract it." Now they are done with him, Camille hopes.

Robespierre ignores Camille's words, instead addressing the club members thus: "I have several times taken up the defense of Camille. I was compelled by friendship to do this, but today I am forced to adopt a different tone. Camille promised to abjure the political heresies, the erroneous, ill-sounding propositions which cover the pages of *The Old Cordelier*. Camille, puffed by the prodigious popularity of his pieces, and the perfidious praise that the aristocrats heap upon him, has not abandoned the path of error that we traced for him and implored him to avoid. His writings are dangerous; they nourish the hopes of our enemies and arouse public malignity. The writings of Camille are condemnable; but notwithstanding, it is necessary to distinguish carefully the person from his works. Camille is a spoiled child who has good dispositions, but whom bad companions have misled. It is necessary to protest against *The Old Cordelier*, which Brissot himself would not have dared to produce, and to preserve Desmoulins in the midst of us. I demand, in consequence, that Camille's paper shall be burned in the presence of this society!"

Camille feels blood rise to his face; he is beset by shock, indignation, rage. He did not expect such an attack on *The Old Cordelier*, not from Robespierre, who read the proofs of the first two editions, who guided his hand as Camille wrote them, who delighted at the attacks on Hébert, and who has patiently defended Camille for the sake of their old friendship.

Burned! Burned by the Jacobins, as Rousseau's *Emile* was burned by the Paris Parlement! Worst of all, is the patronizing, contemptuous tone of Robespierre's voice. Camille cannot resist the retort that now comes to him. He does not hesitate, feeling at once the power of the words; a grenade made of stuff revered by Robespierre, and so well designed to inflict utmost injury.

"That is all very well, Robespierre!" he cries. The stammer is gone; raw emotion drives him. "But I reply, like Rousseau: 'To burn is not to answer!'"

Rousseau himself fired at Robespierre in rebuke for his hypocrisy!

There is stunned silence in the hall. "So be it," says Robespierre, his tone of voice agitated. "We will answer, then, instead of burning, since Camille still defends his writings. If he wishes it, let him be covered with ignominy; let our society restrain its indignation no longer, since he is obstinate in maintaining his diatribes and his dangerous principles. I was evidently mistaken in believing that he was merely misled; if he had been in good faith, if he had merely written in the simplicity of his heart, he would not have dared to uphold works which are proscribed by patriots and welcomed by counter-revolutionaries. Let Camille be judged out of his own mouth; let his words be read to the society immediately."

Camille remains silent, straining to not interrupt.

Now turning to Camille, his eyes ablaze, Robespierre says, "You will learn, Camille, that had you not been Camille, we would not have indulged you so. The way that you have tried to justify yourself proves to me your bad intentions."

Camille cannot restrain himself any longer. "My intentions! But you knew my intentions! Was I not at your house? Did I not leave my proofs for you to read?"

"I only read one or two; I refused the others!"

Their duel of words goes on this way, retort succeeding retort, like rapid passes by swordsmen, while the public watches amazed—these two powerful men, erstwhile best friends. Camille does not once stammer.

Danton is on his feet. "Do not be afraid, Camille," he says. Danton, he sees, is distressed. "Don't be afraid at the rather severe lesson which Robespierre, out of his strong feeling of friendship, has just given you!"

Camille has nothing left to say. He cannot retract what he has written, for it and this moment have redeemed him. He is trembling, from relief. Camille is filled with a feeling of satisfaction and triumph that is altogether new to him. He no longer fears Robespierre.

"Camille," Robespierre says, his voice contemptuous, "is a strange mixture of truth and falsehood, of cleverness and self-deception. Whether the Jacobins retain or expel him matters very little; he is only an individual. The interests of the nation are menaced by two parties, the counter-revolutionaries and the ultra-revolutionaries: Both Camille and Hébert are equally wrong in my eyes. Read the fourth and fifth editions!"

And the secretary reads them while the hall is silent.

No action is taken to expel Camille, but he is resolved: he will not return to the Jacobin Club. He departs alone, for once at peace with himself and the world.

Next day, he reads, the Cordelier's Club has decreed, *Camille*

Desmoulins, already excluded from our ranks, has also lost our confidence, although formerly he rendered great services to the Revolution.

Yet he tells himself that he is safe; Robespierre ultimately will not abandon him. Robespierre has to pretend to deal with Camille harshly, but once he talks to Robespierre and their friendship is reaffirmed, all would be well. And the people are on his side. They will remember him, and they too oppose the terror.

CHAPTER 48

CAMILLE IS NEARING THE stairs to Robespierre's apartment when Eleonore Duplay appears.

"He's not there," she says.

"Of course he is, Eleonore. You mean he doesn't want to see me?"

"He isn't seeing any visitors. He isn't feeling well."

"What ails him?"

"He's been very upset since you attacked him at the Jacobin Club."

"I didn't attack him."

"You attacked him in your paper; you accused him of being behind the terror. Then you would not retract it. He very well knows what you were up to. You tried to use his affection for you to get him enmeshed in your project; then you used that very paper to condemn his policies."

"He and I want the same ends. We have been in this together from the beginning. I had to tell him that his policies are contrary to our shared objectives."

Camille is also here partially at Danton's behest. Danton's distress has made Camille anxious. Danton said, "They weren't going to burn every last copy of your pamphlets. Robespierre was trying to preserve your place in the Jacobin Club by making a symbolic sacrifice of your work. You should have apologized before the Jacobin Club; instead, you put him on the defensive and embarrassed him. Our aim is to stop the terror, not to achieve some personal vindication. You must see him and repair your relationship."

Now, Eleonore says, "He's hurt that you tried to trap him the way you did. And then you quarreled with him in public. You should know that he has to put the welfare of the revolution, of the society, first."

"I did not mean it that way." He takes a step up and, quick as a cat, she scampers up three steps and stands before him. "I need to talk to him. He misinterprets my intentions."

"I'm sorry. He said he can't be disturbed."

"Eleonore, I'm going to move by you, or through you. What are you going to do to stop me?"

He begins to climb the steps, forcibly stepping by her. She remains where she is and he climbs to the landing; he hesitates a moment, then knocks on the door. There is no answer. From inside he hears a chair creak. He knocks again. He hears movement, and the door opens a crack.

"Camille, I can't see you now. Eleonore told you." Robespierre has been listening.

"Max, we need to sort things out. We'll always be together in this. We might as well work it out now."

"Camille, believe me, I understand you, and I am still generous in my regard for you. I'm grateful for all you've done for the revolution and for me. I know how sensitive you are; you're a poet, really, and the direction of things is upsetting to you. You don't speak, you write; that is your special gift. I want to help you; but you must understand that the good of the people must come first. A patriot must be willing to put the good of the country over his own interests, or that of friends or family. I must also deal with Saint-Just, Le Bas, Hébert, Collot, the others." His voice is now strained; an unprecedented show of emotion. "I can't talk any more now."

He closes the door and Camille is left standing. For what seems several minutes, he can't move. There seems to be a terrible truth in what Robespierre has just said, but in precisely what sense Camille cannot grasp.

Early morning: Camille's mother-in-law Annette, whom he adored before he loved Lucile (when she was a child) and he still adores, bursts into their apartment, beside herself. Claude Duplessis, Camille's thoroughly decent father-in-law who cares little for politics, is under arrest! A group of ruffians posing as policemen arrived before dawn and took him away. She says that these "police" shoved her about, pawed her, ransacked their house.

Camille sprints through the streets, his face tear-streaked. He bolts past Eleonore Duplay, and once again he's at Robespierre's doorstep, falling to his knees, now weeping, pleading. Shouting, "Dear Claude is under arrest!"

The door opens. Robespierre is aghast, Camille can see it in his eyes.

"Hébert!" thunders Robespierre. "Camille, stand up! Go home to your wife. Claude will be free today. Stop crying. Go to your wife. I need to go to the Convention." The door closes.

Before nightfall, Claude is back home. He was found in the Carmelite convent prison by Robespierre's henchmen. Camille returns to Robespierre's doorstep, to thank him. Eleonore is nowhere to be seen. He knocks. Calls to his friend. There is no answer; not a sound from inside.

In the coming days, he returns again and again. Eleonore now is there every day. "He is not well," she says, each time. "He can't see you. Maybe later." Camille goes to the Convention, day after day, but Robespierre is absent from there too.

Camille returns to his study and pours his grief and humiliation into the sixth number of *The Old Cordelier*, recounting the unjust arrest and incarceration of his father-in-law. Such a thing, having happened to a man such as Claude Duplessis, who is uninvolved in politics, can therefore happen to anyone. He heaps blame and more condemnation on Hébert.

Yet, still marked by the trauma of his own personal terror wrought by Claude's arrest, he pleads also that the law of kindness be more powerful than that of terror. He declares that, from the first, he has hoped and preached that the Republic would bring peace and happiness rather than misery and terror.

CHAPTER 49

PAINE IS FREE TO wander around the Luxembourg—erstwhile palace ragged and stripped of its royal furnishings, now a prison. The colossal façade and gardens still radiate the old magnificence, at least.

This experience has taken on a surreal quality. The Luxembourg is the prison set aside for foreigners, aristocrats, and educated elites. While the inmates must constantly be burdened by the prospect of any moment and without warning being brought before the Revolutionary Tribunal and condemned to death, life here is weirdly pleasant, even pleasurable. The prisoners are allowed to mix and walk the vast complex. It is said there are about one thousand of them, and many speak English.

A well-prepared dinner, supplied by a restauranteur, is served in shifts, and there are two courses, one of soup and the next of meat and vegetables, plus a half bottle of wine. The meals cost fifty sous, but Paine's friends, who are permitted to visit him freely, make sure that he never lacks the necessary funds. Not only Barlow but also Marguerite and Charlotte come with regularity. Once Marguerite arrived while Charlotte was there, and the three of them had an enjoyable discussion. Charlotte's husband is now freed.

Friends bring him whatever he needs from outside. The relative freedom within the prison allows for plenty of social intercourse, and it is as if the polished gaiety of the now extinct Paris salons is renewed here. Sophie de Condorcet—the Marquis's exquisitely beautiful wife who once maintained a renowned salon of her own—visits frequently, bravely sketching portraits of prisoners to bring to their loved ones.

There are receptions and parties, with social amusements such as bouts-rimés and dancing. There is sex, sometimes worthy of intrigue, gossip, and social scandal. Perhaps here pleasantry is enhanced by enjoyment of life without thought for future. "Eat drink and be merry for tomorrow we die" is the philosophy that most prevails and gives purpose to the inhabitants of this prison.

Marguerite wants to console him not just with talk but also physical intercourse; when he is in the mood, she raises her dress and splays her legs on the mattress, and they do it quickly to minimize chance of scandal. More often he wants only to talk, or to hold her.

Nevertheless, Luxembourg is a milieu that fails to excite or engage him; his incarceration is less tolerable than the constant dread of losing his life. To him freedom is more precious than life. He prefers to receive his friends in the privacy of his cell.

His friend Joel Barlow has been hard at work trying to gain his release but brings nothing but bad news. He reports that, betraying self-satisfaction, Ambassador Morris said to him, "Thomas Paine is in prison, where he amuses himself with publishing a pamphlet against Jesus Christ," referring to *The Age of Reason*. "So be it. He is better off if I do not call attention to him."

In fact, on January 27, one month after his arrival, Paine has completed a preface and postscript to *The Age of Reason*, which Barlow is fearlessly directing to publication. He has dedicated the work to "My Fellow Citizens of the Untitled States," more than anything in hope that this will help bring about his release—the prospect of release being greater for an American citizen than an English one.

Morris does nothing for him. Paine writes to him: *You must not leave me in the situation in which this letter places me. You know I do not deserve it, and you see the unpleasant situation in which I am thrown.*

CHAPTER 50

THE EARLY SPRING OF 1794 is warmer and sunnier than any Camille can remember—the chestnuts are giving leaf, the city squares are abundant with flowers and blossoms, the Seine flows high and muddy while under the bridges the barges passing one after another bump the stone arches.

For two months, since the arrest of Camille's father-in-law, Hébert and *Le Père Duchesne* have been quiet. Meanwhile, these past six weeks Robespierre has again been sick and homebound, and still he will not see Camille.

Suddenly, word is on the street: Hébert shouts in a session of the Cordeliers Club, amid hurrahs, "Père Duchesne has held his tongue and his heart these two months, at sight of moderates, crypto-aristocrats, Camilles—these villains!—in the Convention itself: but I cannot do it any longer; since there is no other remedy, I invoke the sacred right of insurrection!"

A motion ensues to declare a "state of insurrection." The motion is carried and black crepe is hung over the club's mounted copy of the *Declaration of the Rights of Man and of the Citizen*. Over the next days, Père Duchesne resumes to fulminate in print, a new shrillness betraying desperation, fear of death.

The proclaimed "state of insurrection" means that plans for a repeat of the events of May 31 are a foot—to surround the Convention and demand expulsion of Robespierre and other Jacobins, including Camille. But this time, only two of Paris's forty-eight sections prepare to rise. Nor does the Commune join the insurrection.

On March 13, Robespierre returns to the Convention, amid a rapturous welcome. First thing, he mounts the tribune and denounces Hébert and his faction. Then, March 14, a bolt from the blue: Père Duchesne is suddenly ashes. Hébert and his red-capped acolytes, heretofore magistrates of Paris, worshippers of reason, looters and burners of churches, commanders of the revolutionary army, terrorizers of Claude Duplessis, are arrested and cast into the Luxembourg prison.

Lately, Camille and Hébert have crossed pens in mortal combat, and once again Camille can discern the deadly blow that his quill has struck. The narrative spun by cool, austere Saint-Just in explanation for these arrests follows Camille's own poetic license in *The Old Cordelier*: Père Duchesne and his deeds manifest a plot financed by gold from Pitt and the traitorous émigrés; the revolution's enemies hired Père Duchesne to church-burn and found his new sect of atheism, making the revolution odious and thereby undermining the Republic!

Yet Camille is in a low, anxious mood. He cannot bring himself to celebrate his vanquishment of Hébert, notwithstanding that he was behind Claude's arrest, that Camille's hatred for him remains unabated, and that Hébert's demise be Camille's own handiwork. What it demonstrates is that Robespierre has absolute control over the levers of state. And he now acts through his instrument—that preternatural youth, Saint-Just.

Saint-Just too loathes the Hébertists, but, Camille feels, he hates Camille even more; intolerably, he has replaced Camille as the primary object of Robespierre's affection. Camille can see now that there is nothing to stop them, and he appreciates that his own salvation lies only in whatever remains of his friendship with Robespierre.

———————

While the Hébertists awaited trial, a delegation appeared before the Convention to sing in celebration of their incarceration.

Danton was on his feet. "I object! No one should be allowed to sing songs in the Convention. Not on account of incarcerations and trials! Such behavior is undignified and disrespectful."

Everyone was surprised, for such rectitude is out of his character. He sat, uncharacteristically brooding, ill-tempered, as the objection carried.

Danton is berserk, in a rage. Camille, and their friends, Robert Lindet and Jean Hérault de Séchelles, are walking him up and down the Cour du Commerce before letting him go on his way alone, they hope to Louise. Hérault especially is Danton's good friend, and was the valiant president to the Convention who attempted to resist the arrests of the Girondins the previous year. Once a blue blood, he has family who are émigrés plotting the Republic's destruction. Instead, Hérault joined the revolution. He is amiable yet clever. But now Robespierre has taken his measure.

While commissioner on the Rhine, in charge of the Army of the Rhine, Hérault pursued Danton's program to make peace with the Austrians and the Prussians. As a diplomat, he loyally served Danton, and his wit, his warmth, his culture, and his education make him a supremely enjoyable friend. But he was not an effective general. Eventually, Saint-Just (with cold, discreet, cruel Le Bas beside him) replaced Hérault. They improved army discipline, broke off negotiations with the enemy, impelled the army to take the offensive, imposing a ruthless and bloody regime on all who opposed them, and expelled the invaders.

Having returned in triumph, Saint-Just and Le Bas are established in their new role as Robespierre's proxy and Inquisitors for the Committee of Public Safety, the dictatorship. A reckoning was inevitable for Hérault, whose true crime is his friendship with Danton. Saint-Just accused Hérault of treason and incompetence and expelled him from the committee.

Then Danton read a quote in a morning paper (clearly in reference to himself), from the committee's president, the graybeard Marc Vadier, lately a newly converted Robespierre and Saint-Just sycophant: "Now we'll gut this big stuffed turbot!"

"I am not afraid of him!" shouts Danton. "I'll eat his brains and shit in his skull!"

Later, at night, Camille and Danton are back at the Pont Neuf. "Shall we flee?" says Camille.

"You can't mean that. What about your wife's family? Your family and mine? Our remaining friends. We can't take everyone with us. Where would we go? If I go, I shall be thought guilty of the absurd crimes I'm accused of." There are rumors that the Police Committee has uncovered evidence of Danton's financial corruption. "And if France," he continues, "when she is at last free of her king, casts me from her bosom, what country will give me an asylum? Does a man carry his country on the soles of his shoes?" Danton pauses, gazing at the fire-lit water. "I am not afraid of them. Robespierre does not dare take me on. If I fancied he even thought of it, I would crunch up the fellow's vitals. Robespierre! I will take him with my thumb and twirl him like a top."

"So what shall we do? Just wait for them to come and get us?"

Danton falls silent, consumed by thought. Suddenly he turns to Camille, his movement so sudden and large it bespeaks a kind of violence; he is looking hard at Camille. "There is nothing to be done. Resist? No, enough blood has been shed; I would rather die myself. I prefer to be guillotined rather than to guillotine." All at once his eyes are misty. "Don't worry, Camille. I know that they wish to arrest me, but no — they will not dare."

———————

It is from the papers that Camille learns about Hébert's fate. On March 24, the third day of deliberations, Hébert and his circle were adjudged guilty by the Revolutionary Tribunal, and sentenced to death. They were immediately dispatched to a tumbrel.

Long gone were the composure and presence of mind Hébert exhibited when first incarcerated on May 29, 1793, by the Gironde. On the way to his death, Hébert fainted repeatedly. Where were his friends? He saw he no longer had any. The people no longer cared about him.

He screamed hysterically as the executioners forcibly fastened him to the plank and then laid it horizontally on the bench, his neck beneath the blade. Three times the executioners stopped the blade inches above his neck, to amuse the crowd. The papers reported howls, taunts, and laughter. The fourth time they cut off the head. His corpse was disposed of in a communal grave in Madeleine Cemetery.

Reading this, Camille mutters to himself; broken words. Finally, he whispers, "Please let me die well."

CHAPTER 51

CAMILLE WALKS BRISKLY DOWN the Rue Saint-Honoré, a stack of papers under his arm. A few minutes ago, he had a difficult conversation with his publisher, Dessense, who declared that he was refusing to print the seventh number of *The Old Cordelier*. Before, he had only tried to persuade Camille to make alterations (which Camille refused). Now he also gave Camille a few surplus copies of the first through sixth editions that he had stashed away. Something must have given Dessense a real scare.

"Better give them to you, Camille, than burn them, which is what I would have done. If the Police Committee has this premises searched, I can't have them here. I am not so bold as you, Camille, and I have none of the journalist's reasons for personal animosity. Now go on, take them away. Go!"

Curious it is that Camille himself is not afraid. His *Old Cordelier*, the summit of his life's work, is all that matters now, all that gives him joy and relief.

Still annoyed at Dessesne and muttering to himself about their confrontation, Camille looks up and suddenly sees Michele approaching. He taught Camille at the College Louis-le-Grand. The old teacher halts in front of him. "What have you there, Camille?" he asks.

"Only some numbers of my *Old Cordelier*. Will you have one?"

"No, indeed! It is too dangerous; they burn!" The teacher opens his eyes wide and screws up his face in faux panic.

"Coward!" laughs Camille. He is delighted at the response.

"Eat, drink, and be merry, for tomorrow we die!"

———————

March 30, 1794: A letter from his father arrives. Camille had treated life as sport (when he was not at leisure). It was all—the revolution, in particular—an elaborate game he had imagined put on for his personal amusement and professional advancement.

Now, these past six months, he has learned that life is serious business. Deadly serious.

And now, more confirmation. The letter from his father discloses that Camille's mother is dead. He had not expected this news and was totally unprepared for it.

> M. Desmoulins: —
> My dear son, I have lost the half of myself. Your mother is no more. I have always hoped for her recovery, which has prevented me from telling you of her illness. She died to-day at noon. She is worthy of all our regrets; she loved you tenderly. I embrace your wife, my dear daughter-in-law, very affectionately and sorrowfully, and little Horace. I will write more tomorrow. I am always your best friend,
> Desmoulins.

Camille sits in the parlor, unable to move, so great is his despair. He never feels moderately, whether happy or sad. Yet now he is at his lowest point. Overwhelmed by grief, he has arrived at a place that is unbearable.

He and his mother were no longer close, yet this makes the loss more painful. He had hoped he could do something about that, but has not been to Guise for five years. He has not seen his parents since 1789.

Danton visits, pays his respects. Lucile told him about Camille's mother, and asked him to come by.

In the afternoon, after Danton has left, Robespierre suddenly materializes in front of him, in the parlor. Camille stands to greet him.

"I'm so sorry about your mother," says Robespierre.

Is he hallucinating? No, it is Robespierre himself who stands here before him. Right here beside Lucile's harpsichord. "How did you know?"

"Lucile came by. I asked how you're doing. She said you are despondent. You just learned that your mother passed. So, I decided to come and wish you well."

"Please, sit down." They sit and they talk. Not about the revolution, not about the Convention, nor certainly the terror. They avoid Danton, not even mentioning his name; the same for Saint-Just.

They talk about their times as schoolboys. Robespierre is again "Max." Then the talking stops. There is nothing more to say. They are out of topics. Robespierre looks at him intently, with a kind of expectation. Then, all at once, Max is gone.

———————

Late afternoon, Camille visits Danton's apartment. He is in the study, with his nephew. Danton and the boy have been roughhousing a bit, Camille can see. Now Danton is on one knee in front of the fireplace; violently he thrusts a poker into the fire, stoking it.

"Robespierre just came by," says Camille.

"Oh? What for?"

"I don't know. It was so strange. He said he came to offer condolences for my mother."

"That is all?"

"Yes. We just talked about old times. Very strange."

"Yes. He's a strange man. What was said about me?"

"Nothing. Neither of us brought you up."

Now it is nighttime and there is no sleep for Camille. Lucile has been there to comfort him; seated on his lap; hugs, her head on his chest. Finally she laid down in the adjoining room, and now sleep has overtaken her. Fortunately, there are the proofs for the seventh number of *The Old Cordelier* to distract him.

What drives him in this? He cannot help writing words that Robespierre will surely think critical of him. The epigraph is drawn from Plutarch: *Because never have these tyrants failed to judge in order to destroy, under the pretext of slander, anyone who displeased them.*

He compares Robespierre to Octavius, and Danton to Antony. His condemnation is directed at the cowardly Convention as much as at the predators, the perpetrators of the terror. Only he tries to "bell the cat," so he reiterates his claim to liberty of the press.

He feels the terrible past six months have fully reformed him. The Camille of six months ago would not recognize himself today.

Past midnight, a knock on the door. He is surprised that the visitor is Robert Lindet. At around fifty, and with a carriage and build that makes him look well grounded, he is older than the rest of them and moderate in all things, his temperament as well as his politics. Perhaps his maturity has enabled him to remain influential, and retain his honor as well as his head. Lindet is the last remaining moderate on the Committee of Public Safety and friend of Danton and Camille.

"I have been visiting with Danton," says Lindet. "He asked me to come fetch you."

———————

Danton is seated in his study. The fire blazes bright, casting shadows on his scarred face that tonight bears a grim aspect.

When they are all seated, he looks at Camille and says, "The Committee of General Security has issued a warrant for our arrest. They will come this morning, any time."

Camille is numb to this news. He would not have expected to be so calm. It is as though he expected this, and the truth is that of course he did, somewhere in his mind, even felt it was his destiny and his just deserts. Even as Robespierre visited him a few hours ago with condolences for his mother's death.

"Well," he says, "that makes a lot of sense. But apparently we were the last to know. The warrant is actually signed?"

"Yes," says Lindet. "Two of us withheld our names. Ruhr, and I did as well."

"Just so," says Camille, "and Robespierre visited me this afternoon to pay respects for my mother's passing. That was a sham, it seems, unless he wanted to give me one last chance to burn all the numbers of *The Old Cordelier*. It would not have occurred to me to do so. What are the charges?" Danton answers with unrestrained bitterness.

"They have compiled all of the negative rumors and gossip about financial corruption that have haunted me from our days at the Palais-Royal. All these years, those notes Robespierre kept taking! His pockets bulge with them. They fill the drawers in his hovel at the Duplays'. It appears that he organized them and presented them to Saint-Just. 'Friends of Mirabeau boasted loudly of having shut Danton's mouth: as long as Mirabeau lived, Danton stayed quiet.' That sort of thing. In addition, they accuse me of trying to rescue Brissot from revolutionary justice, plotting to restore monarchy with the duc d'Orléans, and laughing at the word 'virtue.'" He laughs out loud. "There was no discussion of my repeated defenses of Robespierre over the years, or all that he has said on my behalf. When Gabriel died, he wrote a letter and professed 'undying love' to me."

"What are the charges against me?"

"You are charged with moderatism," Lindet says. "You are an indulgent."

"Guilty as charged. This is about my writings, *The Old Cordelier*?"

"There were insinuations, nothing explicit."

"So I am condemned for my writings, and for weeping that my friends were unjustly killed by the state. So be it. Too bad I have not better served them. Have others been charged?"

"All of the so-called Dantonists. Besides the two of you, Philippeaux, La Croix."

"Hérault?"

"Yes. Everyone you'd expect."

Now he feels in his throat a knot gathering. "How did Robespierre explain doing this to me?"

"Saint-Just did almost all of the talking in support of the charge sheet. He denounced the Dantonists. Very eloquent, as usual."

"Saint-Just is effective," says Camille. "But everyone knew that he was Robespierre's mouthpiece."

"I spoke to Robespierre privately. I reminded him of his long and intimate relations with the two of you. He said he regards you both as friends, but he can do nothing, either for or against his friends. His entire life has been a continual sacrifice of his affections to the fatherland. Justice is there to defend innocence, and if his friends are guilty, he will sacrifice them with regret, but still he will sacrifice him, like all the others, to the Republic."

"Very well," says Danton. He is now on his feet. "They are irreformable despots. But we still have our heads. I say they do not dare to kill us. We will defend ourselves before the people, for we have been the ones who have truly roused them to positive action, who touched their hearts. Our enemies will see that it will serve no purpose to kill us, and they will not dare. I am ready to face them at the Revolutionary Tribunal. It is only fair, for it was I who conceived and implemented it!"

"I am going back home," says Camille.

"Mind you," says Danton. "I gave Lindet my word that we will not flee. It would be the end of him."

"I have no intention of fleeing. I want to be with my wife. My first concern is for my family. They cannot flee." A sudden thought strikes Camille. He says, "If Robespierre kills us, who will really be left to defend him?"

Daybreak, about six o'clock, all is quiet, then suddenly horse hooves striking the stone roadbed, wheels grind to a halt, then the tramp of boot heels hitting stone and a clang of arms.

Camille flings open the window and sees soldiers bunched

about the street-facing door below. He moves into the adjoining room; Lucile and Horace are still sleeping, the child beside her, their faces peaceful. He cannot bear to wake her, but he must.

"They have come to arrest me," he whispers. She looks at him wide-eyed. Boot heels are outside the door, and there's a hard knock.

All at once she's on her feet. Lucile is fast collecting clothes and other necessaries for his stay in prison. He asks her to pack a book of poems, *Night Thoughts*, by an Englishman, Edward Young, and a locket which contains a tress of Lucile's hair.

He kneels beside the still sleeping child, gently kisses him. Then he stands, and husband and wife embrace. Her face is in the hollow of his neck, and they both are weeping.

"Don't worry," he whispers. "Danton and I, we are ready to fight. We are ready for them. They won't hurt us. I'll be back."

They are banging the door. Lucile opens it and lets them in. The drawing room is crowded with grenadiers, Camille's little family lost in tricolor badged bicornes suspended like crows amid a forest of bayoneted muskets. Camille looks hard at the pale countenance of the officer in his blue greatcoat, faintly mustached and younger than Camille. Not a flicker of recognition or emotion.

Upon descending the stairs, he reaches out and opens the door. Then, in the street, they bind his arms roughly. He looks up and sees not a window opening on either side of the street. Where are the people?

CHAPTER 52

PAINE CANNOT HELP GAWKING, looking for familiar faces in the queue. Today, March 31, he watches police herd new inmates through the Luxembourg gardens; before entering the prison, they are being processed. Paine is the first to notice the erstwhile Minister of Justice and head of the Committee of Public Safety, whose brainchild is the Revolutionary Tribunal. Danton! Disbelieving his eyes, he cries, "Danton?!"

They join hands, clasp hands. Now many astonished faces are gathering around.

Danton says to Paine, "What you did for your country, I tried in vain to do for mine." He pauses, and everyone is silent. Everyone gaping. "I have been less fortunate," he says, "but not less innocent. They will send me to the scaffold; very well, my friends, I shall go gaily." He laughs, not without bitterness. Suddenly he is grim. Raising his gaze, he cries, "I hoped soon to have got you all out of this: but here I am myself; and it is impossible to tell where it will end!" Two guards roughly escort him inside the Luxembourg.

Camille has not seen Danton since they were with Lindet. From noises he hears outside the cell and his observations through the window, he sees that other prisoners are free to move about the complex, not in solitary confinement as he is. From the window, he sees the lawns and terraces where he first laid eyes on Lucile

344

and her mother. What cruel irony that his cell overlooks the gardens of the Luxembourg. Oh what joy, what sadness!

Thusly isolated, absent charge or interrogation and not even receiving a single newspaper, without knowing why he is being treated differently, his mind is overwrought. He thinks, "If it were Pitt who treated me so severely . . . But my colleagues! But Robespierre, who has signed the order for my imprisonment! But the Republic, after all that I have done for her! This is the reward which I receive for so many virtues and sacrifices for her sake!"

Yet his emotions are mixed. He is surprised to be here, yet he appreciates that this fate is what he made for himself. He killed his friends, and so here he is now, about to be killed by a friend. Indeed, it was he himself who killed the king, and the present regime is more oppressive than was the king's. He gains strange consolation by accepting his own fate as in symmetry with what befell his friends and even the king.

Putting thoughts on paper provides some relief. He is at work on what he intends to be the eighth number of *The Old Cordelier* (though the seventh number is not yet published and there is no prospect at of it ever being published). But first, he writes to Lucile.

My Lucile, my Vesta, my angel. Destiny leads my eyes from my prison over that garden where I passed eight years in following you. A glimpse of the Luxembourg recalls to me a crowd of memories of my love. I am alone, but never deserted by thought, by imagination, almost by the sense of the bodily presence of you, of your mother, of my little Horace.

Send me a water-glass, that one on which there is a "C" and a "D"; our two names. Send me a pair of sheets, and a book in duodecimo which I bought a few days ago at Charpentier's, and in which there are blank pages, made expressly for notes. This book treats the immortality of the soul. I have need to persuade myself that there is a God, more just than men, and that I shall not fail to see you again. Do not be too much affected by my ideas, dearest. I do not yet despair of men and of my liberation; yes, my well-beloved, we shall be able to meet yet once more in the garden of the Luxembourg! But send me that book. Farewell, Lucile! Farewell, Horace! I cannot embrace you, but, through the tears which I shed, it seems to me that I hold you still against my breast.

I am going to pass all my time in prison in writing to you; because I have no need to take up my pen for my own defense. My justification is complete in my eight volumes of The Old Cordelier. *They are a good pillow, upon which my conscience reposes, awaiting the tribunal and posterity.*

Where is Robespierre? Robespierre always delivers his treachery by proxy. Can it be that he will not show his face now, after all his history with Camille and Lucile and Horace? Camille's son is Robespierre's godson! Camille begins to weep.

In the evening, he has just written in the eighth number, *Why is it to individuals that one owes one's preservation, instead of to the Republic?* when there is a scrape in the keyhole, a rattling of keys, the door opens wide, and Robespierre enters alone. Here he is! He has not abandoned Camille. For once, Robespierre confronts his victim. Of course, because Camille is his victim.

Camille is seated on the bed, back to the wall. Robespierre sits on the chair facing him. Camille sits up and moves to the edge of the bed so they are seated face to face, Robespierre a little higher.

"How kind of you," says Camille, "to arrange a view of the Luxembourg gardens where I first laid eyes on Lucile."

Robespierre looks agitated; he sits on the edge of the chair. He has grown thinner and paler still. He brings his hands together and interlaces the trembling fingers, to quell fidgeting.

There are no preliminaries, no small talk. He goes straight to the point of his visit. "This is not what I wanted," he says. "I've tried to protect you. But you will not cooperate. I need your help! You have been putting me, indeed the whole Republic, at risk. Still, I am here, still trying to save you. At least this is a good time and place to have an earnest and confidential word with you."

"Let me go home, Max. You can do it. I'm no traitor, neither is Danton."

"Shut up about Danton!" Robespierre hisses. He is visibly shaking, nearly convulsed, the normally pale face darkening. A moment passes in silence, then another. "Not another word about Danton. This meeting is about you!"

Robespierre looks almost pitiful, bent by an internal anguish. He pauses, gathering himself, then he reaches inside his waistcoat and hands a piece of paper to Camille. A note. Addressed to Robespierre. Lucile's handwriting, yet not quite her usual penmanship.

Camille stares; what she has written seems at first blush incoherent.

That hand which so often pressed yours, forsook the pen before its time, because it could no longer hold it to trace your praises. And you have sent him to death! You have then understood his silence!

Yet she is understandably circumspect, not wanting to incriminate Camille or herself. Still, terrible truth underlies what she has written. What Robespierre has now done to them vindicates Camille's rebellion.

Camille bursts into tears; he sobs, and Robespierre hands him a kerchief. He makes himself stop crying and hands back the cloth.

"I will arrange your pardon and your release," says Robespierre, "and your reputation and your offices will be restored, but what I need from you is a demonstration of loyalty to the Republic—a sign of your purity."

"What do you want?" says Camille. Momentarily, he is washed clean of feeling. "*The Old Cordelier*? I agree, now; let's burn them. All of them; every number."

"No. This isn't about that. I need just one thing from you. I need you to testify at the trial. Against the Dantonists." He pauses, their eyes meet, then Robespierre says, "Don't give me that look. You know as well as I do that that they profited from the revolution, from the war. Danton has also conspired with Pitt. He has been to London, I'm sure of it. They are filthy, all of them. Whatever you say will not be used against you afterward. I will guarantee your safety. You have my word."

What Robespierre says hits him like a blow to the head. He wants to agree and go home to Lucille and Horace. He is reeling. Robespierre, he realizes, has won. There is much that matters deeply to Camille. His restored humanism. His redemption. Salve to his battered conscience. But nothing matters more to him than his life, and the lives of Lucile and Horace, and the prospect of a secure future with them. Of course. Robespierre has indeed understood him, and has made an offer that Camille simply cannot refuse whatsoever the consequences.

So, this is it. A Faustian bargain. He should have seen this coming: Trade his honor, his legacy, for his life, financial security, and the safety and security of his family. And in so doing, implicate himself in treason to help vindicate Robespierre, now and for all time, and murder his only remaining friends.

Yet, after behaving thusly, how could anyone, including Robespierre, guarantee his safety? The reckoning he must eventually make would only grow more terrible.

All at once another thought intrudes: Robespierre is afraid of Danton! Danton is right. They don't dare kill us! He needs me to overcome Danton's oratory and tremendous popularity with the people. He cannot defeat Danton without me. And, most of all, he cannot but make us martyrs unless I betray my friends and support these fanciful charges against them, and he cannot bring himself to do that.

"Without me," says Camille, "you can't win. You are out of cards. Why should I do this if without my help you can't win?"

The look on Robespierre's face is not what Camille would have expected in response. He looks a little sad, timid even. He is the domestic cat. "No, Camille," he says, "this is the only way out for us both. The only way I can save us both."

"Save us?" Camille repeats, half with disgust, half with genuine surprise.

"Yes. Save us—"

But Camille spits in his face.

A sudden impulse; it happened before he could stop himself. Now there is no turning back. Robespierre is impassive; he rises, wiping the spittle, and leaves.

It is bedtime. Camille has not slept for thirty-six hours, but still he cannot sleep. He works on a second letter to Lucile. Rises, opens the window, and looks out onto the gardens. Someone is there. A woman. She appears to be mourning. He sees Annette, Lucile's mother. She weeps. He sees her sorrow by her handkerchief and by her veil, which she lowers. He is on his knees, head bowed, straining against the sill and the wall. He calls her name. She disappears. Unable to bear the spectacle?

At last, he sleeps. Kind slumber suspends his woes. Sleeping, he is free, has no more the sense of captivity. Heaven has pity on him. Indeed, he sees Lucile in a dream, with Horace; he embraces her, and then his son.

Suddenly the little one is missing an eye, which wakes him. He is back in his cell, and it is just beginning to grow light. He rises, opens his window, hoping to see Lucile. There is no one, and the thought of his loneliness, the frightful barriers that keep him from Lucile and Horace, the bolts that separate him from Lucile, vanquish all firmness of soul. He bursts into tears. He cries, "Lucile, Lucile, where are you?"

He continues the second letter to Lucile. Only writing to her can keep him whole, he fears. *Socrates drank hemlock; but at least he saw in his prison his friends and his wife. How much harder it is to be separated from the ones you love!*

He writes about his dream, the image of her mother in the garden. *My Lucile, my Lollette! Live for Horace, speak to him of me. You will say to him what he cannot yet understand, that I would have loved him well.*

Briefly he considers relating his meeting with Robespierre, and decides not to take the risk. Certainly this letter, like others, will be first read by his captors and enemies.

He passes nearly the entire day at work on this long letter to Lucile. At last, he finishes. *Farewell, my life, my soul, my earthly divinity. I leave you to the care of good friends—all those amongst men who are virtuous and right-feeling. I perceive the shores of my life receding before me. I see still Lucile. I see you, my well-beloved, my Lucile! My bound hands embrace you, and my severed head rests still upon you its dying eyes.*

He falls asleep while working on the eighth number of *The Old Cordelier*. When he wakes, the room is filled with policemen whom he does not recognize. They order him to pack, and then they take him to a well-lighted and spacious room, a common dining area. All the tables, chairs, and paintings have been removed. Only a chandelier and some lamps remain. Here he is reunited with Danton and the others, some of whom appear sick, a cadaverous pallor. Camille overhears a whisper from somewhere nearby that Chabot has poisoned himself.

Philippeaux, who is perhaps being most unjustly treated, is calm and composed even in this setting. Hérault is the same, the personal warmth and charm unchanged; he embraces a faithful servant, who is no longer permitted to accompany him.

Danton's look is unusually grim, which is alarming to Camille; he is pale and there are dark circles under his eyes. Camille can feel himself starting to panic. He tries to maintain his bearings. He can tell that everything about himself—his exhaustion, his anxiety for himself and Lucile and Horace, his guilt ravaged conscience, everything—can be read in his own anguished face and feverish eyes, eyes which dart about and cannot rest on any concrete thing. Camille is furious, and afraid, yet consoling himself that this is what he has coming to him, his just deserts. He can't make sense of his contradictory emotions.

A prosecutor whom Camille recognizes as from Fouquier's office is introduced (of course his cousin would not intervene on his behalf). He announces that they will be taken to the Conciergerie, the prison beside the Palais de Justice where the Revolutionary

Tribunal convenes, and they will be tried.

But first he will read to them the decree of accusation that was today approved by the Convention with "near unanimity." Who dissented? Besides Lindet?

"The Republic is the people and not the renown of a few men!" the prosecutor declares, and goes on to denounce each one of the accused by name. While the accusations are read, Camille cannot take his eyes off of Danton. He gazes at Danton, his unmoved contempt, as a means to retaining what remains of his own strength, his own composure.

He hears the voice of the prosecutor, yet through it he discerns the somber and austere intonation of Saint-Just. It was Saint-Just, after all, who wrote these accusations for Robespierre, and whose military heroism, dark charisma, false conviction, and will cowed what remains of the Convention into adopting this tissue of lies—almost unanimously!

Danton is attacked worst of all, accused of every manner of crime, public and private. Pummeled by these words, he does not flinch.

Camille hears his own name. Contempt rises in the Saint-Just voice, dismissing him as "a dupe first, and afterwards an accomplice—wanting in character." Saint-Just then proceeds to calumniate him with unremitting venom. Camille can no longer hold on. He is covered in cold sweat; he breathes with difficulty.

Before he knows it, he is shouting; the stutter is gone. He is cursing Saint-Just and Robespierre, this fraudulent process, the cowards in what remains of the Convention.

Someone is rebuking him, shouting at him to stop, to shut up, to get hold of himself. It is Danton; at last, even Danton's composure is gone.

"Very well," says Camille, hardly able to speak, choked as he is by rage and fear. "I go then to the scaffold, because I have shed tears at the fate of so many unhappy people. My only regret, in dying, is that I have not been able to serve them better." His legs collapse beneath him.

Before the prisoners are abruptly ushered into hackney coaches that will bear them to the Conciergerie, Camille hands the letter for Lucile to one Citizen Grosse-Beaurepaire. He is himself a prisoner, but one who will remain at the Luxembourg. Camille pleads that, if possible, he arrange that the letter be delivered to Lucille.

In the Conciergerie, Camille appreciates, dreadfully, that this is the very place which the Girondins had occupied months before. Like the Girondins were before them, whom Camille himself killed, the "Dantonists" are confined together in the same cell.

The jailers still present, Danton says, "I instituted the Revolutionary Tribunal. I ask pardon for it from God and man! My aim was to prevent fresh September massacres, not to establish a scourge for humanity."

Camille decides that he had better prepare a defense. He asks for and receives a pen, ink and paper. He titles the document, *Notes upon the Report of Saint-Just.* Now in a panic, he writes feverishly. Upon reviewing the opening lines, he is chagrined that his despair is so evident: *Saint-Just writes at his leisure, in his bath, in his dressing-room; he meditates on my assassination for fifteen days; and I, I have nowhere even to place my writing; I have only a few hours left in which to defend my life.*

CHAPTER 53

THE COURTROOM IS CROWDED to overflowing. The day unseason-
ably hot, the windows are open, and Camille hears the roaring of
the people, a sound like rushing water. He imagines the throngs
of people, as they were during the trials of the Gironde, Madame
Roland, and Olympe de Gouges. Today the crowd must be greater
still, for the trial of the great tribune, Danton, and Camille, who
incited the storming of the Bastille, and whose pen has brought all
of the foregoing to pass—the overflow from the courtroom spilling outside, encircling the Palais de Justice and extending beyond
along the quays, even crowding the Place Dauphine and beyond,
to the Pont Neuf and the Mint.

It is April 2, 1794, the first day that the "Dantonists" will be tried.

"My name is Georges-Jacques Danton, formerly a lawyer,
afterwards a Revolutionist and representative of the people. My
dwelling will soon be in nothingness, after that, in the Pantheon
of history."

"My name is Camille Desmoulins. I am thirty-three, the age of
the *sans-culotte* Jesus, when he died; a critical age for every patriot."

One by one the prisoners are being made to introduce themselves to the president of the tribunal, Martial Herman, and each
is expressing himself according to his personality.

Camille examines the jury box. He is aware that the jurors have
been carefully selected by Fouquier himself. Camille once visited him
in his office while he was examining a jury list. His cousin was making
a cross beside some names, and beside others he wrote the letter "F."

Camille asked him why, and Fouquier answered, "'F' signifies *faible*, that he is fond of reasoning. We don't want people who reason; we want this business done with. 'X' marks the ones we select."

Camille remonstrated then, and his cousin replied, "This is what the Committee of Public Safety wants; it is not my choice."

Today, the distress is gone from Danton's features. He appears ready to fight. They have rejected the appointed counsel, and Danton will represent them all. The members of the tribunal, side by side in their black habits, faces beneath the black hat brims, look grim, anxious. Fearful? The jurors look expectant. Open minded? Camille can only hope.

Danton gives Camille a nod and purses his lips and winks. The gesture has its intended effect—momentarily Camille has a sense of well-being and optimism.

Danton: "We want to call witnesses; when will the tribunal order the appearance of witnesses we want to call?"

Herman: "It is not yet time to examine your witnesses."

They have assured Danton that he will be heard, but they spend this first day of trial mainly examining defendants other than Danton or Camille. Late in the day, Danton induces them to hear him.

Danton: "I demand that a committee, composed of members of the Convention, should be nominated to hear the protests which we wish to make against the dictatorial methods of the Committee of Public Safety."

"The relief that you request is beyond the scope of this proceeding," says Herman.

"It is not beyond the scope of this proceeding to question the fairness of this very proceeding, to challenge the legitimacy of the indictment, to demonstrate the corrupt motives that give rise to the charges against us."

Camille can feel that the galleries are animated and expectant. He hears the rumble of countless conversations and even expressions of support for Danton. He sees the magistrates' concern and anxiety. They are in over their heads.

"What you ask for is beyond our authority to grant."

"Who says it is beyond your power? You are not the court, the final arbiter of this dispute?"

The galleries are growing restive, color is rising in Herman's face. He rings his bell. "Silence! We adjourn until tomorrow for consultation among us regarding the relief requested by Monsieur Danton!"

Following the trial's first day, Camille is again despondent. Camille imagines Herman in conference with Fouquier and the Committee of Public Safety. What plans are they making for preventing a fair trial for the Dantonists?

Danton says he is "sick of men." This well captures Camille's own feeling. He can't bear to think of where he is, that his life is here, this is his destiny. He can't bear to think about what he will say tomorrow. They are all together in the same cell, the sixteen defendants, and he cannot bear to hear their murmurings about the trial, what's transpired and what's to come.

He wants to fix a distance between himself and the world, and so he turns to the volume he brought with him, *The Complaint: or, Night-Thoughts on Life, Death, & Immortality*, a book of poetry in English, by Edward Young. Yet the book provides no solace. He sits alone turning pages, one after the other. Finally, mercifully, sleep overtakes him. When he wakes, in blue twilight and a little cold, he is refreshed, and optimism returns.

The second day of the trial dawns, and Danton is buoyant. "They have returned!" he says happily. "The people have come to hear our defense." The tribunal cannot prevent Danton's oratory or his examination, in the presence of the people!

Until now, Camille feels, he himself has borne a disproportionate burden of resisting the terror—by means of *The Old Cordelier*. But now it is Danton who bears the full load of dissidence—as he fights for their very lives.

Danton stands before the tribunal, his huge stature, his collar open at the throat, his huge black head thrown back with hair in wild disorder, and his ruddy face bearing a smile of fierce disdain. It is Danton's voice, filled with emotion, wildly sincere, and winged with wrath, that now dominates, commands attention from the courtroom, reverberating. This is the voice that has so often called the people to arms, mustered the levies that would destroy the armies invading France. This voice—that has had the power to move the people again and again—still has, Camille hopes, the power to move them one more time.

Danton speaks, eyes flash, and in reaction the people in the galleries murmur agreement or sympathy, and even applaud. What is more, Camille imagines that Danton's eloquence is being repeated and repeated again from mouth to mouth, the agitated multitude anxious, vaguely terrified at something momentous about to come to pass. Do they seem ready to spill forth and deliver them all?

Camille sees Fouquier, and his cousin looks ill, to be under a terrible strain. He must be thinking that here is a task that may take his measure. He triumphed in the trial of the Girondins, but now there is no Camille to spin the text of his argument, and no defendant has been as formidable or as popular with the people as Danton.

"How have you been able to live so well, buy the properties you own?" asks Herman.

"I sold myself? A man of my stamp is priceless!"

"Danton, we need more than clever rhetoric in response to the charges."

"The government must prove me guilty. Let him who accuses me to the Convention produce the proofs, the semi-proofs, the faintest signs of my venality!"

"You were frequently gone. Doing secret things. Explain your whereabouts."

"I disappeared because I have labored too much; I am sick of life: it is a burden to me. Let me ask the tribunal: Where was Robespierre on August 10?" Indeed, thinks Camille, where is Robespierre now! At this new tack from Danton, Camille feels a jolt of pleasure; he imagines a rumble among the spectators.

"We will ask the questions. He is not on trial."

As though reading Camille's mind, Danton says, "Robespierre was nowhere to be seen, as today. If I were in the employ of Mirabeau—d'Orléans—Dumouriez, I or they could have seized absolute power then. Yet each of them played for supreme power and lost. For my leadership on August 10, the Assembly—the people—made me Minister of Justice, a post I willingly relinquished to remain on the Assembly and avoid charges of dictatorial ambitions."

Danton demands all members of the Committee of Public Safety be summoned to testify under his examination; referencing his accusers, he shouts that he "will cover them with ignominy." "Danton hidden on August 10?" roars he, like a lion in the toils. "Where are the men that had to press Danton to show himself that day? Where are these high-gifted souls of whom he borrowed energy? Let them appear, these accusers of mine: I have all the clearness of my self-possession when I demand them. I will unmask the shallow scoundrels who fawn on Robespierre and lead him towards his destruction. Give me Robespierre himself! Let them produce themselves here."

Herman rings his bell. "Danton," he says, "audacity is no proof of innocence. Your defense should be made in a more orderly manner."

"Who are you to tell me how I should defend myself? You are empowered the right of dooming me. The voice of a man speaking for his honor and his life may well drown the jingling of your bell! Provided that we are allowed to speak," roars Danton, "and to speak freely, I am sure to confound my accusers, and if the French people are what they ought to be, I shall be obliged to ask for pardon for the rascals."

Hearing Danton, and seeing his cousin's and Herman's distress, Camille is filled with excitement. "Ah, we shall be allowed to speak!" cries Camille. "That is all we ask." Camille feels the momentum of the trial has shifted their way, against his cousin.

At Danton's allusion to the potential that the people will deliver him, Herman looks livid, rings the bell incessantly. "Do you not hear my bell?" he cries.

Danton: "A man defending his life despises your bell, and cries aloud."

Herman: "Danton, the Convention accuses you of supporting Dumouriez, of failing to inform it of his intentions and of participating in his plans to destroy liberty, to wit, marching his army on Paris in order to overthrow the government and restore monarchy."

Danton: "My voice has too often spoken out in defense of the people's cause to have to hear this slander. I reject it! Do the cowards who vilify me dare attack me face to face? Let them show themselves! I shall cover them in their own shame. I have said so and I repeat it: my domicile is the void. My head is there, which answers everything! Life weighs heavy, I look forward to leaving it!"

Herman: "Danton, your audacity is the mark of crime. The mark of innocence is moderation. I invite you to justify yourself as to the charges made against you. I invite you to be precise, and above all to address the facts."

"I invite this tribunal, I invite my political enemies, to show me the proofs of these alleged crimes. Then I will respond with precision. My accusers present no evidence, they will not show their faces and testify against me. All I can do is rage against the nothingness of this indictment. Saint-Just, Couthon, Le Bas, these are the three shallow scoundrels who fawn on Robespierre. Let them produce themselves here; I will plunge them into nothingness, out of which they ought never to have risen."

Thus the battle continues, and in louder and louder voice does Danton demand that Robespierre, Saint-Just, Couthon, Le Bas, and a multitude of others be called as witnesses. "I want witnesses! It is," he roars, "what every accused man has a right to demand!"

All at once, Danton appears exhausted. He says, "I am refused witnesses; very well, I will not defend myself anymore. I have also to apologize for any unnecessary warmth I may have shown; it is my disposition."

Herman seizes the opportunity to adjourn. He rings his bell. "Very well. Danton is exhausted. We adjourn until tomorrow!"

CHAPTER 54

NIGHTTIME IN THE CELL, and everyone is subdued, quiet. Each man keeps to himself; some try to sleep. In the fading light, Camille turns the pages of his poetry book. Danton has given the best that he has to his own defense and therefore their collective defense, and the people are not coming to their rescue. There is little the rest of them can do, for Danton's defense is the crux of their collective defense—it is their friendship with Danton that is the underlying crime, the source of their collective guilt. And none of them can match Danton's oratory, personal charisma, and connection with the masses.

Here is the horror: They are all doomed, and each of them in his own way deserves this. Camille can't stop thinking that this is, in a perverse way, justice. No actual traitor resides in this cell. But all are here for good reason insofar as justification remains for the Republic. Camille's final objective was to stop the terror. Too late. The cycle started by Camille with his *Secret History* devours him. Camille finally did try to undermine the Republic with *The Old Cordelier*, and it is his own logic—kill or be killed—that now drives Robespierre and Saint-Just to seek his death. At a profound level, Camille is himself guilty of the very deeds of Robespierre and Saint-Just and their ever-tightening circle, these men who fabricated the conditions for his arrest. Camille spun a false narrative that the queen and the king and the Gironde were traitors. Now it's poetic justice that Robespierre has done the same to Camille.

Danton has lived beyond his apparent means; he has acquired

property in the provinces. The circumstantial evince is that his political offices have been a means to his enrichment. He has not taken a vow of poverty like Robespierre. And Danton has conspired with Camille against the regime. The logic of kill or be killed dictates that Robespierre and Saint-Just must seek Danton's death. Danton has also noted the irony, the poetic justice that he is here, for it was he himself who conceived the Committee of Public Safety as a de facto dictatorship, and the Revolutionary Tribunal as a means to vent the people's rage and bloodlust, and also to cow dissent.

Something like this can be said for all of the prisoners. The other indulgents, like Camille, would in fact vanquish the current regime if given the chance, after they have been participants in its corruption. Those guilty of financial crimes profited at the expense of the public, and profited by corrupting the very regime that is about to kill them. The same logic that led to the murders of Brissot will consume every man in this cell, in which the Gironde themselves were held before they were killed.

Camille's twin satisfactions are that he did not ever renounce his personal campaign to gain clemency for those condemned, and that the cycle must consume even Robespierre before it is complete.

———————

The following day, the court does not convene until mid-morning. Danton rises to speak. "When will we be able to call our witnesses?" he asks again.

They ignore him, and Herman says he wants to hear from other defendants. To Camille, all that is now passing in the trial unfolds dreamlike, fractured; his mind hardly comprehends what is occurring. Hérault testifies, but Camille can follow none of the examination.

Camille is summoned to the stand. The answers he gives he has rehearsed for days. They come out like practiced lines but wooden, absent feeling. He hears fragments of his examination, his own words in response to the tribunal's questions, which, upon responding, he instantly forgets.

"I denounced Dumouriez before Marat did. I denounced d'Orléans first. I commenced the revolution; my death will end it . . . Marat deceived the proletariat . . . What man is there who has not had his Dillon? . . . Since the fourth issue, I have written only to retract . . . I had been encouraged by Robespierre to write the prior editions . . . I unmasked the Hébert faction. It is a good thing that someone did it."

They read aloud passages from *The Old Cordelier*. They accuse him of contempt for the Convention and the committees. For this he has no answer; they are correct. He was and is contemptuous of the Convention and the committees. Still he will not renounce *The Old Cordelier*.

"I have prepared a defense. May I read it?"

"Later. We are finished with you for now."

"No documents have been produced against us!" shouts Danton. "Neither have any witnesses been called. Look at those cowardly assassins," continues Danton, gesturing widely at the tribunal and the prosecutors, "they wish to hunt us to death!"

Fouquier replies that he cannot summon the witnesses whom the defendants desire to examine, since they are members of the Convention. Now all the prisoners begin loudly to demand the right to call witnesses. Camille is vaguely aware of himself emitting the words. They protest against the injustice of this treatment. Danton is on his feet. He is interrupting Herman and the others on the tribunal who are trying to speak. Danton is relentless in his demand to call witnesses. Camille can see that his voice and words are beginning again to stir the crowd.

All at once the tribunal, to a man, is gone. The proceeding is in recess, yet everyone remains in the courtroom. Camille asks someone beside him what has happened.

Herman, he is told, said, "It is time to stop this brawl; a scandal to the tribunal and others who hear you. Regarding witnesses, we will write to the Convention and see what they want carried out."

Danton is beside him. He whispers. "Pull yourself together, Camille. The people are restive. Herman has gone to the Convention to get its response to our demand for witnesses. This is what we want. Things are going our way. Now is the crucial time; the turning point."

The defendants are returned to their cell. Danton is jubilant. "They cannot refuse our demand for witnesses," he says. "Yet they cannot submit any member of the Convention to my examination. We've put them in a box . . ."

Yes, thinks Camille, *maybe Robespierre can't win without me on his side.*

In the afternoon, they are returned to the courtroom. Herman announces a message from the Committee of Public Safety. The members of the tribunal are smiling, appear strangely satisfied.

Herman reads from a piece of paper the committee's message: "'Dillon, who once ordered his army to march upon Paris, has declared that the wife of Desmoulins has received money in order to promote an uprising for the assassination of patriots, and of the Revolutionary Tribunal. The National Convention orders that the Revolutionary Tribunal shall proceed with the instruction to the jury relating to the conspiracy of Lucile Desmoulins and the Dantonists. The president shall make use of every means which the law permits to cause his authority and that of the Revolutionary Tribunal to be respected, and to repress every attempt on the part of the accused to trouble public tranquility and to hinder the course of justice. It is decreed that all persons accused of conspiracy who shall resist or insult the national justice shall be outlawed and receive judgment on the spot."

Danton says, "The Convention cannot have so decreed. That is impossible. The decree is fraudulent."

"What does this mean?" says Camille. Robespierre's retribution against Camille—the completely unforeseen, astounding level of his treachery—is sinking in.

"It means the trial is over," says Danton.

Camille is shouting. He is cursing Robespierre, Saint-Just, the entire government. Yet he is unaware of this but for Danton taking hold of him.

"Camille, stop it! You must calm down. We must be strong to the end."

"Strong! What does any of it matter? They are going to kill my wife. Robespierre is going to murder my Lucile. I myself have killed her!"

He catches a glimpse of Fouquier. His cousin, he sees, is truly shaken, but the stricken look on his cowardly face only more enrages Camille. He tears up his defense, hurls the pieces at his cousin, and lunges at him. It is Danton himself and two others who take hold of him, restrain him, prevent him from trying to kill his cousin with his bare hands.

That night, Camille is confined in a separate cell, as are the other prisoners. Lying still. All at once he calmed down, because of despair. His gaunt, whiskered face twitches. He realizes that this is his last night of life. He heard it said that the jury may not agree — that possibly the majority of them will favor acquittal.

Danton said, in his resolute way, "No, there is no hope."

Camille agrees. His old friends, his cousin Fouquier, and Robespierre, will not permit acquittal, and the prisoners have no advocates. There is no limit to their treachery. Robespierre has gone so far as to proscribe Lucile, as the pretext for depriving her husband, Robespierre's boyhood friend, of due process.

Thinking this, Camille begins to weep. Their intent to murder Lucile has robbed him of any ability to be strong, to maintain dignity in his final hours.

The accused are not even able to defend themselves. Herman decreed that "due to the indecorum, the sneers, and the blasphemies of the accused in the presence of the tribunal, the questions shall be submitted to the jury and the intervening judgment pronounced in the absence of the accused."

For himself, Camille has had enough of life. He is, like Danton, sick of men, sick of life. But what of Lucile? His own ordeal now confronts her. And what will become of Horace? Thinking this, Camille weeps again. For what purpose is a life? In the end, nothing.

Hours pass. Guards come and take him to the waiting room of the Conciergerie. All of the prisoners are now there together. The clerk is there to read the sentences, the paper in hand.

"There is no point," says Danton loudly. "You may as well take us at once to the guillotine. I will not listen to your judgment. We are assassinated; that is enough."

Hearing this, Camille is overwhelmed. He begins to sob. "Lucile . . . my little Horace. . . . Oh, my beloved! . . . What will become of them?" He collapses.

They are all sentenced to death.

Sanson and his assistants arrive to dress them for slaughter. Camille cries out, weeps. Now he finally accepts fully the reality of what is happening to him.

He resists the cutting away of his hair and of his collar; he resists with such violence that his shirt is torn to shreds. At last, the whole team of executioners succeeds in tying him to a chair and finishing their preparations. Camille pleads for the locket with the tress of Lucile's hair. Vaguely he hears Danton ordering that it be brought from Camille's cell. In time, Danton places the locket in his bound hands.

Two tumbrels, drawn by huge gray Normandy horses, stand before them as the gates before the Conciergerie are opened. One by one the men enter the carts, their hands bound. The crowd begins to shout abuse and spit at them. Camille enters the lead tumbrel and Danton follows; they are the last two. They are seated side by side.

"Ignore them," says Danton. "They are Robespierre's hirelings."

The crowd is of such size and density that the carts have to move slowly, through interstices. The people are not here to rescue the condemned men. On the contrary, they curse and belittle them. The fickle people! Camille can no longer endure insults from the people. The people!

He cries, "You are deceived, citizens. Citizens! It is your preservers who are being sacrificed. It was I . . . I, who on July 12 called you first to arms! I first proclaimed liberty. My sole crime has been pity . . ."

The insults do not abate. "Be quiet!" says Danton. "Leave this vile rabble alone."

In the Rue Saint-Honoré they pass a silent, shuttered house: the Duplays' house. Camille imagines that surely Robespierre is there, seated in his darkened apartment, austere, pale, silent, as Camille, his boyhood friend condemned to die by Robespierre himself, whose wife and love will shortly be condemned by Robespierre himself to die, passes by en route to the scaffold.

He must die with dignity, he tells himself. Yet there is no dignity to be had here. Were it his life alone, he would be restrained, even smile contemptuously. But Lucile! Lucile will soon be here at this very spot, to join him in death. His son will be an orphan. A show of strength, of indifference, would be unjust to them. He begins again to weep, tears on his cheeks and neck.

Before them rises the scaffold, and upon it the guillotine, near the old pedestal where once stood the statuette of Louis XVI himself. A wide berth around the scaffold bristles with cannons and armed men. The drums are beating. The sound of the drums batter Camille's soul.

Camille cannot take his eyes off the spectacle before him. The drums beat on, bludgeoning him. Sanson greets the first prisoner led to the platform. All six executioners take hold of the first victim and tie their plank to his body. Together, and at a mutual nod, they lift the board and set it down on the assembly, align the neck inside the lunette, and swing it shut with a clang.

Absent further ceremony, Sanson pulls the string and down comes the axe. The bang! signals that the the first victim is dead. The guillotine is drenched; a lake of blood upon the scaffold;

down the steps flow cataracts of blood. Camille turns his head. He can no longer bear to look.

By the time Camille's turn arrives, he is nearly incoherent, his mind mercifully numbed, paralyzed. He hears his name called out as though from a fog in a distant shore. Danton still is seated beside him, and he nudges Camille. "Get up, Camille. They're here for you." Where is Robespierre? In his hovel. He is never present to witness his treachery.

Two of the executioners wait by the door of the tumbrel, expectantly, as though they were porters and this were a cabriole just halted in front of a theater. It seems odd that no guard is here to take him by force. Camille struggles to his feet, hands bound.

On the scaffold, the blood of the others adheres to his bare feet, yet he hardly appreciates what it means. The thought recurs, once he and Danton are gone, who will there be to protect Robespierre? The executioners seize him and begin to tie him to the plank. He cries out, "My assassins will not long survive me!" His final words.

PART VI

CHAPTER 55

DOOMED! THE GIRONDINS, DANTON, Camille, all guillotined. Paine's turn any day now. He is completely isolated, trapped inside decaying majesty, this erstwhile palace converted to prison. His just deserts for a life of resistance against authority. Visitors are no longer allowed. Paine cannot again see Marguerite or Charlotte Smyth.

Nothing from Ambassador Morris; the United States will do nothing for him, has left him to the whimsy of the Jacobins and their guillotine.

Inside the prison, the festivities are over. Prisoners are prevented from gathering in the courtyards or dining room. Dread permeates the Luxembourg. He wanders the grounds alone. Walking and sleep are the only means to strain against black moods, keep hope.

What is this madness? Here standing before him is Malesherbes! Paine embraces the old man.

"Why are you here?" says Paine.

"I am incarcerated, as are you."

"What for?"

"I defended the king."

"What crime are you charged with?"

"That is my crime. I defended the king."

"That is absurd. What have we come to?" says Paine, in tears. "Even Marat praised your commitment to profession and your valor."

Paine knows he should not say this; he should be careful as he may be overheard. But he cannot help himself. He is so upset that he does not care that he is liable to suffer the same as whatever befalls Malesherbes, for they are guilty of the very same "crime."

They find a bench in the gardens where they sit and speak in whispers, about what went wrong with the revolution, with the Republic. After twenty minutes, guards come and take Malesherbes away by the arm.

Paine does not see him again. He learns that next morning Malesherbes was led into a tumbrel and carried before a pretend tribunal and guillotined at dusk. Paine learns that Malesherbes's sister, daughter, son-in-law, granddaughter, and her husband went to the guillotine with him.

Now Paine's despair is complete. He expects that his own annihilation must be imminent. He gives in to melancholy, spends every waking hour cowering in his room, except when occasionally he must get to a latrine or go in search of food.

He lives in constant terror that his turn has come for the guillotine. How not? Everyone else is dead. Even the women; Olympe de Gouges and Madame Roland. Why Malesherbes and and his family and not him?

Then, in June, the prisoners are gathered in the courtyard, and a new law is read to them and distributed to them on sheets of paper. First, it is disclosed that police arrested a young woman carrying a box with a knife in it near to Robespierre's dwelling; her name is Cécile Renault, and they interrogated her and she confessed to planning an attack on Robespierre. The prisoners are informed that because of this attempt on Robespierre's life, the Convention has passed the Law of 22 Prairiall. Paine listens as the law is read and stares at the printed words. The new law is beyond belief, but in his current condition and in this place, he is now beyond disbelief. This law's target, "enemies of the people," could be anyone. They are vaguely described as including any individual who has spoken critically of the government. The new law deprives those prosecuted before the Revolutionary Tribunal of any defense: no presumption of innocence, no right to testify, no right to examine witnesses, no right to demand evidence, no right to legal counsel, and the tribunal can only choose between two verdicts—acquittal or death. The verdict need not be based on evidence, only on the moral conviction of the jurors.

Every night Paine goes to bed expecting never to see his friends, the world, again. In the coming days and weeks, dozens are taken out of the prison, carried before a pretend tribunal, and guillotined. Many times a man with whom he has just passed conversation is guillotined that same day or the next.

He is moved to a larger cell to share with three foreigners, three strangers, three Belgians named Charles Bastini, Michael Robyns, and Joseph Vanhuele.

Paine falls ill. Cholera.

Delirious, he swims in and out of consciousness, wracked by bodily aches. Illness coupled with despair render him indifferent to whether he lives or dies. Yet, still he survives, thanks to inexplicable charity from these three strangers: the Belgians take care of him. Feeding him broth and seeing to it that his soiled linens are changed.

Once, at night, he wakes; the Belgians are sleeping, and he senses a fifth man in the room. A man at his bedside; it is nighttime, dark, but the man himself is illuminated; like an angel, he emanates light. His hair is lit up, shaded with gold, and resembling a lion's mane. His eyes are even more striking: very wide open, and almost too large for their sockets, still brighter than the rest of this image. A high forehead, a well-defined jaw and chin. William Blake!

"Blake, what are you doing here?" he whispers.

"I came for you."

"And they arrested you? It's good to see you, but I don't want you on my conscience, Blake."

"I am not a prisoner. I have purchased your freedom. I have come to fetch you."

"That is not possible. They would not sell me for any price."

"Thomas, it was your hubris that brought you here. You are not Danton. Your head has a price."

"That may be. But I must stay and take my punishment."

"You can't mean that, Paine. Your incarceration is unjust."

"And so, too, was it unjust for Socrates. He would not flee, and the men who took his life injured themselves worse than they did him, as you see. The men and women murdered by Robespierre will finally vanquish him; I wish to be among them."

"Socrates reasoned that he owed his very life to the state that gave him life and brought him up, gave him a good life. You cannot say the same for the Jacobins. They are thoroughly unjust and they are themselves usurpers. The general citizenry suffer for their oppression, as you do. Thomas, humans have progressed since Athenian democracy. A man must resist unjust government. Yours is no martyr's fate. A willing embrace of martyrdom would run contrary to your message. You elevate the individual; you affirm life and vitality and celebrate life's pleasures. You must leave here and save your own life because this is the principled thing to do.

"And what about the woman you love, Marguerite? Think of her. You will be together in America, with children. There, places in the landscape and the newborn civilization will someday bear the name of the children." Suddenly the image begins to shimmer, and Blake vanishes.

CHAPTER 56

Six o'clock in morning, and the turnkey arrives, reading aloud the day's death list. Wide awake, and on the mend, Paine hears, "Thomas Paine!" Can it really be? Many times he has dreamt this moment, but here and now he is awake; it is no dream. Here since late December, it had seemed he had been forgotten. But Fouquier has now finally picked him. At last, his time has come.

The Belgians, also awake, understand, know better than to try to console him—excepting sympathetic looks. For what kind of consolation could they give? Their own death day is bound to come, could be near at hand.

Even so, he needs no consolation; lack of feeling is what he feels. He is prepared for his life's greatest ordeal. While Paine has emerged from the misery of the cholera, the intangible part of him remains afflicted. It is as if the wellspring of his soul, which animated and gave purpose and order to his life, has dried up. His belief in the cosmic order, a purposeful human existence, in God, even in his own self are no longer present. The greatest source of his despair is that he has been powerless to stop the disintegration of the world as he knew it.

A memory of Blake's visitation flickers. For a few days it had been a source of hope. Yet, he has come to realize, it was but a dream, a hallucination, an emanation from his mind, and bears no relation to occurrences in the physical world.

Paine rises, begins to dress in what, from what he has left, is most suitable for his death day. They are to come for him any time. So, this will be his death day: July 27, 1794, which, being interpreted into the new revolutionary style, means Thermidor 9th, year 2.

Past midnight, now July 28, nobody has come to take Paine to the Revolutionary Tribunal; nor, so far as Paine and his Belgian comrades can tell, have they taken any of the others who were condemned this morning. Meanwhile, Paine and the Belgians sit anxiously, as night proceeds.

They hear tocsin from every steeple, the cannon, galloping horses, rifle shots, and shouts. The city is in tumult. They surmise that a new August 10, or a new June 2, or (perish the thought!) a new September 2 is at hand. One of the Belgians rises, pointing at the window—he has seen something. Outside, there are men on roofs making signals to the prisoners. Signals of hope? They cannot tell.

CHAPTER 57

OCTOBER: PAINE IS SURPRISED that Condorcet's erstwhile protégé Joseph Fouché has come to visit him. They have not interacted since Condorcet introduced them in Madame Roland's drawing room when Fouché was a zealous advocate of his Nantes constituents and loyal to Condorcet. Paine has heard from his friends, and his lover Marguerite, who are now again allowed to visit him, that Fouché is a leading figure in the government. Paine's hope is that Fouché can arrange his release, or, better still, he has come to set him free today.

Fouché has a visage that is, charitably put, eccentric. It is memorable, yet today Paine regards him from a fresh perspective: A prominent beak for a nose; the smiling lips so thin they make a white line. His hair is, however, better groomed than when they first met. The rat's tails are dissolved. Beneath the barely visible eyebrows, the eyes emit a youthful ferocity; sparkle absent warmth. The eyes redeem the awful visage. He is a bird of prey. He has a pistol at his side and is holding a dagger.

Yet this raptor treats Paine with seeming kindness. He inquires about Paine's health and appears relieved that he is better. Fouché seems genuinely pleased that the cell is so spacious. Now that the Belgians have been released, it is generously sized for a single prisoner. Indeed, it was once a bedroom in a palace. Paine is now free to walk the palace grounds and interact with other prisoners, and decent and well-priced food and wine have returned.

"It is France's good fortune that you have survived the terror," says Fouché. "You remain important to her. Your *Rights of Man* is a constant reference of mine. Like Robespierre and his Rousseau."

What the devil does he want of me? thinks Paine. "My condition has improved," says Paine, "but I am hoping that you bring tidings of my release."

"That is my sincerest wish and design," says Fouché, "but it is easier said than done. You remain a controversial figure. Your current American ambassador, James Monroe, is of more help than the last one. And, thanks to me, the guillotine no longer threatens you. I have saved you from that fate."

"So it is said," says Paine. His curiosity gets the best of him, and he asks, "How did you do it?" Nobody who has spoken to Paine knows the full story of Fouché's struggle with Robespierre. "Robespierre was your friend. Yet also you were once dedicated to saving the king and then you voted for his murder. Some of us are not so nimble with our convictions."

"It was inevitable that Capet would perish. Yet the fact that my politics are nimbler than yours must have something to do with why I am free to come and go from this place, and you remain confined here. I will do my best to get you out of here, but it may depend on you." The raptor eyes flash. He pauses, letting that sink in, then he continues, "I will tell you a secret about myself. I have always regarded the conditions of my birth a cosmic error." He pauses. "Ah . . . you are the same. I see it in your eyes. You are from Thetford. I can't imagine it. Actually, yes I can. You and I have much in common. As you know, I was born in Nantes. My family were brawny seafarers; yet, as a boy, at sea I was like a fish out of water, and prone to seasickness. I was thin, physically limited, and had no aptitude for manual labor, I disliked strong drink, and I was bookish. And so a mysterious strength awoke in me which at first made me uneasy—a gift for the art of timely reinvention in order to become greater."

"It is true that I have admired you for your common origins."

"Indeed. My origins are common. I received my education in the college of the Oratorians in Nantes, my only option other than a life at sea like my kin, since I am not a noble. But when I knew it was time to enter politics, I discarded the cassock and the monastic way of life. And so, you see, my *la mort* vote on the fate of Louis Capet continued a pattern."

"I am a man of principles. I will not change them to gain my freedom."

Fouché sighs. "I will tell you how it happened with Robespierre. It is a grim story, but an uplifting one too. You could say that it is a morality play. And I think you will see that what I am going to tell you concerns you. I promise that it concerns you."

Fouché pauses, the dagger falls from his hands, and he raises his eyebrows at Paine. Paine looks back, nods slightly. Fouché begins.

———————

We were indeed once friends, Robespierre and I, in Arras. I taught at the Oratorians' school there. Robespierre and I first met in a circle we called the Rosati. Our little group read poetry to one another, discussed politics and science. Other than myself, Robespierre seemed to have no real friends. His manner put others ill at ease — except for me. I watched him closely, and we grew close as he campaigned for election to the Estates General.

And so after my *la mort* vote on the fate of Louis Capet, I took my seat on the Mountain. I thought — no, I hoped — that Robespierre would be pleased to see me there. My vote had made the difference, after all. Capet was sentenced to death by a single vote, as you remember. Everyone had expected me to vote for reprieve — as you know. I was Condorcet's protégé; I carried to the tribune the eloquent speech that we together prepared, pleading clemency for Capet. But the speech remained unread and I cast my vote for *la mort*. I did it because I foresaw everything that has occurred since. My gift is an animal instinct for what will come to pass, you will see. Yet when I shook hands with Robespierre, he returned only a frigid smile, and then he ignored me. I was undeterred! I took a seat near to Robespierre's perch, even though I knew that I would dislodge one of the Montagne from his regular place. It was I, Joseph Fouché, after all, who personally financed Maximilien's presence at the Estates General! And I had not been repaid. Had it not been for my encouragement, my tutelage, my financial support, Robespierre would still be a country lawyer in Arras, believe me. Yet when he so rudely greeted me after my death vote, it was the first time we had exchanged words since the day he departed Arras for the Estates General, never to return. I remember it well. It was the last day of my friendship with Robespierre.

On that day, in the spring of 1789, I was approaching the front door of the house that Max shared with his sister Charlotte when I ran into a local noble, Dubois de Fosseux, who was leaving the house. I knew his history; his family was no more than two generations from the soil. And so here we are, I thought, nearly at hand is the day when titles and privileges will count for nothing.

"What the devil!" cried Fosseux. He stopped abruptly and examined me head to toe. He was surprised, I saw, that the cassock was gone, and the tonsure was nearly grown in. It had been only about a fortnight since I had abandoned the monastic life. Fosseux raised a forefinger and he said to me, "I blame you for this, Fouché! For what has become of him. Now we'll see what he becomes without me! Let's see how his . . . his . . . zealotry plays in Versailles, if he is able even to make it there!" And he was right. I had exerted a great influence over Robespierre's politics, but now it was doubtful whether he had even the means to travel to Versailles, where the fate of his radical politics would receive many new challenges. Robespierre won election to the Estates General because of relentless opposition to government and inherited privilege and wealth. He opposed the right of the Arras town councillors, including Fosseux himself, to run for election to the third estate delegates, or even to vote in the third estate. "They are nobles," Robespierre argued, "and therefore belong in the second estate. If the privileged are elected to the third estate, they will only represent the privileged, not the third estate." Fosseux correctly perceived that I continuously stood behind Robespierre, urging, encouraging, and informing his speeches. The upshot was that Robespierre was elected one of the third estate's eight representatives from Arras, and Fosseux was not chosen by any estate, and he remained at home. In retrospect, ironically, perhaps this misfortune saved his life. For he is now safely emigrated to a place receptive to his class.

After reprimanding me, Fosseux took his leave, and I entered Robespierre's house. I didn't have to knock. I practically lived there. In the tiny drawing room, I found Robespierre standing beside his sister, and I could see that they were relieved to see me.

"Fosseux will not sponsor me! He has withdrawn his donation," Robespierre said, his voice breaking. Robespierre was due in Versailles for the opening ceremony of the Estates General, and he now had no funds for the journey.

In those days, France struggled to reconcile its internal contradictions. Hence delegates of the third estate, generally poor, were being sponsored by nobility. The nobility knew that aside from any moral imperative, the much more numerous commoners would not long abide their wholly oppressed condition. Robespierre thought that Fosseux would still sponsor him, as he had promised. But Fosseux had now recognized that he could not influence Robespierre, and so he broke his promise.

"I have enough money," I told Robespierre. "I will give it to you." He started to protest, but I insisted. "Max, I want to," I said. "Nothing matters more than this. We'll call it a loan. Repay me when you can." I gave him all my savings and what remained of my meager inheritance—all the money I had in the world, and it was enough to get my friend to Versailles and give him a good start.

I hoped my loan would be well spent, even if it were not repaid—as it has not been. Robespierre, I was sure, would not return to Arras. And I was right. But I was wrong that Robespierre would feel indebted to me. Nevertheless, I did not intend to let that moment in history pass. I had my own ambitions, and I had ideas about how soon enough to recover what I was giving to Robespierre, and more.

I looked at Charlotte. She was crying, her face tear-streaked.

She met my gaze; hers was tender. How closely the sister resembles the brother. She is an Egyptian cat. Ah, the tears, the tenderness, the admiration, and the gratitude that I felt emanating at me.

Once Robespierre was safely on his way to Versailles, a few hours later, I returned to their small house. She was alone, I was sure of it. It was now dark. No lamp was lit. This time I knocked. Immediately, she answered the door. In the semi-darkness I saw that Charlotte had changed into a blue and white dress, which revealed her lovely neck and bosom. I slipped inside the house and took her in my arms. She was perfumed, her hair fragrant; and the small mouth was painted, sumptuous strawberry lips — in contrast to my own mouth, which, until our first kiss, was still untouched by any human lip.

It would have been rash to reveal to prissy Maximilien that it was not I who violated Charlotte; rather, it was the opposite that happened. She aggressively initiated the entanglement when I was still a tonsured Oratorian quasi-novitiate, and a virgin, and indubitably I was not her first lover.

I have asked myself, what did lovely Charlotte Robespierre see in a man such as myself? That I was the alter ego of her brother? It is true, we had much in common, just as we — Robespierre and I — have had with you, Paine. We are all equally ambitious outliers, and prone to self-abnegation in pursuit of our ambitions. Perhaps she felt that I loved her brother, and I was a surrogate for an unholy love of her brother. They had lived as husband and wife, yet probably chastely. Probably, but I cannot know for sure. How else did she gain her experience in lovemaking? I would not hold it against her. But really, I am not the same as her brother. I am not fixed or rigid in my ideas or personal habits. On the contrary.

I must admit to myself, I enjoyed this adventure, but it ended, as it had to. It is not that I did not love Charlotte. I could not. I had taught Robespierre some things, and I had likewise learned from Robespierre. I returned to Nantes, my hometown, and there I began my political career, just as Robespierre, after his education, returned to his ancestral village and there started his political career. But Robespierre and I were not the same. I cannot fathom that Robespierre would ever have married, and in contrast, I am married and plan to have a large family. But I could not marry Charlotte. She lacked a dowry, and she lacked any influence or connection in Nantes. And I felt that because of differences in Robespierre's and my constituencies, and that I needed my politics to remain nimble, of necessity I could not remain too tightly tethered to him. After I broke off the engagement with Charlotte, I told myself, give it time: Time heals all wounds; Robespierre will be glad to have Charlotte back as his helpmate. But my worst fears were realized, of course. Robespierre never forgave me for what I did to Charlotte. I hoped he would be glad to have her back, but I was wrong even in that assumption. He too cast her aside, for that miserable Duplay woman. He did not repay my loan, but much worse, I would find that I could not rely on him to protect me even when I tried to join his circle on the Mountain.

CHAPTER 58

I MAKE NO APOLOGIES for what I did when I cast my *la mort* vote. I perceived change in the political winds, and I did what I had to do to remain relevant and even to save myself. Yet, when the chance came to get away from Robespierre, in the spring of 1793, I took it. He continued only to evince contempt for me.

The provinces were in revolt against the recruitment levy, General Dumouriez had revealed himself a traitor, the army was foundering, and the Convention took action to address the crisis. My deep roots and long experience in the provinces, a relative rarity among the ideologically pure on the left, made me eligible to be one of the envoyés en mission specially selected as representatives of the Convention to investigate all of the départements. Naturally, I was sent to Loire Inférieure, its prefecture being Nantes, my hometown.

Robespierre's Committee of Public Safety summoned me back to Paris on April 3 of this year. By then I had been restationed in Lyon, where I had received news of events in Paris—those of the Girondins who did not flee and Madame Roland and Olympe de Gouges, all guillotined. But I did not expect to find what had become of the Convention. I did not expect what had become of Paris. It was while traveling to Paris that I learned Père Duchesne was no more.

During the journey, I had time to think, and to plan. There was no peace to be made with Robespierre, I felt. I had tried, and he had met my goodwill with unremitting disdain. Our personal history—Robespierre's belief that I stole his lovely sister Charlotte's virtue, only to discard her—and my emergence as an influential deputy on the radical left of the Convention meant Robespierre certainly regarded me as a rival.

Danton, it seemed to me, was a natural counterweight to Robespierre. He opposed the terror, I discerned—though he had helped bring it to pass—the human is a complicated animal, indeed. I had read Desmoulins's strange series of pamphlets, *The Old Cordelier*, and discerned Danton's backing if not involvement. The two of them, Danton and Desmoulins, seemed stricken by empathy. I decided I had no choice but to align myself with Danton. Yes, I agreed: it is time to stop the terror.

But I failed to appreciate that the terror was moving faster than the diligence carrying me to Paris. When I arrived, on April 8, I learned that Danton and all his allies in the Convention were guillotined.

The morning after, I went promptly to the Convention, having hardly slept. I discovered that the delegates now populated benches that were mostly bare. Where once the representatives of the people boldly argued and counter-argued, they were now incapacitated by the terror. They sat mute and anxious, timid sheep who bleated "aye" whenever the Committee of Public Safety demanded one from among them for arrest.

With thoroughness that I had not thought possible, Robespierre had annihilated anyone who resisted him. He had seen to it that every last Girondin, Hébertist, and Dantonist was dead—except Louvet, at large someplace in Paris, and the drunkard Isnard, who fled the country. The once great lights of the Convention had been snuffed out, one after the other, like lamps in a theater.

Even then, the terror continued to unfold while I had been in Paris. Five days after I arrived, on April 13, nineteen more revolutionary notables were brought before the Revolutionary Tribunal and put to death: among them, Gobel, apostatized Bishop of Paris; Hébert's widow; and the widow of Camille. I could not bring myself to confront the guillotine, so I read in the papers: In the tumbrel, Hébert's widow was weeping, and Camille's widow tried to comfort her. Gobel was repentant, begging absolution of a priest.

Pétion, Barbaroux, and Buzot fled Caen. Barbaroux was captured and guillotined after a botched suicide attempt. The bodies of Pétion and Buzot, who had killed themselves, were found in a field, half eaten by wolves.

My erstwhile mentor Condorcet had been hiding, these many months, hunted, concealed by friends, until his presence became dangerous to his protectors. He fled, and in his final days lived homeless, in thickets and stone quarries. Finally, starving, he ventured into the village of Clamars, and was arrested—his wretched condition did not hide that aristocracy was bred in his bones. Next morning, he was discovered prostrate on the floor of his prison cell; dead, self-poisoned.

I realized that anytime Robespierre's police could come to arrest me. And so, my comings and goings were deliberately erratic; only occasionally did I go to the Convention or sleep in my own bed. Yet I knew that none of this would help once Robespierre decided actually to get me.

Including me, the Committee of Public Safety had recalled twenty-two members of the Convention who had been sent out as envoyés en mission. These included Barras, Carrier, Fréron, and Tallien. On their return they each—except me—had called on Robespierre or had written him a letter of supplication, to ask for his help and protection.

I took a different approach from the rest. Eventually, I visited Robespierre in his apartment. I had heard about the surreal experience of climbing the outside staircase, encountering the female gatekeeper, Eleonore Duplay, and gaining admission only with her leave.

Robespierre was seated behind his desk. He had about him an intensely meditative air. The light was dim. Sure enough, the Rousseau bible was near at hand. There was no chair for visitors, and none was brought. I was forced to stand.

I got right down to business. "Listen to me, Robespierre, you can't touch me. I'm not afraid of you. I'm not like the others. I have my own personal army."

"Then why are you here? Your army is in Lyon."

Actually, my army was not in Lyon. The finest of the brutes who made up the revolutionary army in Lyon followed me here. I had been living with them to save myself from Robespierre's terror.

I did not tell him this. Instead, I replied, "The Convention told me to return."

CHAPTER 59

ANY CHANCE OF RECONCILIATION with Robespierre was made impossible by the so-called "Festival of the Supreme Being"—what Robespierre called this travesty—this final descent of the French Revolution—the most important human event ever—to unconscious (or conscious) farce.

On June 8, the terrace of the Tuileries Gardens was converted to an amphitheater, just for this occasion, and the deputies were seated on a semicircle of tiered masonry benches. Before us, a crowd of more than half a million, nearly all of Paris's population. All through the city the houses were decorated with wreaths of oak, laurel, fresh flowers, tricolor ribbons, and flags. The day was noisy—the roar of the people, and the pealing of church bells, booms of cannon and tapping of drums.

I wanted no part of this nonsense. I could take no more. I whispered to myself, "Robespierre, by what authority do you make yourself Pontifex Maximus of the Republic!"

I intended to whisper, that is. I did not mean to say it loud enough for Robespierre and the other deputies to hear me. Yet the other deputies were eyeing me with surprise, and so too Robespierre must have heard, for he gave me a furious look as he dismounted the tribune. But there were no repercussions on that day.

So, by July 14, I had been back in Paris for more than three months, and I had avoided the guillotine. Finally, I went to see it; instinct finally drew me to it. A matter of personal salvation. I had to perceive, to confront, Robespierre's terror. For, I myself could be brought under the knife any day.

Before me, on the scaffold, stood a family of three. Aristocrats. A man and two women; the youngest appeared little more than a girl. "No more women!" someone shouted. Indeed, the women on the scaffold made both a lovely and a pitiful sight. They bore signs of the strain and deprivation of prison life. Yet they remained, in a sense, ideal women. The younger one's arresting, preternatural beauty shone through, even in a ravaged, deranged condition. She was calm. It was unclear whether she appreciated what was happening to her, or, she was indifferent. The older woman, herself a beauty even in this context, was weeping.

I had made inquiries about the condemned. These had been incarcerated nearly two years, since August 10. The man, handsome and noble to the end, gave defiant airs, even now. He was the Marquis de Foudoas, and he was a commander of the Swiss Guards on August 10. What crime had the women committed? The older one was the widowed marquis's sister-in-law, and she lived with him, possibly as his lover; the younger was his daughter. That is all. I also learned that they were neighbors of Charlotte Corday. Yet there was no accusation that any of these condemned had conspired in Marat's assassination. They were already incarcerated when it was planned and carried out, after all.

I could barely look as they were tied to the plank, and the ax dropped, on first the younger—she remained stoic—then the older woman—she was sobbing—and finally the Marquis—still defiant. I had seen beheadings before, but until now I had never appreciated the tremendous quantity of blood let loose from just one.

Next came the underage servant girl of someone who had once been mistress to an Hébertist. When the executioners placed her small body under the blade, there were cries of "No children!" Again and again, "No children!" Yet the execution proceeded.

And so here is the revelation that I gained standing before the guillotine: The people were weary of the terror, and fearful. It had gone too far. The guillotine was now the only instrument of government. Yet even those who wielded it felt menaced by it. Suspicion and mistrust preyed upon every head. And all cowered in fear. There were limits to their insensitivity by exposure. For my part, I had survived, so far. I had survived by an iron will, refusing to yield to the terror, refusing to evince terror. Were Robespierre to discern that I was afraid, I felt, I would have been finished immediately, just as a vicious canine is more prone to attack fear than defiance.

I got into a cab and instructed the driver to take me home. It was still afternoon, yet the streets were deserted, as were the cafés and wine shops. The courtesans had disappeared from the Palais-Royal. Everywhere, virtue reigned supreme, and fear was everywhere perceived, in the creak of a door, an exclamation, a breath. Still, under the hot summer sun, the city seemed expectant, waiting for something to happen. That day was the fifth anniversary of the storming of the Bastille. Surely Robespierre would speak at the Jacobin Club that night.

Bonne, my wife, pulled open the door before I was able to extract the key . . . I am sorry. I cannot relate the crisis of my struggle with Robespierre and ignore the simultaneous crisis—and the torment—of my daughter's illness . . . Bonne had our child in her arm; our only child was crying. I had not been home for a week, sleeping in a barracks with some soldier friends from my time in Lyon.

"So nice to see you," said my wife with mock formality. I might well have interpreted this as rebuke, but I remained silent, did not so much as emit a sigh. I know my wife invariably means nothing but goodwill. But even were she unhappy with me, my sympathy for her would be well deserved. With her, my patience is, in turn, inexhaustible. Yet the source of my affection is so much more than sympathy. Above all, practical considerations are what motivate, what move me, notwithstanding my personal ambition—indeed, ambition animates practical imperatives. I have no illusions that she is an attractive woman. Yet I do not regard her on that term. For me, lust would require a romanticism, an aesthetic concern with respect to one's own life, that is utterly foreign, of no interest to me. I am essentially unmoved by lust for any woman (or man). My wife is a source of security. She is good to me. She the mother of our poor child. We will have more children, as many as physically possible.

My wife handed the child to me, and suddenly the crying ceased. I remember the child's little arm around my neck, and I was surprised that she pulled me to her. She burrowed her face into my neck, and I felt a tremor inside myself . . . as I do now. The fragility of this. Oh delicate life! I felt her skull against my cheek, nose against my neck. She felt so hot. My hand brushed against a foot, and even the foot was hot. The child began again to cry, now more softly.

Bonne asked if I was hungry, if I wanted wine. "No," I replied. "I can't stay long. I have to see Robespierre. Then I'll go to the Jacobin Club." Bonne turned and looked at me, eyes wide, eyebrows raised. On an impulse, I had decided to confront Robespierre with my revelation that the people were exhausted of the terror, that it must end; and make one last effort to broker peace with him.

When I arrived at Robespierre's place, the scene was not what I expected. Two uniformed National Guards stood at the foot of the staircase rising to Robespierre's apartment. Of course, I realized, Robespierre and his cronies must pretend that girl's faux assassination attempt was genuine. The ruse must be played out. After all, her entire family—mother, father, and brothers and sisters—were all beheaded. The Duplay woman stood behind the soldiers.

"Let me by," I said. "I'm Joseph Fouché." I saw that the soldiers recognized me. They parted to let me pass between them. The Duplay woman did not move, but I moved swiftly by her, careful that our bodies did not touch.

"Fouché, you mustn't bother him!" she said, loud enough for Robespierre to hear from within his hovel. She did not pursue me. Stupid woman. Now I knew for sure that Robespierre was there.

At the landing, by the entry to Robespierre's apartment, I knocked on the door. There was no answer. I knocked again, harder. No answer. "Robespierre!" I shouted. "We must speak!" No answer; no movement from within. I imagined him inside, sitting stock still at his desk, a pale, waxen figure. Not even a bead of sweat on the smooth brow. Inhuman. I moved my face close to the door.

"Robespierre," I cried. "The terror must stop. This is what you must announce to the Jacobin Club tonight. Today I watched some executions. The people are restive. They are sick of the terror. It must end. They were outraged at the executions of women and girls and children."

Still no answer came from within. "Robespierre! Do you remember that your first essay for the Academy of Arras was against the tradition of bad blood? You condemned guilt by association. The killing of innocents for the crimes of their fathers must stop. Robespierre!"

And still nothing. "Tonight, at the Jacobin Club, you need to announce the end of the terror. Or else people will suspect you of wanting to be king. They will say you are a dictator. I will see you there, Robespierre!"

I turned and swiftly descended the staircase, striding past the woman and the guards. I felt I was in great danger, yet I had never felt freer.

It was too early to go to the Jacobin Club. Entering the cab, I was again seized by impulse, and gave instructions for a new destination. We arrived at a house; unremarkable, modest in façade and size. I knocked twice before the door opened. Once opened, the door began suddenly to close. I reached out and stopped the action. Charlotte Robespierre stood before me.

"Charlotte," I said. "We have to talk. This is about Max. I want to help him."

Charlotte and I hadn't spoken for five years. She let me pass inside. Inside, the house was immaculate. Everything in order. The floor polished, the curtains looked new. There was even a vase of fresh flowers. Yet I surmised that nobody had come to visit her in a long time.

"Charlotte," I said, "your place is so beautiful, and it's so nice to see you. I should have come sooner."

She said, "What can I do for you?" Her little mouth closed tight; I could see that she was gripped by emotion. She was trembling. I mattered to her, I could see. Love is such an occult emotion.

I replied, "Charlotte, we were once lovers. More than that, we share a love for Max."

"Stop!" she cried.

"Charlotte," I said, "let's go to your parlor. We have to talk."

She turned, and I followed. When we were seated, there was no idle talk. "Charlotte," I said, "why doesn't Max live here? That Duplay woman can't be anything to him. What's going on?"

Tears sprang into her eyes; then glistening lines down the cheeks. They were bitter tears, I learned. Tears of rage. She recounted her humiliation. She came here to make a home for Max. But while living with her, he fell ill, as was his wont, and his delicate constitution was made an excuse for his return to the Duplays. She loved him for what he was, but now these women had turned him into something monstrous; they had made him unrecognizable.

"Charlotte," I said, "I'm here to help recover him for you. To save him. I visited the guillotine today. The people are exhausted by the terror. Max and I, we once shared a vision. The society above all else—above any individual, and especially above the king, and the Church. It was original, bold, and it took nerve. Dissenters, those who would not part with their capital, had to be dealt with, for the society has to be nurtured and preserved above all else. This was the rationale for everything we did. Now, Robespierre has carried it too far. His cult of virtue, his religion, defies human nature. It will destroy us all. I am here to help him, to restore the pragmatism of our original movement."

"Stop it," she cried. "Silence! I know you both better than you think. You'd each of you sooner kill the other."

She sprang to her feet and strode into the kitchen. She opened a drawer, drew out a paper, and brought it to me. I recognized Robespierre's handwriting. The small, neat script. A list of names. Of course "Fouché" was at the top. Fouché, Barras, Carrier, Fréron, Tallien, and others. I counted thirty names. I was, in a way, flattered, honored to be inscribed upon this tablet at the head of those doomed to annihilation. Robespierre, so lacking in imagination.

So lethally banal. Making a list of the remaining intended victims. His final step to absolute dictatorship.

"Where did you get this?" I asked.

"From his desk at the Duplays'," she replied. "I go there when I please. Those horrible women would not dare stop me. He was gone, and I know where he stows the key. But none of them saw me. They were all at the Jacobin Club." She paused, looked at me hard. "I have had this for nearly a month. I knew, and I didn't tell you. I know where you live."

Liquidating those thirty, the final step to absolute dictatorship. Those thirty victims were to be sacrificed, and all that needed to happen was for Robespierre to name them, mark them for arrest, in the Convention.

That evening at the Jacobin Club, Robespierre's speech was worse for me even than I had feared; from the very start, he went for my throat: "I begin with the declaration that the individual Fouché interests me not at all," he shouted. "I was at one time in fairly close touch with him because I believed him to be a patriot. Yet one who refuses to be answerable to the society of the people, is one who attacks the institution of the society of the people. Does he dread the eyes and the ears of the people? Is he afraid that his grim visage will make his crimes all too plain, that six thousand eyes fixed on his own will read his soul in them, will discover there the innermost thoughts which it is his nature to hide?" (This was a tawdry attack, even for Robespierre, condemning my appearance.) "His hands are stuffed with plunder and with crimes." Robespierre concluded, "I summon Fouché to judgment here. Let him make answer and say whether he has upheld or we have upheld more worthily the rights of the representatives of the people, whether he has or we have more courageously crushed all the factions."

I did not take up the challenge to defend myself before the Jacobin Club that night; I fled. I ran, panting, not bothering to hail a cab. The High Priest Robespierre had caused me to be expelled from the Jacobins—for surely, I would now be expelled—and that was equivalent to a decree of proscription.

I arrived back at Charlotte's house and knocked hard, delivered a volley of blows, crying out her name. The door opened, and there she was, a kind of subtle smile on her face. I was breathing hard, could hardly speak.

"Charlotte, my dear. Max has condemned me before the Jacobins. I am expelled from the Jacobins. I am proscribed. Only here. Only here am I safe. They won't look for me here."

She stepped aside, invited me in.

Past midnight, I rose. I was in the room that she had assembled for her brother, wearing a dressing-gown she kept freshly laundered for her brother. I heard from her room her sweetly inhaling and exhaling. I loved her like a sister, indeed like a wife, for saving me. Naturally, I had no carnal interest in her. I would live with the sister under the same roof for an indeterminate time, but I would not lay a finger on her. She, unlike the rest of them, would be spared history's judgment for the French Revolution's treacheries. For she gave me The List.

Quickly I changed into my clothes, then exited the front door into the night. I did not wish to alarm her, and so I planned to return before morning. I reached into the breast pocket of my waistcoat, pinched at The List. It was my only comfort.

Three times I released the heavy knocker, and Paul Barras's door opened. A servant wearing a nightcap. I insisted, I must see the master. Barras arrived in a minute. A light sleeper. He is a military commander and an adventurer, as well as a Convention delegate. He has fought the British in India, survived shipwrecks, and was at the siege of the British at Toulon. He was one of the envoyés en mission recalled by the Committee of Public Safety. In his presence I felt diminutive. He is a big man, and though he has lived a great deal, he has a youthful bearing; a large square head.

By great exertion I kept my voice steady; I could not appear afraid, I knew. So I kind of hissed, bespeaking rage, "In his speech on the anniversary of the Bastille last night, Robespierre incited the Jacobin Club to expel me. I am cast out. Proscribed. It is only a matter of time before the police come for me."

Barras remained silent. He gave a subtle, inquiring look, as though to ask, *Why is this any concern of mine?*

Then I revealed to him about The List. I drew it out from my pocket and showed him. Now Barras was interested, furrowing his brow. His name was next on The List, right below mine.

CHAPTER 60

I DID NOT TRIFLE in contending for my head, nor in long and secret deliberations with colleagues who were threatened as I was. I merely said to them, "You are on The List, as well as myself. I am certain of it; look here!"

All of them were anxious and ready to take action to save their lives. Repeat visits to each others' houses were not safe, and so we had to meet in other places. We avoided the Pont Neuf, as everyone knew that was where Danton and Camille were repeatedly seen together in the weeks before their arrest. Paris is full of hiding places: alleys, groves, hedges, and alcoves, even the obscure café — assuming precautions to avoid being followed.

Tallien required extra prodding; he is younger than any of us by far, less seasoned. When we met a third time, Tallien brandished a letter from his brilliant lover, Thérésa Cabarrús, who was imprisoned at La Petite Force and awaiting trial and inevitable execution.

I took the letter from him. On the paper she had drawn a dagger, and she wrote, *I die in despair at having belonged to a coward like you.*

I did not tell Tallien that I had been with Thérésa the night before and she composed the letter as I looked over her shoulder. She was breathing and spitting fire, and there in that awful place she had maintained her legendary beauty. She wore a light muslin gown with floral prints, the kind Antoinette used to be called indecent for wearing.

She is a noble, born in her family's castle in Madrid and was hiding at her uncle's place in Bordeaux when she and Tallien became lovers while he was envoyés en mission there. Tallien was recalled by the Convention, and he left her in Bordeaux. She followed him to Paris and was arrested. "I was afraid; I felt exposed," she told me. "It was a lapse of judgment." I think she meant both her decision to take him as a lover and to follow him to Paris. She said, "Every day I feel sick hearing when the warden calls the names of those to be brought to the Revolutionary Tribunal. Any day, it could be me. My time will come." She cried, bitter tears. She cursed Robespierre, Saint-Just, the Committee of Public Safety, the Revolutionary Tribunal, but most of all she condemned her lover. "He has abandoned me! The coward!" she seethed.

"He adores you," I said, "but he is afraid. Perhaps you should write to him, tell him what you feel! He does adore you, and this will stir him to action. Only you can free him from this torpor of fear. Do it now and I will see to it that the letter is delivered." All at once she was at her desk.

After he read her letter, Tallien wanted to assassinate Robespierre.

"No!" I told him. "By assassinating him, by this isolated act, you will make Robespierre a martyr, and his system will continue. His popularity will survive, his movement will grow stronger. You will have destroyed the man but not the system, you yourself will be killed, and surely Thérésa will not survive your crime. You will have accomplished nothing; you will have made matters much worse."

"So there is nothing to be done!" he cried. Tallien covered his face with his hands.

"Look at me," I said. "There is a way, and it's the only way. We must legislate his death, just as he did with Danton. Count the votes in your Committee of General Security, even in the Committee of Public Safety, and then in the Convention, and you will see that your determination will carry the day. Every delegate except Robespierre and his henchmen is exhausted of the terror. They all fear they will be next. The delegates also know that the people are on our side. They are sick of the terror. But we must succeed within the system. And we must act before the people rise up. Let's be part of the rebellion rather than be crushed by it."

I knew we would succeed if a majority of the Convention voted for Robespierre's arrest. So, we lobbied the delegates. Control of Paris depended on control of the army. Our revolutionary army is indoctrinated to obey only the authority of the people—of the Convention—to heed duty before personal responsibility. Even my own personal army would never disobey a directive of the Convention. For what is a soldier who will not follow orders but the merest murderer? The great majority of soldiers do not wish to be murderers. The great majority, but you will see that Hanriot and a few others lacked any honor or scruple except fidelity to Robespierre. I will get to that.

So, I broadened the circle of the conspiracy, including even some whose names did not appear on The List. "Count the votes in your committee," I said to each of them. "Refuse him your votes and, by your resistance, reduce him to stand alone."

CHAPTER 61

By the end of July, our child was dead. We wept. Inconsolable, Bonne and I wept and wailed. Fear of Robespierre had prevented me consoling my family as fever burned up our daughter; she could not breathe and suffered and died. My child, tied to a stake and set afire by disease, perished before dawn on July 26. A premonition impelled me and I came, heedless of the risk, and found them. Bonne's saintly face tear-streaked, and the child dead.

The gravesite was sheltered by a bower of chestnut trees, sunshine filtered through shimmering emerald leaves. It was early and already the day was heating. We had no liberty for ceremony. I remember, *thud-thud-thud*, dirt striking the tiny coffin. I felt someone new nearby and turned. Barras's servant. He said, "Robespierre was seen on his way to the Convention."

For three days Robespierre had been hardly seen. He had remained secluded in his apartment at the Duplays', except when he left alone for habitual haunts—long solitary walks in the woods at Ville d'Avray; in the Pantheon, bent before the tomb of Rousseau, sometimes in tears. Lookouts reported that no visitors had come.

Now that Robespierre was on his way to the Convention, I still resisted the temptation to go there. I did not dare. I had set the stage, now it was the turn of my players to act. I returned to Charlotte Robespierre's house. We drank tea, grieved for my dead child. I was literally crying on her shoulder.

Tallien filled me in on what transpired in the Convention. Robespierre denied responsibility for the terror. He spoke at length. He said, "Strange project of an individual man to persuade the National Convention to cut its own throat with its own hands in order to open to that individual the road to absolute power!" Ha! That was well put, and exactly what he did. The idiots in the Convention.

Anyway, a Robespierre crony moved that the speech be printed. This measure would invest it with the Convention's imprimatur. But we had the votes. The measure was voted down! The delegates voted that the Committees of Public Safety and General Security would review it and decide. Robespierre shouted, "What! My speech is to be sent to be examined by the very deputies I accuse!" And, at last, he had given names—in addition to mine. Now all appreciated that Robespierre's aim had been to liquidate his enemies on the committees.

Saint-Just enlisted Barère—always a vacillator and go-between—to be peacemaker. Saint-Just knew Robespierre had not had a good day. By then I had ventured to the Committee of General Security offices. Saint-Just and Barère were in the Committee of Public Safety. Meanwhile, Robespierre read to the Jacobin Club the speech he gave at the Convention before an adoring crowd. This time, he explicitly named his targets for liquidation who had been on The List.

Yet I learned late on July 26 that Barère had secured a deal with Saint-Just. Barère walked into the room where we were seated and announced, "Saint-Just agrees: the terror will end. He will demand it, and the repeal of the Law of 22 Prairial. Then he will make a motion. We all know that the Convention will be pleased to end the terror. Saint-Just will rewrite his speech and show it to the Committee of General Security for approval, before he gives it to the Convention. He'll bring it here. Now leave him alone."

I left alone, weaving my way through the labyrinth of connected buildings into the Tuileries to the offices of the Committee of Public Safety. At last, I passed through the green anteroom and entered the committee's green meeting room. It was incongruously cheerful; the green walls covered with clocks, bronzes, mirrors, tapestries.

Seated alone at the green table was Saint-Just, writing. So charged was his concentration that at first he did not notice me, and I quietly sat down near to him. I marveled at the beauty of the man. The sleek, fine features of his profile. The youthful athleticism of his physique and bearing as he sat on the edge of the chair, bent over his work. The fierce concentration on his handsome face bespeaking artistry and intelligence. Seemingly, there was nothing that this very young man could not do extremely well. He looked up at me, clearly annoyed.

"So you are going to give us Robespierre," I said. "You are, it seems, just as virtuous as other men."

Saint-Just gave me a dark look, brow furrowing.

I continued, "You know that if you denounce the terror, and we vote to end it, the outcome will be our arrest of Robespierre, and the guillotine for him and Couthon."

Saint-Just spit in my face. I drew my kerchief, stood, and made my way to the door. I said, "Then don't do it. It's what I want. I want to see you both die."

What followed is too well known for me to dwell upon it too much. It is remarkable how Maximilien the First perished. Saint-Just broke his promise. He did not show up at the Committee of General Security, he did not announce the end of the terror. He remained united with Robespierre. They stood side by side at the tribune and tried to get us arrested. This time I could not stay away from the Convention. Robespierre could hardly speak, choked as he was by rage. Possibly fear. I am the one who first shouted, "The blood of Danton chokes him!" It began a chant. "The blood of Danton chokes him!"

Robespierre found his tongue and shrieked, "Danton! Is it, then, Danton you regret? Cowards! Why did you not defend him?" That sealed his doom, the idiot.

The accusation passed. We had the votes. Robespierre was decreed "accused" of attempting to be dictator and of masterminding the terror. Robespierre, Couthon, Saint-Just, and Robespierre's brother Augustine were all put under arrest, and slated for trial before the Revolutionary Tribunal.

But Hanriot set them free, at the direction of the Paris Commune. They barricaded in the Hôtel de Ville. Idiots. I had wanted to dismantle the guillotine and send them into exile.

I knew what I had to do and where to go—where I had spent many a night since returning from Lyon in order to evade Robespierre's henchmen, before his sister gave me refuge. When I walked into the barracks, there was the familiar strong odor of perspiration mixed with cognac and wine, which fortified me. These were my men, my army. My trusted right hand, Colonel Brissac, he the foremost among the men under my command in Lyon, first greeted me, as always. I had in hand the Convention's decree that the Robespierrists and their Jacobin supporters were outlaws. I lifted the paper up, the writing facing the soldiers. "Men," I said, "the Convention demands that we muster immediately at the Hôtel de Ville."

Hanriot's and our forces fronted one another before the city hall, cannons facing this way and that. Hanriot himself was nowhere to be seen. Barras spurred his horse forward and cried, "*Citoyens!* Before committing to bloodshed, and the path of endless civil war, hear the Convention decree: 'The Robespierrists and Jacobins are outlaws!'" The decree was duly read.

All at once Hanriot's men turned their cannon and they mixed with our men. There followed quick embraces among men who moments ago stood face to face and ready to kill one another. Hanriot came drunkenly staggering out of the city hall expecting to take command of his army. Instead, he was suddenly confronted by bristling cannon and bayonets all ranged against the Hôtel de Ville.

I first saw Robespierre after the Hôtel de Ville was stormed; he was lying on a table in the council room. He suffered from a pistol-shot wound that wrecked his jaw—a failed suicide attempt—his jaw now bound up with a bloody rag. He clenched the holster. Men taunted and insulted him, "Well, you do seem to have gone quiet all of a sudden!" "Oh, sire! Is Your Majesty in pain?" He did not respond. Yet, the eyes were fierce—the eyes were still alive.

What a pity, I thought. It did not need to come to this! We

would have dismantled the guillotines and spared their lives.

Lebas, one of Robespierre's cronies, was more successful. He lay a few paces away, his brains blown out, and the pistol lying near nearby. Saint-Just was under arrest; he was impassive, cold as ice. Couthon lay unharmed, positioned fetally on a second table.

Early morning, before the Revolutionary Tribunal, the outlaws were arraigned. We did not use that horrible public prosecutor, Camille's cousin, as he was soon to follow these men in their fate. The primary outlaws were Robespierre and his brother—crippled by the broken leg he suffered trying to escape from a high window—together with Saint-Just, Couthon, Hanriot, Dumas, Fleuriot, and sixteen city officials and members of the council general of the Commune. Hanriot had been arrested by some soldiers who struck him with a bayonet and thrust out one of his eyes, which hung by the ligaments down his cheek.

They were all guillotined. At last, Robespierre was lying beneath the blade, and wrenched the dirty linen from his jaw. He cried for pain—oh hideous specter!—then, finally he spoke, to the executioner, his last words, "Quick, Sanson!"

CHAPTER 62

FOUCHÉ LOOKS AT PAINE and shakes his head. He reaches down and picks up the dagger and sheaths it, resolutely. After a pause, he continues, his intonation now signaling lament. "I confess that in the delirium of victory, I felt that the sudden overthrow of the dreadful system which had suspended the nation between life and death would doubtless initiate a grand epoch of liberty; but, in this world, good is ever mixed with evil. How regrettable now, that so happy an event has not contributed to the public good, instead serving as a pretext to glut the hatred and vengeance of those who have suffered in the revolution. And now to terror has succeeded anarchy and vengeance. This has caused me to reflect upon man, and upon the character of factions. There will come a time soon when the cup will have filled, when the excesses of reaction will have placed in jeopardy the revolution itself, and finally the Convention will see an abyss which will yawn under its feet. It could be that a king will be reinstated. This is not out of the question. There remain on this planet Bourbons who were not killed. Even now the crisis is awful—it is a struggle for life or for death. The revolution is being blasted both in its principles and end. And this is what brings me here to your presence. It is, I think, still possible for us—the two of us together, I mean—to save the revolution."

Paine has had quite enough of politics, and he is not sure what to make of his interlocutor, certainly not sure that he trusts him. He knows something about the recriminations, score settling and bloodletting that continues outside this prison, and of the trouble that Fouché is in. Yet he retains the hope that Fouché may be the means of his liberation. So, he says, "What is your plan?"

Fouché waits to reply; seemingly, he is pensive. "I am here to share it with you," he says at last. "But let me start this way. I want to tell you some things about my experience in the provinces. I went to Nantes in the Spring of 1793. The Convention granted me enormous powers; bearing the tricolor cockade and the red baldric, and supported by a sizable detachment from the National Guard, I commanded authority to impose taxes, pass judgments and hand down sentences, summon recruits, cashier generals."

"Yes," says Paine, "such powers can only proceed from a national dictatorship. That is what you all created when you formed the Committee of Public Safety. This was Robespierre's objective all along."

Fouché is suddenly snickering silently; the raptor eyes again lively. "I'm sorry," he says. "You are quite right about Robespierre, and I cannot help laughing at the banality of the term, 'Committee of Public Safety.' That was intentional, of course."

He turns serious again. "Traveling in a coach toward Nantes, alongside the magnificent, inexorably widening Loire—a perfectly clear sunny springtime day, I remember the vineyards, châteaux, wineries, and hovels of the peasants entrenched within the gorge—I meditated on that place's history. I am a learned man, a man who reads books. So I am well aware of the nation's history; I am haunted, intoxicated by it; the history touches me to the very marrow.

"What most struck me then was how the authority of the clergy has remained continuously since ancient Rome's demise. By their education and superior intellect, they insinuated themselves to a position of renewed authority over the barbarians who conquered Rome and Gaul by force."

"The same is true for Britain," says Paine, "yet the English have attained a mixture of power, a king limited by Parliament and a judiciary, and they reformed the Church, absent bloodshed and warfare on the scale perpetrated by the French Revolution. Now the Americans have taken the British experiment to new frontiers. The United States has erected a legal wall between church and state, and its constitution has established a separation of powers."

"No, the British are different. Following dissipation of the western Roman Empire, Britain was for two hundred years returned to its original state of aboriginal wilderness—in thrall of the druids with their magic word view and folklore—and beset by Nordic invaders. Rome and its Church were gone. Just for two hundred precious years; yet this respite from the old world's torments, combined with the immense moat that surrounds their island, enabled the English to imagine a world absent authority superior to the people. In America, even more; the space was virgin. But in France, Rome's authority continued unbroken. Gibbon dates extinction of the western Roman Empire at 476, and the Frankish warlord Clovis first united the lands called France into a single kingdom within twenty years—thus the Lord of the Franks became the first King of France. 'Clovis' is the Latin root for Louis, just as 'Frank' is for France; he was France's first King Louis. And shortly he became the rod of the Church. He was born a pagan, but the chroniclers credit his military victories to his wife Clotilde's god—Christ Jesus—for in 496 he converted to the queen wife's religion, Roman Christianity; this happened after he ordered his men to paint the cross onto their shields and, in an ensuing battle, vanquished the Burgundian tribe. And so, the chroniclers hailed King Clovis—Louis—a new Constantine. The Frankish realm grew, and later, Charlemagne and the Pope forged the axis they called the Holy Roman Empire—a new Christian Roman Empire—and an ages-old structure of authority, hierarchy, and domination was restored."

"So, France, all of Europe, must return to year zero? Everything, all of the old order, must be razed?"

"Here is my point: Hundreds of years later that same Holy Roman Empire is at war with France and must inevitably be crushed; it cannot be allowed to continue, that much the Girondins correctly understood.

"And so, once I arrived in Nantes, I stood before the western façade of the immense gothic Cathedral of St. Pierre de Nantes—the gable of twin towers, lofty, and of heavy proportions; the ornate portals, and the steps and plaza. I listened to the choir from inside. I marvel at Catholicism. I am unmoved by the Christian narrative, once boldly original in its egalitarianism; by the majesty of the architecture and construction, by the beautiful music and artwork, by the psalms and chants, or by the haunting atmosphere of incense and candle wax. I am fully hardened against any of these elements, per se. Rather, it is the object lesson of control at which I marvel. For over a thousand years Catholicism was able to curb and dominate Europeans, subjugate and tame their minds, herd them like cattle and appropriate their productivity, their very selves. Ah, Paine, I see it in your eyes, that here we share common ground."

Paine nods. "I believe that all organized churches, whether Jewish, Christian, or Turkish, are no other than human inventions. Their purpose is to terrify and enslave mankind, and monopolize power and profit. If that is what you believe, then I agree, we have that in common. Yet what I fear most is an exchange of the religion of St. Paul for the religion of Rousseau or Fouché or Robespierre. My faith in humanity is strained by the willingness of the masses to submit to these new faiths. Worse still, submission to a modern state religion. I do not oppose the existence of religion, but there must be a wall erected between church and state."

"Indeed, willingly the people have always submitted. Like yourself, I am a man of reason. But unlike yourself, I do not disdain the people's faith or sentimental attachments to the Church. On the contrary: I stand in awe of the Church, and the people will never change. They still need a church."

"I disagree. There can be another way—"

"Ah, Paine, let me finish. Hear me out. I am not here to debate you. I want you to hear what I have learned, and then we'll see if we can cooperate to save the Republic. You are naïve about a wall between church and state. For the state is inevitably the new church, for it must be. There is merely a struggle between rival dogmas. In my opinion, the Republic must replace the old Church with a new church that is modeled on the old one. The Church is the Republic's rival, and also its forerunner and teacher, and so it must be annihilated. A maximally formidable rival, albeit aged and whose prime has passed, but a rival that must be destroyed. The new church must be built upon the foundations of the old one, just as the cathedral that stood before me in Nantes was built upon layers of ruins of pagan places of worship. The Republic, I am sure, must liquidate the Church. Shall we burn the cathedrals? I thought this to myself then. Destroy them? Perhaps, in time. Not that day. When I arrived in Nantes, I planned only to appropriate the cathedral.

"Like St. Paul, like the Savior himself, I preached to the masses in a courtyard adjoining a spectacular but decrepit ecclesiastical building that is destined for dust. I stood in a Court of Gentiles gazing upon a Christian Temple. On the façade there is affixed a stone exterior pulpit that would be my forum, accessed by stairs within.

"In the evening, I stood triumphant upon the elevated exterior podium. The plaza was filled by the crowd, their faces turned upward to gaze at me, and lit up by torchlight. They looked like an immense herd of white-faced cattle.

"I was nervous. My hands holding the speech that I was about to give were shaking. I began easily, with a generalization, seemingly innocuous, though defining the very achievement and character of the revolution: 'All the people are indivisible, equivalent, and they must be inseparable from the revolution.'"

Fouché stands up now in front of Paine. He continues, gesturing, "I imagined, *Now you are the body of Christ and individually members of it.* But I shouted, 'The revolution is made for the people; and it is easy to understand that when we speak of the people we do not mean that class, privileged by its wealth, which usurped all the pleasures of life and all the goods of society. The people is the universality of French citizens.'

"I imagined, *Blessed be ye poor: for yours is the kingdom of God.* But I shouted, 'The people is, above all, the huge class of the poor; that class which gives men to the country, defenders to our frontiers; the class which nourishes society by its labor. It would be a ludicrous insult to mankind to go on talking perpetually about equality if in respect of happiness there were still to exist huge gulfs between one man and another.'

"I imagined, *Verily I say unto you, That a rich man shall hardly enter into the kingdom of heaven. And again I say unto you, It is easier for a camel to go through the eye of a needle, than for a rich man to enter into the kingdom of God.* But I shouted, 'The rich man can never be a true revolutionary, can never be a genuine republican; indeed, a merely bourgeois revolution, a so-called revolution which does not alter the distribution of property, is nothing but a new tyranny, for the rich man cannot help looking upon himself as kneaded out of a different dough from other men.'

"I imagined, *Repent and be baptized, every one of you, in the name of Jesus Christ for the forgiveness of your sins. And you will receive the gift of the Holy Spirit.* But I shouted, 'Make no mistake: to be genuinely republican, every citizen must experience and effect within himself a revolution equal to that which has changed the face of France. You were slaves of superstition; henceforward your only object of worship must be the Republic.'

"Now here began the truly revolutionary, the unprecedented part of my oration, my manifesto! And I imagined, *Now the multitude of those who believed were of one heart and one soul; neither did anyone say that any of the things he possessed was his own, but they had all things in common.* But I shouted, 'Everyone who is above the pressure of want must contribute to this exceptional levy. The tax must be proportional to the greatness of the country's needs and your means.'"

Fouché paces a few steps, strokes his palms, turns and faces Paine, and says, "Now for the climax of my oration! I imagined, *Nor was there anyone among them who lacked; for all who were possessors of lands or houses sold them, and brought the proceeds of the things that were sold, and laid them at the apostles' feet; and they distributed to each as anyone had need.* But I shouted, 'All the things of which they have more than enough, and which can be useful to the defenders of the country, are instantly to be claimed by the country. Thus, there are people who have a ridiculous accumulation of sheets, of shirts, of table-napkins, and of shoes; all these objects, and others of the sort, can properly be made the subject of revolutionary requisitions. The Republic has the right to annex the excess for the purpose of promoting liberty for all. A republican needs no more than iron, bread, and forty crowns of income. All gold and silver, vile and corrupting metals, which the true republican despises, must be laid at the feet of the Republic, and they will be delivered to the national treasury, so that there they can be given the imprint of the Republic, and, after having been purified by the flames, they will thenceforward circulate only for purposes of general utility. Provide us with steel and with iron, and the Republic will triumph!'

"Finally, I imagined, *From his mouth comes a sharp sword with which to strike down the nations, and he will rule them with a rod of iron. He will tread the winepress of the fury of the wrath of God the Almighty.* But I shouted, 'We shall be harsh in the full use of the authority delegated to us, and we shall punish as treachery, whatever, in other circumstances, you might have been entitled to call slackness, weakness, or negligence. The time for half-measures and backsliding is over and done with. Help us to strike hard blows, for if you fail to do so you will feel them on yourselves. Liberty or death! Think it over, and choose between them.'

"I finished, and there was hardly a sound from the people; only smatterings of applause. Of course, for my message was not one of triumph. They conducted themselves as compliantly as herded cattle! Finished, I stepped from the balcony and into the cathedral. I fell against the wall and slid to the floor, exhausted, sweating. I mopped my brow. I was greatly relieved. I felt that never before in the world's history had anything so original and so bold been proposed. In originality and boldness it surpassed the Christian narrative, the American Declaration of Independence, or its constitution. My proclamation had announced a new order.

"So here I had announced what I believe to be the two pillars

that must sustain the revolution once it matures into a republic —
first, the state as religion; second, the elimination of economic and
social classes and enforced economic equality and lack of need for
basic necessities."

Paine perceives a hardly discernible wink.

CHAPTER 63

"Very clever, Fouché," says Paine, "you delivered your own Sermon on the Mount. But there is a third pillar to your program. Terror. How else could you eliminate heresies and enforce redistribution property, other than by violence? How can liberty abide in such a system? How can freedom of speech be tolerated? What you preached—violent redistribution of private property, enforced by government fiat, and executed by the military—was theft, and state religion cannot tolerate dissent, as the revolution itself demonstrates. These objectives certainly would require violence and murder."

"Ah, Paine, spoken as a true American. The nobility's accumulation of property exists because they have for centuries stolen from the peasants and workers. You and your American friends speak high-flown words. Equality, liberty. Yet your revolution and constitution have stood for only two principles—private property and sovereignty, and sovereignty's purpose the perseveration of existing private property rights. Existing property rights are so exalted in America that slavery continues unabated notwithstanding the high-flown words. And so Americans grow rich through monstrous theft from the black race and other poor. Americans go on about natural laws; yet what natural law justifies the nobility's accumulation of wealth by hideous, monstrous theft from the lower classes?

"So, too, our French Revolution has been deficient in the same way. There has been much talk about about liberty, and about fraternity, but little is said about equality, insofar as money and property are concerned—other than by me.

"So, what is the solution to accumulation of vast wealth over centuries based on unjust systems and force of arms, on theft, on murder indeed, while the great mass of humans suffer shortages and even starvation? Your *Rights of Man* speaks fine words, but it is wanting in solutions. You decry inequality that exists because of religion, monarchy, feudalism, and the merchant class, yet you shrink from the solution that is the only one that can reverse historical injustices that exist after many epochs."

He does not wait for Paine to respond. "So I began by divesting the Church of its ill-gotten gain. Paine, if you ever make it to Nevers, you will see a gothic edifice, which stands on a hill in the center of town, its current form a combination of two buildings, with two apses, at the west end and the east end. This I christened the Nevers Temple of the Cult of Reason." Here Fouché's wink is clearly discernible. "The western apse," he continues, "nave, and transept are the remains of a church originally built in the late Roman Empire. The eastern apse and nave were added in the fourteenth century, but here there is no transept. Also at the east end stands a massive and elaborately decorated tower built in the sixteenth century that may be seen from many miles around.

"It was in the eastern nave that I began regularly to address the people and announce our new order—for I preferred to avoid the transept. I wore the cap of liberty and a simple habit resembling that of the cult we had extinguished. We dedicated the temple to martyrs of the revolution. The internal walls and horizontal surfaces were bare, stripped of the shameful tokens of fanaticism and opulence that were hallmarks of the ancient sect that once ruled French minds. But our plan was that in time, portraits of the revolution's martyrs and revolutionary relics would haunt those old walls, nooks, alcoves, and altars.

"We announced that celibacy was abolished; the priests were required to marry or to adopt a child within a month. By decree of the Convention, and as we transmitted to the people, the people could now divorce as freely as they marry. Christian funeral ceremonies were likewise abolished." Fouché pauses. "Death is an eternal sleep," he says gently, reassuringly, as he did then. "A placard bearing this message was posted upon the gates to the cemetery.

"I personally ordained Bishop François Laurent, formerly the archbishop of the old cult, as archbishop of the new Cult of Reason." Fouché chuckles. "I remember, during the ceremony, Laurent arrived at the pulpit and collapsed, lying prostrate, and I promptly commanded him to rise. I do not wish to be worshipped; that would carry this program too far. I do not want to die violently, an occupational risk of being worshipped. Once Laurent was standing, surrounded by the other clergy standing in semicircle facing the pulpit, I performed the ceremony and he was anointed Bishop of our new order.

"Then I announced to one of the other clergy, 'You may place the cap.' And the one I addressed stepped forward and placed a cap of liberty on the archbishop's head.

"Next day, I stood in the temple square cradling my daughter, amid the ruins and debris of crosses, crucifixes, and images of the saints pulverized by hammers. The occasion was the naming of my daughter. The National Guard were present, a fife-and-drum band playing, and there was a crowd. I gave a signal, and the drum major stopped the music. I thanked everyone for coming, then I proceeded with the ceremony.

"I named her Nièvre, after the department of Nièvre, my ancestral country. She is the one who would die the day before Robespierre's fall." Here his voice is strained. He pauses to gather himself then continues.

"I was well aware that prissy Robespierre would not approve of our Cult of Reason once the news reached the Convention. That was actually partially the point. I also had felt that the victor in this contest would be the one who delivers not only fine phrases but real value to the Republic. My men had been emptying stables of their horses and confiscating sacks of flour. On the estates, the masters had fled, or were converted to agents of the revolution if they were not under arrest, and the bailiffs who once served them were now responsible for exacting adequate levies. I conscripted factories, and set them to work producing equipment and goods necessary for the army. I prohibited all fancy bread, and decreed that only one kind of loaf, war bread, shall be baked.

"These measures enabled us every week to issue five thousand military recruits marching to the frontier, fully equipped with horses, boots, clothing, and muskets. Everyone in that part of the country was hard at work and well fed, and money was flowing to the Convention.

"Now that we had fallen upon the churches, we were dispatching to the Convention wagonloads of golden monstrances, gold and silver ingots formed from broken and melted candelabra and crucifixes, and jewels torn from settings of precious metals. I knew well that hard currency was the Republic's chief need.

"All at once *it* had happened, in my jurisdiction, as I had announced first in my Nantes manifesto: the Nation had replaced the Catholic Church as the new religion."

"Shameful," says Paine, unable to keep silent any longer, "that you defaced the Christian edifices and destroyed the objects of worship. They serve an instructional purpose. And they are beautiful in their own right. They are as deserving of veneration and preservation as the Greek Parthenon or the pyramids, though none of us any longer worship their pagan gods."

"Nonsense," says Fouché dismissively. "I told you I lack any sentimentality for Catholic imagery and art. And our purpose is not to make history of the Church, but to erase it."

He pauses to gather his thoughts. Paine waits, hoping he will get to his point. Fouché continues, "So, here is my plan. First, we will update and improve your *Rights of Man*. The new France needs a new founding document. More than a constitution or a mere declaration. We'll call it a manifesto. And it will be your *Rights of Man*, this time rewritten by Joseph Fouché and Thomas Paine. Your own program was a good start. We will clarify the absolute requirement of equality and we will include solutions and a program for implementation." Fouché is back on his feet, gesturing, as though delivering a speech to a multitude. He is quivering. He continues his oration.

"Your *Rights of Man* is a fine work, so far as it goes, and so too we will capitalize on your reputation. Only you retained your exalted principles—however much some of us may quibble with them—to the very verge of the scaffold, and survived. Your integrity will greatly enhance the credibility of our cause. Once our *Rights of Man* manifesto is perfected, we will need you to write more pamphlets, to elaborate, just as your American Alexander Hamilton did with his *Federalist Papers*, but our message will be different. I have found you an able collaborator. A Parisian, François-Noël Babeuf, believes as we do; he is of lowly birth, yet a man of no meager creative abilities. He writes exquisite phrases: 'A great national community of goods shall be established by the Republic.' 'The right of inheritance is abolished; all property at present belonging to private persons on their death falls to the national community of goods.' 'Every French citizen, without distinction of sex, who shall surrender all his possessions in the country, and who devotes his person and work of which he is capable in the country, is a member of the great national community.' 'The transfers of workers from one community to another will be carried out by the central authority, on the basis of its knowledge of the capacities and needs of the community.' 'The community shall abolish money.'

"Our message will be carried like a torch through the workers' quarters of Paris. Our torch will start a conflagration, a wildfire, so that Paris and the whole country will be consumed in the blaze, and we shall forge a restored and reformed revolution. We shall mobilize the streets by summoning the working-class battalions with the strength and energy of the masses. We will again hoist the tricolor banner of revolt on the Hôtel de Ville!" Now Fouché's right arm with fist is suspended above his head. "The fire will spread through Europe, even England and America! The workers will rise up and vanquish their oppressors!"

Their eyes meet. Says Paine, "You have not fully accounted for your doings in the provinces. What happened on the plain of Brotteaux? Is this the prerequisite for your society of equals? You cannot persuade me that you were not responsible for those atrocities."

Fouché colors. He pauses to think, then seemingly unperturbed, his intonation now mild, he asks, "Have you ever been to Lyon?"

Paine shakes his head.

"Oh, if you ever regain your freedom, you must. The journey there itself is worth the trip. When I last traveled that route last year, it was late autumn, early November. Yet the sun still shone and animated the cool, clear atmosphere. Day two of the journey from Nevers, you are still beside the Loire. I remember, November 10, the river rippled, shimmered, and sparkled in the weak sunlight. The stream was separated from me by vineyards and olive groves. I remember a high stone formation suddenly casting a shadow. I craned my neck outside the coach, to get a better look, and observed a monument to fallen pride and power—the ridge was crowned by the ruins of a feudal castle. I marveled, not at the ruined edifice, but the accelerating pace of human progress. How long past, I wondered, did humans emerge from eons of insignificance, inexorably to dominate the planet? Now the contest will be, inexorably, between nations and between factions within nations; now is the epoch of nation building, of shaping a nation's will, its culture.

"Later, departing the Loire's company, and ascending, transitions of light and shade proliferated; dense masses of forest timber mixed with bright red and gold leaves. Huge fragments of rock scattered among them, as though flung by the hands of giants. Below, in the valley, a slender, shimmering stream. Here and there, under a sheltering ledge, the hut of a goatherd, and near to it a square patch of yellowing cornstalks shorn of their sweet produce.

"I held on my lap a dossier. Repeatedly I examined it. It contained my instructions from the Convention. The Convention declared, *An example must be given to show that the French republic, that the youthful revolution, punishes, most severely of all, Frenchmen who have revolted against the tricolor. There shall be raised above the ruins of Lyon a pillar which will announce to posterity the crime and the punishment of the royalists of that city, bearing the inscription: 'Lyon made war against liberty, Lyon is no more!'* Dreadful, to be sure. Yet my place was not to question. I had to do as the Convention decreed. Certainly it was bitter medicine for Robespierre to swallow that the Convention had given me such a difficult task. But I proved in Nevers that I was up to it. And I agreed with the rationale for such bold action. I am a brutal realist, Mr. Paine. At war with the rest of Europe, France could only deal harshly with insurrection within itself, in the provinces. The Republic was overextended and, seemingly, the local authorities considered it unlikely that the Convention would respond forcefully to their rebellion. Toulon, its arsenal and its forts, were in control of the British, and now under a prolonged siege by revolutionary forces. The English were gathering for an all-out attack on Dunkerque. The Prussians and the Austrians were advancing on the Rhine and through the Ardennes. Civil war raged on in the Vendée. Yet Lyon did not assume the central government's acquiescence. It levied troops, erected defenses about the town, and waited for the national army to arrive. Following a prolonged siege, Lyon was overrun by the revolutionary army."

CHAPTER 64

A MONTH AGO, PAINE began repeatedly to see a young man about the Luxembourg. He looked pale, with sunken eyes and high cheek bones—because of undernourishment, sleeplessness, and worry, Paine surmised. The young man would not meet Paine's eye. For some days, Paine spied that young man with increasing frequency. One day, they were near to one another and the young man turned to Paine and then suddenly averted his eyes and walked away. Paine called to him.

"I can't talk," replied the young man, turning to look at Paine. "My life was over some time ago. I will be relieved to die. I do not deserve to live and, God is my witness, I do not care to. I know who you are. Thomas Paine. Only you survived this ordeal we all have suffered with your honor and your virtue intact. I, on the other hand, have nothing to live for. I deserve whatever punishment awaits me."

They became friendly. Paine learned that the young man's name was the same Colonel Brissac whom Fouché today identified as his right hand, his next in command in his personal army. In time, Brissac told Paine his story. He seemed relieved to divest himself of it.

"The first time I met the commissary," he said, "was the morning after he arrived in Lyon. We stood talking in the great, spacious square, the Place des Terreaux."

At first, Colonel Brissac said only "the commissary" in telling his story. He would not reveal the commissary's identity. Brissac was in prison because the commissary, before the Convention, repudiated him for his doings in Lyon. The commissary condemned the colonel's excesses in Lyon. As a result, Brissac was arrested, to die on the scaffold — to pay with his own blood for the words and the policy of the commissary.

Eventually, Brissac disclosed to Paine that the commissary was Joseph Fouché. "He will get his just deserts, just as I will," said Brissac of Fouché. "He has too many enemies and there are too many witnesses to his crimes. He's a desperate man, for sure, I'll tell you that."

Brissac seemed to be a sedate, thoughtful, unprejudiced, and literate man. Paine imagined that he was unusual among the officers in Lyon, especially considering his youth, though his full head of hair, sideburns, and mustaches were prematurely graying. Certainly he was a young man who was useful to Fouché.

"I was a captain when I first met the commissary in Lyon," continued Brissac. "You can form no idea of the troops there. They were a horde of plunderers and cutthroats, picked up in the bloody puddles of Paris — but their cavalry was superb. It was composed, for the most part, I imagine, of grooms and lackeys of families of rank who denounced their masters and then robbed their stables. There were some from among them picked up every morning sabred in duels among themselves. Yet these brutes had done the bulk of the grim but essential work in vanquishing Lyon."

Hoping to gain a better understanding of the captain and his men, to draw him out, Paine asked, "Were you a part of the siege of Lyon?"

"Yes," he answered. "We were called there from the mountains of Savoy, where we had been in bivouac."

"How long had you been a captain? You are so young."

"I had previously been an officer, or nearly one, under the old government. I was named sous-lieutenant in 1790; I have my brevet, with the fleurs-de-lys of Louis XVI. The course of events brought me back to Chalons. At the time of the general enlistment, claims of preference were allowed to citizens who had already served, and so I was appointed at once to the command of a company. We were marched into Savoy, where we remained a long time, amidst the cold and snows of that country, without provisions, without shoes, and without occupation. At length we descended to Lyon, from the elevation of the Alps, and found a force just arrived from Paris—these brutes called the revolutionary army.

"The morning I met the commissary," continued Brissac, "it seemed a fine day was emerging; I remember it well. The sky was clear, the air fresh, and the green and reddish gold summits of the mountains, glowing in the sun's first beams, were hidden by the mist that was rising from the plain to the east. To our left, not far away, was a cannon, mounted on its limber, and surrounded by artillery sentry. I hardly noticed them, tormented and preoccupied as I was with matters of personal survival, my own and on behalf of my men. Before us, across the square, stood a series of famous buildings designed by Mansard and begun in the reign of Louis XIV; the most beautiful structures in Lyon. The primary edifice was a handsome Baroque château of substantial size, looking nearly like a smaller scale replica of the Louvre.

"Suddenly the cannon's shot boomed—so loud that I was quite startled, and momentarily deafened. The cannonball whistled, and there was a terrible thud and shriek, as the hurtling orb directly hit the château in the midsection, leaving a gaping hole. Loud hurrahs. In the smoke that enveloped the cannon, I saw the artillerists seizing it and pulling it back to its former place."

Relating his story, Brissac's voice was broken; he was nearly in tears. "Need I say more? They were a bunch of criminals! I asked the commissary, 'Can't you do something?'

"I think the commissary forgave my confusion and grief at that moment, for I had suspected that he was a humane man, as I then fancied myself, and I had not seen the Convention's decree for the destruction of Lyon.

"Yet the real reason that I had approached the commissary was an errand of personal self-interest. Later that day, I said to him, 'I must tell you, my men are paid in paper, in assignats, for their arduous and loyal services, while these wretches, without courage and without discipline, are paid in good hard cash. I believe they even may be paid as much as thirty sols.' The commissary said that he would see what he could do to help me, and he did help. We were paid a fair sum in cash from then on."

———————

"A week later," Brissac continued, "late at night, I stood face to face with the commissary. It was after midnight when he summoned me. I had hardly lain down, exhausted by the rigor of helping to maintain civil and military government in rebellious Lyon.

"'You are under my command tonight,' he told me. 'Bring twenty soldiers and follow me.'

"Not thirty minutes passed and I returned, subalterns and the detachment of infantry in motion behind me.

"'So, you are good soldiers, after all,' he said to me.

"The commissary and I rode in front, with a detachment of cavalry from Paris, and the others marched in file, moving quickly through the streets and exiting the gates of Lyon, then advancing between rows of trees. No one else was about. Through the trees the Rhône gave me some relief. The sometime splash and ripple. We moved on and, except the river and the birds, the only sounds were our harnesses and the horses, the gravel beneath horses and men's feet.

"Our destination was a village called Crémieu, reported by spies to have provided aid and comfort to the insurrection. Having proceeded nearly three leagues, we arrived at this village, about equidistant between Lyon and Belley. Roosters had commenced to crow. The air smelled of livestock and smoke. The dawn was breaking when we finally saw someone else. We passed a bare-footed maiden, driving her cow to pasture, having crossed the roadway. She stopped to look at our column passing, putting aside her hair with her hand. Her unmoved, impassive face was striking to me. I turned on my horse and gazed at her for as long as I could while leading troops.

"All appeared peaceful within Crémieu, the villagers scarcely stirring. Pretty white dwellings—they were long with flat red-tiled roofs, with inscrutable shutters, and umbrageous vines creeping along the walls and trellised on pillars, *à l'Italienne*.

"'Make the men load their pieces and surround the village,' the commissary said to me. 'Fire upon all who should attempt to quit it.'

"We obeyed; we enfiladed the principal streets of the village. The commissary and I were at the head of thirty grenadiers with fixed bayonets, ordered to halt a hundred paces from the dwellings. There were paddocks and barns. The commissary ordered goats, sheep, and pigs killed; it was done in their pens, and the dead animals were butchered in one of the more spacious paddocks. The horses were greatly alarmed, I tell you. Yet no one emerged from the dwellings. We roasted the meat on sabers and ate it with knives. Then at the commissary's direction, I ordered a drumroll that restored order.

"The sun was up, and the day was clear, mist rising in the fields. Here the mountains with their forested and gold and yellow crests were closer, and breathtakingly beautiful.

"Now, at last, motion was perceptible within the dwellings. Windows were opened; some ventured out of their doors, mostly to return inside again. Surprise and doubt held back these poor villagers. Meanwhile, it must have been that ominous reports spread about.

"The commissary directed me to follow him with five grenadiers. We went house to house. He advanced with deliberate authority and gruff manner, bearing teeth and bulging eyes. Yet, in truth, we had no fear that true warriors lurked in these dwellings. The first houses were so poor, the walls so naked, the furnishings so miserable, that they rendered me speechless.

"In one of those ruins, however, the commissary saw, upon a smoky mantel, an image of the Savior in an old wooden frame. He appeared overtaken by a blend of rage and contempt. He grabbed the frame and, striking the mantle, shattered it. He then delivered a fine patriotic harangue, preaching that God exists no longer, that Christianity is a miserable superstition, then laid down a twenty-franc assignat, to compensate for the damage.

"We approached the center of the village, where houses of a better appearance told of small proprietors, prosperous farmers, and comfortable townsfolk. At sight of the soldiers, consternation spread visibly, and terror appeared in the countenances of the families. They must have been well aware of what was transpiring in Lyon. The trembling women let fall their arms listlessly on their seats; servants wept. Men stood with colorless faces. Children, sensing that something terrible was amiss, were crying violently, some standing in stupefaction, others held.

"The men were put under arrest. 'Come, citizen,' said the commissary blithely to one of them. 'I am very sorry to inconvenience you, but you must follow us. I have strict orders from the National Convention, and duty takes the place of everything. You must come with us to Lyon.'

"Certainly they were aware of the Jacobins' bloodlust, and that imprisonment of a husband, brother, or father would transition inexorably to the guillotine. Women wept, others cast themselves on their knees or prostrate, and some fainted. The men stammered inarticulately, garbled protestations of citizenship.

"Witnessing all this consternation, the commissary delivered a speech: 'I can well imagine this disturbs you. But, deuce take it, we are not made of stone. Hark ye, I perceive you are honest people, good citizens: some way, perhaps, may be found between ourselves of coming to an understanding.'

"Suddenly the villagers appeared hopeful; there were forced smiles and gaping mouths, and a general movement. The commissary said, 'Have you any money, any savings? If you are desirous to devote it to your country, it is possible I might consent to shut my eyes, and leave you undisturbed.'

"The commissary glanced at me. I tried to appear indifferent, I confess. Now the people were dispersing to access their stores, and surrendering all their money and valuables. The commissary ordered a wretched medallion portrait be taken from an old woman, who wept as she parted with it. The commissary was smiling to himself at his own effrontery. Visits were paid at every principal dwelling in the village, with similar results. Eventually the entire village furtively, and absent resistance, was pillaged in this way.

"The commissary told them, 'Direct me to the curé's house.' He had come, most of all, to apprehend the curé. They told us the curé's house was beside the church. When we arrived, a large tri-colored flag had been hoisted upon the church. Beside it we found the curé's house, a humble dwelling, half concealed by vines. But, said the commissary, he was not fooled. 'Naturally,' he said, 'the curé must have been chief instigator of the rebellion.'

"We crossed a few feet of desolate ground with patches of grass, and passing hollyhocks, and an arbor in ruins; the whole yard was fenced in by a hedge of thorn fagots, and beside it ran a broken wicker-fence, painted green. A child, a boy, in tatters was playing in the sunshine near the door. Nearby, a goat was tied to a plane tree.

"The commissary asked the child, 'Is there anyone in the house?' The child raised his head, and quickly dropped it again, pointing with his finger to the house.

"Inside, we proceeded to a parlor. The curé was seated in a large armchair near the window, a book in his hands; he was an old man, with long white hair. He raised his head, and looked at us through his large spectacles. He bore no emotion.

"'I am well aware of this type of character,' said the commissary to me. 'The chief keeper of mysteries amid the simple minded; self-assured and in control. His presence, his composure, only further infuriates me.'

"'Ah! As for you . . .' said the commissary to the curé, dispatching pleasantries and getting directly to the point, 'As for you, my good friend, I absolutely must bring you with me. The commission finds it necessary to examine you—you must follow me to Lyon, and without delay.'

"Now color was rising in the old man's face. He removed his

spectacles, placed them on the open pages of book, which he set on a nearby table, and endeavored to stammer out a question, without power to finish a word.

"'Come,' said the commissary, 'we have no time to lose; we must set out instantly.'

"The old man rose with surprising alacrity. He was tall and thin, a little bent. 'I think they have nothing to lay to my charge,' he said.

"'You will explain yourself once we arrive in Lyon,' said the commissary, 'but presently there is no other course but for you to come with me.'

"The curé cast bewildered looks at us all, and he said with quavering voice, 'Sir, I am tolerably well liked in this country, and have been assured that, in conforming to the laws—'

"'Don't be alarmed,' the commissary interrupted, 'the law is just.' He was attempting his most reassuring tone. 'Besides,' he added, 'I will take you under my protection—once at Lyon, I will not forsake you.'

"'Well, sir,' said the curé, 'I am satisfied; I shall follow you.' (Naturally, for he had no choice.) He moved toward a corridor adjoining the parlor, perhaps to gather a few articles in a travel case.

"'But now,' said the commissary, with a note of irritation.

"'Be it so, sir; as you will.' The old man halted and faced the commissary.

"'You will have no need of any money,' he said. 'You can't carry your comforts to prison. But you must bring me your money, and I will take charge of it for you.'

"The curé shrugged his shoulders, opened a large cupboard. He leaned in and emerged from it with an envelope that contained two six-livre crowns. 'Here you are,' he said, handing them to the commissary.

"'Come,' he replied, 'you are jesting; you have money in the church. Let's go see.'

"'There is nothing but the ornaments of the church,' the curé said.

"'Oh, very well, we shall see,' said the commissary. In the church, we entered the sacristy. 'Open your stash for us,' said the commissary, striking with the flat of his saber on a panel he discerned was a disguised closet; it returned a hollow sound.

"The curé drew from his pocket a small key, and opened what proved to be a closet door, and in the interior there were large folding doors. Behind them were the sacred vessels of the church, carefully arranged on shelves.

"The commissary was delighted. 'Ah! Very good!' he said. 'Here is money, actually sleeping—what use is there in leaving it here!'

"He unrolled stoles, chasubles, copes; tore off the lace, rented it down the middle, and then ripping the pieces across into sections about a foot long, distributed them to each of the grenadiers present. He then seized a gold chalice, stooped and bent it on his knee, flattening it for more convenient carriage. He did the same with the other vessels, taking whatever was most valuable, and kicking back unwanted items into the closet. When he was finished, he took the old curé by the elbow and, slapping him on the shoulder with his free hand, led him outside.

"Now a child came running up, crying, 'Monsieur le curé, Monsieur le curé.' It was the same child we had seen playing at the door. Suddenly he was enveloped in the folds of the curé's cassock. 'Monsieur le curé, where are you going?'

"'I am going to Lyon.'

"'Ah! You are going to Lyon—and won't you bring me back something?'

"'Yes, I will bring you something.'

"'And what will you bring me? Rosary?'

"The curé embraced him. It seemed the curé had taken charge of this child. The commissary was frowning. I could see that he was annoyed at the scene's sentimentality. He did not know what to do about children.

"'Send back the child,' he barked.

"The curé sent the boy off in the direction of the house. 'He is the son of a native of this place, who has just died in the army,' he said to the commissary.

"'No doubt he fought against the Army of the Republic.'

"The curé responded, 'A very honest man, that man.' His voice was strained.

"It was now broad daylight and drums were beating while we walked back through the village. Yet no villagers were in sight and their houses were closed up and still, as at midnight. The sentinels were relieved, and I reassembled the infantry detachment to march back to Lyon. The commissary and I were again with the cavalry at the front. The curé was in the midst of the infantry of the first rank.

"I expected the curé to collapse, a man of his age marching three leagues at the pace of the troops, and there would be no further need to trouble with him. Yet he kept up, and he never uttered a complaint. It was about three o'clock in the afternoon when we arrived back at the Place des Terreaux. The spacious square was crowded, and drums were beating. There were troops in lines forming a rectangle, maintaining a barricade around a scaffold. The knife of the guillotine fell, *bang!* The echo reverberated along the buildings adjacent to the square. The executioner bore a severed head. It was the hour of the executions. Again, *bang!* Like a sledge upon the anvil.

"The commissary must have been seized by an idea, to produce a lasting memory, for terror was the whole point of this, was it not? He dismounted and seized the curé, taking him by an arm.

"I saw he sensed my gaze upon him; looking up, he said furiously, 'Take your men; you may retire to your quarters!'

"The commissary pulled the curé hard by his sleeve in the direction of the scaffold, handing him over to the executioner. He needed not say a thing in explanation. A mere look and gesture of the head was all that was required, for the prisoner was evidently a cleric. Led by the executioner, the curé mounted the scaffold.

"*Bang!* The echo was awful, and then there was silence. The head of the old curé fell. Then the martial music started up again."

CHAPTER 65

PAINE EXPRESSED DISMAY, AND Brissac said, "I have only begun, Mr. Paine," his head bent, gazing into the pavement, seated as he was on the bench. "December 4. Two hundred men, more or less, were led from the prison and assembled in the Place des Terreaux; they were haggard, dressed in rags, with ample beards and hair greasy and wildly askew. I smelled their stench even from inside the city hall. Their arms were fettered tightly behind their backs. They were strongly guarded on every side by a small army of troops, about four hundred in number.

"A bell was tolling; it was around noon. Now the soldiers were making the men get into a line ranging before the standard of the Hôtel de Ville. Soldiers were shouting and hitting them, though the prisoners were not resisting. The municipal officers came down the steps, the commissary among them, and one of them paused and read aloud the sentence that applied to all of the prisoners: Death.

"Suddenly a woman bolted through the line. She cast herself on one of the men. One of the guards, aided by another, and then another, began to pull her from the man, but she would not let go; she moaned and wailed. The men began to hit her. Finally, after a great difficulty, she was disengaged. Two soldiers carried her away, unconscious.

"When we arrived at the plain of Brotteaux, which fronts the Rhône, the area where it would happen was already cordoned. The sky was gray. I saw the mountains of Savoy in the distance, across the wide slate-colored river and the monotonous plain. There were trees lining this side of the river, and a strong rope was stretched along the trees at about the height of a man's waist. Behind me, a crowd of civilians was gathering.

"The commissary had seen to it that I was there, commanding one of the two detachments totaling two hundred gendarmes, in charge of one hundred prisoners. Another officer led the other two hundred guards escorting the other one hundred prisoners.

"Upon our arrival at the cordon, the prisoners were placed in line, in front of the horizontal ropes and beside one other. Their hands were bound to the rope extended along the trees. At the same time, troops were positioned in a parallel line fifteen paces apart from the line of prisoners. Each detachment was in front of its own set of one hundred prisoners.

"There was a strange silence. Not one of the prisoners was crying out; no one begged for mercy.

"The commissary approached me. I was very distressed. I had not killed before like this. Our eyes met, and he whispered to me, 'This is our burden, don't you see? We must save the revolution. It is for the society. We have to do it. It's not our choice. You mustn't let their suffering count for anything. It can't matter.'

"I laughed. I could not help it. It was such a ludicrous comment. I said, 'But it does matter. Our burden, you say. What about theirs? Everything ends. I have a choice; you are not right about that, either. It is: be where I stand, or join them. I *choose* to stay where I am.'

"When the time came, I stepped away from the commissary, raised my sword; the other officer who commanded the other detachment did the same. I nodded, and then shouted the command, 'Fire!'

"All of the soldiers fired, and those fired upon by my men were instantaneously dead, slumped on the ropes or dangling hideously. It was not the same for the other detachment. You could never imagine anything so horrible. Not one of their wretched victims was shot dead; they hung writhing along the rope and were screaming in unbearable tones of piercing agony. 'Ah, my God!' 'My God, my head, my throat, put an end to me!' 'Mercy!'

"Ten pieces of artillery were fired, to drown the cries—for the crowd of civilians, scarcely two hundred paces off, was itself bawling and shrieking, in horror. I ordered my own one hundred men to re-load, file off on the right flank, and fire. The cries ceased, and all the bodies sprung upon the rope, stiff and motionless.

"To dispose of the bodies, the commissary ordered that they be flung into the river. He shouted, 'Let the bleeding bodies give an impression of terror, and an image of the omnipotence of the people along both banks of the stream, down to its mouth, and, farther yet, beneath the walls of shameful Toulon, under the eyes of the cowardly and ferocious English!'

"On December 20, the commissary ordered the entire battery of cannon at Lyon to be fired in celebration of the fall of Toulon to the revolutionary army, and its complete evacuation by the British. He was joyous. The soldiers were ecstatic, firing their guns, shouting, and drinking to delirium. The name Napoleon Bonaparte was on everyone's lips. The young artillery officer, heretofore unknown to anyone it seems, was being hailed as a hero. For it was he who masterminded the strategy that led to this spectacular victory.

"Next morning, in further celebration, the commissary ordered two hundred more men shot at the plain of Brotteaux, by a detachment now entirely under my command, as Colonel Brissac. He had seen to my promotion. Later that day, in the square, twelve nuns and a priest were guillotined, the ground of the sentence being that they sang hymns."

CHAPTER 66

P AINE DOES NOT NEED to reveal Brissac's disclosures. Fouché knows that he knows. There are many witnesses to Fouché's crimes.

"I would not claim that I was forced to obey orders," Fouché says calmly. "I did what I did willingly, yet it was what I had to do to save the revolution. There was no other way. We were surrounded on all sides by enemies from without whose sole objective was to crush the revolution. Yet even more threatening were the traitors within France who wanted to restore the Bourbons and feudalism. Had we failed, we ourselves would have gone to the gallows and the revolution would have been extinguished. Violence can only be met with violence.

"If the revolution was to be saved, it was inevitable that our class struggle would turn to civil war. We had no choice but to crush the counter-revolutionaries. I did not pursue history. The apparatus of power was handed to me. My position was akin to that of a Roman proconsul. I would have had to have extraordinary restraint, deference, and lack of ambition not to deploy that apparatus to the fullest extent necessary to extinguish the counter-revolutionaries. And I would have been a hopeless idiot and incompetent not to do so. So, I am guilty of murder. Suit yourself. But if you think you would have done anything other than what I did, had you been in my shoes, you yourself are a hopeless idiot. You are no better a man than I am, Paine. I am not Robespierre. I did not kill children, or my colleagues, or anyone innocent of personally intriguing against the Republic. We did nothing more than transform our would-be executioners into our victims, and the energy that propels that cycle is inexhaustible, I assure you.

"So, here is what must happen now if we are to save the revolution again. The workers must be armed. All other classes must be disarmed. We must seize the factories and anything of value in Paris and all of the large farms. We must take control of the banks. We must cancel all the rents and debts owed by peasants. We must confiscate all paper stocks and all printing presses. We must arrest all the bourgeoisie and make them hostages, or kill them. Moderate revolutionaries are more dangerous than open counter-revolutionaries, whom the moderates abet with their fancy words about a people's government, legislatures, liberties, press freedoms, and the like. Separation of powers is a bourgeois sham. What is the rule of law but an instrument of class domination? Politics themselves are malevolent, as you have seen.

"Anyone who has not learned these things from our revolution is a fool. And our revolution will be the one to preempt all others. There must be a powerful dictatorship, yet once society is firmly in control of the workers, and themselves ready to receive the apparatus of power, the leaders will step aside and relinquish power to a society of perfect equality, which will end hierarchy forever!"

Fouché stops speaking at last. He stares directly at Paine, wide-eyed, expectant.

"Be gone, Fouché," says Paine. "Get thee hence. I know not the solution to inequality, but your society of equals is the worst possible world. For that reason, you will fail. We have learned the evil that dictators do. You are finished, Fouché. There will be no stepping aside by any dictator, ever. But you and your dictatorships are as much in the past as is the monarchy. I wager that you will take my place here, and I will outlive you."

EPILOGUE

Paine brought with him from Paris, and from her husband, in whose house he had lived, Margaret Brazier Bonneville, and her three sons, Lewis, Benjamin and Thomas. Thomas has the features, countenance and the temper of Paine. Madame Bonneville arrived at Baltimore a few days after her paramour.

LAMENTABLY, ONLY THESE BRIEF lines, out of an entire book of libels against Thomas Paine, are the basis for Marguerite's cause of action against the author, James Cheetham. Her lawyer, William Sampson, advises that the dead have no claim for libel, even by proxy. She can only sue for libel against herself.

It is June 19, 1810. Marguerite and Mr. Sampson had not yet decided where to have dinner following the summations when a messenger from his office found them and said there was already a jury verdict. She is confident of victory. The New York Court of Common Pleas is not the Revolutionary Tribunal. The United States has no commoners per se, but that is in actuality what these jurors are. Common folk, chosen following questions from the lawyers and the court to try to ascertain their impartiality. This is where justice is to be had, if at all.

The same week that Thomas died, Cheetham announced his libelous biography, *The Life of Thomas Paine*. Marguerite tracked down Mr. Sampson, an advocate of religious freedoms, and he agreed promptly to file suit on her behalf. Mr. Sampson agreed to take the case pro bono—for he anticipated it would enhance his fame and reputation.

The truest words in Mr. Cheetham's libelous "biography" are that, when Paine returned to the United States, the reception at Washington was cold and forbidding. When she and Thomas came to the United States in 1803, the nation he helped found was unrecognizable to him. Even President Jefferson received him without warmth. His erstwhile friends in Congress interacted with him more out of curiosity than friendship.

Worse, the nation's public figures wrote as though speaking at a religious revival. Now it was said that America was founded on religion, pure and simple, not as a *rejection* of state religion and the divine right of kings. America, in its constitution and laws, was now of heavenly origin, a concept alien to Thomas. *The Age of Reason* was enough reason for those of such disposition to dislike Thomas, and so too his association with the French Revolution. When he returned to New Rochelle, the government officials denied him the right to vote on the grounds that while he was imprisoned during the French Revolution, Gouverneur Morris did not recognize him as an American, and Washington had not helped get him free.

Still worse, slavery had taken root in the southern states as a permanent institution, and there was no prospect that women would ever vote in the United States.

Paine's public and writerly life was thus spent mostly in literary feuds. The most public and notorious was with this James Cheetham, who had been Paine's friend and an editor of a republican paper in New York, but abandoned this profession and became the advocate of the British Tory party in America.

This past year, Marguerite was at Paine's side as his health failed and he died a slow and painful death. He wanted to be buried in the Quakers' cemetery, but his reputation had sunk so low that the Quakers denied him this final wish, on account of his rejection of religion. So, she had him buried on the farm he bequeathed to her and her sons in New Rochelle. Only a few remaining loyal friends came to the funeral.

The trial has been a sensation, the courtroom filled with newspaper reporters, and the interested and the curious. Still, the proceedings have been brief. Marguerite took the stand and simply testified to her perpetual platonic relationship with Paine. He was like a father to her, she stated. He lived with her family in Paris for many years, and he and Nicolas collaborated on books and pamphlets. Then Sampson called several ladies of impeccable reputation, whose daughters they had entrusted Madame Bonneville to teach the French language, and each testified to the strength of character and perfect morality of Madame Bonneville, who had been much injured by this Cheetham.

The only evidence offered by Cheetham's lawyers in his defense was a letter from Mr. W. Carver, written in anger, after a quarrel, in which he insinuated that Paine and Marguerite were lovers, because she brought her family to America, leaving her husband in France, and they lived with Paine. Carver testified in the trial, and in his summation Sampson well summarized the course of his cross-examination of Carver regarding his angry letter. "He, with uplifted hand, affirmed, by the ever-living God, the truth of what he testified—and what was that? His letter tells us all: that he and Mr. Paine had a dispute over money; and in their correspondence you may find the crimes and baseness they reciprocally urged against each other. From the same source springs the infernal hint that little Thomas Bonneville had the countenance and features of Mr. Paine. I pushed Mr. Carver farther, and he stated that he and his wife had often gone to visit Mrs. Bonneville and Mr. Paine. Then it was that, seeing the toils in which his honesty and decency had fallen, Mr. Carver tapered off by saying he never had seen the slightest indication of any meretricious or illicit commerce between Mr. Paine and Mrs. Bonneville; that they never were alone together, and that all the three children, the little godson Thomas and all, were alike the objects of Paine's care."

Fearing for his soul's salvation, Carver had to admit the truth of Mr. Sampson's prods in his cross-examination. He testified truthfully. (When Marguerite and Paine came to America in 1803, it was more than ten years since they had become lovers, and like many married couples, the passion was reduced at most to embers and memories. When Carver knew them, the romance was over.)

The jury files into the box. The foreman hands a paper to the bailiff, who hands it to the judge. He reads the verdict. It is unanimous. Cheetham is guilty of libel. The judge assesses a penalty of $150 to be paid by Cheetham to Marguerite. Yet the judge, for no reason relevant to the proceedings, praises Cheetham's book for serving the cause of religion.

She is no perjurer. The claim was legitimate, and the jury's verdict is just, though for reasons other than her lawyer argued to the jury, and which she has kept to herself. A jury, she feels, in their collective wisdom can perceive real truth, even if necessarily unspoken. Paine is the father of her children, and she is his wife — by natural law. Americans still go on about natural laws, now more than ever. Nicolas was an indifferent husband, and an indifferent father. Paine lived with them for years and collaborated with Nicolas on books; and Nicolas welcomed Paine's full collaboration in all aspects of their lives. Whoever delivered the sperm that conceived her sons, the man who raised them, and whose bequest now provides them a means of gaining an occupation in the United States, is Thomas Paine. Benjamin, only fourteen, is already keen for a career in the military and for exploration. So, by natural law, at worst she is a bigamist. So be it. She did not sue Cheetham to restore her own reputation, or to recover money. Rather, unlike Danton, Thomas cared for his "legacy," and now she has begun the path to vindication of whom she has discerned as the only truly great man in the United States after Paine returned to it.

———————

July 5, 1815: After dinner with Wellington in the pretty little house at Neuilly that belonged to Murat (who is now, Fouché thinks, sure to face a firing squad), Fouché and Talleyrand enter the carriage and are off to see the king. Louis XVIII is waiting for them at the Bourbons' château in the same city.

Talleyrand has been Napoleon's chief diplomat, continuously stationed in Vienna. Now he is co-conspirator with Fouché, aiming to determine the very future of the nation, to save defenseless France from invasion by the alliance that destroyed her army, and to try to plant the seeds of a new order in the ashes of the emperor's regime.

They have little in common aside from their love of power and their pragmatism. Talleyrand, like Fouché, has built his career by changing himself and switching sides, as at this moment—from bishop to republican, from republican to emperor's minister. In 1789, at the Estates General, Talleyrand, the Duke of Périgord, was old nobility. He represented the first estate as Bishop of Autun. At just thirty-four years, he wore the violet robe as prelate of a French province, while Fouché, a commoner clad in a shabby cassock, taught mathematics and Latin to adolescents in Nantes. Today, Fouché is the Duke of Otranto (Napoleon gave him the honorary title) but he remains an ascetic and indefatigably ambitious. To Talleyrand, power and distinction seem to have flowed naturally, and they are not an end but a means to pleasures; to wealth, luxury, women, art treasures, gourmet foods, fine wines.

During the ride, with a half-suppressed laugh, Talleyrand discloses that the king, upon agreeing to meet with Fouché, had lamented, "My poor brother, could you but see me, you would forgive me." Between the two of them, Talleyrand and Fouché know everything essential. When, in 1799, Fouché became the Directory government's Minister of Police, an office that was not yet defined, Talleyrand had told him, "The Minister of Police must be a man who minds his own business—and goes on to mind other people's." He had the Police Committee's resources at his disposal. It was an office he would hold through his more than ten years of service to Napoleon. In time, it was Fouché who knew most about the work of other ministers, the Directory, the generals, the whole public policy, Napoleon himself. He shaped the national policy as he executed a policy for himself. Not only is he close to Talleyrand, he is friendly with Wellington, Metternich, the Duke of Orléans, the Tsar, kings.

Fouché is unamused by Talleyrand's disclosure; it is too soon to gloat, and he is not capable of his co-conspirator's polished indifference. Indeed, they themselves have much to lament. When, on June 18, news arrived in Paris of the catastrophe at Waterloo, Fouché was prepared for the worst. Even before Waterloo, he had been in contact with Wellington and Metternich. He knew that Napoleon, who has his own spies, suspected that Fouché would betray him if it was necessary or even expedient. Not long before the campaign, before all the ministers, the emperor had cried, "You are betraying me, Duke of Otranto; I have proofs of it." Napoleon seized an ivory-handled dagger, shouting, "Take this knife and plunge it into my breast. That would be more loyal than what you are doing. If I liked, I could have you shot, and all the world would applaud such an act of justice. You will ask, perhaps, why I don't do this. It is because I despise you, and because you do not weigh so much as an ounce in my scales."

After Waterloo, the emperor hurried back to Paris, as he did after his failure in Moscow in 1812, hoping to retain power. Fouché was ready for him while everyone else was paralyzed—the newspapers were silent, while in the chambers, the streets, the markets, the cafés, the exchanges, the barracks, people could only, with fear, discuss the catastrophe. Immediately, Fouché wrote to Wellington, *The French nation wishes to live under a monarch, but it wishes that that monarch live under the empire of laws. The sovereign shall receive the scepter and the crown from the hands of the nation.* Fouché told the other ministers, and his allies in the Chamber of Representatives, that Napoleon will demand to be dictator. "We can and we must deny him what he wants. We have the votes."

Napoleon faced his ministers in the Silver Room of the less prominent Élysée Palace, instead of the Tuileries. He was not the same Napoleon, and he was still the same. In some ways, they now saw him for what they should always have seen. He wore the same blue uniform with the long white waistcoat underneath, covering his no longer round stomach, and the white doeskin breeches now fitting somewhat loosely over thighs above the stumpy legs, and the Hessian boots. His hair had become thinner, yet the singular lock still hung down in the middle of his broad forehead, but lighter and more fragile. The once supple face and plump neck now seemed to sag, and the eyes revealed fatigue, age, and anxiety. He harangued as before, about the great armies he was still yet to raise—in a fortnight he would lead a new army of two hundred thousand against the Allies and, if necessary, requisition all the carriage horses in the country. Fouché sat silent, for he knew he needed to say nothing; all knew it would be hard to extract two hundred soldiers from the exhausted populace.

Meanwhile, in the Chamber of Representatives, Lafayette fulminated, issuing memorable words that delivered the coup de grâce: "The bones of our brothers and our sons bear witness everywhere to our loyalty to this man. In the sandy deserts of Africa, on the banks of the Guadalquivir and the Tagus, beside the Vistula and on the icy plains of Russia, during the last ten or twelve years three million Frenchmen have perished for the sake of this one man! For a man who today still wishes us to shed our blood fighting against Europe. We have done enough for him; our duty is to save our country." Thunderous applause. Then the chamber issued a demand for Napoleon's abdication.

At last, in the Silver Room, before the ministers, Napoleon looked at Fouché, evincing not sadness but hatred. "Write to the gentlemen in the chamber," he said. "Tell them to be easy; they are going to have their way." He retired to a room, and Fouché scribbled a note to Lafayette that Napoleon would abdicate. The emperor returned, bearing his written abdication, and handed it to Fouché without a word. Less than three days after Napoleon's return, he was finished, vanquished by Fouché. For Fouché was ready for him. He had the votes.

Fouché's proposal that the chamber at once appoint a provisional government, a Directory elected by the chamber, was accepted, and he himself was elected, and made President of the Directory. There was no one else who knew as much and so many as he did; and, after the news of Waterloo, Fouché had led them to this point. He is now chief executive of the nation. Yet Fouché is a man who knows his limitations. He will not make the same mistakes as Robespierre and Napoleon. He is about to relinquish the pinnacle he has just attained. Yet this interlude has served its purpose. Wellington, the king, and Talleyrand understand that only he, Fouché, can open the gates of Paris to the Allies, and so he was admitted to the secret meetings tonight.

Unlike Napoleon, Wellington appeared in the vigor of his prime, and he was taciturn. His shoulders are broad, a muscular chest. He is not short, and the body is well proportioned. The forehead not too high, a long face, strong jaw, and a Roman nose that completes the resemblance to Julius Caesar. His full, black head of hair is only beginning to show signs of lightness at the temples.

Fouché, smitten, set out to persuade the conqueror that he and Talleyrand were indispensable. He painted in lurid terms the situation in Paris and strength of the opposition to the Bourbons. Talleyrand cut him short and made a firm offer—a complete amnesty for them and all their friends, the Foreign Ministry for Talleyrand, and the Ministry of Police for Fouché. Wellington was indifferent to these terms; he wanted what they wanted—to prevent futile resistance by French partisans and to avoid the need for the Allies to take Paris by force. It was already agreed that Louis XVIII would be restored to the throne.

The co-conspirators have reached their destination, and they exit the carriage. Talleyrand is lame, and so he places a hand, thin and pale and heavily ringed, on Fouché's shoulder as the two men walk inside. The king is waiting, beside him a servant and loyal noblemen. The king is fat, and coughs asthmatically. Talleyrand introduces Fouché, omitting that he was among those who killed the king's brother. No pleasantries are exchanged. Fouché kneels, kisses the king's hand, and swears loyalty in the name of God.

Later that same evening, Fouché returns to Paris, and joins his colleagues in the Tuileries Palace. They suspect nothing. He has in his pocket the warrant for his appointment as King Louis XVIII's minister.

Next day, Allied troops enter Paris and occupy the Tuileries Palace. The king arrives to reclaim the throne. Carnot, the most loyal of Napoleon's loyalists, confronts Fouché. "Traitor, where am I to go now?" he says. "Wherever you please, you hopeless idiot," answers Fouché.

ACKNOWLEDGEMENTS

THE AUTHOR WOULD LIKE to thank Kelly Huddleston, David Ross, Craig HIillsley, and Cam Terwilliger for all their invaluable help and advice: Craig and Cam, who helped to bring the characters to life, to forge the shape, and make it shine; and Kelly and David, who believed in *Children of Saturn*, and made the novel their own and beautiful to behold.

SELECT BIBLIOGRAPHY

CHILDREN OF SATURN IS a novel, a work of fiction that is a product of the author's imagination. But two things can be true at once. The French Revolution proves the adage that truth is stranger than fiction. Most of the facts dramatized in this novel are supported by the written historical record. The rest are plausible. All of the characters actually lived. Much of what they say in *Children of Saturn* is adapted from their writings (we may assume that, like others who write, what they wrote they also said) or historical records of their public statements. The following works stand out as sources of inspiration and information:

Billington, James H. *Fire in the Minds of Men: Origins of the Revolutionary Faith*. Basic Books, 1980.

Carlyle, Thomas. *The French Revolution: A History*. London, 1857.

Cheetham, James. *The Life of Thomas Paine*. New York, 1809.

Claretie, Jules. *Camille Desmoulins and his Wife*. London, 1876.

Conway, Moncure Daniel. *Life of Thomas Paine: With A History of His Literary, Political and Religious Career in America*. London, 1893.

Davidson, Ian. *The French Revolution: From Enlightenment to Tyranny*. Profile Books, 2016.

The Diary and Letters of Gouverneur Morris. Charles Scribner

Sons, New York, 1888.

Fouché, Joseph. *The Memoirs of Joseph Fouché, Duke of Otranto, Minister of the General Police of France*. London, 1825.

Hibbert, Christopher. *The Days of the French Revolution*. William Morrow, 1999.

Israel, Jonathan. *Revolutionary Ideas: An Intellectual History of the French Revolution from the Rights of Man to Robespierre*. Princeton University Press, 2015.

Jordan, David P. *The King's Trial: Louis XVI vs. the French Revolution*. University of California Press, 1979.

Keane, John. *Tom Paine: A Political Life*. Grove Press, 1995.

Lamb, Robert. *Thomas Paine and the Idea of Human Rights*. Oxford University Press, 2015.

Lawday, David. *The Giant of the French Revolution: Danton, A Life*. Grove Press, 2009.

Lewes, George Henry. *The Life of Maximilien Robespierre: With Extracts from His Unpublished Correspondence*. London, 1849.

Linton, Marisa. *Choosing Terror: Virtue, Friendship, and Authenticity in the French Revolution*. Oxford University Press, 2013.

Methley, Violet. *Camille Desmoulins: A Biography*. E.P. Dutton, 1915.

Nelson, Craig. *Thomas Paine: Enlightenment, Revolution, and the Birth of Modern Nations*. Penguin Books, New York, 2006.

O'Gorman, Frank. "The Paine Burnings of 1792–1793." *Past & Present*, vol. 193, no. 1, Nov. 2006.

Paine, Thomas. *Common Sense, The Crisis, and Other Pamphlets, Articles, and Letters*. Library of America, 1995.

"The Place Des Terreaux, An Episode in the French Revolution." *The Dublin University Magazine: A Literary and Political Journal*, vol. 19, 1842.

Rickman, Thomas. *The Life of Thomas Paine.* London, 1819.

Schama, Simon. *Citizens: A Chronicle of the French Revolution.* Random House, 1989.

Scurr, Ruth. *Fatal Purity: Robespierre and the French Revolution.* Henry Holt, 2007.

Taylor, Ida Ashworth. *The Life of Madame Roland.* London, 1911.

Thiers, Louis Adolphe. *The History of the French Revolution.* London, 1881.

Thomas, Chantal. "Heroism in the Feminine: The Examples of Charlotte Corday and Madame Roland." *The Eighteenth Century,* vol. 30, no. 2, University of Pennsylvania Press, 1989, pp. 103-118.

Vale, Gilbert. *The Life of Thomas Paine: Author of Common Sense, Rights of Man, Age of Reason, With critical and explanatory Observations on His Writings.* New York, 1853.

Van Alstine, Jeanette. *Charlotte Corday.* London, 1890.

Zweig, Stefan. *Joseph Fouché: The Portrait of a Politician.* Viking Press, 1930

Made in the USA
Monee, IL
09 November 2024